Seven Days of Rain

M. Jonquil

Exile Creek Publishers

ISBN 978-1-7341138-1-5

I. Wednesday Evening

Harry

I almost didn't go to the chess club that night. The chess club meets every Wednesday from about six to ten, and that Wednesday was the day before Thanksgiving. I suspected they weren't even having a meeting. But it was a gloomy evening and I had nothing else to do and certainly no plans for the holiday. After an hour or so of moping, I drove over to the north side of town and was mildly surprised to find that the lights were on in the dingy little church basement where they held the meetings.

There was hardly anyone in attendance. Not that there ever was much of a crowd at the chess club, but that night it was just the real hard-core enthusiasts – and the lonely guys with nowhere else to go, guys like me. There were three games going on at two separate tables. A few of the players looked up when I came in. No one greeted me, although I'm enough of a regular that I knew everyone in the room and they all knew me. Chess players, especially when they are playing chess, are not the most sociable creatures.

There was a seventh guy in the room: Norm, the unofficial president of the club. Norm was sitting off to the side doing a crossword puzzle. That's what Norm did at the club: he almost never played chess. Norm had some kind of loose affiliation with that church and he had been entrusted with a key to the basement meeting room, and he opened and closed the place for the chess club every week. Without Norm there would have been no chess club. We all used to worry about that from time to time because Norm was pushing seventy and had already had one minor heart attack.

I walked from table to table watching the moves of all three games. In the meeting room there were these plastic tables with folding metal legs. Each table was just large enough for two chess boards and four opponents.

The club provided vinyl, roll-up boards and plastic pieces, the standard sets you would see at any weekend tournament. During the rest of the week, when the room was used for other purposes, the boards and sets were stored in a battered cardboard box in a small cupboard under the stairs leading down into the basement.

Of the six guys playing that evening, two were rated high enough to have earned the title of expert, one was a class-A player, two were about my strength, class-B, and one was class-C or perhaps a bit weaker. Actually, the United States Chess Federation doesn't use the terms class-A, class-B, class-C anymore; nowadays they say "first category" players for class-A and "second category" players for class-B and so on. I may not have been quite as old as Norm but I was old enough to be stuck on the old terminology. Heck, it took me years to adjust to digital chess clocks and to algebraic notation; and I still own dozens of chess books from my early years, all written in descriptive notation.

Experts, at least, are still called experts.

With two exceptions, all the guys in that room that night were as old as me or older. The exceptions were one of the experts, a tall guy with an abrasive sense of humor and a deep obsession with chess, and the class-C (or "third category") player, Rob, who tended to chew on his raw, ravaged nails between moves and who needed after every game to climb the stairs and step outside the building to smoke a cigarette.

No one was using a clock and the games were going slow and if I had had anywhere else to go I would have left, but I didn't have anywhere else to go except back to my empty apartment so I stayed and watched and wondered if I would even get to play a single game.

Then Maddie came into the room.

Maddie

I almost didn't go by the chess club but I was striking out everywhere else and if there's one thing you can say for sure about the chess club it's that there will be men there – losers, of course, but quiet and sober losers – and after the sleazeballs I had already encountered that night (a few I had even considered going home with, I was getting that desperate) and with the fact that my last few stops of the evening were going to be bars where the men were likely to be even more drunk and more sleazy than the likes of which I had already suffered, I decided on a whim what the hell why not take a chance, why not swing by the chess club.

There was almost nobody there. Can you believe it, even chess players have lives it turns out, places to be, families to be with on a holiday. They were doing better than poor Maddie, obviously.

I asked Norm for a game but he was too into his crosswords. Norm was old but I had never seen him as completely out of the question. I remember looking at him that night, thinking: If I wanted to, I bet I could become the highlight of his later years, the best thing that's likely to happen to him between now and the day he dies. I could be the smile on his face when he breathes his last. If he had any money, which I doubted, he would leave it all to me. If the dummy would just get his nose out of his crosswords.

The six guys playing were all regulars I had seen before and they were all duds in my book, either too married or too out of shape or too clueless or too into chess – those last two things being more or less interchangeable.

Then I noticed this other guy standing off to the side. I didn't troll the chess club often enough to know every single one of the regulars, but the more I looked at him the more I thought I'd seen him there before. He had short gray hair and a dense, close-cropped gray beard. He was a little under average height – which was maybe why I hadn't paid him any attention on previous visits: he was an inch or two shorter than me, and I usually don't go for men who are shorter than me. But he looked to be in pretty good shape for his age and he was clean and sober and it was the night before Thanksgiving and I was determined not to spend this one alone, not after what happened the year before; and he had a half-friendly face, maybe even a handsome face if a gal could wipe some of the sadness off of it.

Harry

I had seen her at the club exactly twice before. The first time was about four and a half months ago, the second time was just over two months ago. It was rare to see a woman at the chess club, so of course she stood out. I mean, she would have stood out anyway – she was not unattractive. I mean, she had a lively, expressive face and from certain angles she was what anyone would call good-looking.

She ignored me completely as she had done the two times I had seen her before. She went straight over to Norm and asked for a game. Norm startled: he had been so engrossed in his crossword puzzle he had never seen her coming. Maddie asked him again for a game. "Not right now," he said automatically. Then he gave her a long look as if she were hiding a secret. He said, "Do you happen to know a four-letter word for all right, third letter K?"

Uncertainly, Maddie smiled and laughed. Her eyes flew all around the room. She noticed me.

"Jake," I said.

She said, "Pleased to meet you, I'm Maddie."

"No," I said.

"No?"

I said, "My name's not Jake. It's Harry."

"Okay," she said, her uncertainty growing by leaps and bounds, her eyes glancing toward the door.

I said, "Jake is the word Norm's looking for."

Norm piped in, "Is it really?"

I nodded.

Norm mused, "Jake means all right...I never knew that...or maybe I knew it and forgot...that seems to be happening more and more lately..." He laughed at the predicament of his failing memory while checking to see if the word fit into his puzzle. "Well, look at that," he said; "I'll be darned, that must be it."

Meanwhile Maddie was looking me over like a horse she wasn't at all sure she wanted to bet on.

After a long look, she said, "Would you like to play with me?" The way she said it made a few heads turn. I received more than one wry, warning glance.

The general consensus at the club was that Maddie was crazy. Personally I had no opinion on the subject, having seen her so seldom. But I'd heard her talked about several times, chess players being the gossips that they are, despite their general unsociability. The story most often told about Maddie was how she "went after" Otto, one of the club's strongest players, how she started "taking lessons" from him. Otto was a big, broad-shouldered guy with blond hair who laughed at his own jokes. He was also a bit of a showoff over the chess board. When he deigned to play a lowly B-player like me, he made a point of reading some magazine or the newspaper, never took more than two second to move, and lost hardly ever. In short, Otto had an ego you couldn't miss — and when Maddie started to "go after" him, he basked in the attention. But Otto was also married. Very much married. He was a late-bloomer in that department, being fairly recently hitched, even though he was only about a decade younger than I was – and he talked about being married quite a lot. So, one night at the club, in the middle of Maddie's lesson from Otto, Maddie exploded. I wasn't there to see it but that's what I heard. Maddie let Otto know in no uncertain terms that she was thoroughly sick and tired of hearing about Otto's adorable wife, about Otto's wonderful marriage. Maddie stormed out.

Next week she returned with a bouquet of flowers, placing them directly across the board where Otto was playing, and offering her most heartfelt apologies. Dirt clung to the stems as if she had picked them out of someone's yard. By all accounts, Otto was completely flummoxed. He gathered up the flowers, placed them on the table beside his board, and tried to brush away the dirt. He played on, attempting to ignore Maddie, his face growing redder and redder. Maddie pulled up a chair and sat beside him, happily chattering away as if all was forgiven. Otto soon resigned his game, one of his few losses at the club, and exited. Maddie pretended not to notice.

At the chess club, being crazy was not in itself an unpardonable offense. Like most chess clubs, ours had its share of strong chess players who were mentally unstable, to put it kindly. Mostly, these guys were on the perimeter of the club, so to speak, stopping by only occasionally – but when they did stop by they were there to play powerful, sometimes chaotic chess and they were always welcome. It's probably still that way at the club, assuming Norm has kept his health.

Maddie unfortunately had earned the "crazy" label and she was also a weak player and, to make things worse, she was considered an unserious player, one who was unwilling or unable to improve.

If she had asked any of the other guys in the room that night if they would like to play with her, they would have said no. Except Norm. Norm would have said yes if he had solved his crossword puzzle. Norm made no judgments about anyone. But Norm really couldn't function until he had solved the puzzle he brought with him each week to the club. The other guys, they would have said no – and if later you asked them *why*, they would have said "because she's crazy." That was the word they used to dismiss Maddie.

I figured they were being too hard on her. I said, "Sure, I'd like to play."

Maddie

He wore no ring. You see that all the time in bars of course. But no one takes his wedding ring off to go to the chess club, right? I knew before the pieces were set up, before a word was spoken that he was lonely, that he dreaded the holidays – the immediate one, Thanksgiving, and the ones to follow, Christmas and New Year – maybe not as desperately as I was dreading them but he was dreading them quite a lot. So I knew right away that I had him. The question was: did I want him? No. Actually, the question was: did I think I could do better than him in the few stops I had left, or was he my best available option.

Some of these chess losers, if they will be so kind as to sit down across from you at all, will not speak a word while the game is being played, as if the fate of the world hung in the balance – give me a break! To be fair, they are not all like that: some of them have enough social skills and enough perspective to actually play chess and at the same time carry on a limited conversation.

Harry was one of these. In fact, it was hard to determine where the limits of his social skills lay. He was quiet and guarded, didn't offer much, but he could be drawn out – for instance, I soon discovered he was a great one for reading, a collector of books – also, he had a knack for gently turning the conversation back toward the other party, as if he were genuinely interested, so that I found myself talking quite easily with him, telling him things about myself I wouldn't ordinarily tell a man so soon. Or, in most cases, ever.

We sat at a table all to ourselves. Oh, I caught plenty of vibes from the other two tables. I knew perfectly well what most of them thought of me. Sometimes I think their distrust of me, their *fear* of me – because that is ultimately what it was – was what kept me coming back to their sad little gatherings: I couldn't help messing with them, getting under their skin, into their heads.

Anyway, Harry was a pleasant surprise and I began to hatch a plan.

Harry

I don't remember much about the chess we played. It was far from serious. Maddie was constantly prone to dropping pieces – that's a term we chess players use: it means leaving pieces unguarded and open to capture. I kept pointing this out to her, kept urging her to take back her latest move.

Maddie was a talker. I know a lot of the guys at the club hated that. I have to say I didn't mind it and it would have been silly for me to claim that I did: much as I like chess, the club for me when I could muster the morale to go was more about getting out of my apartment, being around other people.

She told me about some early miscarriages she'd had. This was completely out of left field – and in the back of my mind I began to wonder if maybe she wasn't crazy after all. Who tells stuff like that to a stranger? She told me that due to complications of the miscarriages, she couldn't risk having children. She told me how sad this made her.

Then in the next instant she was telling me about a cabin on a lake where her family vacationed when she was young, about a checker board set up on a gnarly maple table inside a screened-in back porch, about a rope swing that went far out over the water, about how all the other kids, her brothers and cousins (she had no sisters), how they would swing to the furthest reach of the rope then let go and it was as if they were flying and they would plunge screaming into the water, the freezing cold water, screaming with delight, into the "mirror of the sky" as she put it, and how she alone could not bring herself to let go of the rope, how she clung so tenaciously so desperately against her own will, her arms clutching the rope to her chest, her fists balled up under her chin, how she tried and tried to let go, how an older kid or a grownup had to always be stationed at the starting point, the huge, slanting, overhanging branch of a massive willow oak, from which all the children flung themselves into the air, someone had to stay there to fend her off from the tree and to catch her when she came whooshing back, spinning helplessly at the end of the rope, whimpering, defeated.

Maddie

I knew it would be hard for him to just up and leave with me if I asked him to. I couldn't tell for certain how many of the vibes from the other tables this Harry was aware of, but I could well imagine the looks he would get from his fellow chess losers if I offered such a direct invitation. So, the first part of my plan was simple enough. I looked around in my purse for something to write on, found an unpaid parking ticket and wrote on the back of it *Meet me at McFall's in 20 min*. He glanced at what I had written, studied me a long time, nodded.

I didn't like the long look he gave me. It was insulting. Why was a guy like him, fifty if he was a day, obviously lonely, hesitating even for one instant when a gal like me makes such an advance?

The second part of my plan wasn't too complicated either. I had a few more bars to hit, as I've already mentioned, and I was going to hit them with Harry in tow. If anything better came along, Harry could always be cut loose. (He didn't know it but he had just increased his chances of being cut loose with that long look of his.) Meanwhile, he could buy me drinks.

Harry

I had no idea where McFall's was — or even, for that matter, what it was. I assumed it was some kind of bar or club or restaurant but I had never heard of it before. I was already in my car, sitting in front of the unlit church — unlit except for the small, rectangular basement windows — with the motor running. I had hung around inside for five minutes after Maddie left. Not knowing where this McFall's place was, I didn't know how long it would take to get there, and Maddie had said to meet her in twenty minutes.

I thought about calling my son. He was almost thirty, he got around town more than I did — which wasn't saying much, but I figured he'd know. Then, as I was dialing, I recalled Charlie's inevitable first move when he needed information like I needed: he would whip out his smart phone. I had one of those, too. Was holding it in my hand, in fact, about to call him.

Charlie used to tease me about not using my phone to get information. I use it, I used to tell him, it's just that I didn't grow up with any kind of phone in my pocket, much less a smart phone, and for people my age it's not always the first thing we think of.

I used my phone to get the address for McFall's. Charlie had told me the phone could guide me to anyplace I chose, but I'd never accessed that particular "app," as they say, and didn't know how. Where did I ever go?

McFall's turned out to be about five minutes away, on a seedy stretch of the old industrial road that runs along the river. I thought about going back down to the church basement for ten minutes or so, but I was afraid of being drawn into a game. I pulled away from the curb with the idea that I would kill time by aimlessly driving around town. But that seemed juvenile somehow. In the end I decided to drive straight to McFall's and to sit in my car in the parking lot and watch to see what kind of people went in and out of the place.

On the way, I tried to puzzle out why someone like Maddie would want to spend time with someone like me. I had been working on this problem ever since she flashed me her note. Maddie, I guessed, was about mid-forties. She was said to have an attractive figure, although that was hard for me to judge, as I had only seen her three times now and each time she wore multiple layers of brightly-colored and loose-fitting clothes. (She once appeared for a lesson with Otto wearing a skimpy exercise outfit, claiming to have just come from the gym. This occurred on a night I was not at the chess club, but it was talked about frequently, both by members who had been present and by others like myself who had merely heard about it. According to reports, there was not a drop of sweat on her that night and she wore her usual heavy layer of makeup.) As I mentioned, Maddie had an expressive face and from some angles she looked appealing. However, there seemed to be a lot of conflict mirrored in that expressive face, a lot going on beneath the surface, and even I, with my limited experience of her, had noticed times when a cloud passed over her and she didn't seem very pretty at all. Still, she was young in my book, articulate, at times vivacious. Her hair was blonde – although with dark streaks, which probably was an indication that she colored it – (but I had been told by my own sister, who shows not a hint of gray, that this is common, that many women color their hair). Maddie's eyes were a disarming blue, warm somehow, although I had always understood that blue was supposed to indicate coolness, and she held her eyes open wide and seldom blinked.

My first guess as to why she wanted my company was, of course, that she was lonely, same as me. That feeling can get overwhelming around a holiday like Thanksgiving, which is supposed to be all about spending time with family and friends. I understood that all too well. But usually, I'd found, when you think someone else is thinking the same as you, you are mistaken.

The trouble was: I had no other guesses. So I decided to go with what I had. She was lonely, I was lonely. Thanksgiving was sort of the kick-off to the loneliest time of the year, a season that peaks at Christmas and New Year but does not end there, oh no: the loneliness slogs on through the cold dark days of winter toward the final insult, the last day of the loneliness season, Valentine's Day, another one of those concocted holy days designed to put a Christian face on an older pagan tradition, commemorating a possibly mythical saint, and now little more than a silly excuse to spend money on mostly empty tokens of affection, but deeply painful nonetheless if you happen to be alone. I did not look for Maddie to see me through the entire season. But if she could comfort me and I could do the same for her on this Eve of the Season of Loneliness – and perhaps we could go so far as to see each other through the next awful day as well – I was open to it, I was game.

Maddie

He rolled into the parking lot ten minutes early. I thought *Isn't he the eager beaver?* And then another voice inside my head quipped, *The eager beaver-snatcher, do you mean?* Inwardly I laughed at the joke, although really I don't have a dirty mind and I hate it when unseemly and unbidden thoughts spring up like that and I chastised myself for thinking this one.

McFall's had an outdoor patio that ran down one whole side of the building. A wall of lattice separated the patio from the parking lot. It was a cool, damp November evening but they had a blaze going in the fire pit and I was sitting outside, at a sticky, wobbly table-for-two just behind the wall of lattice, so that I could see Harry pull into the parking lot but it wasn't likely he could see me. Which was just as well: I was sitting at that little table with a guy who'd offered to buy me a drink the second I walked through the door. I'd said, "Sure, handsome." He was tall and skinny, as skinny as a drug addict, except for his arms, which he obviously liked to show off. He had bulging biceps and wiry forearms with veins as big as termite tunnels snaking under the skin, and every inch of his arms all the way to the backs of his hands was covered in tattoos. Despite the chill, he wore only a t-shirt with the sleeves cut off so that his arms were on full display.

When I saw Harry pull into the parking lot I thought: *Shit, how am I going to lose Mr. Tattoo when we've just started on these drinks?* But then I noticed that Harry wasn't getting out of his car. Was he on the phone with somebody? It didn't look like it. It looked like he was just sitting there. I remembered the long look he gave me at the club when I flashed my note and I wondered if he was having second thoughts about the whole thing. This got me riled up against Harry but Harry wasn't within reach, so I took it out on Mr. Tattoo.

I asked him if he'd built up his arms by lifting weights in prison. He said, darkly, "I ain't never been to prison, only jail."

"My my, aren't you the model citizen."

I kept at him and it wasn't long before Mr. Tattoo was endearing himself with little nothings like "You sure got a mouth on you, lady; I can think of a lot better things you could be doing with that mouth" and finally "I ain't got time for a bitch like you" before slouching off to find a bitch more worthy of his valuable time.

It all worked out perfectly because just as Mr. Tattoo made himself scarce, Harry got out of the car.

Harry

The place was just this side of being what we used to call a dive. I kept asking myself: why would Maddie come to a place like this? I kept hearing the guys at the club answer: *because she's crazy*. Why would she invite *me* to a place like this? Did she think this was the sort of place I would enjoy?

There were more people coming and going than I would have expected on the night before Thanksgiving, but then not many of these people looked like they had happy homes filled with smiling faces to go back to at the end of the night. Okay, so maybe it was my kind of place after all.

Inside, there was canned music turned up way too loud. The kind of music I guess they call hip-hop. Not really my thing. Fortunately, I found

Maddie on the patio where the music was not so oppressive.

I saw she had a drink and I said, "You started without me."

"Only one," she said.

I sat down. "Does someone come to the table?"

For some reason, this momentarily confused her, then she said, "No. You have to order your own at the bar."

I asked what she was drinking. She had to repeat it to me twice because I couldn't believe I was hearing it right. I went to the bar, got another *sin fizz* for Maddie, whatever the hell that was, and a beer for myself. I paid in cash: that was all they took.

Back at the table, Maddie and I attempted to make small talk.

"Feels like rain coming."

"I think the temperature is dropping, too. Good thing they have that fire going."

"You're a beer drinker, then?"

"Not really. Red wine is more my thing. But…" I would have said *red wine didn't seem like the drink to order in a place like this*, but I caught myself, not wanting to come off sounding stuck up or talking bad about a place that Maddie might like; instead I fibbed, "but tonight I felt like something different so I went for the beer."

The strange thing was: Maddie seemed to intuit my true meaning. She said, "I'm sorry about inviting you to such a shankhole, it's just that…" And then she had a similar moment to mine where she caught herself about to say something I might not like or fully understand. Except I had no ability to intuit her thoughts. She trailed off without ever finding a new direction for her unfinished sentence, resuming with, "I'm sorry — we can go somewhere else if you'd like."

"No no, this is fine," I hastened to assure her.

Maddie

I've been with plenty of guys who, if there's an awkward moment or two in conversation, they can't recover from it. An awkward moment leaves them uncertain, wary, sometimes even bristling and accusatory, like it's always the woman's fault, like a woman is never supposed to let that happen. Harry wasn't like that. Not like that in the least. Awkward moments left him vulnerable, does that make sense? They embarrassed him, and he was not good at hiding his embarrassment. His instinct was simply to get past the moment – he didn't blame me, he didn't blame himself, he had no interest in blaming anybody, because blaming wasn't solving – and he trusted the other party, in this case me, to cooperate in good faith to muddle through and get past the awkward moment. I found this genuinely endearing about Harry, while at the same time noting that it was a trait that could well be used against him.

Is everyone such a calculator as me? Sometimes I wonder.

Harry

She asked how I got interested in chess, and I mentioned my Uncle Stanley who taught me how to play when I was seven or eight.

"And do you stay in touch with your Uncle Stanley?"

"Uncle Stanley's dead, I'm afraid."

"Sorry to hear that."

"It was years ago; he died peacefully...and he lived a good, long life – he was ninety when he passed. So, how about you?"

"How about me what?"

"How did you get interested in chess?"

"That's a funny story," Maddie said. But the story she went on to tell didn't seem funny at all. Something about an ex-husband who taught her the moves but not much else about the game so that he beat her easily then actually gloated when he won and mocked her as stupid.

"Well, I hope he had other redeeming qualities," I said when the story ended.

"Not really. Marrying that creep was one of the biggest mistakes of my life. But I was young and stupid – we both were. So how about you?"

"How about me what?"

"Married?"

"Not married, no."

"Ever been married?"

"Yes, for nineteen years."

Maddie studied me. "What did she die of?"

I said, "Maybe I left her for someone else, maybe she left me."

"I don't see that in you," Maddie said softly.

I sighed. "An accident on the highway. It was foggy and there was some ice and a tractor-trailer jackknifed. There was a pile-up, seven vehicles including the truck. Two fatalities, Suzanne and a three year-old girl in another car. The highway patrol determined that no one was to blame." Maddie reached across the table and patted the back of my hand.

I said, "I get a Christmas card from the truck driver and his family every year. I never respond. I feel bad about that but I don't know what I would say."

Maddie

I knew I was going to have to dump poor Harry. Too bad, but I don't like sharing a bed with a ghost. The plan now was to get us both out of there as fast as possible, hit the few places remaining, squeeze a few more drinks out of Harry, and leave him at the last stop. I threw back half my drink; Harry had hardly touched his beer.

Just then Mr. Tattoo reappeared on the patio. He must have already struck out with every other female in the establishment. The only surprise, really, was how quickly it had happened. His face darkened when he caught sight of Harry sharing a drink with me. Mr. Tattoo noticed me eyeing him and he approached the table, smiling contemptuously.

Harry looked where I was looking and we both watched Mr. Tattoo take one careful step after another — he was having to put a lot of his limited mental capacity into walking straight.

When Mr. Tattoo reached the table, he slurred, "Hey grandpa, thanks for keeping my seat warm — now take a hike."

Harry glanced at me. "Do you know this guy?"

"Never saw him before."

"Lying bitch!" the tall man spat.

Harry smiled, looked the man over, asked, "What's that you're drinking?"

"Fuck off, grandpa."

"You fuck off!" I shouted.

Harry took a deep breath. "Friend," he said, "if the lady wanted me to leave, I would leave. But she wants you to leave. So don't make any trouble, just walk away." His voice was calm but suddenly more resonant than I would have thought possible for such a soft-spoken man. There was no belligerence at all in his voice but there was this quality to it – I'm not sure how to describe it – a kind of steely self-assurance as if he had a long acquaintance with command, an utter conviction that he would be obeyed because the consequences of disobedience were too terrible to even be contemplated.

My skin turned to goosebumps and a chill ran so far down my spine that it made me wriggle in my seat. (Thank god Mr. Tattoo was too drunk to catch the wriggle – who knows what he would have made of that!) I watched Mr. Tattoo. Was he at least sober enough to hear the tone of Harry's voice? Harry had been careful to remain seated so as not to unnecessarily antagonize – but couldn't Mr. Tattoo see the way Harry was sizing up his state of inebriation, how Harry had nonchalantly taken hold of his beer so as to be ready to throw it in the tall man's face? Couldn't the bleary-eyed idiot see how Harry was tensing to spring?

Mr. Tattoo turned and walked away.

Harry

Out in the parking lot, Maddie said, "Let's take your car, we'll leave mine here." She seemed to know exactly where I had parked my car. A chill wind rustled her many layers as she lead the way, and minute raindrops were condensing out of a gathering mist.

"Okay," I said, opening the door for her. "Where are we going?"

"I don't know, just drive."

We drove.

Maddie said, "There's a few other places we could go. Do you want to? They're a lot like the place we just left. I thought it might be a good plan to try them out but I'm not sure I want to anymore?"

"Go to another bar?" I all but whined, making a face, but Maddie ignored me.

"I can't believe how you handled that scumbag. I can't believe how calm you stayed. How in command you were. Did you used to be in the military or something? Weren't you scared? What were you going to do if he wanted to fight?"

"I was never in the military," I said.

"But what were you going to do if he wanted to fight?"

I said, "He was pretty far gone — I think I could have pushed him over and he would have had a hard time standing back up."

"Have you been in bar fights before?"

"No of course not, never." Then a thought occurred to me and I glanced at Maddie and asked, "You?"

"Me what? Been in a bar fight?"

I nodded.

"Never," she declared.

Even I could tell she was lying.

Maddie

Harry was suddenly very interesting to me. I knew it was a million to one I would find anyone more interesting at the places that were left. Okay, so maybe sleeping next to the ghost of his wife wouldn't be so terrible after all. Or maybe he had a guest room we could use.

I said, "Let's go somewhere you can drink some good red wine — know anyplace like that?"

Harry kept his eyes on the road. He spoke not a word.

Harry

God was I confused. Part of me was rock bottom certain that I didn't want to have anything more to do with this Maddie — what with the seedy bar, the odd story about her ex-husband who taught her chess, the belligerent drunk who clearly knew her, despite her claim to the contrary. I wanted so much to tell her: *Look, let's circle back so you can pick up your car and maybe I'll see you some night at the chess club.* I was on the verge of saying it. But something kept me from speaking.

Fear of going home alone to my empty apartment. Fear of waking up there alone next morning, Thanksgiving Day, with nothing to do and no one to share the day with. Sure, there was that. But that was nothing new. Minus the special sauce of it being a holiday, those were the typical fears of a lonely old man who had also, to be perfectly frank, gone too long without having sex; those were the typical fears of a lonely, horny old man.

But there was something, too, about Maddie. Something beyond the simple, basic fact of her being female. She possessed an unpredictability that, despite my better judgment, I found more than a little intriguing. And she had shown that she could be insightful, although I suspected that her keen ability to read people did not run so deep as to make her compassionate. And she was persistent – look how she kept coming back to the chess club where, she must have sensed, she was not generally welcome, look how she kept coming back to the game itself after her bad experience with her ex-husband – that was something to be admired, right?

Yeah right. Or maybe all my rationalizations about Maddie were no more than smoke. Maybe it all boiled down to the simple, basic aforementioned state I was in.

Maddie had thrown something out there and she was waiting for me either to rise to the obvious bait or to call it a night. What else could I do? Did I even have a choice? I rose to the bait.

I said, "There's a bottle or two of red wine at my place – if you're interested?"

Maddie

By the time he answered I was fuming. First, the hesitation at the chess club, then that long sit in his car after he pulled into the parking lot at McFall's, now this. Who did this loser think he was?

"Stop the car," I said.

"You all right?"

"Stop the car," I repeated, cold as ice.

He stopped the car.

I got out, slammed the door, walked away.

Harry

Okay, I thought, *the guys at the club were right — she's crazy…now what do I do?*

Maddie

I had no idea where I was or which way my car was or how far I was going to have to walk to get back to my car. The street before me was dark and empty and already glistening from the light rain. This was NOT the way this night was supposed to unfold. I started bawling. And then I stepped on some broken pavement or maybe I missed the edge of a curb and I turned an ankle and I went down in a heap. And then it started to really rain, a cold, mean-spirited downpour.

And there was Harry standing above me. It was too dark for me to see the expression on his face. "Let me help you up," he was saying; "I'll take you to your car." He was practically shouting to be heard above the rain which was fast becoming a torrent, but even so I could hear this note of kindliness in his voice, like he was talking to an invalid or to an inmate from an insane asylum. He was reaching down a hand for me to take.

I slapped his hand away. I wanted to screech at him. That he was a loser. That I deserved better than him. But only sobs escaped me.

The wind picked up and the rain began to fall at a slant.

"C'mon," he said, taking off his jacket and attempting to shield me from the weather. "Let's get to my car."

I couldn't very well just sit there: I let him help me up. My ankle was tender and I let out a moan.

"You've hurt yourself," Harry said.

After a few tentative steps I knew it was nothing serious but — I can never resist — I played it up a little. Harry wound up putting an arm around my waist, so that I could lean on him, and we marched like that through the rain, Harry holding his jacket above our heads, trying to cover us both but mostly covering me. His arm around my waist was surprisingly strong.

Back in the car, Harry stammered his apologies. He hadn't meant to sound so forward, hadn't meant to suggest that I was "loose" or "easy" — those were his actual words — hadn't meant to "presume." He started to talk about himself, about how loneliness often clouded his judgment, but he quickly put a lid on that kind of talk. In case I hadn't already figured it out, here was another clue: Harry was not his own favorite topic of conversation.

We were parked beside the road. Rain drummed on the roof and washed across the windshield. Harry's short gray hair was plastered to his scalp. In the poor light, his hair, wet as it was, looked almost black. The motor was running and the heat was on; nevertheless, Harry was shivering. I thought this was odd because I felt fine. But then it occurred to me that I was wearing more layers than Harry was: his jacket lay in a heap on the backseat, too wet to be of any use. Also, Harry was drenched whereas I was relatively dry.

I thought it was sweet of him to think I had been insulted by his invitation due to my maidenly modesty, of all things. He genuinely did not have the slightest clue as to what had actually set me off. Men! — they're so dense — how do any of them make it through the day?

When I told him I'd love to go to his place to share some wine with him, he refused to believe me. He kept insisting that he should take me back to my car.

Harry

It was as if a bunch of the guys from the chess club were suddenly sitting in the backseat, acting like the chorus from some ancient Greek play, warning me: *she's crazy, get clear of her, drop her off at the seedy bar, then get the hell out of there, go home and be by yourself and count your blessings.* On the other side of the argument there was this: the memory of walking in the rain with my arm around Maddie, of the contours of her body leaning against mine.

It was tough but I kept my mind focused on the message of the chorus all the way to McFall's. Not that McFall's was very far — less than five minutes.

The rain was falling harder. I didn't know which was Maddie's car and she wouldn't tell me. We circled the parking lot and politely argued back and forth. The situation was getting ludicrous. Also, my resolve was failing fast. Here was an attractive, younger woman flat out saying she wanted me to take her home – wanted *me* to take her home. As we circled, I happened to notice Maddie eyeing this one green hatchback, sort of a wide-bodied mini-van, every time we passed it. The rear of the hatchback was festooned with bumper stickers, protesting all sorts of tyrannies and espousing everything from world peace to an uprising of wiccans. Maddie eyed this vehicle with trepidation not far removed from dread. In spite of this – or maybe because of this, given Maddie's peculiar nature – I decided this must be Maddie's car, and I pulled into an empty space beside it.

Maddie went pale. She stared straight ahead. She said something that I couldn't hear and had to ask her to repeat.

"Don't make me go there," she quavered.

"Go where?"

She cast a furtive glance toward the car. "I can't be there for Thanksgiving," she said in a terrified whisper.

Moments passed. Sometimes I'm slow on the uptake. Finally, it dawned on me what she was saying. "Maddie, are you living out of your car?"

"I can't be there for Thanksgiving," she said again, the edge of hysteria coming into her voice. "I won't survive it."

I backed out of the parking space and we headed for my apartment. Somewhere along the way Maddie started making small talk: pointing out little oddities in the passing scenery, making humorous observations about one person or another from the chess club, offering wry comments about people in general. By the time we got to my apartment, Maddie was acting as if the exchange about her living out of her car had never happened.

Maddie

It surprised me that Harry lived in an apartment. I had him pegged for wandering around some rambling brick ranch house full of his dead wife's bric-a-brac. The apartment was both Spartan and cozy – certainly large enough for one person, but by no means was it overly spacious. It was arranged like a townhouse. On the ground floor was a living room, a dining area, and a cramped kitchen. At the top of the stairs, I could see the door to the bathroom, ajar. I guessed there was enough room on the second floor for two modest bedrooms. One long wall, running from the front to the back of the apartment, going from the living room all the way through to the dining area, contained nothing but shelves of books. From floor to ceiling it was an unbroken wall of books.

The furniture was sparse and simple. An L-shaped couch and a chair arranged around a not-very-large flat screen TV. These all looked new – or newish at least. Below the TV was one of those electric heaters made to look like a miniature woodstove. There were two unmatched end tables and a pair of reading lamps, also unmatched. The dining room table looked like something Harry might have found at the dump. Or maybe it had been left behind by the previous tenant. Its tilted surface was made of scarred, cracked oak. Two beat-up wooden chairs stood beside the table. A folding metal chair leaned against a wall. Also in the dining area, off in a corner, was a small wooden table with a chessboard inlaid into its surface. A set of wooden chess pieces stood on opposite sides of the table in four neat rows: the starting position.

Under the front window in the living room and under the back window in the dining area were low shelves, brimming with more books. There was an additional reading chair and a floor lamp arranged beside the front window.

The place was well-dusted. The pine floors and the throw rug in the living looked as though they had been recently vacuumed. A faint lemony scent wafted from the kitchen, as if Harry was in the habit of scrubbing the vinyl floor in there every Wednesday before hurrying off to the chess club.

When we had pulled up in front of the place, the rain was falling in sheets. Harry had said, "Nothing to do but run for it – see you at the front door." He reached into the backseat and handed me his jacket. Then he got out on the driver's side and ran for it himself.

Inside the apartment, he kicked off his shoes but made no fuss when I kept mine on, tracking footprints across his clean pine floors. He flipped on some lights and went straight to the thermostat and turned up the heat. Harry was one of those conscientious people who turned the lights off and the heat down whenever he left his apartment – why was I not surprised? He returned to the little foot rug just inside the front door and stood there, streaming water. He was shivering again.

I laughed and said, "Go put on some dry clothes."

He looked at me in amazement. "Aren't you soaked?"

I held out his dripping jacket and he nodded and took it from me and hung it on a small rack of hooks beside the front door. He turned to me and said, "How's your leg? – didn't you hurt it? Looked like it was your ankle."

Running through the rain, I had forgotten all about that. I put some weight on it now and it actually did still hurt, at least a little, and I winced, trying not to overplay it. "Tender," I said, "but I think it's going to be all right."

"Good good," he said. "I'll just run upstairs and change then, if you don't mind."

"Not at all," I said. "In fact, I heartily encourage it. Take your time – I'll just be browsing your books."

Harry

Pulling on some dry clothes, a feeling came over me like this had to be a dream. Or a hallucination of some kind. Maddie could not be downstairs in my apartment. And in fact it was so quiet downstairs that it was almost possible to convince myself that no one was there. Then a floorboard squeaked. Then I heard someone running water in the kitchen sink. It was not a dream. I finished dressing, sat down on the bed, tried to take a minute to think things through.

Clearly, there was no possibility of changing my mind, of dropping Maddie off at her car after all. I supposed I could gently question her about other places where she might spend the night – perhaps with a friend or a family member or even in a shelter. If she did stay here, my plan was to fix up the living room couch for her to sleep on. Under no circumstances should she and I wind up in the same bed together. Having made a firm resolution on that subject, I put on a pair of slippers and went downstairs.

Maddie

You can tell so much about a person by the books they keep, assuming they keep any books at all – and if they are the sort of person who doesn't keep any books that says quite a lot about them too. Harry had not exaggerated about being a collector. He displayed, I'm guessing, at least fifteen hundred volumes on the shelves in his living room and dining area. It was hard for me to judge how many — there might have been two thousand books on those shelves. The books were arranged by subject, and the subjects were diverse. There was a whole section devoted to every aspect of chess, of course. There was a section devoted to history — particularly to medieval history, the Napoleonic Wars, and the American Civil War, along with stray books from various other historical periods. None of these were heavily academic volumes; rather, they were the kinds of texts an intelligent, inquisitive lay reader would be drawn to — mostly trade paperbacks and mostly, judging by their condition, purchased in used bookstores or in thrift shops. This was true of the books in all his subjects of interest: modern physics, space exploration, Darwinian evolution, birds and dinosaurs, human behavior, the nature of consciousness, economics (mainly critiques of capitalism and globalism), myths and folktales, world religions, atheism, baseball. Other subjects, too, but these were the main ones that caught my eye. Oh, and speaking of things that caught my eye, in amongst his books on WWII, as if placed there deliberately as an act of camouflage, I found a particular volume of essays that made me do a double-take — could staid old Harry possibly be into...? I would have to find a way to work that volume into the conversation.

One very telling fact about Harry's books: there was not a single work of fiction in evidence, leaving out the collections of folktales. Could Harry really be so interested in so many subjects and yet have no interest at all in fiction? I heard a creaking floorboard above my head and all of a sudden it dawned on me: the fiction must be upstairs.

It occurred to me that while Harry was changing I ought to catch up with my medication. I went into the kitchen and, filling a glass at the sink, popped a quick antidepressant. Then, since I had been drinking and expected to drink more with Harry, I added a couple of caffeine tablets. Otherwise, I knew, that tricyclic I was on mixed with alcohol would make me drowsy.

Back to the living room. Other than bookshelves, the walls, I noticed, were almost bare. There was a framed reproduction of Van Gogh's *Starry Night*. There was a framed photograph, poster-sized, of some sort of celestial object, a kind of misshapen galaxy. There was a simple wall clock: black numbers and black hands sweeping around a circular white face.

On top of a wooden stand near the front door was a small framed snapshot of a young man possibly in his mid-twenties. The young man bore more than a passing resemblance to Harry — this was Harry's son, I guessed. I picked up the photo for a closer look, wondering if I could catch a glimpse of Harry's dead wife in the son's features. Just as I was beginning to form a picture of her, Harry appeared at the top of the stairs.

Harry

She was studying the picture of Charlie. It occurred to me for a horrifying second that maybe Maddie knew Charlie from somewhere.

"Your son?" she said, almost as more of a statement than a question.

"Yes. That's Charlie."

"Living, I take it."

Involuntarily, my head flinched backwards at the question.

"Sorry," Maddie said, laying a hand on my arm, "sometimes things slip out — sorry. He looks nice. Does he live close by?"

"He lives right here in town."

"Will you be seeing him tomorrow for Thanksgiving?"

I hesitated. "Um, no."

Maddie's eyebrows went up. She waited for more.

"I see him from time to time but not…It's just that…During the holidays Charlie…Charlie does his own thing…"

Maddie said, "And it's obviously not something you're comfortable talking about."

"No, I'm not," I said.

"What a mysterious man you are," Maddie said.

That dragged a short laugh out of me. "More confused than mysterious, I'm afraid."

"Oh we're all confused," Maddie said, suddenly quite earnest.

I wondered if now was a good time to ask her about her own family and friends, about other places where she might spend the night. But before I could formulate the first question, Maddie said, "I'm cold! Are you cold?"

"A little," I said. "I turned up the heat, the place will…"

"Tell you what," Maddie said. "Why don't you fire up that adorable fake wood stove and pour us both a glass of red wine?" She kicked off her shoes and settled herself on the couch, pulling her legs up underneath her.

Maddie

It had been a snap talking to Harry at the chess club, then a little harder at McFall's, but now he felt closed up, like he had withdrawn into himself, like he wished I wasn't there. Part of him, anyway, wished I wasn't there. You didn't need to be a psychic gypsy fortune teller to see that there was another part of him, simmering beneath the surface, that very much wanted me to be there. It would have been easy to get mad at the surface part of Harry — it had already happened to me a couple of times and in varying degrees that night — but then where would I be? Alone in my car surrounded by the dark and the cold and the rain, and Thanksgiving rolling in like a tsunami. No thank you. My goal — my *job*, actually: I saw it in that moment as my job, in the sense that you work at a job to get nourishment, to get shelter in order to live — was to look past Surface Harry without rancor and to make contact with Simmering Harry.

It was slow going. Talking about himself made Harry uncomfortable, and he seemed to have lost the knack of effortlessly turning the conversation to me. Now his inquiries were rather a little too focused — who else did I know in town (subtext: where else might I spend the night). *Really!,* I wanted to chide him, *if I had anyplace else to go would I be living in my car? — would I be here?* But comments like that would have been contrary to the performance of my job, and I kept them bottled up.

The wine he served was a mid-range California merlot. I praised it continually, while still trying to be subtle about encouraging Harry to drink more. It was my hope that the wine would allow Simmering Harry to shine through. But it was clearly in Harry's mind to not lose control of the situation and, that night at least, he was a slow drinker.

Once I got him onto the subject of his books, the conversation flowed more easily. Harry was pleasantly surprised to learn I shared some of his interests, had read some of the same books — (although I was careful not to mention the one book that had particularly caught my eye). He was good at describing a book without making it tedious. He had a gift for briefly stating the gist, for touching on a few interesting facts, for pinpointing a book's key strengths or weaknesses. He was so good at it I had to ask him: "Are you a teacher?"

"Me? No."

"What do you do?"

"I'm a block mason."

"You're pulling my leg."

"No, really."

"Let me see your hands," I said.

Hesitantly, slightly amused, he presented his hands to me, palms upward. I slid my fingers then my palms onto his. His hands were hard and rough and I noticed for the first time all the little cuts and scrapes on his fingers. His hands were also very warm.

"Well, you must be the most well-read block mason in town," I said, "maybe even in the whole country...does all this reading help you in your work?"

He gave a short laugh. "It doesn't make me a better mason, I'll tell you that. But it does give me something to think about on simple jobs where there's plenty of time to think."

I asked him what he thought about, but that was a mistake, that kept the focus of the conversation on him longer than he liked. He clammed up and I had to find a new way forward.

I said, "Where'd you leave the bottle? In the kitchen? I'll get it. Drink up, I'll pour us both another."

It was touch and go like that for I don't know how long. Outside, the wind was becoming erratic: now and again rain pelted Harry's front window. Meanwhile, Harry's ridiculous electric wood stove hummed and shimmered, creating a very poor imitation of a fake fire; but it radiated warmth, and the faint orange light it put out was at times almost comforting. And Harry, I felt, was slowly warming up to me. And to my delight I found that I was warming to Harry.

Harry

Despite her claim of being cold, Maddie had removed her light checkered overcoat while I was upstairs and at least two finely woven and intricately patterned sweaters. (Each time I had seen her, that's how she was dressed: in colorful insubstantial layers – I might have already mentioned this.) The overcoat and sweaters lay in a messy heap at the far end of the couch. Now a scarf and another sweater came off and joined the heap.

She had no family or friends in town. She had arrived here months ago to take on a new job at the hospital. She was a councilor specializing in helping patients adjust to major health-related life changes: for instance, stroke victims who might never fully recover or the newly blind or amputees. The job was being funded through a federal grant, but the grant was eliminated as a result of some budget battle in Washington, and Maddie found herself out of work. She was like many mental health professionals, she said: prone to mental health issues of her own. She said this with a hopeful smile, as if trying to convey that she trusted me to understand, trusted me not to leap to any judgment about her. When the job disappeared, she found herself spiraling into depression, unable to make a decision about what to do next – in the meantime the little bit of money she had was dwindling.

At some point in the conversation, she asked me what I did and when I told her she seemed incredulous. She wanted to see my hands, wanted proof that I really did lay block for a living. When I showed her my hands, she touched them, placing her hands right on top of mine. It seems silly to say, but this excited me tremendously. I tried to hide it, not sure how successful I was at that. I had not been touched so intimately by a woman since…well, since Suzanne. And yes of course I know that holding hands or touching hands or whatever it was we were doing was not in itself all that intimate. But it was the setting that made it seem so: the dim light, the red wine, the rain outside, the two of us sitting along together face to face on the couch.

It was with great effort that I recalled my resolve not to wind up in bed with Maddie. I pulled my hands away. I forget what we had been talking about but my sense of the conversation was that it, too, was spilling over into intimate territory – and I abruptly moved the subject to safer ground. Maddie seemed disappointed, almost chagrined. She jumped up to get the wine bottle, found it in the kitchen, poured us more wine.

Maddie

By the time I convinced Harry to open a second bottle I was maybe two glasses ahead of him. By then I had noticed his small collection of music CD's. I couldn't make heads or tails of his musical tastes — best I can say is that he seemed to like both well-known and little-known artists across any number of genres. Harry didn't have anything to play music on other than the DVD player hooked up to his television. I selected a jazz CD and played it low. Someone named Plas Johnson. It was good stuff.

When Harry returned with the fresh bottle I said, "Do you know what I'd really like to do?"

"What?" he said guardedly.

"Play a game of chess."

That made him laugh. "I don't think chess mixes well with alcohol."

"Maybe not for you," I said, "but I've never tried it — maybe the wine will loosen up my inhibitions, make me more creative. Can we try? Please?"

So Harry pulled his wooden chess table out of its corner and we placed the two wooden chairs from his dining area on either side of the table. Harry flipped on an overhead light. I made him turn it off. I wanted the lights to stay low.

Harry

She picked up a white pawn and a black pawn and held them for a moment behind her back. Then she presented her two closed hands for me to choose one. I chose the left. It held the white pawn. I set up the white pieces on my side of the board.

I opened with my queen's pawn as I usually do, moving it two spaces forward. Maddie countered by moving her king's pawn one space. Slightly unusual but certainly playable. As I made my next move (queen's bishop pawn up two spaces) Maddie said, "What shall we play for?" I didn't know what to say to that.

Maddie said, "Back in middle school, we used to play spin the bottle, and the winner got a kiss. Did you ever used to play spin the bottle for a kiss, Harry?"

"Um no," I said.

"What was the prize when you played?"

"I, um…never played that game," I mumbled.

"Not ever?"

I shook my head.

Maddie regarded me skeptically, sure I must be either lying or pulling her leg. After a while she said, "You really never have, have you? Well, how do you like that?…I thought everybody…" Her voice trailed off as some memory distracted her. "The prizes became a lot more interesting by the time I got to college," she said with a throaty chuckle.

I shifted uncomfortably in my seat.

Maddie stared into my eyes, then at the chess pieces, then directly at me again. She gave me a lascivious smile. She purred, "Tell you what, Harry, if you win you can do whatever you like to me, how about that?" I stammered something about maybe that wasn't such a good idea. Maddie waved my objections aside. "Don't worry," she said, "it's not the same deal if I win, I see you don't trust me enough for that – if I win all you have to do is let me kiss you, but if you win…it's anything you like."

I have to say, the stakes excited me, aroused me, despite every attempt I made to keep my mind off of sex. The best thing to do, of course, was to purposely lose the game. But before that thought had even fully formed in my mind, Maddie anticipated it and told me I'd be cheating if I didn't play to win.

"You too," I said.

"Of course."

The trouble was: Maddie was such a bad player it would have been hard to tell if she was making bad moves on purpose.

Before move ten, she was down a knight for a pawn. By move fifteen she had lost one of her rooks and had gained only another pawn. On move twenty she was checkmated. With each capture, with each maneuver that strengthened my position and weakened hers, I felt a powerful sexual tension grow in me. By the time I played the final move, trapping her king, my heart was racing and my dick was bulging against the zipper of my pants.

Maddie rose, walked slowly around the table until she stood beside me. "Anything you want, that's what we agreed to…what do you want, Harry?"

I was as tongue-tied as a bashful teenager.

Maddie

I wanted very much to ask him about that book of his that had so caught my attention, but something told me the time still wasn't right. Meanwhile, Harry sat there hopelessly confused. It was charming in a way, hilarious in a way, but also sad that a man like Harry, a mature man, yes, but good-looking and personable despite his years, sad that he had starved himself sexually for so long, so that when an opportunity like this presented itself he could do nothing but blush and sputter.

Since he seemed incapable of telling me what it was he wanted, I went for the old stand-by: I turned him from the table, knelt between his legs, pulled his throbbing penis out of his pants and took him in my mouth. I haven't met a man yet who doesn't like that. Harry was no exception. Thank goodness he was clean down there; with older men, you never know (younger men, too, for that matter). Harry was circumcised – and I have to say I like that better. He wasn't particularly big but he wasn't small either – just your average run-of-the-mill penis, a size I kind of prefer. For instance, I could fit all of him into my mouth without gagging, just barely but I could do it, and I did exactly that from time to time just to let him know that I could. What can I say? Sometimes a gal likes to show off. Anyway, some guys really get excited by that. Mostly, I stroked the lower part of Harry's penis with my hand and used my mouth and tongue elsewhere, especially on the tip which in Harry's case was exquisitely sensitive. I've often wished in such moments that I could feel what the man is feeling – I think it must be different from when a woman gets her clit licked – and now that familiar wish flowed through me like an electric charge as Harry shuddered and gasped and moaned.

Yet no matter how I excited him – and I found there were a lot of little tricks I knew that excited him – I couldn't make him cum. I got him pretty close a couple of times, but each time he would take my head in both his hands and gently pull me away, whispering *no no no*, softly but fiercely. I had long since undone his belt and trousers, had slipped off his shoes and completely removed his pants and his underpants so that he could open his legs wide and I could get to him easily without fear of pinching his balls inside his clothing. After one of those times when he pulled me away, I decided to give my knees a break: I stood up and straddled him, face to face. He had partly slid down onto the chair and I sat on him high enough up so as not to squash his member. I was still wearing most of my clothes but as I lowered myself onto him I could feel the shaft of his penis pushing upwards along the crack of my ass.

"What's the matter, Harry?" I wheedled.

"Nothing nothing," he pleaded. "It's wonderful."

"Why don't you cum?"

He was blushing. "It…it wouldn't be right…not in your mouth…"

"But, Harry, I don't mind, I want you to."

"No," he insisted. "It wouldn't be right."

I looked straight into those flinty gray eyes of his. "Do you want to fuck me?"

More blushing.

"You do, don't you? – of course you do."

He made some excuse about not having any condoms in the apartment and I told him that maybe, just maybe I might be able to find one in my purse.

Harry

Sometimes I'm slow on the uptake – have I already mentioned that? I think most guys would have clued into the possibility that Maddie could be a prostitute much sooner than I ever did.

Maddie

It flashed across his face that he thought I was a hooker. I wanted to slap him. If a gal uses her body from time to time because she needs to to survive…in my mind that's a different thing from prostitution. I admit there can be a slippery slope but, if said gal keeps before her a few basic principles, she can, I believe, steer clear of moral hazard. The first principle is: if she's not having fun herself, she shouldn't do it. In other words: on some level you have to truly like the person you find yourself with. For instance, I would have frozen to death on the street, I would have slit my wrists in my car before I spent a minute with Harry in his apartment if I had not felt some attraction to Harry. The second principle is: give freely, don't make it a transaction, leave it up to the other person to give in kind – or not. But I have found that if the first principle has been assiduously followed it is rare to be disappointed when following the second principle.

So much for Maddie's Theory of the Interpersonal Barter Economy. Actually, though, it helped me in that moment to remember and to think through my basic principles. It kept me from slapping Harry.

Instead, I laid a hand on either check, patted him gently, and said, "I'm not what you think."

He told me it was uncanny how I could read his mind; I told him he had an especially open face, which was true.

He started to make some noise about how he didn't think it was such a good idea for the two of us to have sex but I cut him off. His dick was still hard as a hickory pole. Pointing to the clock on the wall, I said, "Would you look at the time!…getting close to midnight…drink up, Harry, it's nearly Thanksgiving."

I lifted myself off of him, retrieved my glass, pretended to drink. I wanted to give him a chance to catch up.

"Anyway," I said, "you've already had your prize for winning. If you want to do something else to me, you have to win another game."

Harry was already slipping on his underpants and trousers. "I…I don't think I like those stakes," he said. "It kind of puts me on the spot and…I'm not good at…I'm not used to…"

"It's okay," I said, setting up the pieces for another game. "We'll play for something else if you like…let's see, what will it be…I know, let's play strip chess."

Harry

She described the rules for strip chess as if any schoolboy ought to know them. If a player's piece got captured, he or she forfeited an article of clothing and had to remove it. If either player got checkmated, he or she forfeited all of their clothing. Simple.

Maddie had the white pieces this time. Before we began, she topped off my wine glass. I pointed out that she seemed to be wearing a lot more articles of clothing than I was.

"More of a challenge for you," she smiled and pushed her king's pawn forward two spaces.

I responded by pushing my king's pawn forward one space – opening as black with the same move Maddie had used in our first game. Maddie played her queen's pawn up two. I did the same with my queen's pawn. These are the standard opening moves of a French Defense. Maddie captured my queen's pawn and I took hold of my king's pawn, preparing to recapture. But Maddie said, "Uh-uh...an article of clothing first, if you please, mister." I thought for a second then loosened my belt. "You're supposed to stand," Maddie said. I stood and removed my belt. "Kind of sexy the way you did that," Maddie teased, taking the belt from me.

I sat down and played my move, capturing her pawn. Maddie stood and removed a vest. She handed it to me.

"Maybe we should turn up the heat," I suggested.

"Maybe we should," Maddie agreed.

No more pieces were captured for at least the next ten moves. I played solidly, developing my knights and bishops, castling on the kingside. Maddie's moves were unusual but more incisive than in our first game. It suddenly dawned on me that she was playing some kind of system – (had she learned it from Otto?) – whereby she was lining pieces up against my king and preparing to castle her own king on the queenside. As soon as she castled queenside I sent my king's knight to that side of the board, hoping that it would find an opportunity to lunge forward. Unfortunately this also had the effect of leaving my king badly undefended. Maddie immediately launched a pawn storm on the kingside. The next capture occurred when Maddie sacrificed a pawn to open lines against my king. She stood and removed a gauzy blouse. She was probably winning after the pawn sacrifice but she misplayed the attack and I was able to make use of one of her own advancing pawns to shield my king from her heavy pieces. But she was intent on breaking through. She threw everything at my kingside, ignoring my threats in other areas of the board. For instance, she completely missed the fact that a bishop was hanging. When I captured it, Maddie removed her billowy cotton pants. Underneath was another layer of pants but so shear that I could see not only the shape of her legs but the actual color and cut of her panties, which were turquoise and bikini-style, riding low on her hips and high on her thighs. Her legs were shapely and fit, not exactly the legs of a dancer but the legs of someone who had probably done a lot of yoga – or went to the gym a lot: I recalled the story of her showing up at the chess club in skimpy workout clothes. The next chess piece to go from the board was Maddie's queen. Here's how that happened: Maddie moved a knight to the center of the board with the obvious intention of throwing it into the attack against my king; I countered by shifting a bishop so that, if the knight moved, her queen would be exposed to capture; Maddie, not seeing past the attacking possibilities of the knight, overlooked the "pin" as we chess players say.

I suggested that the queen ought to be worth at least two articles of clothing. Maddie gave me a smoldering look and said, "Oh at least…in fact I ought to be punished severely for losing my queen like that." She gave me a pair of socks: she was still wearing another pair. Resuming play, Maddie was able to capture my bishop, and I gave her my pullover sweater, which left me wearing only a t-shirt on top.

Once Maddie's queen had been captured, her attack fizzled and her position collapsed. Over the course of ten moves I made nine captures and Maddie one by one handed over her clothes until she was left wearing only a bra, the shear pants and the turquoise panties, also one sock. As the layers peeled away, I was becoming more and more distracted by the sight of her. She was generously curved yet slim – the kind of slimness that comes from a lot of effort.

I was still more or less fully clothed. Her king was boxed in a corner, and I had such an overwhelming material advantage that even a player of my limited strength could calculate any number of quick checkmates. But I had become entranced by the strip show. It wouldn't do to checkmate her and capture all her remaining clothes in one fell swoop – I had to take possession of them one at a time.

Playing chess, Maddie hardly took any time to think. She plunked down her pieces with lightning speed. Personally, I hated to play that way: I was never any good at what chess enthusiasts call "blitz." It always took me a long time to think through even simple tactics, much less to be able to grasp the basics of the underlying strategic situation. Too long when playing against other serious players, which was why I lost so often. But to make it a fair contest against Maddie, I was doing my best to play as quickly as she played. From my point of view, it was making a tense situation even worse.

The dim, shadowy light was another distraction.

Maddie gave up the bra next and I saw for the first time her full, round breasts. Imagine a statue depicting an immense crying goddess, imagine the shape of the teardrops on her cheeks – I don't know how better to describe the shape of Maddie's breasts. To a man like me, lonely and longing, the sight of them was nothing short of miraculous.

When her shear pants came off she made a small performance of it, turning slowly, swaying her hips, sliding the material side to side as the pants slowly descended.

Maddie was down to one pawn and her king, one sock and her panties. She traipsed to the board and without the slightest hesitation shifted the pawn forward. Absent-mindedly, I maneuvered a knight into position to capture the pawn, which was now blocked by one of my pawns and was therefore unable to move. Maddie remained standing so that I could gawk at her to my heart's content. Or maybe, with all the rapid-fire captures, she had simply grown tired of sitting, standing, sitting, standing. She studied the board, and her body was stunningly beautiful. But something was puzzling her. I glanced at the board.

"I have no legal moves," Maddie said.

It was true. Her pawn was blocked. Her king was not in check but with my last move I had inadvertently attacked the only other safe square that remained to her king, and she had no other pieces. She couldn't move her king without putting herself into check – not allowed by the rules of chess.

"Isn't that stalemate?" Maddie asked.

I felt myself going red in the face, frustrated at my own carelessness. I had to admit that it was stalemate: the equivalent of a draw.

Maddie

At first I thought: he can't possibly be so worked up, he must be kidding. I couldn't believe it mattered so much to him that he failed to beat me: I thought Harry had more going for him than most of the losers at the chess club. But as soon as I said that to myself, I decided I was being too idealistic. Harry was a man after all: they are all the prisoners of their egos.

When I asked for my clothes back, he refused to give them, claiming that according to my own rules I had "forfeited" them.

"So, I guess you get a free show indefinitely, huh?" I challenged, swinging my boobs a bit to further mesmerize him.

"We...we'll play another game – you can have a chance to win your clothes back."

"How will it work? If I capture one of your pieces I get one thing back? And what do you get if you capture one of my pieces?"

He shook his head. "Not like that."

"How then?"

"If you win – or even if you draw – you get all your clothes back."

"And if I lose?"

Tiny beads of sweat had appeared on Harry's forehead. "Anything I want," he said.

Ah, so the demon wanted out of the dungeon. I was about to see the dark side of Harry, assuming he won. I couldn't wait.

Harry

Maddie started to set up the pieces for another game. I had to remind her that it was my turn to play white. I used the advantage of the first move to do my best to dominate the center. Maddie occupied a nearly equal share of the center and defended it solidly, developing her minor pieces to active squares. Both sides were poised to castle when Maddie unexpectedly threw another pawn into the battle for the center. This weakened her kingside and led to a series of exchanges that left her one pawn down, with her pieces slightly scattered. She chose that moment to castle kingside. I castled the opposite way and soon had my queen, both bishops and a rook all bearing down on her king's position. There was no hope of defense so Maddie tried a counterattack against my king. But her pieces needed time to get organized; meanwhile my attack was advancing at full speed. I sacrificed a bishop to strip away the two remaining pawns in front of her king and checkmate followed a few moves later.

"Well played," she said.

All this occurred while Maddie sat up very straight in her chair, putting her magnificent breasts on full display, no doubt to distract me. And distract me they did – there were moments when I felt they were hypnotizing me – but they also served as a kind of goad. I wanted those breasts, I wanted that body of Maddie's as my prize. And now I had won the jackpot.

Maddie said, "I'm not going to help you out this time, you have to tell me what you want."

I stood up. "Come upstairs," I said.

She moved to obey me without uttering a word. I notice for the first time, apropos of nothing, that the lone sock she still wore was pale green with narrow horizontal stripes of orange and yellow. I beckoned for Maddie to lead the way. It took no special feat of mindreading for her to know why I wanted her to go first, and as she climbed the stairs she put on an enticing show for me, swinging her hips, moving her ass which was so perfectly defined by those skimpy turquoise panties.

She paused at the top of the stairs, not knowing which door to enter. "To the right," I said, my voice a husky whisper. The door to my bedroom was half closed. She pushed it open and walked in. The room was dark except for the glow of the living room lights which had lit our way up the stairs and some faint hints of street lighting coming in through the closed blinds of the window.

Maddie reached behind her with both hands, touched my arms, took hold of my wrists, pulled my hands in front of her and guided them to her breasts. Suddenly, my hands felt bloated with heat, as if my hands were blushing. Or was the heat coming from her? – I couldn't tell. But when she purred *Mmm, Harry your hands are so warm* I had my answer. Her breasts were soft, pliant; and the worry flew into my brain as I squeezed and rubbed and stroked that my hands were too rough, that I was causing her pain. But she cooed *Oh Harry that feels good*. And the thrill in her voice left no room for doubt. Her nipples stood out as firm and as hard as acorns in winter.

She turned in my arms so that we were facing one another and she threw her arms around my neck. She kissed me hungrily, thrusting her tongue inside my mouth. She tasted of red wine mixed with some chemical flavor I couldn't identify – I chalked it up to those strange sin fizzes she'd been drinking at that bar.

"Harry," she whispered. "Do anything you like to me. Anything. Everybody hides something they want that they don't think anybody else will understand. Whatever it is you want, I'll understand and I'll never tell another soul. I'll give it to you, Harry, I want to give it to you."

Maddie

I felt a thrill run through my whole body when I told him in the dark that he could do anything. I understood to my core the danger I was putting myself in – What if this Harry turned out to be a really sick dude? – but it was the danger, the potential for danger that gave me the thrill. It was rolling the dice with my safety on the line based on nothing more than my reading of a stranger – usually I was pretty good at reading strangers, but sometimes I had been spectacularly wrong.

Harry's rough hands moved slowly up and down my back. Mostly he touched me with his fingers and I could tell he was self-conscious about the roughness of his hands, afraid that they might scratch me or something. His fingers found my panties; his hands slipped inside and he fondled my ass, delicately at first but with growing enthusiasm. My panties slipped further and further down until finally I gave a small shake and they fell to the floor.

I would have undressed him but I thought he might be getting a kick out of having me naked (except for one sock) while he remained fully dressed (minus the few articles of clothing I had managed to win from him at chess).

He said, "It's been a long time for me."

I put my cheek against his and nodded. He kissed my neck.

"I want to see you," he said. He stepped away from me. For a moment I thought he was going to flip on an overhead light: I squinted to be ready against the sudden glare. But he opened a closet door instead, reached in and activated a pull-chain light, then pushed the door far enough closed so that the light in the bedroom was about equal to a dim lamp. He gazed at me.

"Turn around," he said.

I slowly turned for him.

"Sit on the bed."

I sat.

"Stand up again."

I stood.

"Good god you're beautiful," he said.

I laughed. "You're not so bad yourself, mister."

He shook his head. "Broken down old man," he muttered.

"Hardly."

He continued to drink in the sight of me. I couldn't remember the last time a man looked at me with such longing and such appreciation: I have to say it made me feel singularly good, like I was a celebrity or even a goddess.

Harry said, "I feel like I'm in a dream."

I moved toward him. I kissed him, lightly this time. "Maybe this *is* a dream, Harry — you should go with that feeling...what have you always dreamed of doing with a woman?...this is your chance to do it."

Harry

Maddie couldn't know it, but she was touching on a tender spot.

When Suzanne and I married, Suzanne was twenty-four and I was thirty-two: eight years between us. (Suzanne's fundamentalist parents were scandalized that she had taken up with such an older man and, even worse, a Catholic; then they were scandalized again and all their fears about the moral depravity, not to mention the wild prolificacy, of Catholics appeared to be confirmed when Charlie was born, full-grown and healthy, not quite seven months after our marriage.) At the beginning of our marriage and for perhaps our first ten years together, Suzanne portrayed herself as uncomplicated and innocent or, rather, she really was those things: they were a true reflection of who she was — just not, I'm afraid, a complete reflection of who she was. For instance, during those first ten years, she seemed to have no particular interest in sex. When we did have sex — which wasn't too often — we always did it the same way: with me on top and with the lights off, and it never took more than a few minutes. But sometime after ten years together — don't ask me exactly when — Suzanne began to want more from me. But she didn't know how to tell me or how to say what it was she wanted. She grew frustrated, and I was too dense to understand why and, although we rarely fought, there was a growing tension between us, which, of course, only served to make the situation even harder to escape from. Sometime after Suzanne turned forty, her mindset became, I think, it's now or never, and she started seeing a therapist. Whatever they talked about, it helped Suzanne; it transformed her. Suzanne grew wiser, freer, bolder. In bed, at her urging, we made the first few, tentative explorations of other possibilities. I was delighted but also still terribly confused. I'm ashamed to tell it, but after one of those small forays I asked: *Dear, is this the menopause?* It's a wonder Suzanne didn't slap me. Soon after, she sat me down and told me I needed to go with her to one of her therapy session. I said I would think about it.

Two days later she was hit by a truck.

In the eight years since Suzanne's death — (eight years: the difference in our ages) — I'd had plenty of time to go over all of this. It had become clear to me, for instance, that twenty-four year-old Suzanne was interested in vastly older me because she thought, she hoped, mostly unconsciously perhaps, that I, her husband, to whom she vowed both love and obedience, would impose upon her a whole new universe of sexual pleasures which until then she possibly had only imagined in the abstract — the steamy details being too sinful — and all of it would happen at no peril to her image of herself, not to mention to her immortal soul, because it would be her wizened, worldly husband imposing his will on her, and to refuse to comply would be tantamount to disobeying scripture.

Unfortunately for Suzanne, she picked the wrong accomplice. Sure, I was nearly a decade older than she was. But I had been a shy, bookish kid who had grown into an awkward, self-conscious, tongue-tied loner of a teenager and, sad to say, I never really found my way out of that. When Suzanne and I started dating, she was a virgin and I might as well have been, ignorant as I was. My sexual experiences till then had been few and far between and all with girls as socially challenged and as clueless as I was. I knew next to nothing. Also, I had been raised Catholic — Catholic in the days when sex outside of marriage was some kind of sin, mortal or venial, I could never remember which applied to illicit sex, and even inside of marriage one was never supposed to forget that the purpose of sex was procreation, not pleasure. Suzanne's fundamentalist upbringing could not have been much different. Do religious organizations still teach that nonsense?

Of course it occurred to me during those first ten years of marriage that maybe there were other things Suzanne and I might try in bed. Sex was everywhere in the culture, then as now, so it didn't even require much imagination on my part for these "other things" to enter my mind. But I honestly thought that Suzanne didn't like sex, that she only put up with my occasional friskiness out of a sense of marital duty. The part of me that was interested in "other things," maybe even keenly interested, slowly that part of me atrophied.

I'm not saying I recalled all this in detail while I stood there taking in the sight of Maddie. But on some level it all flashed through my mind.

Here's another worry that was flashing through my mind: Maddie, I assumed, had sex all the time, or at least as often as she wanted it, and, for her, sex was boring – regular sex, I mean. She was looking for something kinky, surprising. Then at the other end of the spectrum there was me. I had gone so long without sex that I was more atrophied than ever. I wasn't especially interested in any kind of kink, wasn't looking for the wild or outrageous. I just wanted a quiet, affectionate sexual encounter.

I tried to say something along those lines to Maddie – not the part about her having sex all the time but the part about me wanting to take things slow in bed.

Maddie wasn't buying it. She reminded me that *anything I wanted* had been my terms in our last game. I had to admit that was so.

Maddie said, "If we all we did was have vanilla sex, I'd just be one more in probably a very long line. I want you to remember me, Harry. I want this to be a night you'll never forget."

I tried to protest that there was no "long line," but Maddie laughed me off. But here was the thing: even if I knew what dark sexual fantasies were lurking inside me, I had no intention of opening myself up on that subject to a stranger, a stranger who might possibly be crazy, and who also might show up at the chess club some night and tell everybody all about it.

Meanwhile, Maddie was saying, "It turns you on that I'm naked and you're dressed, doesn't it? Gives you a feeling of power over me, yes?"

I agreed that it did, although really it boiled down to the simple fact that Maddie was wonderful to look at while I was a lot older, and I worried that she would not find my body very attractive.

"What else would give you that feeling of power?"

I needed to come up with something and in the moment an irrational idea took hold of me. I determined that I would make up something kinky that was not really anything I ever longed to try – that way, if Maddie spread it around the chess club, I reasoned (although that is clearly not the right word), it wouldn't be as embarrassing because it wouldn't be my real secret. I said, "Would you let me tie you up?...on the bed?"

Maddie

Alarm bells! It's almost never a good idea to let a stranger tie you up. Correction: it is *never* a good idea to let a stranger tie you up. Things can get out of control. Bad things can happen. Also, there was something not quite right about this request of Harry's, almost as if it were not genuine. I couldn't put my finger on it.

"Think of something else," I said.

He looked confused, disappointed, out of ideas.

"Doesn't 'anything' mean anything?" he wanted to know.

"No of course not," I said. "For instance, 'anything' doesn't include leaving permanent marks or drawing blood or inflicting serious injury."

Harry looked appalled. "Jeez!" he exclaimed. "I didn't have anything like *that* in mind...oh my God...what kind of sicko do you think I am?..."

I took him in my arms, ran my fingers through his hair, pulled his head slowly downward until his lips were touching by breasts. "Calm down, Harry," I said; "it's not a reflection on you, it's just...oh never mind...what were you going to use to tie me up with?"

It was a small relief to see that he had no idea. It would have been a very bad sign if he had immediately whipped out the handcuffs and the braided ropes. After a moment of casting about Harry said, "I know! I have this collection of cloth belts. They might work."

"Cloth belts?"

He detached himself from me and opened the door to the closet and rummaged inside. With the closet door more fully open, the light in the bedroom got brighter. "Here they are," he said. He held up eight or nine woven belts each with two metal rings at the end to cinch the belt.

"How do you happen to have a collection of cloth belts?" I asked with as much nonchalance as I could muster. "I noticed you were wearing a leather belt earlier."

"Oh I never wear these," Harry said. "It's just that Suzanne used to give them to me."

"She did, did she?"

"Yes," Harry said, blinking guilelessly in the extra light spilling out of the closet.

"Close the door the way you had it," I said.

Harry nudged the door shut a little past halfway.

I asked, "You never lived here with Suzanne, did you?"

"Here?...no. We rented a place on the edge of town when we were first married, then for years we had a house together. I sold the house after she died. Actually I sort of lost the house after she died...it was a rough time."

"Do you believe in ghosts, Harry?"

"Ghosts? Me? No!"

"I do," I said, "but I think they're every bit as attached to places as to people."

He looked at me quizzically.

"Come here," I said. "Put those belts down...hold me."

He stepped toward me, tossed the belts onto the bed, took me in his arms. The oversized t-shirt he was wearing gave little clue as to his physique, but once again I couldn't help noticing how heavily muscled his arms felt. If he had been wearing his shoes, we might have been the same height, but Harry was in his stocking feet so I was slightly taller – still, it felt like we were a good fit.

Harry began to mumble into my ear, suggesting that maybe it wasn't a good thing for us to sleep together, maybe he ought to make up the couch in the living room for me. I actually considered the idea for a second or two. But then I got to imagining how such an arrangement would play out: me by myself on the couch downstairs, him by himself in the bed up here, each of us listening for the other to creep along the stairs – and it would have to be him creeping on the stairs since he was the one suggesting the arrangement – and what if he never worked up the nerve? – no, that didn't strike me as any fun at all.

I slipped a hand inside his pants. He had gone limp, but that state of affairs was soon corrected.

"Nothing doing, mister," I told him. "You won something from me fair and square. I'm not going to have you saying to everybody at the chess club that Maddie doesn't pay up on her gambling debts."

"I would never..." he started to say, not catching that it was a joke.

"If I let you tie me up, do you promise to play nice?"

Harry

She wanted to go over the ground rules again about no permanent injuries, et cetera. Of course I agreed. She did not want to be gagged, but blindfolded would be okay if I got a kick out of that. I agreed about the gag, told her it hadn't crossed my mind to gag her or to blindfold her either. She wasn't into anal sex and preferred I didn't go there. That was disappointing to me. I confessed to her that I had never experienced anal sex and was somewhat curious about it.

"Really? Never?"

"Never."

She thought this over. She said, "I have to say, it's not much fun...at least not for the woman...at least not in my experience."

"Oh," I said.

"Tell you what," she said. "Ask me again later and we'll see."

"Okay."

Before I tied her up she wanted me to undress for her. "You can put your clothes back on after I'm tied if that's your thing," she said. "But I want to see you first, Harry...I want to see you for who you are."

I pulled my t-shirt off over my head.

Maddie said, "Wow, Harry, for an old guy you're really built."

I said, "Thanks, I guess."

She laughed. "You know what I mean...you're not really old...but most guys your age have totally gone to pot...but you..."

I looked down at my naked upper torso. "I lost a lot of weight after...well, when things changed in my life...then when I got on my feet again I went back to laying block, so..." I shrugged.

Maddie said, "Those lucky blocks."

I was slow to figure that out.

"Never mind," she said. "Not a funny joke...how old are you, anyway?"

"Let's not get into all that," I pleaded. "Not now."

I took off the rest of my clothes. I stood before Maddie, naked. With each heartbeat, my dick drooped slightly then bounced back to full erection. Maddie looked me over.

"Turn around for me," she said, grinning.

I turned for her.

She mimicked a man's voice. "Nice ass, strong legs...you'll do."

I felt myself beginning to blush. "Is that how men act?...is that how I acted?..."

Maddie laughed again. "It's just the way it is, Harry. And to some extent it goes both ways. It used to really bother me when men treated me like that, but now I see I'm going to miss it when they stop."

Maddie

I assumed he wanted me face down on the bed and I arranged myself that way without bothering to ask. I tucked the two bed pillows under my hips to give him a better show. He bound my wrists first. He was such a gentleman about it, adjusting the metal loops so that they weren't digging into me, careful not to make the restraints too tight, asking if they felt all right. I said they felt fine. He tied each of these belts to the bedposts at the top of the bed. There seemed to be enough slack so that I could wriggle my hands out if things started to get out of control. That helped to reassure me.

He bound my ankles next. He cinched these a little tighter. I speculated: *maybe he thinks a woman's ankles are less delicate than her wrists.* But when he took hold of my ankles and pulled me downward on the bed, so that the belts at my wrists tightened and lost all their slack, I felt a surge of panic. I tried to grab hold of the belts in an effort to retain some slack but I was too slow. "Hey, wait a minute, Harry!" I cried but he was already busily fastening to the lower bedposts the belts that held my ankles.

"Is it all right?" he asked again, still the seeming gentleman.

"Actually, they're a little tight," I said. "There's no way I can get out of these."

"Isn't that the point?"

Suddenly I had a sick feeling in the pit of my stomach.

"Take a minute to get used to them," he said. "If you still think they're too tight, I'll loosen them."

"I'd like you to loosen them now, please."

"Take a minute."

He stood beside the bed, gazing down at me. I watched him over my shoulder.

He said, "Now that I have you like this, what should I do with you?"

He had become utterly unreadable to me. Was he actually asking *me* that question? Was he asking himself? Did he really have no idea, or was he some psycho toying with his newest victim?

"Harry…please…" I wheedled. That wasn't the way I wanted my voice to sound: I wanted to sound more confident, more in control. At least I wasn't begging. Not yet.

An idea seemed to occur to him. "I'll be right back," he said. Then, smiling, "Don't go anywhere."

I thought: *oh shit, he's headed for the kitchen to get the knives.*

Instead, I heard him go into the second bedroom. I had caught a glimpse inside that room when we first came up the stairs. It looked like Harry was using it for storage and perhaps a small office. He flipped on a light in there, adding very slightly to the light in the room where I was bound. I heard him shifting things around, as if he were searching for something in a stack of boxes.

I thought about how to free myself. I knew there was no hope of pulling against the belts: that kind of movement would only tighten them further. I needed to create some slack, especially in the belts securing my wrists. I tried to shimmy forward on the bed, but the belts around my ankles pulled too insistently the other way. I tried to stretch my body: that helped a little. I tried to shimmy sideways to create slack on just one wrist: that gave me something to work with.

Meanwhile, Harry had grown quieter, as if he'd found the thing he was looking for and now he was tinkering with it. My imagination was providing me with plenty of images of what that thing might be, each a more horrific torture device than the last.

Even with the slack I had created at one wrist, I could do no more than touch with my fingertips the metal loops that kept the belt tight. There was still no way for me to work the belt back through the loops. Then a thought occurred to me. What if I pulled myself along that one belt until I was able to reach its far end, where it was tied to the bed post? Perhaps I'd be able to untie it. I pulled, dragging myself minutely forward. I strained as hard as I could against the other three belts and they tightened remorselessly, cutting off the circulation in my feet and my other hand.

I heard Harry making his way down the stairs. The renewed thought of kitchen knives freaked me out and for an instant I thrashed wildly against all four restraints. It was a panic reaction but there might have been some sense to it: perhaps one of Harry's knots at one of the bed posts would work loose. What made no sense – what was totally crazy – was this: as I thrashed I became suddenly aware of my naked ass, my exposed cunt wagging back and forth and I couldn't help myself, I grew moist with excitement. None of

Harry's knots worked loose.

When the panic subsided, I resumed pulling myself toward the one bed post. The thrashing, it turned out, had created yet a little more slack. My fingertips found the knot at the far end of the belt. I stretched even further. My arm was nearly pulling out of its socket. I struggled to undo the knot. I heard Harry's footstep on the stairs. The knot gave ever so slightly. I resisted the urge to try to yank myself free: that would only make the knot harder to untie. I worked my fingers into the center of the knot and probed for its weaknesses. The knot gave a little more. As if possessed of little minds of their own, my fingers at once understood the workings of the knot and the knot came free. I whipped my hand across the bed to unbind my other wrist. But there was Harry's voice just behind my ear, saying, "What's going on here?" And my free hand was pulled away, the belt still firmly clasped around its wrist. I tried to struggle but I found that I was exhausted. "No no," I whimpered as Harry retied the belt to the bed post. I felt a sudden chill and realized I was drenched in sweat. I buried my face in the bed coverings and wept.

Harry's voice was saying, "I haven't used this thing in so long the batteries were dead. Luckily, I had some spares in the junk drawer in the kitchen."

Then there was a click and a flash.

Harry

She turned on me with such fury I nearly dropped the camera. "Don't you dare take my picture like this!" she screamed.

Her timing was terrible because just as she turned and screamed I snapped another picture.

"Goddamn you!" she wailed.

I couldn't understand what the problem was. I tried to reason it out with her. I wasn't physically hurting her in any way: no marks, no blood, no permanent injury. She'd said she wanted this to be a night I would always remember — well, now I would have the pictures to help me remember. I was hoping she would let me take a lot more pictures.

Maddie refused to be reasoned with.

Also, I didn't know what to make of her incessant demands and pleas to be untied. Did she mean it? Or was she playacting in order to emphasize her helplessness and therefore to heighten my supposed sense of power? My guess was the latter, because otherwise it hardly stood to reason – I mean, she had just agreed to let me tie her up; so how was it possible for her to be so freaked out about it? Then again, this *was* Maddie pinioned before me in all her naked glory. How many times had she already signaled that I should not expect fully rational or consistent behavior?

I happened to notice that she had shifted somehow on the bed so that the pillows which had been under her hips were now more or less under a thigh. This shifting had caused the belts at her ankles and one of her hands to tighten dreadfully. Perhaps this was part of the problem. I took her by the hips and re-shifted her on the bed, then I made sure none of the belts was tight enough to cause her any harm. All the while Maddie protested that she didn't like what we were doing, that she wanted to be free. I reached under her to readjust the pillows. The edge of one of the pillows was damp. I thought it might be sweat because I had noticed that Maddie was sweating. Operating out of what I can only describe as instinctive curiosity, I touched my fingertips to the whiskers under my nostrils and sniffed. There was no mistaking that oceanic scent. I thought: *she's playacting for sure.*

I wasn't certain I could pull it off but I decided to go along with the dramatics. I gave her a playful slap on her lovely round upturned bottom, told her to hush up, that I'd untie her when I was good and ready. She gasped at the slap, stared at me wild-eyed over her shoulder. But she obeyed me, she quieted down. Now what was I supposed to do?

Her anger about the camera I took to be genuine. I had already set the camera down on the nightstand and planned to take no more pictures.

I climbed onto the bed, knelt between her legs. She'd said no to anal sex so that was out, but if I simply took her in the normal way from behind would that be too close to her idea of vanilla sex? Anyway, if Maddie really had a condom in her purse, we had both forgotten it – and this seemed like an awkward time for me to go traipsing yet again down the stairs. What I really wanted to do was just to look at her. Her prone figure, her pale skin in the dim light was like a vision from an extraordinary dream. But the situation, I felt, called for more than looking.

I touched her with the tip of a single finger, touched her just above the crack of her ass. My finger strayed upward along her spine. Goosebumps rose on her flesh. I felt the coldness of her sweat. I touched her like that as far as I could comfortably reach, almost to between her shoulder blades, then I laid my whole open palm on her back and slowly slowly moved my hand downward, scratching her soft creamy skin ever so gently with the abrasiveness of my hand. Maddie undulated from side to side like a partly hypnotized python, displaying what I took to be pleasure. I lifted my palm when my hand arrived at her ass but I kept that one fingertip in contact with the little ridges of her spine and continued to move my hand downward. The tip of my finger slipped between her flexing cheeks until I found the tuckered depression of her asshole. I circled it and circled it with my finger. Maddie shivered.

The other cloth belts I'd pulled from the closet lay in a tangle at the foot of the bed. I picked one up, doubled it, and folded part of it into my hand so that a small loop of cloth hung down. I touched Maddie lightly with this part of the belt, tickling her back and sides, all the while gazing at her. She arched her back, straining to look over her shoulder, curious to know what I was touching her with. "Ticklish?" I asked. Maddie eyed the belt, said nothing, turned away. She seemed to have grown tired of pretending to be afraid. I continued to lazily tease Maddie with the end of the belt, sometimes letting it slide across her ass and between her legs.

Maddie

When his hand came down on my ass, I winced and shut my eyes so tight I saw tiny sparkles against the insides of my eyelids. I don't think I cried out but I'm not sure – maybe I did. One thing I was sure of: hard as that slap was, that was not the full force of what Harry could do.

My reaction was…complicated. On one level, I loved it. It got my juices flowing. What can I say? I have a fetish about getting spanked. It has always turned me on. (I suspected Harry had the same fetish: the book I had spied on his shelf downstairs was what gave me the clue. When I offered him anything he wanted, I'd pictured him turning me over his knee and punishing me like an errant schoolgirl – not this!) Even now, if I truly trusted Harry, a good spanking would have made me cream the bed, would have left me begging for him to take me any way he liked.

On another level, Harry's slap sobered me. If he was not to be trusted, there was no use struggling. I needed to keep my head clear and preserve my strength. If things started to get too far out of hand, my only recourse, as far as I could see, was to scream for help — scream until he gagged me. Maybe the walls in these apartments were thin. Maybe a neighbor would hear and call the cops. Maybe Harry would get spooked.

It was a good sign that he stopped snapping pictures when I told him to. Or was I grabbing at straws? — might he be saving the resumption of that particular form of violation for later?

I could have kicked myself that I had not established a safeword with Harry. If we had a safeword in place, I would know exactly what kind of predicament I was in right now. Either Harry would have untied me, or not. If not, he would have demonstrated his unreliability, and I would know I was in serious trouble. Why *didn't* I establish a freaking safeword?! Too sure of myself, I guess. Too sure I had seen through this guy. Seen him as a harmless older man, an amateur to whom it would have been tedious to explain the whole concept of a safeword. Too sure I knew what he wanted.

His rough hand on my back felt gentle and warm. When he touched my asshole, I thought: *uh-oh, here we go, he's going to start taking what he wants.* But he did no more than touch me. When he started teasing me with one of those cloth belts, I thought: *he'll be whipping me with that thing in a minute.* I could almost feel that belt coming down on my ass, almost wanted it. But the whipping never happened.

It occurred to me that maybe I was not in so much trouble after all, maybe my initial panic had caused me to overreact to the whole situation. I decided to try something, to test that hopeful possibility.

Harry

I kept casting about for something kinky to do to Maddie but I wasn't coming up with much. The only thing I could think of was to "go down" on her, as they say. I know times have changed, but people used to think that any kind of oral sex was really pushing the boundaries. I have to say, I used to think that — still do, I guess, in the back of my mind. Kneeling there between Maddie's legs, I hesitated about initiating that kind of thing. What did I know about giving a woman oral sex?

It was at that moment when Maddie rescued me. She motioned for me to put my head close to hers, like she had something to tell me. I leaned forward until I was partly lying on top of her and partly supporting myself with my arms, my dick poking into the small of her back. She made a kind of purring sounds, as if she couldn't be more content. She kissed my cheek and nibbled my ear. She said, "Harry, darling, I'm absolutely loving this and we can get right back to it in a minute but I drank so much wine I really gotta pee – you need to untie me for just a second so I can go pee."

"Oh," I said. "Sure."

I slipped off the bed and untied her ankles then her wrists, working in the reverse order of how I'd tied her. When her feet and hands were free, she rolled over onto her side and gave me a long, solemn look. "I'll be right back," she said and she glided off the bed and into the bathroom.

Maddie

I glanced quickly into Harry's medicine cabinet on the off-chance he might have something in there worth popping. No such luck – his medicine cabinet was even more boring than I feared: aspirin, ibuprofen, Tylenol, Tums. I don't know why, but I often get the urge to steal things out of people's medicine cabinets. Stealing anything from Harry's would have been next to impossible since the only place I might possibly conceal the loot was in the one sock I was still wearing. I chewed a couple of Tums. But that didn't quite stifle the urge, so I dry swallowed a pair of aspirins.

I looked at myself in the mirror. I noticed the stub of a white hair at the corner of one of my eyebrows. I tried to pluck it with my fingernails but I couldn't get enough of a grip. If Harry had a pair of tweezers anywhere in that bathroom they were well hidden.

I purposely did not look at myself more generally – that kind of looking, especially around the holidays, especially in the bathroom of a stranger who, moments before, might have been a serial killer, that kind of looking could only lead to introspection which could only lead to recriminations and depressive thoughts. Safer to focus on details, the more minute the better.

However I did want to take the opportunity to commune with my reflection to this extent: I wanted to ask myself what to do with Harry. (As soon as I thought of Harry, I heard once again his footstep on the stairs. I was surprised to hear he was coming *up* the stairs: he must have slipped down them so quietly I never heard him.) He had proven himself to be trustworthy. Maybe the thing to do was to set up a safeword and let him have his way with his cloth belts again. But something told me his heart wasn't really into bondage. Maybe I should let him take me up the ass as a reward for not torturing me or killing me. Probably not, I decided — unless he became wildly persistent about it — it's never been fun for me; and why should Harry be the only one having fun? I turned my mind away from what I *should* do and instead concentrated on what I wanted to do. Oddly, I found, that what I wanted, after the tension of the last few moments, was what Harry had started out saying he wanted: quiet, affectionate sex — in fact, I wouldn't have minded in the least if we left out the sex. Cuddling with Harry until we both fell asleep seemed like perfect bliss — the two of us together in his nice warm bed in his nice safe apartment while outside the rain fell and the temperatures dropped and the holiday demons preyed on the weak and the lonely.

Harry

When she came back into the bedroom I was sitting on the edge of the bed. The cloth belts were back in the closet. The pillows were propped against the headrest. Maddie's purse was on the nightstand. Against my will, my erection had faded.

Maddie said, "You brought my purse upstairs." The faintest trace of a question was in her voice.

"You said you might have a condom — I didn't want to go through your purse, so I…"

"Oh…right…"

"But now…I'm not so sure…I mean…I'm sorry…I might not be able to…um, perform…"

Maddie

He looked so dejected, so defeated.

I plopped down beside him on the bed, threw my arms around him. "Oh Harry, it's okay — we can just cuddle."

"I'm such a..."

He was absolutely still and silent. He gave no indication at all that he was crying. But tears dropped from his cheeks.

My eyes watered: I'm so prone to crying when other people cry. "No you're not," I sniffed.

He looked at me with infinite sadness. "You should be with a much younger man...I'm, I'm no good for anything I'm afraid..."

It's got to be hard to be a man — no pun intended. They are so quick to be aroused and so proud of themselves when their dicks swell, but oh how their pride — not to mention their confidence — crumbles at the first hint of a droop. And, even worse for them, there is simply no convincing way for them to fake arousal.

I might have told Harry that the problem he was experiencing happens all the time to all kinds of men, young and old alike. He should relax, have a sense of humor about it — the problem might just fix itself. But I knew his main take-away from such kindly intended remarks would have been that Maddie was a "loose woman." Screw that. Still, I wanted to help Harry — he was so forlorn.

"C'mere," I whispered into his ear. I turned down the bed and slipped in under the covers, pulling Harry after me. I took him in my arms and snuggled the whole length of my body against his. That felt good. "Hold me," I whispered, and I felt his strong arms circling me. I gave him a long, tender kiss. Slowly, slowly his lips responded to mine. His hands rested motionless in the middle of my back, like warm lumps of clay. I tugged on one of his arms until his hand was in mine and I guided it to my breast. I applied gentle pressure to his other arm, urging it lower and lower. Both lumps of clay came alive and Harry was massaging my nipples, fondling my ass. Meanwhile, I planted a dozen little kisses all around his face, his neck, his ears. I rolled him onto his back and straddled him, dangling my breasts before his eyes.

I had been careful not to lay a hand anywhere near his penis, so as to avoid drawing his attention to what might or might not be going on down there. I still thought that was the best policy. I sat across his hard, flat stomach, leaving his man muscle to work things out for itself. My plan was to prime him for a few more minutes, then to nonchalantly slide downwards, scope out the situation. If there was no improvement or minimal improvement, my plan was to keep sliding downwards and do what I could to set things right with my hands and my mouth. He'd already shown that he liked that.

Harry continued to knead me with his hands. I told him how turned on he was making me, told him how handsome his face was, how beautiful his body was, how sure his hands were. I let an occasional moan escape me. I got so into my little act that I failed to notice the gleam that had come into Harry's eyes – all sadness had vanished, replaced by a kind of thankful adoration. His hands suddenly shifted and he took me by the hips and lifted me. He settled me so that the tip of his riotously erect penis was poking into the underside of my pubic mound. He slipped a hand under me and tried to guide himself into me.

"Whoa there, cowboy!" I cried, trying to sound like I was making a joke.

Harry gazed at me, a distracted grin on his face, as if he were beholding the image of a goddess.

"Let's get that condom on you," I said.

The condom was, of course, an important consideration. But the real reason I needed to slow things down was that I was so dry Harry would have torn me to pieces if he had forced himself inside of me. While I struggled one-handed to get the condom out of my purse, my other hand was furiously working my clit, trying to get some juices flowing.

"Harry," I said, "if you would just ever so gently pinch my nipples…no – you're rubbing them…I need you to…ow, now you're *poking* them, stop that!…I need you to pinch them, to gently pinch…a little harder…a little harder…yes, yes, just like that, yes…"

The floodgates opened and I was ready for sex.

I yanked my purse onto the bed, dropped it onto Harry's chest and, using both hands, dug out the condom then tossed the purse aside. I made no pretense of not knowing what to do with the thing. I installed it on him with well-practiced if not exactly professional dispatch. My hurry was not because of any burning need I felt; rather, I worried that Harry might at any moment suffer a relapse. I took hold of Harry's penis, stretched up high on my knees, positioned myself, pointed Harry in the right direction and, with a wiggle of my ass, sank down onto him.

Harry made a quavering *oh* sound, as if he had just found the keys to a car that had been sitting in his driveway for years, unused. Looking down on him in that dim light, with my body casting a shadow partly across his, it seemed to me that Harry could pass for quite a younger man. In my mind I made him so. This was not too much of a stretch given Harry's impressive upper body build – if only his close-cropped hair and beard had not been so insistently gray.

I leaned forward, placing my hands on the pillow on either side of Harry's head, until my face was just above his. His hands stroked my hair, my cheeks. His touch was gentle, reverential. He stared into my eyes as if he were searching for the answers to life's great mysteries. I rocked slowly forward and backward, letting him move inside me. "Don't!" he urgently whispered. Then he croaked, almost begging, "Please?...for a minute?... please be still..." I was still. I felt his penis filling me up and I knew he was doing okay with his erection.

"Is this good for you, Harry?" I cooed.

"Yes yes, this is wonderful – you're wonderful..."

"You're pretty wonderful yourself, mister."

I slipped a hand down to my crotch. With a single fingertip, I touched the base of Harry's penis. He made the quavering *oh* sound again. I hummed into his ear and I purred, "You feel so good inside me, Harry." All of this was more or less distraction so that I could finger myself again, keep myself lubricated. I figured we'd stay like this awhile, then I'd offer to let Harry be on top.

Almost unconsciously, I started to rock once more. Forward and back, forward and back. I felt Harry slip halfway out of me then plunge back in. *Oh oh oh* Harry quavered. His hands moved to my hips and they forgot all about being reverential. His fingers dug into my ass. Suddenly, he was thrusting into me, lifting his hips – and me – entirely off the bed. His *oh's* turned into *ugh's*. He came with such pent up energy that, if he hadn't been wearing a condom, it would have felt like a volcano going off inside me. Even so, it was pretty volcanic.

I crouched over him, studying his face. Inside me, his penis was rapidly shrinking. Were we in for a round of fresh self-recriminations – this time over the issue of premature ejaculation? No, we were not. Harry looked perfectly satisfied, perfectly sated. He did possess the wit or the manners or whatever to ask, "Did I go off too soon?" I kissed him on the forehead. I said, "No, darling, that was perfect." And for one brief instant I felt the ghost of his wife not only in the room but speaking through me. That should have creeped me out but, strangely, it didn't; if anything, it made me feel more connected to this man, this Harry, to his life. I rolled off of him, thinking: *great, that took a lot less time than I expected — now I can get some sleep.*

II. Thursday, Thanksgiving

Charlie

I called to Alexis that I was going out for a walk. It was Thanksgiving morning. The bank where I was a teller was closed, of course, but Alexis had agreed to work a partial shift at the hospital, covering for a co-worker who had called in at the last minute supposedly sick, so our plans for the early part of the day had flown out the window and I had nothing in particular to do until five-ish, when we planned to leave for Alexis' parents' house, about an hour's drive to the west. We'd been assigned to bring pies, but the pies were already made. Alexis and I had baked them together the evening before, doing almost everything from scratch: an apple pie, a pumpkin pie, and, my favorite, a strawberry-rhubarb pie. Actually, I had done most of the baking. Alexis had pulled a twelve-hour shift at the hospital and was feeling tired. I had cheated most on the pumpkin pie, using canned pumpkin pie mix. On the plus side, and to partially appease Alexis, who was getting more and more into a health food kick, the apples, strawberries, and rhubarb were all certified organic.

Sometime during the night a cold westerly wind had picked up. There was no trace of last nights' rain except a few stray clouds fleeing rapidly toward the rising sun and a maze of rippling puddles in the street.

It was not in my mind to drop in on Dad when I set out on my walk. Alexis probably wouldn't have believed that – but it was true. Okay yes, I did walk in the general direction of Dad's apartment, but there is also a coffee shop in that direction that I sometimes used to visit, as well as Greenleaf Park, a place where Alexis and I were always saying we should spend more time.

The coffee shop was actually open but I didn't stop in. The park felt rather lonely – too chilly and too early for most people to be out. Maybe that's what made me think of Dad: the lonely feel of the park, the early hour. Dad gets up every morning at six o'clock. Doesn't matter if it's a workday or not, doesn't matter if his alarm is set or not – he's just always up at six. So I knew he'd be awake. And I knew he'd be by himself in that book-crowded apartment of his. And it was Thanksgiving, and somehow it didn't feel right to leave Dad out of the picture altogether when we were planning to have dinner with Alexis' family.

You couldn't help noticing that Dad's apartment complex was dated. It consisted of a scattering of small, two-story buildings, all of them showing their age. Within each building, the narrow units were set up like town-homes. At least there was some space between the buildings and ample parking — nowadays, to increase density, they would no doubt pack the buildings closer together and minimize the parking; in that respect, Dad's complex had aged well. I noticed both his car and his work truck parked in front of his building: further evidence — not that I needed it — that he was home. I rang the bell.

I rang again.

I heard hurried steps fumbling down the stairs.

The door opened a crack and there was Dad, his close-cropped hair looking almost disheveled. When he saw it was me, he opened the door further. He was wearing a pair of gym shorts, hastily thrown on by the looks of them, and nothing else.

"Charlie!" he said, his voice all kinds of weird. "Is everything all right?"

"Everything's fine, Dad. Happy Thanksgiving."

"Oh yeah right Happy Thanksgiving."

"Are you okay, Dad?"

"Me? Yeah sure I'm fine…how are you?…are you okay?…and what about Alexis?…how is Alexis?…is Alexis okay?"

I peered at Dad a long time, trying to figure out what was going on. Then, just as I spoke the words *He's fine, Dad — Alexis is fine*, I heard a woman's voice calling from upstairs, "Who is it, Harry?"

Harry

Charlie's eyes practically popped out of his head — it made me think of the cartoons I used to watch with him sometimes when he was a kid. Then an enormous, silly, lopsided grin spread over his face. He said, "Damn, Dad — good for you…but pardon me, far be it from me to interrupt anyone's fun…call me later if you get a chance." And with that he backed off the front stoop and walked away with his hands in his pockets and such a spring in his step you'd have thought he was the one who had scored.

I closed the door against the cold morning sunlight. Maddie was standing at the top of the stairs, completely nude except for that one sock, pale green with stripes. "Who was it?" she repeated.

"My son, Charlie."

"Your son? Well, where has he gone?" Then, accusingly, "Did you send him away?"

"No," I said. "He...it's just that...he might have heard your voice. He said he didn't want to intrude..."

"Call him back," Maddie ordered.

"I really think it's best if I don't..."

"Call him back this instant, Harry, or so help me I will." She started down the stairs.

"Okay okay," I said and flung open the door and called to Charlie. I invited him in for coffee – he's a big coffee drinker. He demurred. Maddie, listening at the top of the stairs said, "Tell him I really want to meet him." I said, "My...um, friend would really like to meet you." I think Charlie could sense that I was being put up to this and that I wished he would go away. But I could see that his curiosity was getting the best of him. He said, "Okay sure, coffee sounds great."

I turned to Maddie. I said, "He's coming – hurry up and get dressed."

Maddie disappeared, then reappeared a second later. "My clothes are downstairs," she hissed.

And there was Charlie coming through the door.

Charlie

There was an x-rated flash at the top of the stairs. There was Dad standing just inside the door in his oddly-hitched gym shorts, looking for all the world like a criminal caught red-handed. He waved me into the living room, awkward and confused. He said, "I'll just have to run upstairs and get dressed." But then he didn't go upstairs; instead, he followed me into the living room. "Actually," he mumbled, "I have to collect a few things down here first." A motley assortment of women's clothes were strewn around that chess table of his, Dad's shoes and belt among them. I glanced at the position on the board. "Looks like mate," I said, trying very hard not to smirk.

Dad collected the women's clothes, blushing uncontrollably. I looked at his lean, muscular body, watched the unconscious grace of his movements even as he struggled in a situation which obviously caused him extreme embarrassment but which, by my lights, was no cause for embarrassment at all. I thought: *I love you, Dad; I'm glad I'm your son.* He fled upstairs, his arms full of women's clothing, leaving his belt and his shoes behind, also a sweater that I was pretty sure belonged to him.

I went into the kitchen, filled Dad's copper-bottomed kettle, and set it on the stove to boil. His drip-system coffee-maker – the pot and the cone, both made of white porcelain – were on prominent display on a shelf beside his kitchen window. I took down the pot, placed it in the sink and ran hot water in it from the tap. Both the kettle and the coffee-maker were presents from me: I had been trying to educate Dad on the subject of coffee. Coffee filters turned out to be in a drawer beside the refrigerator. The coffee itself was in a corner cabinet. There was a plastic container of instant, about three quarters used up; there was a bag of generic grocery store-brand ground coffee, "breakfast blend," almost full, but at least the bag had been opened; and there was, way in the back, the organic, fair-trade whole bean coffee I had given to Dad over a year ago, its vacuum seal intact. I sighed. I poked around in his other cabinets for the electric coffee grinder I had also given him. It was nowhere in sight. Meanwhile, the kettle was close to boiling – also I didn't know how long Dad would be and I didn't want him to find me rummaging through his kitchen. I pulled out the breakfast blend and measured out enough for a full pot of coffee.

I heard water running in the bathroom above my head. I heard someone on the stairs. The kettle whistled and I switched off the stovetop.

The someone on the stairs turned out to be Dad. He came into the kitchen, wearing a rumpled pair of khaki trousers, a pullover sweatshirt, navy blue, and a pair of black slippers – his usual outfit for hanging around the house. He said, "My…friend wants to freshen up a bit before she comes down."

"Does your friend have a name?"

"Maddie." Dad said.

I blinked at him. "Just Maddie?"

"Yes," he said. "Just Maddie…." His eyes moved around the kitchen. "I would have done all this."

"And where do we know Maddie from?" I asked, as if speaking to a recalcitrant child.

Dad turned on me the full force of that steely, fatherly gaze of his. "Son..." he said, his voice dark and calm and full of warning.

"Okay okay, I'll stop clowning around."

"Good," he said. "Why aren't you pouring the water?"

I just shook my head. I've been over all this with him before. Once the water boils it then has to cool a bit. Boiling water is good for tea, not coffee. Also, once one does start to pour water over coffee grounds, it is important to keep the grounds soaked at all times – do not let air get to the coffee grounds; pay attention and keep pouring in water a little at a time so that the filter inside the cone is always full to the top.

While I ministered to the coffee, Dad opened a cabinet and got out three mugs.

"How does Maddie like her coffee?" I asked.

"Dunno," Dad mumbled, shooting me a dark glance.

"Hmm," I said.

Maddie

The chess table was back in its corner. The two wooden chairs once again stood beside the beat-up oak table in the dining area. Harry's son sat on one of the wooden chairs; Harry sat on the collapsible metal chair that had been folded against a wall. The other wooden chair they had reserved for me. Harry stood when I got to the bottom of the stairs and his son, a moment later, followed suit.

Harry said, "Maddie, this is Charlie. Charlie, Maddie."

There is actually an etiquette to performing an introduction like that – and most people aren't aware of it. Assuming there is always some difference in the social status of any two people, etiquette requires that the more important person be addressed first and also last. So that if the palace gardener, say, were being introduced to the Queen of England, it would go like this: Your Majesty, please allow me to present the palace gardener; lowly gardener, you may now grovel before Her Majesty, the Queen.

It's a little thing but it's something I always have my antenna up for. It might have been unconscious, it might have been unintentional, no more significant than the flip of a coin, but Harry placed my social status above that of his own son, and damn if it didn't make me feel like the freaking Queen of England.

Charlie was slim like his father, not as broad in the shoulders but about half a foot taller. He had brown hair with a slight curl to it. I wondered if Harry's hair would show a curl if he wore it longer – (I thought about Harry's hair and decided that it would not). Charlie had the same square, handsome face as his father, but without the fierce gray eyes – Charlie's eyes were a prankish, moody brown. Long lashes and heavy lids gave them an almost feminine quality. Unlike his father, Charlie was clean-shaven – and when he shook my hand I found that his grip was anemic and his palm was softer than mine.

Three mugs of coffee had been placed on the table. Also on the table was a small bowl containing packages of sugar marked with the logos of various fast food restaurants. Also, there was a half-pint container of low-fat milk. Harry did not have any artificial sweetener or any half-and-half, let alone cream.

"I'll just drink mine black," I said, sitting down.

"Best way to drink coffee," Charlie opined.

Harry obviously liked to load his with milk, and beside his mug were three empty sugar packages.

I noticed that Charlie sometimes made a small humming sound after he spoke, as if asking *don't you agree?* – he had done it just then when making his pronouncement about the best way to drink coffee. This little verbal tick of Charlie's seemed to get under his father's skin.

Charlie and I said polite things about how pleased we were to meet one another. "I've heard so very little about you," I said; "I know you live here in town but, tell me, what sort of work do you do?"

Charlie spoke briefly about being a bank teller – for the time being at least, until he got himself through school: he was planning to take courses at the local community college.

Charlie was quick in conversation – much quicker than his father – and before I could ask what he planned to study he had switched the questioning to me: "But tell me about yourself...Dad and I don't talk much, unfortunately...I can't say that I've heard anything at all about you...how long have you and Dad been seeing each other?"

Harry

I felt my face flush when Maddie answered, "Oh we met for the first time last night...at the chess club."

"Really?" Charlie said, like he had just been handed a juicy piece of gossip.

"Actually," I said, "that was, I think, the third time we've seen each other at the chess club."

This time it was Maddie who said, "Really?" in much the same tone of voice.

"I noticed you the first two times, maybe you didn't notice me." It slipped out before I had a chance to think. I flushed even redder.

There was a slight, awkward pause in the conversation, then Charlie jumped in with, "Well, I think it's great that you and Dad have *started* seeing each other — I hope it continues...and what do you do, Maddie, if I may ask?"

"I'm between jobs at the moment," Maddie said from behind her mug. "Hey, this coffee's not half bad."

Charlie sent me a multi-layered look. The top layer was a look of concern: *Who is this woman?* Beneath was a look of satisfaction: *See how people appreciate it when you take a little trouble over the coffee.*

Charlie did not allow another awkward pause. "At any rate, you like chess, I gather."

"Fascinated by it. I've found it gives rise to so many interesting positions. Wouldn't you say that's true, Harry? But how about you, Charlie?...you must play – you're dad must have taught you."

Charlie grinned, not missing the double entendre — and my blushing discomfort continued. "Yeah sure, Dad taught me when I was a kid but I never took to it...baseball either." Ruefully, Charlie shrugged.

"Do you know what just occurred to me?" Maddie said. "Since I have the two of you sitting here together on Thanksgiving morning, there's a mystery you can help me clear up."

"What's that?" Charlie said. But I already knew what it was — and in that moment I knew that it did not just occur to her: it was Maddie's whole reason for insisting that Charlie should be invited in.

Maddie continued, addressing herself to Charlie, "Harry told me last night that you lived right here in town. But he also told me that he spends Thanksgiving alone. What's up with that? Is it true – or was Harry just playing on my heartstrings?"

Charlie took a deep breath and glanced my way, inviting me to speak. I muttered something about me not being very good company around the holidays.

Maddie regarded the two of us, clearly expecting more of an explanation.

When no further explanation was forthcoming, she prodded, "And yet here you are – and I don't see anyone fleeing your company."

"It's complicated," I said.

Charlie rose from the table. "Anyone want more coffee?"

Maddie

Complicated! I could have smacked Harry right in his gray whiskers. Aside from the fact that I can't abide it when a man says that to a woman – *it's complicated, dear, you wouldn't understand* – there was absolutely nothing complicated about this situation: Charlie was gay and Harry didn't approve. And yet they clearly had an affection for one another. Here they were making themselves miserable – and over what? A trifle. So, Charlie was gay. Big deal, Harry, for God's sake look at a calendar, let's see if you can figure out all by yourself which millennium you are living in.

What was most frustrating of all was that neither of them would talk about it. How were they ever going to get past it if they refused to talk about it?

Charlie picked up immediately on my mood – he cleared out pretty quick, saying "great to meet you" and "Happy Thanksgiving!" and, to Harry, "I'll check in with you in a day or two – if that's all right?"

"Of course, of course," Harry said, closing the door. He turned to me and, casting about for something to say, remarked, "That's great you got to meet Charlie." He couldn't have sounded less sincere. I regarded him in stoney silence. He crossed to the dining area and started clearing away the coffee mugs. "Did you get enough coffee? – there might still be some left in the pot...that Charlie sure makes a good pot of coffee..." Harry ran water in the sink and washed all the coffee things. I got the feeling that a dirty dish never stayed that way long in this place.

Harry emerged from the kitchen drying his hands on a dish towel. "We should see about getting your car away from that parking lot, don't you think?...should we go right now?"

Suddenly, all my anger left me; I felt tired and blue. I had moved from the dining area to the living room while Charlie was saying his good-byes. As Harry spoke, I sank onto the couch. I said, "I suppose you'd like to get rid of me as soon as possible, remove the disorder from your cozy little hidey-hole."

Harry made as if to speak but no words came out. He looked down at the dish towel in his hands as if discovering it for the first time. For an instant it seemed he would go back into the kitchen to hang the thing up properly but some wild spirit came over him and he tossed the towel over his shoulder through the kitchen door. He joined me on the couch.

I wouldn't look at him at first. But I could feel his gaze on me and I soon felt like an adolescent averting my own gaze. We made eye contact and he put a hand on my knee.

"Okay yes," he said, "there's a part of me that feels just like you say, I wasn't going to admit it but what's the point, you see through me so clearly. That part of me is small and scared – I'm sorry, I can't help it, it's part of me. But...but..." He faltered, he looked away. "Dammit!" he said, struggling to find whatever words he was looking for, or struggling with himself.

"We can go now." I spoke softly but did not stir.

"Maddie." He said my name as if he were alone, contemplating someone he remembered from long ago. Then: "Maddie," – this time addressed to me – "last night was...what I mean is...oh hell, I don't know how to say it – when I woke up this morning I felt alive, does that make sense?...not just happy, or not even happy really, but alive. I haven't felt like that in a long time – no! that's not right – I haven't felt like that ever, not like I did this morning. I looked over at you still sleeping and I was scared, I was terrified because...because I could see how out of place you are with me, and I thought: in this one moment I'm alive but Maddie will soon move on and this is the one such moment I'll ever know."

He was gazing at me again. I gazed back, trying to figure him out. He was undoubtedly sincere. Sincere in the sense that he believed this feeling he was describing was true. The feeling itself was another matter. Clearly, it was an overreaction to one night of sexual shenanigans, a night which in fact had ended rather anti-climactically – for at least one of us.

I patted his hand, still resting on my knee. "We had some fun, Harry. I wouldn't make too much of it."

"Yeah, he sighed, "I kind of figured that's how you'd be about it." He said this with an air of such resigned hopelessness that I was able to resist the urge to take offense.

I said, "I feel like you're telling me two different things: you'd like me to go and you'd like me to stay."

He thought this over. "I suppose I am," he said.

"I can only do one of those two things."

Harry

I took that to mean that she was leaving it up to me to decide. Later, it occurred to me that Maddie might have been saying, right then, that she had made up her own mind, that it was clear to her how this thing between us would have to play out.

I said, "I wish you would stay."

"Part of you or all of you?"

"Part of me," I admitted. "But the part that's not small and scared."

Maddie reached right into my crotch and grabbed my dick through the fabric of my pants. "I think I can guess which part, mister."

She kissed me playfully and sprang up from the couch. She bounded into the kitchen. "It's Thanksgiving! What are you going to fix me later for dinner?...Actually, if you're really nice to me, maybe I'll help." I heard various cabinets open and close, I heard the refrigerator open. "Jeez, Harry, what do you do for food around here?" She popped her head out of the kitchen.

I said, "I usually don't have much of an appetite." She frowned at me like I was speaking a foreign language.

"But today I'm starving," I said.

We went cruising in my car, looking for a restaurant that was open on Thanksgiving morning. It turned out, there were lots of eateries open, especially fast food. I drove past several of them, looking for something more upscale.

"Harry," Maddie said, "I'm not picky."

The next place we passed was a Biscuit Den. "Those are my favorite,"

Maddie said; "let's go there."

The Biscuit Den was a small place, maybe half-full. There were one or two solitary men hunched at the counter; a few silver-haired couples in the booths along the back wall; two couples sitting together, also well past retirement age, at a table in the middle of the floor.

Maddie picked a tall, square table by the front window. The table top was so small you wouldn't have been able to fit a regulation-sized tournament chess board on it. The chairs were such that you had to climb up into them. I thought that people had stared at Maddie and me when we walked in, because of the difference in our ages — and I mentioned this under by breath to Maddie.

"Nonsense," she said.

There was one waitress on duty and one cook at the grill behind the counter. The waitress was busy explaining something to the elderly foursome in the middle of the room. She was having to shout.

Maddie said, "You never told me how old you are."

"You never told me, either," I said.

"Guess."

In the bright morning light coming through the window, I studied Maddie's face. There were care lines under her eyes and radiating from the corners of her eyes. And there were those worldly blue eyes. Her lips were chapped and one side of her lower lip was slightly irritated because she had a habit — I had noticed — of biting it as if she were perpetually anxious. Maddie was fair-skinned and lightly freckled — or rather, she once must have been freckled: she had the look of someone who had spent many careless years under the sun, so that her freckles were becoming small blotches. This was even more evident on her neck and on the little bit of her upper chest that was visible. These areas were beginning to take on an almost leathery look. I tried to call to mind her exquisite, slim body from the night before. A slew of vivid images flooded my brain — but in every circumstance, even while we played chess, the light had been dim.

I'd be the first to tell you I don't know much about women, but one thing I know is this: in a situation where you are called upon to guess a woman's age, you can't go wrong underestimating by at least ten years.

I said, "Between thirty and thirty-five. You can't be a day over thirty-five."

Maddie hesitated ever so slightly and a look of disappointment flashed across her face. But then she smiled and even laughed and said, "Well,

Harry, you've got a real talent for guessing ages."

"I have?"

She became suddenly pensive. "I used to think I looked young for my age, people used to always tell me how young I looked for my age. But you hit the nail right on the head." She sighed. "I must be slipping – I turned thirty-five a week ago."

"Happy birthday?" I didn't know what else to say.

The waitress chose that moment to appear at our table. She asked if we wanted coffee and we both said yes and the waitress ambled away. Maddie looked about to cry. I hid behind the menu.

Was Maddie playing me? Was she really older and trying to make me believe she was still thirty-five? I glanced quickly over the top of the menu. I couldn't be sure. Her distress seemed real enough, but those worn features…. Maddie caught me looking at her and tried to put on a brave smile. Whatever age she was, dammit, I'd hurt her. I should have told her she looked twenty-five.

The waitress returned bearing two cups and a full pot of coffee. We ordered and, when we were alone again, Maddie said, "So, what about you, Harry – how old are you?"

Now it was my turn to hesitate. I thought the difference in our ages was bad enough when I considered Maddie to be in her mid-forties. It crossed my mind to lie – more than crossed my mind: I was sorely tempted to lie – but in the end I thought: *what's the use?*

"I'll be sixty at my next birthday."

Maddie's eyes widened. "Sixty! Really?!"

I nodded my head sadly.

She said, "Wow, Harry, you look great – seriously, you do." She went on for a while about how she never would have guessed, which only served to make me feel worse about guessing her age so accurately.

The food was slow in coming and we struggled to find things to say to one another. Maddie downed cup after cup of coffee. I breathed a sigh of relief when the food finally arrived: the regular breakfast plate for me; for Maddie, four eggs, scrambled, with a double order of bacon – and a biscuit, of course.

Maddie attacked the bacon first, picking it up with her hands. She explained between bites that she was a vegetarian, sort of: she ate fish and fowl but never the flesh of mammals, except for bacon — bacon was too much of a temptation. Then she covered her eggs with ketchup and dug into them with a fork, using the biscuit to help scoop them up.

She noticed me watching and, mouth full, said, "Sorry, Harry, I can't help it – I always eat like this the morning after sex."

The foursome in the middle of the room might have been hard of hearing but every one of those four heads turned our way.

Maddie

The bit about always having a voracious appetite the morning after sex wasn't a complete lie – but I did somehow forget to mention the fact that I had been cutting down on food lately in an effort to make my money last longer.

After breakfast, outside the Biscuit Den, Harry mumbled something and I had to ask him to repeat it.

"Do you still want to...stay?" he asked.

"Why? Are you having second thoughts? Do you want me to go?"

"I've already said I want you to stay."

"Then why the question?" I really had no clue.

He mumbled again but this time I heard him: "...because of my age."

"What about your age?" I demanded.

"I'm...you must think I'm..."

"What?"

"Horribly old."

I took his face in both my hands and gave him a big, sloppy, wet kiss on the lips right there in the parking lot.

"Does that answer your question?"

Harry flushed so red I was afraid he was going to have a heart attack. He hustled us into his car, glancing furtively toward a group of people sitting inside the restaurant. I hadn't noticed them before.

Traffic was light as we pulled out onto the highway. Harry suggested that we go pick up my car. I told him I didn't see why we needed to rush.

Harry glanced at me. "Aren't you concerned that somebody might break into your car or, I don't know, vandalize it? That McFall's place was sort of...what I mean to say is...um..."

I couldn't help chuckling. "McFalls is a creep pit – sorry about inviting you there," I said.

"Oh no, nothing like that – not at all," Harry tried to assure me.

"My car will be fine," I said, waving away all concern. "What we should do is find a grocery store – who knows how late things will stay open today."

We were on one of those commercial highways, lined on either side with chain stores and strip malls. It was amazing how many places were open, all varieties of business. Didn't things used to be different? Didn't most shops stay closed for Thanksgiving? When did it change?

I said some of this to Harry. He said, "I was thinking the same thing."

I looked at him. "You're like me, aren't you? – when the holidays roll around you hole up and hide, don't you?"

Harry nodded. I patted his leg.

We found an open supermarket and strolled through its aisles. Harry pushed our clunky, rattling shopping cart. Neither of us knew what to get; neither of us had any enthusiasm or confidence about cooking a holiday meal. We kept it simple: some fresh veggies (my idea), a couple of potatoes to be baked in the microwave (Harry's), several bottles of red wine (both), a can of cranberry sauce (Harry's), a roasted chicken (both – the store did not carry pre-cooked turkey and neither of us had any idea what to do with an uncooked one), half and half (mine – on my own, I would have selected heavy cream, but I thought it would be too rich for Harry: I was hoping to lure him away from milk in his coffee with half and half), butter for the potatoes (Harry's – a good omen for success with the half and half), a dozen eggs and two packs of bacon (mine – and oh how Harry's eyebrows shot up when I placed them in the cart).

On the highway once again, Harry said, "We'll drop the food off at my apartment then go get your car, okay?"

"Okay," I said, "but we have one more stop to make – pull in here."

We pulled into the parking lot of a chain drugstore. We sat in the car and after a minute Harry asked, "Is there something you need?"

"No – there's something you need, mister."

Harry looked puzzled. I was on the verge of enlightening him when he figured it out for himself.

He came back a few minutes later, blushing furiously, holding a small plastic bag that appeared to contain a single item. I looked suspiciously at the size of what he was holding.

"How many did you get?" I asked.

"I got a box," he said.

"How many are in the box?"

"I…I don't know…I didn't look."

I took the plastic bag from him and glanced inside. I said, "Trojans –

well, at least you got a good brand. But, Harry, this is a box of three. Didn't they have any bigger boxes?"

He didn't know.

I shook my head. "Well, we'll keep this one but go back inside and buy a bigger box."

"Go back inside?"

"Yes, Harry, and buy a bigger box."

"How big?"

"I'll leave that up to you, tiger."

Charlie

Alexis was gone by the time I got back to our apartment. I was tempted to call him at work to tell him about Dad. Actually, I knew calling was out of the question – for multiple reasons. But maybe it would be okay to text?

No, it would not be okay.

Alexis hated to be bothered at work. Even a text had better be important. And any news about my dad – short of that he was dead – Alexis would not have see as important. The only thing newsworthy Alexis would have found in a text from me about my dad and this woman Maddie would have been the news that I had been to see my father – and Alexis would not have been please.

Dad had made it clear that he didn't like Alexis, and Alexis in turn wanted nothing to do with my dad – not for himself or for me, either. Alexis' argument was that if my dad rejected my choice of partners, then he was rejecting me, personally, and my lifestyle. I agreed with that to a certain extent. Dad had never been able to fully reconcile himself to my orientation. I thought maybe we were making progress, slow progress – but then Mom died and I was still only nineteen and Dad, outwardly, turned to stone. I found out later – around the time Dad lost the house – that inwardly Dad had fallen apart same as me, maybe worse than me. But by then I had fled that place, the house of my childhood, which had become so full of Dad's brooding silences. I fell into a series of unhealthy relationships. I seemed to have a knack for it: back then you could show me a crowd and I would pick out the wrongest guy in it, and be attracted to him. So, Alexis' argument that Dad was really rejecting me and my lifestyle anytime he rejected one of my boyfriends was maybe a bit shaky – but Alexis didn't like to hear about my old boyfriends so I never got around to setting him straight on that.

It worried me sometimes that Dad didn't like Alexis any better than he liked the others. Maybe Dad had simply fallen into the habit of not liking any of my boyfriends; maybe I had conditioned him over the years with my poor choices. But I was certain I had opened a new chapter in my life when I met Alexis. Alexis wasn't like the others. He was far better looking, for one thing. Okay, yes, he had a few flaws, but in my heart I knew that he was worth the effort to try and fix.

Still. I wished there was someone I could share the dirt with about Dad. I thought about calling Aunt Fran, Dad's sister. She'd certainly be interested. We kept up with each other through Facebook (but not Twitter: Aunt Fran had some kind of grudge against Twitter) and she also used to check in from time to time by phone. She never failed to ask how Dad was doing. (She called Dad, too, and they talked, but Dad never was much for talking about himself and that tendency of his had only gotten worse since Mom died – and of course Dad was not on Facebook, or Twitter either for that matter.) Aunt Fran urged me all the time to look in on Dad, to spend time with him – but she didn't have the first clue about my situation with Alexis.

Yes, she would certainly be interested to hear about Dad and Maddie. But what, exactly, would I tell her? What did I know about this Maddie? Nothing really, other than the fact that she was significantly younger than Dad. And how would Aunt Fran take this news, ardent churchgoer that she was? Would she be happy for Dad, that maybe he was coming back to life, or would she feel it was her duty to reprove him?

Well, finding that out would be part of the fun, wouldn't it?

I whipped out my phone. Out of habit, I pulled up Aunt Fran on Facebook before dialing her. There she was, she and Uncle Milt, squinting in the bright sunlight, both wearing tropical colors like costumes that simply did not suit: off on a Caribbean cruise, in celebration of their forty-fifth wedding anniversary. Damn!

Did my newsflash about Dad warrant interrupting such an adventure? No, it did not.

I *liked* a couple of Aunt Fran's photos, all the while hoping that she and Uncle Milt were having a miserable time.

Maddie

I used to rate Thanksgiving dinners on a scale of one to ten, one being the kind of fiasco that involved smashed dishes, a broken window or two, a visit from the police. I stopped keeping score when it became depressingly obvious that, year after year, I had the world's worst luck when it came to Thanksgiving dinners. And then of course there was last year — my latest relationship in ruins, my medication all out of whack, no dinner at all, no job (I had been fired outright from that one, let's not talk about the reasons why), no home, nothing but a cold night alone in my car, nothing but pills and booze and waking up two days later in the hospital cursing myself for being the biggest failure in the history of the world: if suicide is the mark of a failed life, then a person who fails at suicide... All that happened in Minnesota. Minnesota is a dark place, especially in winter.

Thanksgiving dinner with Harry was quiet, low-key. In the back of my mind, I kept waiting for it all to go wrong — but it kept going right. Cooking was minimal and Harry took care of most of it, but the few times when we were together in his cramped kitchen there was no tension, no strife. During the meal, we talked mostly about books. We discovered more and more books that we had read in common. Harry impressed me with his thoughtfulness as a reader and with his memory. He was fascinated by my ability to make what he saw as surprising connections between books in widely different fields. I randomly played Harry's CD's one after another. The music was eclectic, covering a wide mix of genres and time periods, but uniformly good. In my mind I kept trying to match Harry to this rather remarkable selection of music. I could almost do it, could almost see the match — but not quite. Finally, I asked Harry about it.

"All of that is from Charlie," he explained. "Mostly from Goodwill stores and second-hand music shops, things he thought I would like."

"And do you like them?"

Harry frowned as if puzzled. "I used to play them because Charlie kept insisting that if I was going to be alone so much it couldn't be healthy for it to also be so silent. There was a period where I didn't even own a radio or a TV.

"I took Charlie's advice, I played them. But books were my true refuge. The music felt like a distraction. That CD player used to be upstairs and I'd play the music there, not very loud, while I stayed down here reading.

"So, to answer your question, I don't know if I like them or not, I'm only now starting to hear them."

I thought to myself, *Maddie, this is quite a breakthrough – this is the most comprehensive statement Harry has made about himself since you met him – good show!* (Sometimes, unaccountably, I speak to myself using a British accent: I've never understood why I do this.)

We realized toward the end of the meal that we had forgotten to get anything for dessert – no pie, no ice cream, nothing. In the past, I have witnessed only marginally dysfunctional Thanksgiving dinners spiral hopelessly out of control over a crisis such as this. Harry merely shrugged.

I said, "Red wine is a perfectly good dessert in my book."

Harry grinned. "Not much more for me – I have to go to work tomorrow."

I refused to believe him.

"Really – I have to," he said.

"Blow it off."

He laughed. "Not possible." He gave me a few details about the project his crew was working on, how behind schedule it already was, how desperate the contractor was to get the foundation completed.

"I heard on the radio when we were driving it's supposed to get into the high twenties tonight. Won't it be too cold to work outdoors?"

Another laugh. "It'll be forty degrees by ten o'clock – I checked – plenty warm enough to lay block. I plan to be there at nine."

"Well, what am I supposed to do?"

Harry seemed puzzled by this question. "You can stay here, if you like. What would you normally be doing?"

"What do you mean by 'normally'?"

Harry hesitated. "I guess I mean what would you be doing tomorrow if you and I hadn't met."

I felt a weird pressure behind my eyes. *Where would I be right now if Harry and I hadn't met?* – the question waylaid me. I felt a chill spread through my body like I was walking past a graveyard. I hurried to reassure myself – *I'd have simply gone home with someone else* – but a bleak memory of Mr. Tattoo sprang to mind and the chill only gripped me harder. Would I have settled for that? For something worse? Or would I have wound up in my car? And then what?

Harry gently touched my arm. "You okay?"

"Who me? – I'm fine, I'm great!"

"You looked for a second there like you'd seen a ghost."

Harry

I tried to remember last year's Thanksgiving and the one before that. But I found I had hardly any memory of them – just a vague recollection of feeling blue, otherwise nothing. I thought that if I could remember those last couple of Thanksgivings this one with Maddie would stand out as being pretty good. And it was pretty good, don't get me wrong, better even than pretty good – but it didn't compare to all the Thanksgivings from years ago when Charlie was young and Suzanne was, I thought, happy.

Part of my trouble was that, off and on all that day, I found myself preoccupied with sex – and my preoccupation only became more intense as our Thanksgiving dinner drew to a close. I hadn't experienced anything like this jittery tension since I was a teenager. Would we do it again tonight? That was without doubt a dumb question because I knew I wanted to and Maddie couldn't have sent a clearer signal: she was the one after all who had sent me into that store to buy condoms. Still, like a nervous teenager, I wondered. Also, *what* would we do exactly? Would Maddie want to make another attempt to get at my dark side? Would she want to reveal some aspect of her own dark side? Also – and these were the thoughts that really made me jittery – would I satisfy her (dimly in the back of my mind I suspected that I had not fully achieved that the night before), and, scarier, would I stay hard the whole time?

All of that was floating around somewhere in my head.

When dinner was over, I itched to clean up the kitchen but worried that Maddie would read into it something nefarious. I tried to satisfy the urge by stacking all the dishes in the sink and rinsing them. But the compulsion grew until finally I blurted out, "I'm not going to be able to stand it, I have to wash the dishes – please don't take it the wrong way."

Maddie grinned like the Cheshire cat. "I was wondering how long you'd be able to hold out," she said.

I *harrumphed* and hurried into the kitchen. When I came back, Maddie had filled both wine glasses and had switched on the fake wood stove. She said, "Last night I thought this was the hokiest thing I had ever laid eyes on but tonight I have to say it is starting to grow on me. as it a gift from Charlie?"

"No," I said. "I found it in the dumpster at a construction site where I was working."

Maddie laughed. "No, really, where did you get it?"

"Really, I got it out of a dumpster."

For some reason, Maddie found this hilarious — she could not stop laughing. Finally she said, "That priceless, Harry."

I started to say that I failed to see the humor, but that only set her off again. In response to my dour expression, Maddie, cackling, patted the couch beside her. I sat and waited. I thought: her laugh has a slightly hard edge to it. Eventually Maddie settled down, offering an unsteady apology. We sipped wine. We listened to Charlie's music. We necked. The fake wood stove churned away.

"Thanks for agreeing to play with me last night," Maddie whispered.

"Thanks for asking."

More wine, more music, more petting.

"Harry, tell me about what's going on between you and Charlie."

Maddie

Immediately he became tense, evasive. When I pressed, he said, "It might be best if you left that alone."

"But, Harry, there's such obvious affection between you two — whatever the disagreement is about, there has to be a way to bridge it."

"I'm asking you to change the subject." Harry's gray eyes were cold and hard.

"Do you want to go outside and look at the stars?" I couldn't think of anything else to say — and there was that color poster on Harry's wall of some sort of lopsided galaxy.

"Sure," Harry said. Then: "You might want to put on a few more layers — it's already getting cold."

We went out through the back door. We stepped off a narrow concrete stoop and walked along a concrete walkway and then across a patch of grass until we were far enough away from the building to see a wide swath of the sky — but in no direction could we see all the way to the horizon. It was a clear night but the lights of the city drowned out most of the stars. There was no moon.

"I like to look at the stars," I said. "Even when there's only a few."

Harry remained silent, staring upwards.

I rattled on, "Sometimes I can make out Orion but I don't see it tonight. Orion's about the only constellation I know."

Harry said, "I think it rises a little later this time of year." He pointed almost straight up. "That might be Cassiopeia but I'm not sure, the stars are so dim."

"You must like to look at the stars, too."

"Yeah," he sighed. "Mostly I forget to look – but they do help keep things in perspective."

"Exactly," I said.

We went back inside talking about how fantastic the stars were to look at when one was far away from the lights of any city. I motioned toward the poster on the wall. "What is that?"

"That," Harry said, "is a pair of colliding galaxies." His tone suggested that this was all the explanation anyone should need. But when he caught the questioning expression on my face he continued, "Apparently it's not an uncommon phenomenon, galaxies colliding – I read about it."

"Of course you did," I said. "But why...?"

"...hang a picture of such a cataclysm on my wall?"

He started to explain but I'd already figured it out. I cut him off, "More keeping things in perspective...whatever bad day you're having doesn't amount to much when you consider the inconceivable number of bad days on the countless worlds of those two galaxies...Is that the reason? – something like that?"

Harry nodded. "Pretty much exactly like that."

I studied the swirling colors of the poster. "Also it's beautiful," I said.

We had both worked hard to change the subject but I think we both felt that the subject of Charlie still hung in the air. I think that's what caused Harry to say what he said next.

"What about you..didn't you say you had brothers?...and cousins?...have you been in touch with them today?...do you need to borrow my phone?...I haven't noticed you with a phone."

Harry

Maddie's family — what remained of it — was thousands of miles away, on the West Coast. One brother was living; the other died while in the army — not in combat but as the result of an accident during a war game. "How senseless is that?" Maddie wanted to know. Her mother was living but resided in a state mental hospital: Maddie reported that she was completely deranged. Maddie's father had abandoned the family when she, Maddie, was young, and Maddie retained only the vaguest memories of him — he was a tall man, who towered over other people, with a prominent nose and very big hands. Maddie had lost touch with her cousins. She'd canceled her phone service to save money; her phone was buried somewhere in her car.

I urged her to borrow my phone and to call her brother.

"Actually, that might not be a bad idea," she said. "You really don't mind?"

"Of course I don't mind."

I handed her my phone, told her she should go upstairs so that she could have a private conversation. Upstairs she went, phone in one hand, wine glass in the other.

Alone, I sat in front of the fake wood stove. As if by its own accord my hand reached out and flipped the switch to off. Until yesterday, I had been alone for a long time and thought that I was thoroughly sick of being alone but now after Maddie's brief invasion of my solitude it was as if I missed being alone — this made no sense but I could not deny it was how I felt — and even the hum of the fake wood stove was suddenly too much company. The guys at the chess club thought Maddie was crazy? They should get a window into my head if they wanted a look at crazy.

Charlie! Why did Maddie keep bringing him up? What was there to say about Charlie? Of course I didn't like it that he turned out to be gay. What father would? But I didn't blame Charlie for it personally. I understood that it was part of him — like some people have red hair or a stammer. I had long ago gotten past the notion that it was a sickness or a condition that could be cured. And I sure as hell didn't see it as any kind of sin: religion didn't come into the question at all, no matter what my sister Fran might sometimes intimate. So, I had accepted the fact — but I still didn't like it.

And I especially didn't like the new man in Charlie's life, Alexis. Didn't like him the minute I met him. Didn't trust him and didn't like him. Charlie once tried to explain to me that I wasn't being fair to Alexis, that I was lumping him in with Charlie's boyfriends from the past, who had not always been nice to Charlie, that I was only *pretending* to have finally accepted him, Charlie, for who he was, and that I was *projecting* my unhappiness with Charlie for being gay onto Alexis. I told him, "Sorry, son, that's not what's happening." It was clear that Charlie didn't believe me – he thought, like he often used to think, that I was not in touch with my own feelings. I couldn't say that I blamed him. For years, while he was growing up, that would have been true of me – not in touch with my feelings and not interested in getting in touch. And I'm sure things only got worse after Suzanne died; thankfully, I have no clear recollection.

One more possible cause of the rift that had formed between Charlie and me: As the parent of a grown child I knew how tough it could be sometimes to see him as a grown-up and not as a child. The memories of those days when he was a child were still so strong. It had never occurred to me before that maybe the grown child experiences something similar: he can't always see past the Father-image of his memories to the fallible, malleable man who had been there all along hiding behind the curtain.

Without the warmth of the fake woodstove, the house felt slightly drafty. I got up, checked the thermostat, nudged up the temperature a degree or two. I wandered into the kitchen to make sure there weren't any dishes I'd missed. There weren't. I noticed that a lot of lights had been turned on, and I moved around the downstairs of my apartment turning off most of them. I peeked through the front window, was puzzled momentarily by the strange car parked between my cay and my work truck – it was Maddie's, of course.

The CD player ran out of music and I popped in another disk without bothering to notice what it was.

Maddie

No answer at Freeman's. Not a big surprise: it was Thanksgiving and of course he wouldn't recognize the number – he probably wasn't picking up. I left a voicemail, very short, just: this is Maddie, hope you're having a good holiday, call me back at this number, we need to talk.

I had not spoken to my brother in six months, at least. As far as he knew, I'd settled into my new job and everything was peachy.

I made the call from Harry's bedroom, sitting on the bed. It occurred to me that Freeman might see the call, listen to the voicemail and call right back, so I waited.

It was really sweet of Harry to trust me with his phone. Many men I've known would never have done that – too many secrets to be discovered on a phone. Of course I rooted around in Harry's. I didn't expect to find many secrets but you never know. He had practically no contacts. There was Charlie, some person named Fran, a few others who looked like business contacts. I felt sad for Harry. The only messages he sent or received were to and from Charlie – and they were few and far between. His recent phone activity was sporadic. The only apps were the ones that had been pre-installed.

I stood up, tossed the phone onto the bed and, moving quiet as a cat, or, more fittingly, a cat burglar, prowled around the upstairs of Harry's apartment. When I first came up I'd flipped on a light in the bedroom, so it was easy to see in that room. I looked through all his dresser drawers, silently sliding them open and closed. The oddest thing I found was that he had an entire sock drawer devoted to such things as Ace bandages, wrist braces, elbow braces, knee braces, etc. I thought: *I guess that figures given his age and the work he does.* I crept into his spare bedroom. It was dark, of course, but some light leaked in from across the hall. There were boxes of miscellaneous junk Harry must have salvaged from the house he'd lost. I saw them as a treasure trove – but too rich to explore in that ill-lit room and in the time available to me. There was a small desk in one corner where it looked like Harry kept track of bills. On the desk was a laptop computer, turned off. I went back into the bedroom, retrieved the phone and, using it as a flashlight, quickly rifled through the desk but found nothing out of the ordinary.

And then like a bolt from the blue it dawned on me: Harry had offered to let me stay here tomorrow while he went to work. What was I doing? I had all the next day to snoop to my heart's content. I exited the spare bedroom with the idea of going directly downstairs and rejoining Harry, but something stopped me. I swerved into the bedroom. I sat on the bed. Harry was a sweet, decent guy – and he trusted me. He trusted *me*!

I had a decision to make.

I wasn't proud to admit it but in the past my instinct had been to make guys pay for trusting me. I supposed I figured if they were as dumb as that, they got what they deserved. But over time I had come to see this instinct as self-defeating. Sitting there on Harry's bed, thinking those thoughts, it did not escape me how silly it was to say what I was saying — something so obvious: taking advantage of people (men, in particular) who trust you can be self-defeating — but for me, in the life I had led so far, coming to realize this had been a slow discovery. I resolved that it was time for a new direction — or, rather, I wanted to make such a resolution. But would I keep it? That was the thing I was trying to decide.

It fell silent downstairs for a moment then new music came bouncing up from below. It was a sort of fusion between jazz and Brazilian samba, vaguely like bossa nova but with an entirely different kind of energy, very danceable.

Freeman wasn't calling back; my mind wasn't making any binding decisions on the question of trust, or on any other questions. The only thing I could say for certain in that moment was that I very much did not want to be sitting alone in a room by myself on the night of a holiday — especially not with music like *that* canting and capering beneath my feet.

Harry

Maddie returned carrying the wine glass but not the phone. She wanted to know what the music was. I told her I didn't know. Rather than inspect the CD case herself, Maddie went to the wine bottle and filled her empty glass.

"Do you dance, Harry?" she asked.

"I'm terrible at it."

"I thought you'd say that," she said.

She stood there, swaying her shoulders, bumping her hips, gauging me. I could practically see her mind at work: how bad at dancing was I, really? — could she persuade me? — did she want to? It didn't take her long to give me up as a bad bet. She downed half the glass then placed it beside the bottle and started to move. I thought for an instant that this was a show for my benefit — but, no, this was Maddie dancing for the sheer joy it. She danced without the slightest hint of self-consciousness, as if she were alone, and for some reason this excited me and made me feel even more present in the room with her. The music took her over. I marveled at her ability to translate music into movement and maybe, for a brief instant, I lost myself watching her as she had lost herself to the music.

I was the first one back. Maddie still danced as if in a trance. Her forehead glistened with sweat. Instinctively, she threw off a gossamer layer of clothing. Then she was back, too. One moment she was not aware of me watching her; the next she was. Her movements by slow degrees became less fluid, became more intentionally provocative. She glanced at the clothes lying on the floor. She smiled at me.

Maddie

For years, starting when I was a teenager, I used to fantasize about being a stripper. There were times when I would dream about it, night and day.

Harry

One music track ended and another began. It was the same style of music – spicy, with a Latin beat – but slower, almost sultry. I think Maddie was already toying with the notion of stripping for me, and I think it was this new track that decided her to do it. Watching her, I regarded it – and still do – as a kind of minor miracle that this particular music started to play at this particular moment.

Maddie had stripped for me the night before during our second game of chess – but this was different. This show, this gift that she gave me was as different from the night before as, I don't know, a grand feast is different from a midnight snack. I think it would be tiresome to describe Maddie's performance in detail, but it was enthralling to watch. I'll only say that the layers were removed more slowly the closer to nude she approached, and this was delightfully tantalizing. When only her bra and her panties remained, Maddie made use of her sheerest garments as if they were veils, draping them around her while she – slowly slowly – removed her underthings and then danced for me in a state of semi-nudity. That was the part of the performance that aroused me most. Her movements were always fluid, graceful, were blithely erotic and at the same time profoundly sensual, were frankly indecent without ever becoming outright lewd. When finally she stood naked before me, breathing heavily, smiling radiantly, her last veil fallen to the floor, we were both surprised to realize that the music CD had some time ago run out.

Maddie had danced in the space between the living room couch and the dining room table – the most open area in my apartment. The couch was actually faced away from this space. I had started out watching her by twisting my body and looking over my shoulder, but sometime during the performance without even being aware of my movements I'd turned and knelt on the couch, resting my arms on its back. Maddie glided around to the front of the couch and, kneeling beside me, threw her arms around me and we kissed passionately. Maddie practically tore my clothes off. "Take me," she groaned in a husky voice. "Take me, Harry, fast and hard the way you like it." If this was still part of the performance, I was as spell-bound by it as I was by all the rest. I twisted us both around and laid her down on the couch and sprang between her legs, as eager as a young man. She hugged my ribs with her knees and inner thighs. Her hand found my dick and was guiding me into her. At the last moment I arched away. "The... condoms..." I gasped in a strangled voice. She gazed up at me with a smile I could not read. She said, "You're a sweet man for remembering, Harry." She slipped out from under me, retrieved one of the packages I'd purchased earlier that day, and in a very short time I took her just the way she'd begged me to.

Maddie

He rolled off of me, looking like he was content to spend the rest of the night sleeping there on the couch.

I slapped him on the shoulder. I said, "Oh no, mister, you don't get off so easily – this night is just beginning."

He gave me a languid, dreamy puppy-dog look, reminded me that he had to go to work tomorrow.

"Too bad, mister."

"What...what's left to do?"

I looked at him a long time. I searched for any hint of callousness or selfishness but found none, at least not in connection to his latest remark – I mean, Harry was a man after all and if I looked hard enough I was certain to find those traits in him. On the other hand, it was difficult to believe he could he be so clueless as to think what he'd just done to me on that couch was the kind of sex a woman enjoyed. He stared back at me so apparently free from guile that finally I decided, what the hell, I would just ask him. So I did.

He looked confused, maybe a little embarrassed, but to his credit he did not get defensive. He said, "Um…well…you did kind of say that's what you wanted…"

"I was giving you what you wanted, Harry."

"Oh."

"I thought that if we got the old slam-bam-thank-you-ma'am routine out of the way early maybe in the next round you'd settle down and relax a little and go a little slower."

"The next round?" Doubtfully, He glanced along his reclining body to his utterly deflated penis.

"After an interlude," I said, "for recovery."

His eyelids sagged. "I'm afraid I'm likely to fall asleep during the interlude."

"Too bad you don't dance," I said.

Harry let out a soft chuckle and closed his eyes.

I dragged him to a sitting position, tugging on his arm since he wasn't wearing any clothes to grab hold of.

"Should I make you a pot of coffee?"

He shook his head. "Can't drink coffee this late at night, I'll never get to sleep."

"That's sort of the idea, mister."

Another shake of his head, a slow, lazy smile. "No, really…coffee this late at night gives me a headache, makes me jittery…I won't sleep a wink."

I contemplated feeding him a couple of caffeine pills. Would he believe it if I told him they contained only naturopathic ingredients designed to improve stamina? I figured he might. But a small voice inside me said it was too dirty a trick to play. Usually, I don't listen to that voice but this time I did.

"Maybe if I just took a short nap…" Harry suggested.

"No way," I said, but he was fading. Then I got an idea. I gently slapped his cheek to get his attention. I said, "Go get that camera of yours."

Harry

At first I resisted. I didn't want to have to drag myself up the stairs. But once I got moving, the realization that Maddie was going to pose for me took hold and by the time I got to the top of the stairs it was all I could do not to take them two together.

I retrieved the camera from the spare bedroom. I'd hung it up in there during the day while I was tidying the upstairs. I noticed that my hands were shaking slightly from excitement. Downstairs, a new music CD started to play. I paused in the upstairs hall, took a few deep breaths, attempted to calm myself.

When I returned to the living room I found Maddie lying on the couch, giving me a centerfold pose: she was on her side, one elbow propped, her head resting on her hand, one leg tucked beneath the other, toes pointed, both knees bent ever so subtly, her other hand nonchalantly covering most but not all of her sparse brown pubic hairs.

It occurred to me that possibly she had done this kind of modeling before, she seemed so poised, so professionally *arranged* on the couch, but I did not have the courage – the balls, really – to ask her.

While I fumbled the camera out of its case, the cover off the lens, Maddie asked, "I can trust you, can't I, Harry?"

"Trust me?" I almost blurted before it dawned on me what she meant. She was asking: could she trust me not to post nude pictures of her all over the internet. I nodded. I said, "I would never do anything to hurt you or to embarrass you."

She seemed to sigh at that, almost wistfully, and it puzzled me.

I snapped a picture of her, then another just the same because I was afraid my hands had not been steady enough. I moved a little to one side to get a different angle and snapped another picture, then I moved the other way and clicked off a few more. She held perfectly still and let me photograph her from as many angles as I desired. Her only movement was to turn her face toward the camera when I asked her to. When I was done there was a pause. For the first time, the music came fully into my head. It was a species of the blues I had never heard before: quiet, understated: a rich, mellow (older) male voice, a single guitar masterfully played, every song a slow dirge yet, somehow, replete with the memory of happiness.

Maddie said, "You're in charge here, mister — you tell me how you want me."

At first I was timid about directing her how to pose. Timid and on some level embarrassed. I'm like a lot of lonely guys, I guess — I look at porn on my computer from time to time. The poses I suggested for Maddie came from those empty, enticing hours. And I could tell from Maddie's con-spiratorial grin — *you dirty old man!* — that she knew it. She posed for me on her knees, her shapely inviting ass up in the air, she posed on her back with her legs closed then with her legs spread wide apart, she posed bent over the arm of the couch, she posed standing, she posed while cupping her breasts, while fingering her vagina, on and on — each pose exactly as I directed. She smiled for me, she pouted for me, she sneered at me, whatever I wanted.

We moved from room to room. In the kitchen, while posing bent over as if looking for something in a lower cabinet, Maddie discovered a cloth apron. She held it up in front of her, balled in one hand. "This wasn't Suzanne's, was it?" "No," I lied. She put it on and I took a series of pictures with her front covered but her sides and her rear exposed, the thin apron strings accenting and further sexualizing her bare skin to a surprising degree.

I got very excited about the possibilities of semi-nudity. I told Maddie to go find her panties and to put them on. I waited for her in the kitchen. I was so into what we were doing that my directions to Maddie had moved far beyond making suggestions — now I was flat out giving orders. And Maddie was obeying. And it was turning me on like nothing I had ever experienced before. I took more pictures in the kitchen. Sometimes Maddie's breasts were exposed over the top of the apron, sometimes not. In some shots I allowed her to wear her panties normally, in others I wanted them arranged to look like a thong, in still others I wanted them lowered and rolled into a narrow cotton band that covered nothing but the barest strip of her upper thighs, or I wanted them down altogether, Maddie's legs spread as far as they would go, her panties stretched between her ankles. She posed in front of the stove with pots and pans as if cooking, she posed while sitting and then lying on the countertops, she posed on her hands and knees on the floor.

After one of those kneeling poses, Maddie gave me a long, slow inspection as if I was overlooking something obvious. She crawled toward me, walking on her knees, her body upright, her hands off the floor. She touched my fully erect penis and, smiling, licked it and put it in her mouth. It shocked me to realize that I was both hard and naked: I had grown entirely oblivious to the state of my own body.

Maddie was giving me the slowest blowjob imaginable. In fact, she was hardly moving at all, just holding my penis in her mouth. Then I got it: she was posing. I snapped away.

We spent a lot of time in the kitchen. Afterwards, on our way to the bedroom, we spent a lot of time on the stairs.

We experimented with other articles of clothing, both Maddie's and mine. We experimented with various pieces of furniture. We experimented with light and shadow.

It must have gone on for hours but it felt like no time went by at all, and the event that finally broke the spell was when the output screen on the camera blinked *memory chip full*.

Maddie

Earlier, I had taken the liberty of smuggling the small box of condoms upstairs so that they would be close to the bed if needed. I don't know why I did it secretly instead of just telling Harry that I was doing it – a tiny manifestation of one of my many compulsions, I suppose.

That whole posing gig – what can I say about it? At first I thought I was doing it just to keep him awake. At first it bored me. But as I watched Harry lose himself more and more in what we were doing, watched him grow more comfortable with saying what he wanted from me, more assertive about how he said it, more nonchalant about pointing that camera and – *click click* – taking what he wanted from me, taking my naked image from me, as I watched him become ever more excited, watched him swell up, literally and figuratively, his excitement flowed into me like a slow tide and I, too, lost myself more and more in what came to feel like a peculiar and intimate dance between us or, perhaps, a ritual.

The experience of being exposed to him like that was unexpectedly delicious, better than any stripping fantasy I had ever had. Not exposed in the sense that I, mostly, wasn't wearing any clothes – although that was part of it, of course. It was more about being exposed to him on the score of what he might do with those pictures. It occurred to me – somewhere near the top of the stairs, I think – that I must have made up my mind about how to react to Harry's trust in me: I would not punish him for it; instead, I was giving him my trust in return, as a gift, and the realization of this made me almost cry with happiness, which in turn made me immediately accuse myself of being drunk. I *was* a little drunk – I'm not gonna lie.

In the bedroom, after the camera ran out of memory and Harry, finally, was forced to put it down, we turned off the light and sat together on the bed in the semi-dark and held each other and rocked, slowly slowly, like survivors of a shipwreck washed up on an island we had all to ourselves.

I don't know what was going on in Harry's mind, but I had not forgotten my initial reason for keeping him awake. I took hold of his hand and said, "Let me show you some of the places I like to be touched."

We started with the wonderfully sensitive places just behind my ears, my right ear especially for some unfathomable reason. We moved by slow degrees to my clitoris, skipping over my breasts – I'd decided to save those for another time, for their own special lesson. Guiding just the tip of Harry's finger, I demonstrated for him how I liked my clit to be stroked. Harry was good at it as long as I was guiding him – almost right away I started to get wet – but as soon as I left him on his own, he became unsure of himself, of how much pressure to exert or, even, where exactly he was supposed to be stroking. It was as if he was completely ignorant of female genital anatomy – was this possible in a man his age? – a man who had been married for *how many* years? I continued to tutor him and by slow degrees he got better.

While he was apprenticing down there, I slid my free hand behind his neck and pulled his face to mine. "Here's how I like to be kissed," I said; "I'm going to kiss you like I'm the man and you're the woman." He looked doubtful but before he could protest I pressed my lips to his. I smooched him, rolling my lips on top of his, overdoing it just a bit I'm afraid, then I used my lips to part his and gently explored him with my tongue. He tensed and I pulled away. I said, "You don't like that." I meant it to be a question but it didn't turn out to sound like one. Harry croaked, "I…I…I'm not sure." I said, "I like a man who's a little bit pushy – but not too much." "Oh, um, I see," Harry sort of bleated. He looked like he was getting the wrong idea so I tried to explain: "I mean, that's how I like a man to kiss me in bed…I wouldn't want some strange man to kiss me like that out of the blue." I wasn't sure how much that helped.

Harry had completely lost track of what he was supposed to be doing with his finger down below and I set him once again along the right path.

"Kiss me," I said, and we kissed like sisters. I pulled away and tweaked his nose. I said, "I'm not being the man anymore, silly, that's your job now."

"Oh," Harry said, flustered, "…I thought we were still…I thought you were…oh never mind."

"And don't stop what you're doing down there, either," I ordered.

But it turned out Harry wasn't good at doing two things at once — at least not those two things. When he focused on kissing he wasn't half bad, although he quickly developed a tendency to be slightly too over-active with his tongue — but my poor clit found itself pining for attention. When I reached down and set his finger in motion again, his kissing became abstract, mechanical: a gal could have more fun lipwrestling with the Tin Man from *The Wizard of Oz*.

I almost said that to Harry, and right away I was glad I didn't. It would have been mean and it probably would have undermined his confidence, which seemed pretty shaky to start with.

Instead, I sighed and lay back on the bed so that kissing became out of the question. I preferred him to concentrate more on his finger skills than his kissing. Except Harry took my movement as an invitation to climb on top of me and I had to push him off twice, my hand against his chest, before he got the message that I really meant it. I think he was slightly miffed and confused.

"I want you to stay right where you are," I murmured, trying to appease him with a low, sexy voice; "I like what you're doing…and besides I want to look at you."

Immediately he became self-conscious — both about touching me and about me looking at him, at his naked body. I sensed that he was blushing, although the light was too dim to tell for sure.

"You're such a beautiful man," I said in a quiet, marveling tone. I would have said the same thing to any man in that moment, in that situation — but in Harry's case I really meant it. His features were quite nice. He had a well-shaped nose, good cheekbones, expressive lips, a forehead that was not too high and not too low. The dim light only accented the fact that his eyes were rather romantically deep-set. His short gray beard gave his chin maybe a little more definition than it really possessed (but I had a hunch his chin was full enough all on its own), and his hair and beard together framed a face that displayed an appealing mix of sensitivity and strength. Add to that Harry's powerful, trim body and there truly was sitting before me a beautiful man.

Meanwhile, despite his self-consciousness, or maybe because of it, Harry's finger landed exactly on the right spot and involuntarily I made a small noise as if I were happily and unexpectedly tasting one of my favorite flavors. He'd found the spot and he had the pressure about right but, of course, he had no clue about when to shift from slow up and down to rapid side to side – he would have needed to be inside my skin to have a clue about that. I placed my hand on top of his and together we masturbated me.

Harry

I thought maybe I was hurting her. Her eyes were squeezed tight shut and the expression on her face looked more like a grimace than anything else. But her hand was right there with mine, egging me on. I imagined my rough finger must feel like sandpaper on her sensitive parts. Did she *like* to be hurt? I was sitting beside her on the bed – sort of an odd position for sex, if what we were doing could be called sex, but this was where Maddie said she wanted me. Acting more or less on its own, my free hand – the one not ravaging her vagina – strayed across her body until it got the notion to fondle her breasts. I remembered what Maddie had told me to do the night before, and gently I pinched one of her nipples. She shivered, she writhed under the touch of my two hands. I was on the verge of telling her that we needed to stop, that it didn't matter whether or not she was turned on by pain, this wasn't good, when she emitted a series of humming noises, each one longer and more intense than the last. Her eyes were still narrow slits, and her grimace had given way to a look that suggested she was off in a world of her own – or, perhaps, she was so intensely present inside her own body that it was the rest of the everyday world that had drifted away, not she. The humming noises reached a peak and Maddie held herself there, rapt in that moment, poised on the edge of release, holding herself back, savoring the anticipation, and there was a split second when I held my breath, when it seemed she might not be able to stop holding herself back. Then she gave herself up to it and a deep, slow, throaty laughter came pouring out of her, rising and falling, and with each rise another release. It went on and on. I watched her, amazed. I had never seen anything like it. It was a revelation to me.

Maddie

Some men are into cunnilingus; most men, in my experience, are not. More's the pity. My radar in this regard is pretty well attuned, if I do say so myself, and Harry had given ample indication that he was most definitely of the latter persuasion. And please don't ask me what the indications are, I couldn't tell you: little things, subtle things, the shifting of an eye, the arching of a brow, subliminal body language — you'll just have to believe me, some gals can sense these things.

I would have loved it if Harry had gone down on me just then — he might have brought me off bigger than the first time. But I knew he would never do it on his own. And I sensed it would be asking too much of him if I suggested it.

In fact, I was surprised to see that Harry was looking thoroughly worn out. This was disappointing because I was feeling on top of the world, I was feeling like a million bucks, ready for a million fucks. I considered trying to re-energize him with a blowjob. Possibly it would have worked, but something made me hesitate. Harry didn't look just sleepy. He looked weary, bleak.

"You okay?" I asked.

He smiled, he patted my leg. "You taught me something tonight," he said. "Thank you."

I glanced at the digital clock on the nightstand beside the bed. How on earth did it get to be so late? I thought about Harry having to do his mason's work all day tomorrow in the cold. I thought about his age: he was suddenly looking not so young.

"Maybe it's time we turned in," I said.

"Yeah, maybe so." A hoarse whisper.

We arranged ourselves naked under the covers, side by side, not touching, like two corpses in the morgue. I couldn't stand it. I turned to Harry, I slipped my arms around him. I nibbled his ear. I wasn't necessarily trying to arouse him: I was convinced that was a lost cause for the night. I suppose I was just burning off some sexual inertia after a very pleasing orgasm. I cooed into his ear, "Thank you so much, Harry, for this wonderful Thanksgiving...I can't remember a better one."

But he was already asleep.

III. Friday

Charlie

Black Friday. My branch was open but I wasn't working there that day. I was at a training class for new tellers. The class was in the basement of our main branch in a special training room set up to look like a bank lobby. We were going over do's and don'ts during a robbery.

The morning session had to do with the most common scenario: a single robber approaches a teller and hands over a note or makes a verbal demand for money. It was basic stuff but I was having trouble concentration – my mind kept wandering to the subject of Alexis, to the seemingly perfect evening we'd spent with his family, to the way it all went terribly wrong afterwards.

Stay calm. Do exactly as the robber says. Give the least amount of money possible. Make sure you include the bait money and/or, if your branch is so equipped, the dye pack and any tracking devices. Do not activate the alarm while the robber is watching you; wait until he has left your window. Under no circumstances should you attempt to confront the robber or to pursue him once he leaves the bank.

Stay calm, do exactly as the robber says. Somewhere in the back of my head I heard the rest of the lesson but mostly I was stuck on those two first points. The robber is a potentially dangerous and violent man – stay calm, do exactly as he says. That had been my mistake with Alexis last night. I had not stayed calm. I had not let him have his way. What happened last night was my fault, really, because I had not done those two simple things.

During our lunch break, I texted him *Im not mad anymore are you*. Alexis did not respond.

The trouble started on the drive home from his parents. Actually – let me back up a minute – they weren't really his parents. Actually what I mean is: his mom was really his mom, but his dad was only his step-dad. That Thanksgiving was my first time meeting them, plus Alexis' two older sisters. Alexis' step-dad, it turned out, didn't like it anymore that Alexis was gay than my dad liked it that I was gay. In fact, Alexis' step-dad steered clear of us as much as he could and, when he was forced to be in the same room with us, was openly hostile toward us both (Alexis' mom and sisters shielding us and scolding him at every turn). My dad, at least, the time or two he met Alexis, made an effort to be civil – and on his worst day my dad never treated me the way Alexis' step-dad treated Alexis. So, naturally, I made a comment or two in the car going home. Perhaps I was a little drunk on the white wine and schnapps and holiday brandy Alexis' mom had on offer – and yes I had taken a little something to calm my nerves before meeting Alexis' family – so I'm not exactly sure what I said. but it couldn't have been too bad, I don't think. Probably, I questioned why we were spending time around Alexis' step-dad while we treated my dad like some kind of pariah. Alexis and I got to arguing. One thing led to another.

In the afternoon we practiced bank takeover situations involving multiple armed robbers. Real actors were brought in to play the robbers; we tellers took turns being either tellers or customers. Sometimes the actors wore ski masks, sometimes they let us see their faces. There were six of them: four men and two women, all dressed in dark clothes. Sometimes they claimed to be armed but showed no weapons, sometimes they waved around fake handguns, except for one guy who in the armed scenarios brandished a fake Uzi.

This was more engaging and I didn't think about Alexis as often as I had in the morning, except when I was forced to raise my arms above my head. Then the pain from the bruises on my upper left arm reminded me of the night before, of Alexis' fury, of how he grabbed me. I was glad no one could see the marks. I would have been mortified.

Maddie

In Harry's spare bedroom I found a laptop computer inside a computer case on the floor beside the small desk where he paid his bills. I powered up the laptop and tried out a couple of obvious passwords. *harry123* – small "h" – did the trick. I got onto the internet and accessed my email. My inbox was brimming with unanswered messages. I opened every one that looked like it might be a response to a job query or application. (I'd sent out my resume to all kinds of places since losing my job at the hospital.) There weren't many of these responses and none of them bore good news. All the other messages looked like junk, certainly nothing urgent. I opened a new-message box and typed out a message to my brother:

Hey Freeman, Called you last night from a friend's phone. You didn't answer. The East Coast job didn't work out. I may be heading west again soon. May need to crash on your couch again. I know Abigail doesn't really like me but I hope she won't mind too much. Just wanted to give you a head's up. Hope you had a happy turkey day. Love, M

I hit send. Then I got to thinking that I should have added something else. I opened another new-message box. I typed:

Not a sure thing yet I'm headed your way. Still one possibility I'm looking into. Will let you know.

I hit send again.

I sat in front of Harry's compromised laptop. I itched, I ached to delve into that machine — so many secrets to be discovered on a computer. But something held me back. *That's weird*, I thought and went prowling around his apartment, but every time I felt the urge to poke into something that might be private — and the spare bedroom alone held boxes and boxes of mysteries — a stronger urge stopped me. "What the fuck is going on?" I said aloud.

I went into the bathroom and looked at myself in the mirror. I'd already eaten — bacon and eggs, what else? — and showered. I was wearing no makeup. All my makeup supplies were in my car. I took a long look at myself with no makeup and decided I didn't particularly like what I saw. On the other hand, I didn't *hate* my looks — not like I had so many times in the past. I opened Harry's medicine cabinet and once again inspected his charmingly ordinary collection of over-the-counter medicines. How could anyone live like that?

This reminded me about my own collection of pills in my purse. Had I taken my anti-depressant at all yesterday? I couldn't remember. Now was the time for my first dose: midmorning after a meal. Yet I made no move to locate my purse. I searched inside my mind for that erratic darkness that assails me and can threaten to overwhelm me when I'm off my meds or when, for whatever reason, something shifts in my body chemistry and the meds send me spiraling out of balance. The darkness was nowhere to be found. The thought crossed my mind that maybe I'd hit upon my own natural cure, maybe I didn't need the pills.

I slammed shut the medicine cabinet. My un-made-up face wheeled into view. "Oh no you don't," I said to myself. "We've made that mistake before. Go get the pills."

I got the pills and returned to the bathroom. I watched myself swallow two. (You can't be too careful with yourself.)

I stood there brooding about the last time I decided to go off my meds cold turkey because I thought I'd found true love. I wound up driving my boyfriend's car head on into a concrete highway divider. To this day I'm not sure if I was trying to kill myself or if I was just trying to escape the darkness inside my head – or maybe that's a distinction without a difference. I totaled the car, of course. I was the only occupant and by all rights the crash should have killed me: I wasn't wearing a seat belt, but the air bags saved me anyway. I walked away from it – was carried away from it, actually – with nothing worse than two badly sprained ankles. I found out later that my boyfriend had never bothered to insure the car, or even to register it. I found out, too, that he was married – a minor detail he'd neglected to mention, the prince.

"Hey!" My reflection snapped its fingers at me, breaking the spell of memory. "Enough of that, that's in the past. Let's find *new* ways to screw up this time, okay?"

"Okay," I said, putting on a brave smile. I don't think my reflection was fooled.

Harry

Our job was to build a basement foundation on a steeply sloping lot. The back wall was to be made of twelve inch blocks, nineteen courses high. It was a new job: we were starting off of the footer, and the first couple of courses of that back wall and of most of the side walls had to be lifted over steel rebar sticking out of the footer every two feet. And it was a complicated foundation, with lots of corners: slow work.

We laid up the first few corners and ran strings to rough check for level. We would have done this in any case, but I think many of us already sensed something was off – you lay block for a living you develop an eye for these things – I know I sensed it. The footer turned out to be nowhere close to level.

"That's bullshit!" our foreman fumed. "Don't those bastards own a laser? How the fuck did they get so far off?!"

Our foreman was an excitable fellow, and too young to remember the days before laser levels, when concrete footers got poured out of level all the time.

So, it was a slow start on a cold morning. We had to set up our own laser, find out exactly how many inches out of level we were dealing with, take down most of the corners we'd already built, then cut a lot of blocks to even out the first course.

We were using two laborers on that job: one to carry block and, eventually, to help set up scaffolding; the other to mix and carry the mortar. Usually, the masons are waiting on the laborers. That morning it was the other way around. The laborers were jogging in place, blowing on their hands, wishing they had something to do. Meanwhile, we were all of us being paid by the block – which essentially meant we were hardly being paid at all, since not a lot of block was being laid. Tempers were rising, and the foreman's excitable nature was not helping.

Back when I had my own company, I would have sent one of the laborers for coffee and doughnuts. It's amazing how well hot coffee and warm doughnuts go down on a cold morning, especially when things aren't going exactly right. I would have quickly located the lowest two points of the footer, laid up corners there, and set guys to work laying stretcher blocks between those two corners. Then I would have worked, corner by corner, from there to the highest point, cutting blocks as I went.

But it wasn't my job to run and I let things play out as the younger men saw fit.

It was nearly eleven o'clock – a good two hours into our day – before the crew fell into a steady work rhythm. If the temperature ever reached forty degrees, it wasn't by much. The sky started out gloomy and gray and only got grayer as the day wore on. The wind never stopped blowing.

I wasn't as fast anymore as some of the younger guys but then I wasn't as sloppy, either. (Maybe when I was their age I was just as sloppy and not even aware of it – as many of them seemed not to be aware: depressing thought.) But I was still useful. Because I could lay blocks so true and mortar lines so even, it usually fell to me to lay up the corners. On this job, because there were so many corners, the foreman was tackling a few of them himself. The foreman's name was Doug and, despite his anger issues, it had to be said he was a highly capable mason. But he wanted me to lay the back corners, which were the tallest – it was important that they stay plumb, and even a slight inaccuracy from one course to the next, over nineteen courses, could add up to a lot.

So I didn't get a lot of thinking done that morning. Too many distractions – the cold and the wind, the tension among the crew which never fully dissipated, the strain of lifting twelve inch blocks, the concentration needed to keep the corners exactly plumb, the challenge of staying ahead of the other masons, who were filling in between the corners almost as fast as the foreman and I laid them.

Still, thoughts of Maddie were never completely absent from my awareness – memories of her at least, if not fully formed thoughts: image after image of her, as if dozens of those pictures I'd snapped of her had been transmitted not to the memory chip in the camera but directly into my brain. There were other memories, too – the smell of her, the pungent, earthy scent of her as she lay exposed to me on the bed; the feel of her, it was still astonishing to me and, yes, shocking to me that this woman I hardly knew had let me touch her in such an intimate place; the deep, exhilarating sound of her laughter as she climaxed; the sadness that overtook me afterwards.

Maddie

Without realizing it, I was making myself crazy in Harry's apartment. I wanted so much to snoop but I couldn't bring myself to do it. A dozen times I sat in front of that laptop of his, teetering on the edge of plunging into it or else turning the damned thing off. I never did either.

Harry had taken his phone with him when he left for work, so at least I was spared that temptation.

To my amazement I found myself in the kitchen, washing up my breakfast dishes. That's the moment when it became clear to me that I was making myself crazy. I decided I needed to get out of there. I decided to go to the gym and put myself through a tough workout.

If you ever find yourself living out of your car, keep in mind the following necessities:

- You need to locate a couple of clean, safe places where you can go to the bathroom and where your repeated use is not likely to be noticed. At least one of these places should be available 24/7. An all-night Laundromat, I have found, is often ideal.
- You need to have a place to shower. If you expect to remain in

the same area long-term, you might consider signing up for a class or two at a local community college. First make sure they have a gym, with shower facilities, and that all students have access. If college isn't your thing, I recommend you find a commercial gym, nothing fancy or upscale, someplace where the monthly membership is cheap.

That morning Harry had gotten out of bed at the ungodly hour of six o'clock. At first I thought he was just getting up to pee. But when I heard him padding down the stairs, then a few minutes later caught the first whiff of instant coffee, I realized he was up for good. I rolled over and went back to sleep. The next thing I knew, the daylight coming in through the window was noticeably stronger, although still not particularly bright, and I heard the sound of the front door being gently pulled shut, then the sound of a truck starting. I got up and went to the window in time to see Harry's truck rolling out of the parking lot. The sky was a gray mess. The wind was trying to tear the last few leaves out of the trees. It looked cold out there.

When I went downstairs I found all the dishes from the night before put away. In the drain board now were an orange juice glass, a coffee cup, a spoon, a bowl – no doubt for oatmeal: one of the few staples Harry kept in his house. There was a note on the kitchen table. It read:

Please make yourself at home. Will be back after five, sooner if it rains. Dinner tonight?

It was written in oddly formed block letters, like the work of a child, I first thought, but that didn't quite describe it; like the work of a peasant who perhaps had learned to write late in life, who had never grown fully comfortable with writing – yes, more like that. Capitals were written like capitals and all the other letters were written the same way, only smaller. But beyond the handwriting there was something missing. The note should have included phrases like: *Sorry I have to work. Wish we could spend the day together.* And perhaps the last sentence could have been more formal – something like: *Can I take you to dinner tonight?* One might even have hoped for a *may I*, coming from Harry.

I read the note over and over again. He had not signed it, nor had he named me at the top. The note could be read as a polite way of saying: *Please be gone from my house before five o'clock today.* But I didn't think that was Harry's intent. One highly important clue was the fact that he had left a spare key on top of the note. He wanted me to stay, but something was going on.

It occurred to me that this hyper-inspection of Harry's note was in itself a form of snooping, but no part of me resisted it: I concluded this must be an acceptable means of peeking behind the façade and trying to catch a glimpse of the hidden Harry.

I recalled Harry's abrupt weariness the night before. Could whatever had come over him then still have been oppressing him when he wrote this note?

I went to the kitchen window and looked outside. I felt sorry for Harry having to work in that wind and that gloom. But something told me it probably wasn't bothering him all that much: something in his tone of voice the night before when he said he'd be at work before nine let me know he relished working in the cold — I supposed you'd have to, on some level, if you were willing to spend decades toiling as a block mason. And in any case the weather that day probably matched his mood.

"Okay, Maddie," I said aloud, "we said we were going to the gym — let's go!"

But I didn't go.

This often happens to me. I'll resolve to do something positive, then I'll resist doing it. I wandered along Harry's long line of bookshelves, looking for clues to how his mind worked in the way he'd ordered his books. Snooping again, but this was another acceptable method. I took down the book that had caught my interest so keenly two nights ago, my first night in Harry's apartment, the book that made me suspect that Harry might share my preoccupation with spanking. The book was a collection of essays by Daphne Merkin called *Dreaming of Hitler*, and right on the front cover it advertised: "includes the famous essay 'Spanking: A Romance'."

Harry's copy was a paperback. The pages were just beginning to yellow at the edges. The binding showed almost no wear at all — if anybody had opened this book, they had been careful to leave no sign. I had read and re-read Merkin's spanking essay many times, back when I owned my own paperback copy of this book, but I had barely glanced at the other essays. I dropped in on a few of them now, turning to randomly selected pages. Nothing else caught my interest. Which is not to say that Daphne Merkin isn't an interesting writer — it's sad but her spanking essay has ruined all her other writing for me: if she is not writing about our shared fixation then I'm moving on. But it wasn't just that. There was a half-hidden, half-formed thought nagging at the back of my head. It wouldn't allow me to concentrate.

I let my eyes roam aimlessly across Harry's shelves, pretending not to care if the nagging thought clarified itself or not and, sure enough, I was able to fool it, and when it ventured ever so slightly into the open, I pounced on it. Here's what it was: it was the realization that I'd had two nights ago that all of Harry's books were non-fiction and the assumption that I'd made that he must keep all of his fiction upstairs. But was there any fiction upstairs? To be certain, there were books upstairs — not as many as downstairs, and not arranged on shelves but stacked on the floor and on his nightstand and in the spare bedroom on top of boxes. I had to know immediate if any of those books were fiction. I flew up the stairs, I examined every book. Every last one was non-fiction. What did this say about Harry and about how his mind worked?

Harry

Things settled down after lunch. As the back wall grew higher and there became a need for scaffolding, my work actually got easier. Before then, the foreman had expected me to work on those two all-important back corners plus several others. But once I was off the ground, even by just a foot or two, my only concerns were the two back corners plus the next closest two, which were also pretty tall. To get to any of these spots, all I had to do was walk along the scaffolding from corner to corner to corner. It was not expected of me that I should climb down off the slowly rising scaffolding and attend to any additional corners.

There was a better mood among the crew now. We were making good progress. Bellies were full. Doug, the foreman, had knocked back his usual two shots of whiskey with lunch and this had temporarily doused his anger — not to mention some of his skill as a mason. Doug was a drinker with loads of experience, and he was able to function at work, so far, because he was clear-eyed about the effect alcohol had on his abilities: he tasked a couple of the younger, more promising men on the crew to carry on building all the corners not given to me.

It was a good time for me to think. Before Maddie came into my life I had been reading a book on the Sumerians, those ancient people of Mesopotamia who are said to have built the first city, Ur. In fact, just before going to the chess club that Wednesday I had been reading about the ziggurat of Ur, modeled after the great ziggurat of Babylon, the inspiration for the Tower of Babel, and I recall looking forward to contemplating both structures the next time I laid block, reflecting on how similar my work was to the work of men who had lived something like five thousand years before me, how the knowledge and skills had been handed down generation to generation. Now here I was laying block and, although I had not entirely forgotten the ziggurats of Ur and Babylon, my thoughts were not so much on the work of ancient masons; instead, I wondered about their home lives, about the women they loved, or at the very least slept with. Did those ancient Mesopotamian masons know how their women liked to be touched? Did they regularly experience the thrill of participating in the acts that a woman might need to find her own release? Did they understand that a man's orgasm did not necessarily bring about an orgasmic response from a woman? Why hadn't *that* information made its way down to me?

The memory of Maddie riding me our first night together. My explosive ejaculation. Maddie's words to me afterwards, when I worried that I might have gone off too soon: *No darling that was perfect.* Exactly the way Suzanne used to say it. Except Maddie did not pretend to go off herself, as Suzanne so often did. And Suzanne *was* pretending – after years of quietly suspecting, I knew this now with the certainty of a revelation. How repressed we both were, Suzanne and me. And what a fool I was.

I tapped another block into place, checked for plumb and level, moved along the scaffolding to another corner. One of the young guys filling in between corners stopped me. "You okay, Harry?"

"Yeah, fine."

"You look down in the dumps – this weather getting to ya'?"

"Maybe so," I said.

I paused to watch him lay a few blocks. I'd noticed earlier that he sometimes struggled to keep his line straight and even.

"Your mortar's too dry," I said. "It dries out fast in a wind like this. Mix in a little water – it will make things easier."

He nodded to show his appreciation for the tip. I moved on.

Maddie

When things went bad this latest time, when the job went bye-bye, when I had to make a decision about hightailing it back to the West Coast, one more failure in my wake, or trying to tough it out here, and it was obvious that the money wouldn't last, that I'd be sleeping in my car pretty soon, I went shopping for a gym. The cheapest one I found was a hellhole, complete with roaches – I would not have been surprised to learn there was a meth lab in the basement. The next cheapest turned out to be just what I was looking for. It wasn't devoid of grunge but it was miles ahead of the first place, it lacked the bugs, and it was for real. The clientele was mostly men, of course – that is always the case at any run-of-the-mill gym – and the men were wholehog into body building (also tattoos). The few women who haunted the place were of two types: the hardcore gym-users who were nearly indistinguishable from the men, and the girlfriends of the male body builders. Both types of women sported their own tattoos. What I liked most about the place was that almost no one hit on you or bothered you. You could go in there and do your own thing and everyone else was doing their own thing, too, and they left you alone. I don't think the owners would have cared if I'd flat out told them I was homeless and using their gym as a part-time roof over my head with a bathroom and showers. I think they probably suspected. Also, I think at least a few other gym members were in the same boat I was in. I spent a lot of time in that place before I ran into Harry.

(Exercise is often a good antidote to depression. I know it works for me. (Sometimes.))

I surprised myself by actually going to the gym on that day after Thanksgiving – Black Friday as they say in retail. Wandering around Harry's apartment, as soon as I started backsliding on my resolution to go to the gym, I thought I was done for, I thought I would never work up the will power, and then, having caved on that good intention, I'd probably also cave on the whole not-snooping-on-Harry thing. I could see it happening. I'd pry into every corner of Harry's lonely life and find all his sad, sordid secrets – who didn't have them? – and lose all respect for him, losing all confidence in him while at the same time despising myself for doing what I was doing, for my weakness, for my betrayal of Harry. By the time Harry got back from work – I imagined him stooped and weary but with a hopeful gleam in his eyes since he was coming home to me – by the time that happened, assuming I hadn't already fled, I'd be a hot mess, full of rage at Harry for who knows what, for having secrets in the first place, for not hiding them better, for letting me victimize him as I would have been doing all day; and of course full of my old familiar self-loathing. Oh yes, I could see it quite plainly. One more potentially good thing in my life transformed into a train wreck. I saw it all play out as if it had already happened, as if I were viewing it from the vantage point of memory – not surprising, I suppose, since I have played out similar scenes with other men. Or, granting that the coming blow up with Harry was still in the future, I saw it as inevitable, one more sorry reflection of my fate – always me, standing alone in a hall of distorting mirrors.

The next thing I knew, one of those distorting mirrors turned into an opening door and I walked through it and found myself in the parking lot in front of Harry's apartment and I got into my car and drove to the gym.

Harry

A cold, light rain began to fall around four o'clock. We were already as high up on the back wall as it made sense to go in one day. The lowest mortar joints needed time to set before we placed any more weight above them – or the mortar would start to squeeze out the sides. Despite being "down in the dumps," which I was, my heart gave a small leap of joy when the foreman called to the laborers to start cleaning out the cement mixer.

While we were cleaning up our own hand tools, the foreman gathered the masons together. He told us how the developer on this project was really breathing down his neck.

"I need to make a show tomorrow," he said.

Some of the guys objected. Tall and heavy as some of these walls were, it really wouldn't hurt anything to let the lower joints rest until Monday – in fact, it was the smart thing to do.

"Yeah yeah, I know," the foreman said, "I don't plan to lay many block tomorrow but the developer's got to see somebody out here…just a couple of guys for a couple of hours. Who's in?"

The man to my left, turning up his collar against the wind and the strengthening rain, said, "Supposed to be more of this tomorrow."

"We'd just be making a show," the foreman said, his ruddy face growing hard with anger.

No one said anything.

"Who's in, goddamm it! I got to be able to count on a couple of you bastards! How about you, Harry? You'll be here, won't you?"

I winced, I rubbed my shoulder. I said, "Sorry, Doug, but you've got to give me until Monday to get over lifting all those twelve inch blocks – in case you hadn't noticed, I'm no spring chicken anymore."

It was all I could do to keep the truck at no more than ten miles above the speed limit on the interstate. At the bottom of my exit ramp, I came close to running a red light. I said to myself *Whoa there, cowboy*, echoing Maddie from our first night together. It was strange how thinking about my time with Maddie both disheartened me for my past failings with Suzanne and exhilarated me when I dared to think there might be the possibility of a better future.

Approaching home, I passed the Biscuit Den where Maddie and I had eaten. I said to myself: *That's where we ate breakfast together on Thanksgiving morning.* I considered stopping somewhere to buy flowers. Was that too corny? I decided that Maddie would think it was too corny. Besides, I didn't really want to take the time to stop.

Turning into my parking lot, the first thing I noticed was that Maddie's car was gone. I parked where her car had been. I sat in my truck a long time thinking through the ramifications of this. I had not expected this. I kept asking myself how I had missed the possibility of this. My hands on the steering wheel felt colder than they had all day.

The door to the apartment was unlocked. The note I had left on the dining room table had been moved to the couch in the living room. Beside the note, a book lay open, its splayed cover facing upward. The key I had left for Maddie was still there on the table.

Maddie

I sort of lost track of time at the gym. By the time I got back to Harry's the last light was fading from the sky. Harry's truck was in the parking lot and so was his car, but all the front windows of the apartment were dark. I climbed the couple of steps to his door, my legs still a little shaky from the grueling workout. The door was unlocked. Inside, there didn't seem to be any lights on at all.

"Harry?" I called, but there was no answer.

I left the front door open behind me and crept forward through the feeble light that trickled in from the parking lot. I found Harry slumped in an upholstered chair beside the couch in the living room. For a moment I thought he was dead. His mouth hung open and the light was too dim to determine clearly whether or not he was breathing. I was afraid to touch him, afraid to speak. I turned on a floor lamp that stood between the chair and the couch. It was one of those lamps that had three different settings for brightness. I turned the switch only one click, to the dullest setting. If Harry was dead, I didn't want to see the death pallor on him. But, to my great relief, I saw in an instant the slow rise and fall of his chest.

A book perched crookedly on Harry's upper leg. *Dreaming of Hitler*. It was open to the title page. I had not noticed this earlier but now I could see that someone had written an inscription there. Harry's hand rested on top of the book, making the inscription impossible to read. I was struck by the intricate pattern of thick blue veins on the back of Harry's hand.

Harry?" I said again. His brow clouded, his mouth partially closed, but he didn't wake up.

I slipped the book from under his hand, turned it around, and read, "Dearest Harry, Here's a book I hope you will find…intriguing. S."

What an idiot, I thought. *How could I have missed that? She was the one with the fetish, duh.*

I closed the book and placed it on the couch. Harry startled slightly but continued to sleep. His weathered face looked so sad he might have fallen asleep while crying, or in mourning. I moved silently away from him; I shut and latched the front door.

I was wearing a hooded sweatshirt. Beneath that I was still in my gym clothes, and they clung to me, still heavy with perspiration. It had felt so good walking out of that gym, knowing that I had a place, however temporary, to go home to, that I had no need of their showers – I fervently hoped that someone at the gym noticed.

When I came back to the living room, there was Harry staring at me as if in a trance. Nothing had changed about his features, except his eyes were open – hard, blank, gray, wide-open eyes. The eyes of a mannequin or a figure made of wax. They made him look even deader and even sadder.

Then two things happened: something came to life in him – and his phone, tucked into his shirt pocket, rang. I like to think it was the sight of me that woke him fully, that brought him back to life – and maybe it was. His eyes flared first with amazement, then with joy. He barely had time to half-form a smile before joy gave way to doubt – *was he dreaming?* – then the phone rang. That's how I remember it: in that order – but really everything happened almost simultaneously.

He slipped the phone out of his pocket. He was so intently focused on me it was clear he meant to turn off the phone. But before he did he glanced at the screen. He looked again, more carefully. He swiped the screen to take the call.

Harry

It was an odd time for Charlie to call. Actually, it was odd that Charlie was calling, period. I knew immediately that something was wrong. His voice sounded distant and shaky. He wanted to know if he was calling at a good time, worried that he might be interrupting something. "It's fine," I assured him; "I'm always happy to hear from you."

He sighed or sobbed into the phone – I couldn't tell which – and in the voice of a little boy said, "Daddy."

I was startled by the ferocity and confusion of my response. I was at once repulsed to hear my own son, a grown man, reduced to such a pitiable state while in the same moment I desperately wanted to take him in my arms and comfort him.

"What is it, son? What's the matter?"

"Can you come get me?" Still the little boy voice.

"Where are you, son?"

Maddie

We walked through the entry doors to the emergency room, Harry in his dusty and mortar-splattered work clothes and me in my gym shorts and zipped-up hoodie. Charlie sat in a corner by himself.

We had taken Harry's car to get there and I had to practically fight Harry for the keys to let me drive. When he hung up the phone, he was crazed. But not with worry – with anger. I kept asking, "What's wrong? What happened to Charlie?" And through gritted teeth Harry kept saying that he didn't know, that Charlie didn't say. But it was clear to me that Harry knew plenty.

We approached Charlie, and Harry said, "You okay, son?"

Charlie stood stiffly, using both hands to push himself up. He offered a weak smile. "Thanks for coming. Both of you. Good to see you again, Maddie."

I told him it was good to see him, too.

Harry was clearly waiting for an explanation.

Charlie said, "I thought I broke a rib but turns out I only cracked it."

Harry said nothing.

"I fell down a flight of stairs…tripped over my own feet…it was such a stupid mistake…"

I noticed that he said "mistake," not "accident."

"Where's Alexis?" Harry asked, cold murder in his eyes.

"He's, um, working…in a different part of the hospital."

I said, "Charlie, do you want us to help you get home?"

Charlie hesitated, glanced with trepidation at his father. "Actually, I was hoping I could stay with Dad…just for a day or two…it's silly, I know, but all of a sudden the stairs at my place make me nervous."

Harry

Maddie offered to drive my car back to the apartment so that I could ride with Charlie. I offered to drive Charlie's car for him, but he said he was fine. On the way, I told Charlie that Maddie was also staying with me.

He said, "That's great, Dad. I'm glad for you." He pondered a moment, said, "I should go back to my own place, shouldn't I?"

"Hell no, son, you're coming home with me."

Charlie simmered with a question. "So..." was all he could finally manage.

We both carefully kept an eye on traffic through the windshield.

I said, "I have no idea how long this thing with Maddie will last...I suspect it's kind of temporary...I suspect it will be over in a couple of days, maybe sooner."

"She's not a...?"

"A what?"

"I mean...she's not taking advantage of you, or anything, is she?"

I said, "Given the difference in our ages, maybe you ought to be worried about me taking advantage of her."

Charlie shot me a skeptical glance. "Given the difference in your ages, it usually works the other way around."

I laughed. "Listen, Charlie, if Maddie was out to fleece someone she'd be looking for richer game than me."

"Okay, fair enough," he said.

We drove in silence for several heartbeats. I wanted so much to make Charlie confirm what I had long suspected and now knew for certain must be the situation with Alexis. But now was not the time. Now was the time to get my boy home and to help him heal.

I said, "The spare bedroom's full of junk, sorry. But the couch is supposed to open up to be a bed. But I've never tried it, so I don't know how it works."

Out of the corner of my eye I saw Charlie's face relax into a small, sad, appreciative smile. Had he sensed my simmering questions the same way I sensed his? Was he relieved that I was not going to put him through the third degree? I think so – that's how I read his smile, anyway.

We made it back to the apartment before Maddie did. Charlie looked tired and his hair was a mess. I asked if he wanted to lie down or maybe take a shower.

"No, Dad, I'm fine."

"Probably a dumb question, anyway, right? About taking a shower? Are you all taped up?"

"Actually, no," Charlie said. "I asked about that. The nurse said they used to do that but they don't anymore. Turns out it's a bad idea to constrict the ribs if there's a break or a crack. I'm supposed to breath deep and expand my ribs as much as possible, makes it less likely a lung will collapse."

"Well, how do you like that?" I said. "Years ago I took a fall off a scaffold and cracked a rib or two — or maybe I broke them, I don't remember anymore — and they taped me up pretty good."

"Yeah I remember," Charlie said.

"Do you?" I said, surprised. "That was a long time ago — you were just a little kid."

"I remember," Charlie declared. "You broken 'em, and you went to work the next day. Mom was so worried — and so mad at you."

We both fell silent.

Charlie said, "*You* should get a shower. You look like you came straight from work."

"I'll wait for Maddie," I said. I was beginning to wonder where she was. Actually, I was beginning to relive the feeling I'd had when I came home earlier and thought she'd left for good.

Charlie peered at me, unable to read me. I retreated into the kitchen, uncorked a bottle of red wine, placed three glasses on the counter, filled two. When it comes to drink, Charlie takes after his mother: not much taste for it — where wine is concerned he prefers a sweet, chilled white to any sort of red. But I had no white wine in the house. On the other hand, given the circumstances, I didn't think he'd turn down a drink.

Back in the living room, I handed Charlie one of the wine glasses. He hesitated, took a small sip, set the glass down on the coffee table. The place felt oppressively quiet. I went to the CD player and popped in a CD. It turned out to be the music that I thought of as Brazilian, the music Maddie had danced to last night. Stripped to.

"Do you like that one?" Charlie wanted to know.

"Um, I sort of picked it at random," I said, flushing. Then, seeing Charlie's disappointment, I added, "But I've been listening to a lot of them lately. Maddie and I both have. And we like them all so far."

Charlie

Maddie came barreling in, carrying several large sacks of fast food.

"Who's hungry?" she sang out. "Harry, you *must* be – out in the cold all day, having your way with who knows how many blocks. I know I'm starving. How about you, Charlie?"

I caught Maddie's odd turn of phrase about the blocks but figured it must be some (hopefully filthy) inside joke she shared with Dad, and I restrained myself from prying. Dad's expression reminded me of a cocker spaniel who'd just caught sight of his beloved, long-lost mistress. If he'd had a tail, he wouldn't have been able to control himself, he'd be wagging it a mile a minute.

Maddie came to an abrupt halt. "Who put that music on?"

I pointed to Dad, who suddenly looked flustered, who stammered something about not paying attention to which CD was which.

Bumping her hips, Maddie cast upon Dad a conspiratorial smile, conspiratorial and at the same time lascivious. "I love this music," she announced, her voice deep and suggestive.

Dad hurried to her side and steered her toward the table in his little dining space. She glanced at me over her shoulder, threw me a wink and a smile.

Dad put out paper plates while Maddie emptied the sacks of food, making a pile in the center of the table. She noticed us watching her and said, "I didn't know what anybody liked, so I got a couple of everything."

The pile continued to grow. Maddie said, mock defensively, "Don't send me for food when I'm hungry!"

"Who sent you?" Dad teased.

"Okay, so it was my own idea...but you have to admit it was a good one!"

"Sure sure," Dad and I said together.

Dad poured Maddie a glass of wine and we settled around the table.

"Where's yours?" Dad asked me, meaning my wine glass. I nodded to the coffee table, where I'd left it.

Dad started to rise. "Do you want me to get it for you?"

Before I could say anything, Maddie said, "What are you doing drinking wine, Charlie? Aren't you on some kind of pain medication for your rib?"

"Well yes, but..."

Dad slapped his forehead. That was a slightly weird gesture, especially coming from Dad. Was he nervous around Maddie? Yes, that was part of it. But it wasn't just nervousness. He seemed at times almost to be putting on a show for her, like he was trying to match her physicality and demonstrativeness — natural traits in Maddie but not so much in Dad. Anyway, Dad slapped his forehead. He said, "I totally didn't think of that. Why didn't you say something, Charlie?"

To myself I went, *Totally?*

To Dad I said, "I didn't think of it either, to tell you the truth." (I guess, really, I was speaking to Maddie, trying to cover for Dad.) "Anyway the pills they gave me are supposed to be pretty mild."

Maddie had already emptied half her wine glass. She jumped up, filled a glass of water for me at the kitchen tap, set the glass before me, then retrieved my wine glass from the living room and emptied it into hers. "What'd they give you?" she wanted to know.

Harry

Charlie and Maddie got into a detailed discussion about pain medications. It seemed to me that Maddie's knowledge of and enthusiasm for anything remotely narcotic might cause Charlie to raise an eyebrow or two. "Maddie used to work at the hospital," I broke in at one point; "that's how she knows so much about this stuff." Meanwhile, Charlie was rattling on about oxy-this and aceta-that to a surprising degree himself. To me, they sounded like a pair of drug addicts.

At one point, as Maddie was draining her second or perhaps third glass of wine, I got up from the table and changed the music. I put on something called "*Iris*: Music from the Motion Picture." It started off slow and dreamy then turned into a series of quietly soaring orchestral pieces. Charlie and Maddie continued to talk right over it.

"Anybody ever heard of a movie called 'Iris'?" I said, hoping to change the subject.

Charlie had no clue about the movie. He just knew he liked the soundtrack, couldn't remember where he first came across it, thought I'd like it, too.

Maddie's only response was: "Open another bottle of wine, would you, Harry."

Charlie

Dad is not a hard man to read. Or maybe he is, maybe I just know him too well, being his son.

Maddie made him furious with her offhand remark, speaking to him as if he were her personal servant. I knew by a subtle shift in the tenseness in his bearing, the hardness of his voice, the coldness of his eye.

"I'm going to take a shower," Dad said, and he marched upstairs.

"What's eating him?" Maddie wondered. "Did *I* say something wrong?"

I shrugged. What other response was there?

Maddie and I continued to carry on a conversation. She opened the second bottle of wine herself. We ate our fill and packed away all the leftovers – there were plenty of leftovers – and threw in the trash the shamefully abundant paper waste. Maddie asked me to select more music, but I opted to play the "Iris" soundtrack again, feeling we had not given it a proper listen. The second time through it had its moments but it also at times sounded tired and repetitive to me. I was a little taken aback by how quickly Maddie drained that second bottle.

All the while I was remembering innumerable scenes between my mom and my dad that had played out along parallel lines to the one I had just witnessed between Dad and Maddie. Either Mom or Dad would do something or say something to set the other one off. It could be the tiniest thing. They rarely had major fights – like shouting at one another or calling names, still less was there ever a threat of physical violence. No, their way of fighting was much more low-key and, perhaps, much more damaging over time. The random tiny thing would occur, would set one of them off – and there would follow hours, days, sometimes the better part of a week when one would simmer and silently fume while the other pretended to be (or actually was) oblivious to any trouble. This was not the norm, it didn't happen all the time, but often enough. Generally, people saw them as a happily married couple. And I suppose they were. While at the same time they weren't. Growing up, I started out thinking that they were, but as the years went by I came more and more to suspect that they weren't. Maybe it would have been better for all concerned if they'd fought in the usual way.

The plumbing did not keep any secrets in that apartment of Dad's. We heard it when the water to the shower stopped, then when the trickle down the drain pipe came to a halt. We did not hear the bathroom door open – or I didn't anyway. But it wasn't hard to miss the quiet *thud* of the bedroom door.

"Do you think Harry's going to come back downstairs?" Maddie asked, her eyes shiny with drink.

"Probably not," I said.

IV. Saturday

Charlie

Next morning I woke to an ominously silent apartment. Or was I simply remembering the silences of the house I grew up in? I wandered into the kitchen and put on water for coffee. I rooted through Dad's cabinets until I found the coffee grinder I'd given him. But I did not grind the coffee right away. I always do that after the water boils and while it is cooling. I went to the living room and looked out the front window. Dad's truck was gone. I checked my phone to be sure of the day of the week – it was, indeed, Saturday. I yawned and stretched, and it felt like somebody was sticking a dull knife in my side – also my shoulder was still sore. I found a carton of orange juice in Dad's refrigerator and washed down a pain pill, not bothering with any glass. I considered taking a second pill – the discharge nurse had said I could take as many as two at a time – but decided to wait and see. The kettle whistled and I turned off the burner.

Maddie appeared just as the first mug was ready to pour. She wore a plaid bathrobe that I vaguely remembered being a gift from Mom to Dad. It was a plaid of fine red lines interwoven with navy and gray on a cream-colored background. I tried to recall if I ever saw Dad wearing it and found that I could not. One did not have to look too hard to see that Maddie was wearing nothing underneath.

I poured and handed the mug to Maddie and took down another mug for myself.

"You like yours black, as I recall," I said.

"Actually I prefer a little cream." She opened the refrigerator and brought out a small container of half-and-half. "We picked some up at the store the other day," she explained. "Hungry?"

"Not really. You?"

"Not really."

"Any idea where Dad's gone off to?"

"I was going to ask you."

I shrugged. "He was gone when I woke up, looks like he took the truck."

"Yeah," Maddie sighed. "I peeked out the bedroom window, I saw."

"It's probably none of my business," I said, "but are you two...all right?"

Maddie looked at me a long time. We were sitting across from one another in Dad's dining space by then. "What does all right mean in your book, Charlie?"

"Never mind, I shouldn't have asked."

"Are you asking did we fight last night? – did we screw?"

"Look, I apologize for asking."

Maddie reached across the table and patted my hand. "Sorry," she said. "I'm a little hungover...I get testy sometimes when I'm hungover."

We sat for a few minutes each thinking our own thoughts. Maddie got up and refilled her mug; she motioned with her eyes toward my mug and when I nodded she topped me off.

She sat down again and said, "He was out cold when I went upstairs. It would have been pointless to try and wake him. He'd had a long day yesterday – and a long night the night before."

I used to have a hard time thinking about my mother and my father having sex. Not that I thought about it all the time. But it's one of those images that sometimes pop into your head, unbidden, especially when you're growing up, especially when you're trying to figure out why your own thoughts about sex seem to be so different from everybody else's. The thought of Mom and Dad having sex used to panic me, used to make me feel slightly queasy. The thought of Dad and Maddie, however, for whatever reason, didn't bother me at all. In fact, I noticed in my heart a certain pride for the old man, also a kind of tenderness toward him, for the loneliness I know he suffered after Mom died, for the feat of enduring it and for the attempt now of trying to find his way past it.

"I think you're good for him, Maddie," I said, maybe expressing a hope more than an honest opinion.

"He has a funny way of showing it," Maddie said, "running off to work on a Saturday morning without even a peck on the cheek for good-bye." Absent-mindedly she adjusted the bathrobe, which had fallen partially open. "Do you think that's where he went? – to work?"

"I don't know where else he would have gone," I said. "He doesn't go to a lot of places."

"The chess club," Maddie reminded me.

"Yeah, that and work...as far as I know those are the only two things that get him out of the house."

"I made him mad last night somehow, but I'm not sure how."

"He can be a hard man to read," I said.

Maddie was surprised. "You think so?"

"Well, not for me personally, but I think a lot of people have a hard time reading him...you know? I mean, he kinda doesn't fit into any neat category: he's a construction worker but he collects books and reads widely and voraciously; he's thoughtful and I've often seen glimpses of how articulate he must be inside his own head, but he tends not to say very much and at times, I swear, he can be downright clueless."

Maddie nodded. "And at other times he sees right through to the heart of the matter." She studied me carefully.

Since they picked me up from the hospital, the whole time I had been with Dad and Maddie, deep in the back of my mind, I'd felt almost naked, covered by the thinnest veil of lies. Maddie was inviting me to step out from behind the veil.

Maddie

I didn't think I'd get anywhere with Charlie. He wore the same closed-up, tight-lipped expression that was already becoming familiar to me after only a few days with his father. But the longer I looked at Charlie the more convinced I was that Harry's hard determination didn't come naturally to Charlie's softer face – with those pouty lips, those coltish brown eyes.

Charlie shook his head. "I can't talk about something like that with Dad." He spoke in low tones as if he were standing at a graveside or huddled inside a confessional.

I nodded to let him know I understood. "You *should* talk about it, though...You need to find someone you can talk to."

He stared into his coffee, his eyes growing moist, his two hands cradling the mug. One hand drifted loose. Almost imperceptibly that hand moved toward me. I slid my own hand across the table. The moment we touched, Charlie's fingertips curled around mine, pulling our hands closer together. His hands were longer and narrower than Harry's and, as I think I might have mentioned, much much softer.

"Between us?" he asked.

I nodded.

"If I tell you about it, it's because I'm trusting in you...I'm not...I'm not looking for some secret way of talking to my dad about it without actually having to talk to him."

"I understand," I said.

He seemed on the verge of tears when he started, but the more he said the further from crying he strayed. His voice became – not hard exactly – but emotionless, almost droning. I knew the place he was at. The things he needed to talk about could only *be* talked about if you locked away your feelings, turned the pain into mere words. Oh yes, I knew that place.

Everything seemed to click when Alexis came along: the two of them seemed so right together. Charlie had been involved in a few flings, mostly unhappy, and in one serious relationship, also unhappy, before Alexis and, yes, technically Charlie was rebounding, since that other relationship had ended not quite a month prior, but he would have sworn there was not the slightest hint of desperation in his feelings toward Alexis. "But, then again, sometimes I'm good at fooling myself," Charlie said with a rueful smile. Alexis was a couple of years older than Charlie and, when it came to relationships, far more experienced. And oh, how beautiful Alexis was with his jet black eyes, which were really deep deep blue, and his dramatic mane of black hair. People remarked all the time about Alexis' Latin good looks, although his background was actually Eastern Mediterranean. They met at a march to kick-off the town's LGBT Pride Week and before that week was out they were living together. Charlie moved in with Alexis – Alexis would not even consider the alternative, although Charlie's place was both bigger and cheaper. Maybe Charlie should have seen that as a sign of trouble right from the start, but he was too smitten. Another bad sign: Alexis had few friends, if any, and it wasn't long before he was finding fault with Charlie's friends, alienating many of them, isolating Charlie more and more. And of course Charlie's father loathed Alexis, loathed him immediately, even before the real trouble started – not that they ever saw much of each other – but Charlie had chalked that up to his father's inability to accept Charlie for who he was. So many signs.

The first incident occurred about two months after they'd moved in together. This was before Charlie got his job as a bank teller. He was working two part-time gigs – one as a waiter in a hotel restaurant, the other as "customer service representative" for an on-line marketer of flooring products. Both jobs sucked, but at least at the restaurant you got to interact with your co-workers, and one night after work Charlie was invited by some of the other wait staff and kitchen staff to go out for drinks. Charlie called Alexis and urged him to join them. Alexis said no, suggested coldly that Charlie should come straight home. Ignoring the odd coldness in Alexis' voice, Charlie replied he would just stop in for one quick drink, then he'd be there – and that's what he did. Alexis met him at the door with a fist to the gut. Charlie crumpled, fell to the floor and Alexis stood over him, fuming and swearing. Later, Alexis apologized, promised it would never happen again. But then it did happen again. There followed another apology, another promise. Time went by – a week, maybe two – then another incident: a kick, possibly aimed at the groin, which left a sizeable bruise on Charlie's inner thigh. It seemed to come out of nowhere, and it was for the craziest reason. Charlie would never forget what caused it, it was so ridiculous. The thing they had been arguing about, which had started as an innocent discussion, was this: when friends drop by who are smokers at what point is it asking too much to make then go outside to smoke – if you're in a first- or second-floor apartment that's a no-brainer (they go outside) but what if you're in a fifth-floor apartment, no elevator? – is it reasonable for your friends to expect that they should be allowed to sit by an open window and smoke? That's what Charlie and Alexis had been arguing about. And the real irony was: fewer and fewer of Charlie's friends were dropping by, so the entire subject was fast becoming moot. Not to mention the fact that their building had an elevator.

I think Charlie would have described every last violent incident if I had let him. But I could see that going over each attack at that level of detail would only serve to get him worked up. I didn't think it could be the least bit cathartic for Charlie to relive every painful memory – he was too close to it all. Instead, I got him talking about the patterns of Alexis' behavior, and possible causes. As to patterns, all Charlie could say for sure was that the attacks were occurring with greater frequency. As to causes, Charlie's first response was to ask if I thought he, Charlie, was to blame.

"No, Charlie, I don't."

"I mean, obviously the cause is that Alexis is angry...but maybe the deeper cause is that I'm setting him off somehow, not being sensitive enough to his needs..."

"Is he drunk when he hits you?"

"No."

"Not even a little?"

"Sometimes he's had a drink in him, sometimes not."

"Does he do drugs?"

The slightest hesitation, a shifting of the eyes. "No, never."

"What's his work environment like? Does he have good days and bad days? Do the attacks always happen when he's had a bad day at work?"

"I've never noticed a pattern like that?"

"Do they happen right after he comes home from work?"

"Once yes...the other times, no."

"Are you sure? I was with a guy once who was a freaking monster when he came home from work...but he didn't beat me."

"Yes, I'm sure. You're not talking about Dad, I hope...?"

"Jeez no, Charlie — your dad is a lovely man."

"Glad to hear you say that...he *is* a lovely man, I'm glad you can see that in him."

"How about this?...Do the attacks always happen when there is a dispute about your friends, even if the friends are no more than hypothetical chain-smokers?"

Charlie did that thing people do with their eyes — looking off to the side when they are trying to remember.

"Now that you mention it," Charlie said, "that might be a pattern."

"I'll tell you two more patterns I suspect — you can tell me if I'm right or not."

"Go ahead."

"Alexis is always careful to hurt you in places that don't show, isn't he? For instance, I bet he never hits you in the face."

Charlie looked glum. "Do you think he's doing that on purpose?" His voice became suddenly very small.

"Classic behavior for an abuser like Alexis," I said. "Textbook."

"So...he *plans* these attacks...?"

I shook my head. "I'm not saying that, Charlie — I don't know if he does or not. But I *am* saying I bet you're not the first person he's done this to: he knows how to avoid suspicion and how to keep himself out of trouble."

Charlie looked lost in thought, but he shot a quick glance my way. "You said you had *two* more patterns...what's the other one?"

I squeezed his hand. "The attacks are getting more violent, aren't they?"

Charlie gulped and nodded.

Harry

When I got to the jobsite it was just Doug and the two laborers he'd cowed into working on a Saturday.

Pulling my trowel and level out of the back of my truck, I called to Doug, "Where are the other guys?" Yesterday he had bullied and cajoled at least three of the masons on the crew into saying that they would be here.

Doug acted like he didn't hear me.

The wind lacked some of the gustiness of yesterday but made up for that by being steady and raw. On the plus side, the rain that had been forecast had not materialized, and the sun was making every effort to break through the ragged gaps in the clouds.

Doug was thoroughly miserable. Of course, he was angry at the masons who had so far failed to show up. Also, he was apprehensive that the developer would appear at any moment and not be sufficiently impressed with his "show." Finally, the flush on Doug's face looked to be more than just a reaction to the biting wind. The way he dragged his feet, the way he hung his shoulders, the way he kept scratching the top of his knit hat like he was trying to make a very deep and painful itch go away, told me that Doug was hungover. I hadn't often see Doug like that on our usual Monday through Friday work schedule – but the poor devil probably couldn't hold himself back on a Friday night, and so here he was suffering the consequences on a Saturday morning.

I wasn't hungover but I have to say I also wasn't in such a great mood. First, there was Charlie to worry about. Alexis was beating Charlie – I guess I'd known that for awhile but had somehow kept myself from believing it. In a way, it was a bit like having to come to grips with Charlie's "orientation," as they say, all over again. Only this was worse. What did it say about my son that he let his gay lover beat him? Where was his self-respect? What kind of man was he that he didn't fight back? And was there anything I could do to help him? If so, I couldn't see what it was – at some point a man's got to be able to take care of his own problems, right? I had a lot to process when it came to Charlie.

And then there was Maddie. Despite myself, I still felt a nagging resentment toward Maddie: it wasn't just the way she'd spoken to me but the fact that she'd spoken that way in front of Charlie. "The way she'd spoken to me..." Part of me knew just how petty I was being. But that simply made the part that was resentful dig in deeper. I wanted so much to get over it. I was impatient with myself to get over it. And frustrated with myself that I'd ever let such a trivial thing upset me at all. Meanwhile, I had to admit, watching Doug suffer *did* slightly help to brighten my mood.

Doug had set the two laborers to waterproofing the outsides of the block we'd laid yesterday. Doug himself was doing the work of a laborer, carrying blocks, stacking them close to where they would be needed, in the hopes that a mason or two would show up – maybe he felt his hands were too shaky to lay any block himself. With me there, he told one of the laborers to start mixing mortar.

A passenger car rolled into the development, bumping slowly along the unpaved road, and Doug eyed it nervously. It pulled in beside my truck. After a minute or so, one of our masons emerged, a guy whose name was Mike but whose nickname on the crew was Slim – because he wasn't.

Doug scowled. "Where are Cory and Travis?" he demanded, naming the other two masons who said they'd work.

"They ain't doin' so good this morning."

Cursing, Doug swung the two blocks he was carrying onto a low scaffold – except he missed his aim with one of them and it struck the edge of the wooden plank and bounced back. Doug was too slow to get completely out of the way. A corner of the block clipped the top of Doug's nose. Then the block landed square on his foot.

Doug howled. He was able to kick his foot free from under the block. There he was hopping on one foot, holding his nose, blood seeping through his fingers. The sun chose that moment to shine its full light on our small patch of earth.

An expensive-looking SUV appeared at the entrance to the development. Doug didn't see it right away. When he did, he frantically waved to the newly arrived mason to get to work. "Make it look like you've been here awhile," he honked.

"Hey, Mike," I called, "grab the first aid kit out of my truck, will ya'? It's in the cab, behind the passenger seat."

Doug refused to be tended to while the developer scrutinized us from behind the rolled-up, tinted windows of his SUV. While Mike and I laid a couple of eight-inch blocks, Doug himself carried buckets of mortar to us, one-handed, his other hand holding a navy-blue bandana to his nose. Limping, he winced at every step.

When the SUV finally rolled away, I persuaded Doug to sit down on some of the blocks he'd stacked, and I took a look at his nose. It was an ugly scrape but nothing worse. The bleeding had pretty much stopped. I cleaned up the cut with some gauze and some antibiotic ointment and put a band-aid on it. I told Doug he ought to go have his foot looked at – plenty of tiny bones in the foot, not too unlikely he broke a few of them. But he wouldn't hear of it. "So what if I did?" he wanted to know; "What are they going to do about it? Put a cast on my *foot*? What's that going to help? Screw it – if I broke it, it'll heal on its own." I was not surprised. I could picture a lot of guys in construction, myself included, saying the same thing.

Mike wandered over. "We going home, Doug?"

Doug looked up at me. "What do you think, Harry?"

"The forecast this morning was for wind and rain until noon, then clearing. I bet that developer's got a tee time set up for one o'clock; I bet he swings by here one more time before lunch."

"Let's stick it out till lunch," Doug said.

Mike gave me a dirty look and went back to work. The laborers were none too happy, either.

Honestly, I had no idea what the developer was going to do. I hadn't even checked the weather forecast in any great detail that morning. I was being selfish, that's all. I wanted an excuse to be out of my apartment and I wanted the calming, focusing tasks of masonry so that I could enter into that mental space where I was often able to think my own thoughts with peculiar clarity and, sometimes, to clear away unwanted emotions. Also – it was small and mean of me, I know – I was still getting a kick out of watching Doug struggle through the morning.

We labored on. The wind continued steady but the sky showed more blue and fewer clouds with every passing hour. When the sun was near the top of its arc, Mike nudged my shoulder. "Would you look at that!" he said. There it was again, the developer's SUV. This time the great man got out of his vehicle. His clothes might or might not have been a golfing outfit. He waved until Doug acknowledged him. He gave Doug a big thumbs-up, got in his SUV and drove away.

Mike said, "That's it, boys, pack it up, let's go home."

Doug limped over to where I was working. "Damn, Harry," he said, clapping me on the shoulder, "you called that right on the nose."

I smiled at him, thinking he was making a weak pun – but Doug was oblivious to his own paltry wit.

Maddie

After our talk, Charlie took a quick shower but he had no fresh clothes to put on. I offered to go with him to his apartment and even to go inside with him while he gathered some things. Charlie was reluctant. He was confused about what he should do.

"I shouldn't be imposing on you and Dad like this," he said.

I protested that his dad would certainly not agree that Charlie presented any sort of imposition – and as far as I was concerned, I was a guest in Harry's home myself. But Charlie waved my words away.

"You know what I mean," he said. "Three's a crowd."

I drew breath to argue further – except I *did* know what Charlie meant, and I appreciated his tone: it was clear he bore no malice, cast no moral judgments.

"You can't go back to Alexis," I insisted.

Charlie sighed. "There's more to it, to Alexis and me, than just the violent parts. There are still times when he can be very sweet, in his way. I don't know that I'm ready to give up on us, and on that side of him."

"Charlie, have you and Alexis ever been able to discuss his problem? Does he even admit that he has a problem?"

Charlie made several false attempts at a reply. "The short answer is: no we haven't – I've tried, but the anger shield goes right up on his side – and no he doesn't."

"Charlie, you *cannot* go back unless and until Alexis agrees to certain conditions." I held up a hand, ready to tick them off.

"Can I hire you to represent me?" Charlie joked.

"Charlie, this is serious – now, as to the conditions…"

"It *is* serious, I know it is." Charlie touched my arm. "I just can't talk about it anymore right now. I'm going out for a walk."

But by then I was in full protection mode. "You can't go out in weather like this with what you're wearing! Listen to that wind! And I'm not the least bit certain that the rain has stopped for good."

"I'll put on my windbreaker."

I whooped at the ridiculousness of the idea. "That flimsy thing?!"

Charlie moved toward the door, windbreaker in hand, but I headed him off.

"You are not leaving this house until you put on one of your father's heavy coats!"

Charlie looked at me like I was crazy. "I wouldn't fit into anything of Dad's."

"Nonsense. You two are practically the same size." (Charlie was taller but Harry was broader in the shoulders.)

I saw an idea flit across Charlie's face. I said, "As God is my witness, Charlie, if you make a dash for the back door I will tackle you so hard you'll have more than one broken rib to cry about."

His frown was overcome by an astonished grin at having been read so presciently, then laughter sprung out of him like water out of a fountain. I couldn't help it: I started laughing, too. That set Charlie off further which only set me off further and soon we were falling all over ourselves, holding each other up, tears streaming down our faces, we were laughing so hard.

Charlie went out the front door carrying an umbrella and wearing a charcoal gray woolen overcoat with large black buttons that fitted him rather well, I thought.

Harry

The additional hours of work, between the two visits from the developer, had been good for me. In that time I came to understand the real reason for my anger the night before. It had to do with Maddie and Charlie hitting it off so well and with the way they had left me out of the conversation, going on about a topic (drugs) that I knew next to nothing about; it had to do with the fact that Maddie was closer to Charlie's age than to mine. A lot closer. Not that I was jealous of Charlie or saw him as a rival. But the way those two rattled on together had been an uncomfortable reminder of how far apart Maddie was from me – in age, in interests, in lifestyle, anyway you wanted to look at it. Obvious, once I'd seen it – and I shook my head, while tapping into line one of the last blocks of the day, at my perpetual slowness.

I took my time driving home that day, knowing I had some apologizing to do.

Here was the first thing Maddie said when I came through the door, her words a furious rush: "Harry where have you been I'm worried about Charlie."

"What's going on?! Is he having trouble breathing? Where is he?!" (I thought maybe his lung had collapsed.)

"He went out for a walk – and he's been gone for well over an hour."

I instantly relaxed. "That's just Charlie," I reassured her. "When he was a teenager he'd spend morning, noon and night out walking sometimes."

The next thing Maddie said was: "What lovely flowers! Aren't you sweet!"

She took them from me, she gave me a peck on the cheek, she admired the bouquet – what the florist had called a "spring mix," never mind that it was November – then Maddie handed the bunch of flowers back to me to be put in a vase. I had prepared an entire little speech, my apology, but all of a sudden the time did not seem right for an apology.

One-handed, I searched through the cabinets in the kitchen. I was not looking for a vase – I already knew I didn't own one – just something to hold flowers. I found a glass pitcher that Suzanne used to serve iced tea in. It wasn't ideal: the mouth of the thing was too big. But it was all I could find. I filled the pitcher with water, dumped in the flowers, and set it in the center of the dining room table. The flowers splayed randomly to the edges of the pitcher, creating a weird circular pattern that even I could see was not too pleasing.

"What if he's gone back to Alexis?" Maddie fretted.

"Did he say anything to make you think he would?"

Maddie considered. "No, not really," she said. "But when I offered to go with him to his apartment to pick up a few of his things, he didn't want to go."

I tried to make sense of Maddie's reasoning. If Charlie *didn't* want to go to his place, wasn't that a good sign? Maddie read my thoughts.

"He has no clothes except what he's wearing," she explained. "No personal belongings, not even a toothbrush or a comb. If he intended to stay here, even for a day or two, wouldn't he want to make a run by his apartment?"

"Okay. I can see that."

"Maybe we should go over to Charlie's place and make sure he's not in any trouble."

I frowned. "Alexis is a son-of-a-bitch but I don't think he's *that* dangerous."

"Alexis just last night put your son in the hospital."

"What if we go over there and Charlie's not there but Alexis is?

—actually maybe that wouldn't be such a bad thing…"

"So that you can put Alexis in the hospital?"

"Something like that. Sure, why not? I have to say the thought has crossed my mind more than once since yesterday."

"Harry, you know that's not a solution."

I shrugged. "How do I know until I give it a try? Maybe the son-of-a-bitch needs a taste of his own medicine."

Maddie stared at me like I was plotting an assassination. "I can't believe I'm hearing you talk like this."

I came so close to saying to Maddie that she would understand if she'd ever had a child of her own – I can only imagine the stupid, hurtful fight those words would have lead us into. That's one of the few good things about getting older: sometimes your brain gets out ahead of your mouth – not all the time but sometimes. Instead, I said, "It was your idea to go over there."

"Okay, but you convinced me: bad idea."

"I suppose if you're really worried about him I could call him."

Maddie placed both hands on top of her head in a gesture that might have indicated: *I can't believe this thing is so empty*. She said, "You know, it's weird how you forget about cell phones when you don't carry one with you all the time. Have you ever noticed that?"

I would have told her that I hardly think about cell phones even though I do carry one, but Maddie was impatient to find out about Charlie. "Call him, call him!" she urged.

I pulled up his name and rang his number. No answer. I left a voice message: "Hey Charlie, it's Dad…um, Saturday a little after noon…um, call me…okay thanks, bye."

"You're so charming over the phone," Maddie teased.

"I hate leaving messages."

The phone chirped to let me know I had a text. It was Charlie, of course. I read his message aloud: *walking thinking will see you guys later today promise*.

Maddie nodded, satisfied. Then she noticed the flowers on the table. "What the hell is *that*?" she said. She carried the pitcher and the splayed flowers into the kitchen. I heard water running in the sink. She emerged a minute or so later with two wine bottles pulled out of the recycling bag. She'd split up the flowers to make a pair of elegant arrangements spilling out of the top of each bottle. She placed one on the dining room table.

My phone chirped again. Charlie: *will text when I am nearby*.

Maddie said, "I think this other one would look spectacular on the nightstand beside the bed. What do you think, Harry?"

My phone chirped another time: *don't look for me for hours.*

Maddie smiled. "That son of yours is a very thoughtful lad...why don't you come upstairs with me and see what you think of the flowers?"

Maddie

Charlie returned a little after sunset, his cheeks a bright rosy red from being out in the wind so long. He wanted to know if we were hungry; he suggested that we make an early dinner of the leftovers from the night before. Harry and I exchanged guilty glances.

"Actually," I said, "your dad and I kind of had a late lunch...we sort of ate all the leftovers...mostly me – I was famished!"

"Oh," Charlie said, surprised and disappointed. But he continued to eye his father and me, and I could see him taking in the glow that must have been emanating from the two of us. "Oh," he said again, this time surprised but upbeat. "That's great, that's wonderful, now I don't feel so bad."

"About what?" Harry was genuinely puzzled, the lummox.

"About..." Charlie started to say, making a gesture with his hand toward the blankets folded up on the end of the couch. "...nothing nothing, don't listen to me."

Harry frowned.

"I'm just saying I feel much better after my walk, that's all...hey, nice flowers!" He motioned toward the wine bottle/vase perched in the center of Harry's battered oak table.

I put on my most demure smile while at the same time sending Charlie a quick wink. He flashed back *stop trying to make me laugh!* Meanwhile Harry was fretting about what Charlie would have for supper. "I'll call for take-out, we can get something delivered – what do you want, Charlie?"

What Charlie wanted was not to cause any trouble. He went into the kitchen to see if he could scrounge up a meal. I called after him, "I can already tell you what's in there: oatmeal – and a couple of eggs in the fridge...and, oh yeah, I think there's some canned soup in one of the cabinets."

Charlie called back, "Oatmeal, eggs and canned soup – perfect! I was having cravings for those three things the whole time I was walking."

"I'm sending out for pizza," Harry insisted. "Maybe we'll have a slice with you."

In the end Harry won. Even Charlie had to admit that sending out for pizza was the least amount of trouble.

Charlie said he wanted to "freshen up before dinner" and retreated upstairs to the bathroom.

Harry wandered over to his wall of books and, hands behind his back, perused the titles. Was he surprised to find Daphne Merkin back in her place? Did he even notice? I became aware of an odd energy in the house — or, I should say, it felt odd to me. I tried to center in on it, to understand it. Part of its oddness had to do with the uneasy comfort both Harry and Charlie seemed to find in it — and as soon as I perceived that, it was like someone had slipped a secret decoder ring onto my finger. Each of them was remembering, reliving the familial life they had shared with Suzanne. I felt Suzanne's presence. She was not possessing me, exactly, but she was occupying the same space as me. Whether Suzanne was a real presence or if I was being swayed by the combined power of the memories and desires of father and son, I have no way of knowing. In the moment Suzanne felt truly present. I reminded her gently that she had never lived in this house: perhaps I felt the need to insure myself against any attempt on her part to actually possess me. Suzanne made no acknowledgement. It occurred to me that she might not be aware of me at all — to her I might be no more than a window she found herself gazing through. I felt the current of her desire — it clouded my thoughts like a person's breath clouds a pane of glass — she strained to inhabit the place and time that I in that moment inhabited, ached to be once again in the presence of her husband and her son. Harry continued to stand with his back to me. Charlie, hiding out in the bathroom, hiding a truth from his father that his father already knew, was there in the house and at the same time not there. It all seemed so familiar to Suzanne. How much of Charlie had she figured out while Charlie was growing up? How far ahead of Harry had she been on that? How had she dealt with it inside herself? How had she addressed it with Charlie, with Harry? I found myself floating away from myself as I pondered those questions — but, somehow, through the act of pondering, Maddie, the window, cast a pale reflection back toward the gazer, who could not recognize herself in what should have been her own reflection — and Suzanne fled.

I would have fallen to the floor if I had not been able to steady myself against the back of the couch. Next thing I knew, Harry was beside me, his strong arms and powerful grip handling me like a sack of mortar for which he happened to have fond feelings. I put my arms around his neck and hung on until the room stopped swaying.

"What is it? What's the matter?"

"Nothing's the matter...I'm fine – it was just a touch of vertigo."

Harry half carried me to a chair but I was already feeling better and I stayed on my feet.

"I'm fine, really," I insisted.

Harry begged me to sit.

I made some lame joke about how he'd worn me out upstairs even more than I realized. Harry could not be distracted from his confusion and his concern.

Charlie

I stared at myself in the bathroom mirror. People say my dad and I look alike. Personally, I have always had a hard time seeing it. My dad and Aunt Fran – now those two look alike: the same square face, the same intense gray eyes. Me: when I try to look intense, it never works out – I wind up looking either demented or constipated, or both. Mom could never pull off intense either: her features were too soft. Mom's natural expression was *accommodating*. I have always seen more of Mom in me than Dad.

But that day standing in front of that mirror I thought, every now and then, that I was catching glimpses of Dad after all. Maybe it had something to do with walking around for hours in his coat. Or maybe, sadly, I was forgetting my mother's face – and Dad's was the only one left to compare myself to. *No it's the coat*, I insisted.

Gingerly, I pulled off my shirt, inspected the long red welt across my ribcage. It was darkening, turning purple. Also, there were the remains of bruises on my upper arm.

I frowned into the mirror. "This has got to stop," I said. I said the words softly, so as not to be heard outside the bathroom. "Alexis, this can't happen anymore, this has got to stop." I said it over and over again, practicing.

"One way or another, this is *going to stop*."

Maddie

Poor Harry looked worn and frazzled. As if he didn't have enough to worry about with Charlie, now he felt he had to hover at my side to keep me from face-planting myself. And, of course, there were other things going on in his head concerning me. He'd never told me what had angered him the night before. I tried to go over the events of last night in my mind but they were fuzzy: perhaps I had had a bit too much to drink. Anyway, I didn't think it mattered. Whatever had happened last night was a minor glitch, soon forgotten. The more worrisome vibe coming from Harry was the weariness that had begun two nights ago, the night of Thanksgiving. What was the cause of that? To me, that was the deeper puzzle. In bed this afternoon the weariness seemed to evaporate, only to reappear, descending on Harry like a fog, like a full-blown depression, once our lovemaking was over. I urged him to tell me what was the matter, but he only smiled sadly and stroked and petted me and told me each time with me was a new revelation. I told him again what I'd said to him before: good sex is rollicking fun but he shouldn't make too much of it.

Charlie was still hiding out in the bathroom at the top of the stairs. I motioned to Harry to follow me into the kitchen. Since we were in there anyway, I decided to open a bottle of wine: it turned out to be the last one. I poured us each a half-glass and volunteered to make a run to the grocery store.

"No, I'll go," Harry said. "Besides, that reminds me – I never paid you for the food last night."

"Harry, that was my treat."

Harry shook his head. "You can't afford to do something like that..."

"Listen, Harry, just because I'm living out of my car doesn't mean I'm completely destitute. It was my treat and that's that! Also I'm going to the grocery store! – you stay home with your son: the two of you should talk."

Harry was decidedly not pleased. I don't know what distressed him worse, letting me pay for things or the prospect of having to talk with Charlie about his situation with Alexis. Actually, I did know – and it had nothing to do with who bought the groceries.

"Did he talk to you?" Harry wanted to know. "Did he admit to you what's been happening?"

"We talked but it was confidential."

I watched Harry's mind move all around that statement – was there some honorable way for him to probe into what Charlie had said in private? He decided that there was not, and he made no attempt. *Yay Harry*, I thought — *yay me for finding Harry*.

"But I will tell you one thing."

"What's that?"

"I'm only telling you because it's something Charlie *didn't* say — in fact he lied about it — so I don't think the privilege of confidentiality applies." (I had been turning this argument over in my head all day.)

Harry waited.

"Alexis is doing drugs."

"Are you sure? What makes you think so? Wait a minute...how do you know Charlie was lying?"

"You're just going to have to trust me on this one, Harry."

Charlie

Dad called to me that the pizza had arrived, and when I came downstairs I found that Maddie was gone. I cast a questioning glance Dad's way.

"She's making a run to the grocery store...we're almost out of wine."

"Heaven forefend," I said. (That was one of my little catch-phrases, more or less recent, and I wasn't sure I was going to keep it — I guess everybody has them — some people thought this one was funny when I used it right; some people never saw the humor: it was my first time trying it on Dad.)

Dad smiled uncertainly.

The pizza box was on his beat-up dining table. He faded away into the kitchen and came back a moment later with a china plate.

"You okay, Dad?"

He made no answer, handed me the plate, went back into the kitchen, emerged with a glass of water, and set it down at the place where I had eaten the night before. In the meantime, I had flipped open the pizza box and pulled out a slice: Veggie Delight.

"Thanks for remembering I'm a vegetarian," I said — just to say something, just to try to get him to speak.

"Maddie's a vegetarian, too," he said. "Sort of."

"Oh yeah? Sort of?"

But he didn't elaborate.

"You worry about her when she leaves, don't you? You worry she won't come back."

"Do you want ice in your water?"

"Actually, if there's any wine left I wouldn't mind some of that."

Dad eyed me skeptically.

"I stopped taking the pain meds," I explained. "I don't need them, I have hardly any discomfort. So it's okay for me to take a drink."

Harry

In that moment I saw a terrible downward spiral in store for my son. Maddie was right: Alexis *was* a drug user. Charlie was planning to hoard his pain medicines, pass them on to Alexis. Meanwhile, Charlie would manage the pain from his injury with some combination of alcohol and over-the-counter medicines. Where else could this lead? — it would only give Alexis more incentive to harm Charlie.

With a sinking feeling in my gut, I poured Charlie a glass of wine; I poured more into my own glass as well.

"Maddie says we ought to talk," I said, sitting across from him.

Charlie had just taken a bite of pizza and was moving the slice back toward his plate, threads of cheese stretching away from his mouth. He chewed, he swallowed, he sipped his wine. "Maddie told you everything, didn't she?"

"Maddie told me you two talked and that it was confidential."

Charlie studied me, trying to gauge my level of truthfulness. I turned the wine glass in my hands. I said, "Charlie, I may not have been the most clued in dad when you were growing up…there were plenty of things I was slow to figure out…about you and your mom both…and I guess I didn't always react the right way in every situation…but about what's going on now, between you and Alexis…I don't really need Maddie to explain it to me…I kind of already know."

Charlie dropped his gaze. Suddenly, he couldn't meet my eyes.

After a long silence, he murmured, "I wish Mom were here."

Another silence. "Me too," I said — but not with my whole heart: I wondered if Charlie could hear that.

Charlie started to say something. My phone buzzed. It was a number I didn't recognize, an unfamiliar area code. I knew Maddie didn't have a phone but still it occurred to me that it might be her. I left the table and swiped the screen.

It was a man, asking for Maddie.

"Maddie's not here. Who's this?"

"This is Freeman."

"Who?"

"Her brother. Freeman. She called me from this number, left a message, told me to call back, so I'm calling back. Where is she?"

She's...listen, I'll tell her you called...I'll have her call you back."

"Who are you?"

"She should be back pretty soon...I'll have her call you."

I ended the connection.

Charlie was watching me. "Someone for Maddie?"

"Her brother."

"She has a brother, good for her."

The remark hung in the air between us. Did Charlie feel that his mother and I had cheated him somehow by never providing him with a sibling? If so, I'd have to mark it down as one more thing that someone close to me was feeling that I'd missed for all these years.

I came back to the table and now Charlie was looking me straight in the eye.

"I'm going to handle this problem with Alexis, Dad. I'm going back there tomorrow and I'm going to take care of it. Can we just leave it at that? Please."

Those big brown eyes of his looked so soft and vulnerable, it was hard for me to see how he stood a chance against a jackal like Alexis. Yet I nodded. I felt there was no other answer to give.

Charlie said, "Tell Maddie that's my plan, would you?...maybe after we've all turned in for the night?"

Maddie

Shopping with Harry on Thanksgiving, he had asked about my wine preferences. I told him my pocketbook usually dictated my preference: the cheapest. His reply, I remember, was, "Cheap wine's hard to drink." I suppose in his own head that sounded kind of snobbish, but I didn't take it as anything other than the truth. He hastened to add: "I used to drink cheap wine all the time when things were bad, don't get me wrong." I assured him I wasn't getting him wrong. He said, "Nowadays I've graduated from cheap to inexpensive." He was being modest: he selected several wines, all reds, at least one rung above inexpensive on the hierarchy of cost – merlots and blends, mostly.

Standing there in the wine aisle by myself, picturing Harry and Charlie back at Harry's apartment, hoping they were finally figuring out how to talk to one another, I found it difficult to place in my cart bottles of wine that cost three times as much as the cheap stuff at the far end of the aisle. I noticed a sign that said if you bought six bottles you got a ten percent discount, and that helped a little – but, damn, this was going to set me back. What was I thinking when I said I would do this? I drifted a little further down the aisle. Would Harry notice if I bought something slightly cheaper? I decided to chance it.

It had been in my mind to pick up some actual groceries, too, but now the old money worries were assailing me and I went through the checkout line with exactly six bottles of red blend.

While I stood in line, I got that feeling you sometimes get when you're being stared at. I glanced all around. A tall man two checkout lines away was doing the staring. Our eyes met. I recognized him immediately: Mr. Tattoo. I wasn't positive that he recognized me – in fact, I was pretty sure he didn't, and that was why he was staring: he was trying to figure out where he knew me from. I looked away and, turning, suddenly became fascinated with the magazines and tabloids in the rack in front of the counter. His eyes were still on me; I could still feel them. His line was moving faster than mine, and the next time I glanced his way he was already paying for his purchase: a twelve-pack of beer, what else? I averted my eyes until I was sure he was gone – the last thing I wanted was for him to feel my gaze on his back.

I tried to chat up the cashier – a boy of perhaps nineteen – but there was a line behind me, and he didn't know what to make of me. When he totaled my purchase I took as long as possible digging cash out of my purse, pretending to look for exact chance. On my way out, I stopped to study all the different brands of cigarettes, cigars, and other tobacco products in the glass case beside the manager's booth. Who knew they still sold snuff? – I wondered who bought it. I paused at the exit door and scanned the entire parking lot. No sign of Mr. Tattoo. I made my way to my car.

I got out of the parking lot without incident, but I couldn't help noticing a pick-up truck which had sprung to life as soon as my car started moving. One side of its battered front bumper was held on by tie wire. Also, one headlight was wildly mis-set – so that when the truck fell in behind me on the road, the light from that headlight streamed through my rear window and glared back at me from my own rear-view mirror. Had I seen this truck before? An image flashed in my head of this exact same truck crookedly parked outside of McFall's. But I didn't believe it was a true image – more likely, it was a mirage brought on by the panic that was beginning to grip me.

The truck was riding my rear bumper. Its wayward headlight was on me like a spotlight. I felt pushed to go faster and faster. I found myself racing toward Harry's apartment, but was that a good idea? Mr. Tattoo, in that checkout line, had looked mean and sober, stone cold sober. Could Harry fend him off in that state? Would Charlie be any help at all? Or would Mr. Tattoo intercept me in front of the apartment before I could even make it to Harry's door? I cursed the fact that my phone was shut off. If I had a working phone I could call ahead, alert Harry and Charlie. Hell, if I had a phone I could call the police.

The traffic light I was approaching turned red. I thought about running it, but there was too much cross-traffic. As I applied the brakes, I hurriedly locked the door beside me and made sure all the others were locked as well. I could feel the deep vibrations of the truck's engine directly behind me.

Charlie

The wine was gone – Dad had evenly shared it out between the two of us. There was more than half of the pizza left. I had stopped at two slices, and Dad kept saying maybe he'd have one later, "when Maddie got home." It broke my heart a little each time he used that phrase. I wasn't picking up a feeling from Maddie that she thought of this place as home – and even though Dad himself had said that "this thing with Maddie" was probably temporary, it was plain that he was beginning to hope against hope – and I worried for Dad how hard he would take it when Maddie moved on.

With the subject of Alexis off limits, we didn't find much to talk about at first. Dad asked me how my job was going. He listened with half an ear and an eye toward the door, waiting for Maddie's return, as I described my recent training on what to do when the bank gets robbed. I asked how his work was going. "Fine, fine," he said.

Then he added: "That's one thing I don't regret not teaching you."

"What? Masonry?"

He nodded. "It's backbreaking work."

"I thought you liked it."

"I'm not saying I don't like it…I'm just glad you're finding your own way, that's all."

I thought of some smart-ass things to say about my enviable career, my brilliant path through life so far but kept them all to myself.

"Are there things you *do* regret not teaching me?"

He studied his scraped-up hands. I noticed he had a large blood blister under the nail of his right thumb.

"Baseball."

"What'd'ya mean, 'baseball'? We used to play catch in the backyard all the time. Don't tell me you don't remember…"

"Of course I remember," he said. He smiled involuntarily, and I smiled too. "But I never took the time to really teach you the game, never took you to ball games…you never played Little League."

"I was into soccer."

Dad brooded. "I always suspected your mom steered you in that direction instead of letting you choose for yourself."

In the past, I would have taken that as code-speak for: *your mom is to blame that you chose to become gay*. Now I was able to hear Dad more generously.

I thought over what he said. I said, "Yeah, maybe."

Dad was watching the door again, or perhaps he was just staring into space. "I never really understood soccer."

"It's pretty simple, Dad."

"Yeah yeah, you kick the ball around and try to score goals — I get that. What I mean is I never understood the finer points, the nuances, the strategy — hell, off-sides is a mystery to me…I just never understood soccer the way I understand baseball."

Maddie

It was a long light, and the longer I sat there the madder I got. What the hell gave this Mr. Tattoo the right to terrorize me? Okay, I let him buy me a drink and then I didn't play nice with him at McFall's the other night. Big deal. The way he'd reacted proved he didn't deserve better treatment — not that that even mattered. The point was: a brush-off in a bar, deserved or undeserved, did not give this sleaze-bag or any other the right to intimidate.

The light turned green. I didn't move. From behind the growling pick-up truck, I heard horns complaining. Eventually, all the vehicles behind us went around. The light turned red.

I unlocked my door. I got out of my car. I marched to the side of the truck. I had no view of the driver: all the windows were tinted, even the windshield. I threw myself against the glass of the driver's side door. I pounded, I screeched, "Come out of there, you son of a bitch! How dare you! I will fucking tear you limb from limb!" In my fury, I looked for something to damage. I grabbed the nearest windshield wiper and twisted it until it looked like the broken leg of an insect. I tried to rip it completely off but it wouldn't come loose. The radio antenna, however, was a different story. I made a furious effort to stab my way through the side window with it.

The truck lurched into reverse. I crouched forward and lunged after it. It shifted into forward and turned to the right, bouncing hard onto the sidewalk to go around my car and avoid my onslaught. I threw the crumpled antenna after it.

I noticed a car idling in the central turning lane, a long, boxy sedan. An elderly woman rolled down the window and beckoned me to come to her. Her car was facing the opposite direction from mine: she must have been driving the other way and pulled into the turning lane and stopped when she saw there was trouble. I waited for a car to go past, then I crossed to the center lane.

"Are you all right, dear?" she wanted to know. She wore enormous glasses and her hands shook – whether from fright or from some medical condition, I couldn't tell. She looked, frankly, too old to drive. But – I give her credit – she alone had the courage to stop when she saw someone in possible need of help.

My hands were shaking, too. I heaved a big sigh and said, "I'm better than I have any right to be – I just got away with one of the stupidest stunts I've ever pulled in my life."

"Did you know the person in that truck?"

"Not really."

"Was the person threatening you in some way?"

"He was tailgating me."

"Tailgating?!"

I thought: *this is too complicated to explain; I'm just going to let this lady think I'm crazy.* But from the expression that was forming on her face, I could see she didn't think I was crazy at all: she gazed at me in wide-eyed wonder like she was in the presence of a celebrity or even a superhero.

"I've always wanted to do that," she confided. "I've always wanted to do to some tailgater exactly what you just did!"

Harry

"What else do you regret not teaching me?"

Charlie could see that I was worried about Maddie, and I could see that he was trying to keep me talking to distract me. That was what he was doing on one level at least. On another level, this talk we were having, these reminiscences we were sharing, was filling some need for him. I sensed he was mustering strength for his confrontation with Alexis. For this, he needed to reconnect with his past – not with his childhood so much as with the stable family existence Suzanne and I spun around him, mostly real but part fabrication, for nineteen years. So, that's how our conversation went: Charlie and I each distracted in our separate ways by immediate worries, while simultaneously we delved whole-heartedly into our shared past.

"I wish I'd gotten more involved in your religious upbringing."

Charlie emitted an incredulous hoot. "You cannot be serious! Dad, one more side in the Holy Wars would not have done anybody any good."

He was referring to the bitter feud between Suzanne and my sister Fran, a feud that Charlie was the center of for most of his life. Suzanne has been raised in a small Pentecostal church that Fran dismissed as a cult. Fran and I had been raised staunchly Roman Catholic. I fell away from the faith early, doubting on instinct, without the mental tools or the knowledge to make any defensible case for my lack of belief. The further from the church I strayed, the more firmly Fran attached herself to it. We were like two kids on a playground see-saw – except each of us only went in one direction and neither of us would admit we were the one going down. (That, essentially, has never changed.) When Suzanne and I first started dating, I pretended to consider joining her church and she pretended to consider my – (woefully unformed, even in my early thirties) – reasons for doubt. At the time, neither of us knew we were pretending to the other – but it is clear to me now that we were. When Charlie came along, all that changed. As soon as she suspected she was pregnant Suzanne insisted that we get married. I happily agreed, although both churches gave us trouble and in the end we were married at City Hall. As soon as Charlie was born, Suzanne was adamant that he be given a firm religious foundation. My sister Fran had the same idea. The endless struggle that ensued is what Charlie calls the Holy Wars.

"I should have been more forthcoming with you about my own doubts," I said. "I should at least have put my foot down with your Aunt Fran and kept her from interfering."

Charlie thought it through at some length.

"No Dad, I think you played that one exactly right."

I shook my head. But before I could speak Charlie continued, "First of all, it's not like Mom and Aunt Fran were at it all the time – most of the trouble seemed to happen around the holidays."

"Yeah, but there was always so much *tension* between them, even when there were no outright hostilities."

"I don't know how you would have fixed that, Dad – short of banning Aunt Fran from our lives completely."

"Your Aunt Fran certainly has her opinions," I said. "And she's not shy about sharing them."

Nodding, Charlie said, "And as to how you felt about religion, that was never any secret to me. If anything, your silence on the subject amidst all the bickering made your position that much stronger – or that's how it seemed to me, growing up."

"Your Uncle Milt was every bit as silent as I was, and you'll never find a more devoted Catholic."

"Do you think he really is?"

"Of course I do."

Charlie ruminated on this. "Okay, maybe so. Devoted. But do you think he really believes anything, deep down?"

I hesitated to give an opinion.

Charlie said, "I think if Uncle Milt had been born a Hindu, he'd be devoted to Hinduism; if he'd been born a Buddhist, he'd be devoted to Buddhism. I don't think he's ever given a thought to what he believes, not a single day in his entire life."

"I'm sure you're being unfair to your uncle," I said without conviction.

"I'm just saying he's like most people – how is that being unfair?"

To this I made no reply. Outside, night had fallen.

Rising from my chair, I said, "Maybe I'll start wrapping up that pizza – sure you don't want another slice?"

Maddie

Back in my car, tooling along, no one following me, I found myself taking detour after detour. I kept shying away from the thought of going back to Harry's apartment. *No big deal*, I told myself, *I just need a little time to unwind*. But I knew that wasn't really it. The altercation with Mr. Tattoo had rattled me, all right, but I was swiftly getting over it. Did these detours have something to do with Suzanne? I turned over the possibility in my mind, and I had to admit that, yes, whatever had happened earlier with Suzanne was causing me to hesitate about going back. It was not that I was afraid of Suzanne. I did not see her as fundamentally malicious, and I believed she bore me no ill will personally. But it seemed merely prudent to gather my wits and my mental integrity before subjecting myself again to her strange pressures.

I thought all this about Suzanne, believed it, while at the same time laboring under the very real likelihood that I had imagined the whole thing.

(I've rarely seen evidence that others have this dual track – sometimes multi-track – playing in their heads as incessantly as I have.)

Okay, so the non-existent ghost of Suzanne was spooking me.

But that wasn't the whole reason for these detours, either – maybe not even the main reason. What was the main reason, then? The main reason was Harry.

He was a sweet guy but I couldn't see spending the rest of my life with him. Actually, what I couldn't see was spending the rest of *his* life with him. He had aged remarkably well so far – but what would be his condition in ten years, twenty years? Being anyone's long-term caregiver was not for me – I was temperamentally unsuited to the task – I had long ago come to that realization. I was good at counseling people in distress, especially on a short-term basis, but not at caring for them. Keeping one's professional distance, some people called it – and maybe for some people that's what it truly was: a willful shutting down of one's natural instinct to nurture the sick, the wounded – but for me, I knew, it sprang from a fundamental lack of compassion.

The best case for Harry and me was that I would winter over with him while I continued to look for work. Maybe we'd stay together for as long as next spring. But sooner or later that next job would come along and, wherever it happened to be, that's where I was headed. Meanwhile, every time Harry and I screwed I could see him tumbling deeper down a rabbit hole of his own devising, confusing good, old, workaday carnal satisfaction with some fantasy about everlasting love. He was going to be hurt when I left, and the longer I stayed the worse his hurt was going to be.

Driving along yet another detour, six bottles of red wine jangling quietly in their plastic bags on the floorboard in front of the empty passenger seat, it became clear to me that the kindest thing I could do for Harry was to never go back.

Charlie

Dad emerged from the kitchen. The pizza was put away, the delivery box had been flattened and folded and placed in the recycling bag, the plate I had used was drying off in the drain board. Dad had filled our two wine glasses with water but only I was drinking any.

"Where *do* you think I stand on religion?" Dad wanted to know.

I said, "Not to put too fine a point on it, you think it's all a crock of shit – same as I do."

Dad frowned. "We really should have talked about it while you were growing up."

My eyebrows shot upward. Dad looked at me, said, "What?" I must have been staring in amazement.

"You're not going to stand there and tell me that you, of all people, had your own secret religion the whole time I was growing up. Are you?"

He sat down across from me at the small table. "No, Charlie, I wasn't going to say anything like that. But I don't dismiss religion as a 'crock of shit,' either, as you so eloquently put it. And I don't recall ever feeling that way when you were growing up, even when your mother and your aunt were doing anything *but* showing Christian kindness to one another."

And for the first time in our lives, Dad and I had a conversation about religion. He told me what a great experience it had been for him to grow up surrounded by the certainty of faith. He'd felt uplifted and protected by supernatural forces who were ultimately good and caring – God, Jesus, the Holy Spirit (whatever that was), the angels and the saints – although God could sometimes be mysterious and even terrifying. Dad told me about the beginnings of his doubt. There was no crisis: it was more of a natural progression, starting in his early teens, as his brain formed, as his reading habit took hold, as he found himself each day more and more able to think for himself. He said: "At some point it became obvious to me that most of what passes for religion is based on fiction, stories. It was so obvious I thought everyone must see it, I thought the adults around me must be playacting, like they did about Santa Claus for the benefit of little kids. What a shock it was to find out that so many otherwise reasonable people were dead serious and, by my lights, completely irrational on this one subject. It still shocks me every now and then to this day. People get so caught up in their religion, I often wonder if I'm the one missing something obvious."

"Sounds to me like you think it's all a crock," I said. I was half joking –
but as soon as I said it I wished I hadn't: it brought such a look of sadness and
disappointment to Dad's wintry eyes.

"No, son, that's too easy. I mean, if that's what you truly believe then
so be it, I don't mean to criticize. But for my part, I'm convinced there's
something deep and meaningful about religion – maybe I saw glimpses of it
when I was young and believed all the stories – but somewhere along the
way I lost sight of it, and now it simply baffles me."

"From what you're saying, it sounds like you equate religion maybe a
little too much with Christianity. What if Christianity's not your thing,
Dad? The world's full of other religions. Maybe you should try being a
Buddhist of something."

Dad gave me an uncertain smile.

"I'm being serious," I said.

"Have *you* looked into other religions?"

"Yeah some...a little...actually no, not really...maybe one day I'll get
around to it."

Dad made a small gesture with his hand, indicating the wall of books
that was mostly behind me.

"I have," he said. "Not that I was trying to *be* a Buddhist or a Muslim or
anything like that – but I have read about a lot of them."

"Didn't find any that were convincing, huh?"

Dad shook his head. "No more convincing than the stories in the Bible."

I said, "If I ever do get around to looking into different religions, I think
I'll start with Zen."

"Why is that?" Dad asked.

"Cool name," I said.

Dad frowned.

"Kidding, kidding – seriously, what I like about Zen is that they're
saying if you train your mind a certain way, if you work hard at it, you'll
attain enlightenment: so, it's like a thought experiment that you can
actually try and see what happens. With other religions, usually, you don't
get to find out if they're true or not until after your dead."

Zen, Dad informed me, was a form of Buddhism. I guess I knew that.
Dad went on to explain that many people consider some forms of Buddhism
– Zen, for instance – more of a philosophy than a religion. Dad said he was
unclear about the distinction and tended to lump all forms of Buddhist into

the general category of religion. The Zen notion of enlightenment was called *satori* and it had to do with "seeing into one's true nature."

"That could be useful information to have," I quipped.

Dad shrugged. "Many Buddhist schools of thought say that one's true nature is in fact Emptiness, whatever that's supposed to mean. Not sure if Zen follows that or not."

"Oh," I said. Then: "I feel like I went through my empty phase my senior year of high school. Didn't much care for it. Think I'll work on being full, instead."

Dad chuckled.

I started to ask a question, stopped, started again, stopped. Dad patiently waited. I asked, "Do you think Mom still exists...on some level?"

I expected Dad to think about that one a long time; instead, he answered right away, "I don't know, Charlie."

I said, "There are times I feel she's close by, like she's watching over me, trying to anyway. Do you ever get that feeling?"

All Dad would say was: "There are times I miss her, times I vividly remember her."

"You think she's gone don't you?"

"I honestly don't know, son."

Our conversation sputtered on to other topics but it became increasingly hard work for both of us. Eventually, Dad rose from the table, walked to the living room, and looked out the front window.

Maddie

I was parked on a residential street. On one side of the street were modest two-story homes, set close together. On the other side was a tiny neighborhood park. I was on the same side of the street as the park. If the plan was to spend the night in my car, this felt as close to an ideal spot as I was going to find in the immediate vicinity. I was not altogether sure what my plan was. Probably it was wishful thinking to even suppose that I had a plan. All I was doing was "trying it out," this being along in my car again.

I sat in the driver's seat, in plain view of anybody walking past – but the sidewalk was empty. My car was arranged as follows: the very back, just inside the hatchback, was so piled full of my belongings that the entire rear window was obstructed. The seat directly behind me had just a few items of bundled up clothing strapped across the windows, so that it looked from the outside as if the car was crammed full of stuff, from the hatchback all the way to the headrests of the front seats. In fact, the backseat was a cocoon of blankets with my favorite pillow in the center. And I had rigged up a short black curtain to hang from the ceiling just behind the front seats. This curtain could be lowered into place so that someone looking in through the windshield could not see me in my cocoon. I had spent many a cozy night in that space – also many nights fending off demons.

I was reluctant to climb back into my cocoon. I wanted to first experience the familiar silence, the chill working its way into the car, the loneliness, the recriminations for being along – what was the matter with me, how did my life spin so far out of control? – I wanted to experience it all with my hands on the steering wheel, ready to make a quick getaway if it proved to be too much.

There were lights on in some of the homes across the street; others were dark. Decent, normal people living their lives. I envied them and pitied them at the same time – mostly I envied them. Your chances of spending the night in your car unchallenged are much greater in a neighborhood of modest homes. Too many suspicious eyes watching the street in poorer neighborhoods. And don't even think about well to do neighborhoods: more suspicion there than anywhere else. However, even in a neighborhood of modest homes it is always good practice never to park directly in front of someone's house – you are bound to draw attention to yourself.

The car made quiet, sporadic ticking sounds as the engine cooled. It was a chilly night but no worse than that, and the wind had finally spent itself. I pulled my anti-depressants out of my purse. I was up on my dose for the day, but I wanted to count how many pills I had left. I spilled them into my hand then carefully placed them back into the plastic bottle, one by one. Enough for almost a week. I already knew that but it was reassuring to double check.

An image of Harry appeared in my head. He was alone in his apartment, wearily pacing. "Can't you just be happy for what we had?" I asked him but he made no reply.

Some ideal places to spend the night in your car: truck stops, interstate rest areas, the parking lot of a 24-hour Wal-Mart or similar establishment. Personally, I'm partial to truck stops.

I thought about the six bottles of red wine. A couple of them had twist-off caps. But I was certain that if I drank alone in my car that night from a bottle of wine and if that bottle had a twist-off cap, it would be the subtle tawdriness of that last seemingly insignificant detail that would make the whole picture too pathetic to bear, and I'd find myself toppling off some cliff's edge which I could sense was dangerously close at hand. As for the corked bottles, I was sure there was a corkscrew somewhere in my car and equally sure that I would never find it. Too bad. The windshield was clouding. I touched it with my fingertip, drew a slanting line in the haze.

Another image of Harry, dejectedly sinking onto the edge of his empty bed, pulling back the covers, burying his face in the sheets, taking in the smell of the two of us together.

I was going to need to check in with my psychiatrist next week to get my prescription renewed. I was still using the same West Coast gal who helped me so much before I came East. She preferred face to face electronic communications but would settle for a regular phone call. She knew about my job falling through but not about me living in my car. Since I discontinued phone service I had been managing communications with her through my old laptop, connecting to a network at various coffee shops or sometimes the library. But the last time I turned on the laptop the screen was nothing but blue fuzz. I had been meaning to turn it on again, to see if the problem had gone away – but fear of the likely outcome had kept me from performing that particular test. Like the corkscrew, the laptop was buried somewhere in my car.

Getting my next prescription filled had definitely been in the back of my mind when I imagined wintering over with Harry. That computer of his was going to be the short-term fix for my communication problem. And I could, more or less, truthfully claim to have a roof over my head – although on that score my line to my psychiatrist would have gone something like: *Oh by the way my living arrangements have changed… yes, I'm staying with a friend I made at the hospital while I was still working there…she has graciously offered to share her two-bedroom apartment with me…her name?…Harriet…she's a very sweet woman, older than me, an amazing hard worker: she works double shifts all the time, drags herself home only to sleep…if she's here during one of our talks I'll introduce you but don't count on it.*

Oh well, a week was potentially a long time – maybe some other opportunity would come along before my pills ran out.

I could see my breath when I exhaled – odd: one minute I couldn't, the next minute I could. The windshield was heavily fogged over. My hands, I suddenly noticed, were icy cold. I pulled my sleeves over them and rubbed them together. My ears felt as fragile as fine china and the tip of my nose was growing numb. It was time to climb into the cocoon or make my escape back to Harry. I teetered on the edge of a decision. Both options attracted me and at the same time repelled me.

Another image flashed into my head: me in Harry's house, alone. This was not a made-up scene; this was a memory. Me, on the morning after Thanksgiving, trying to work out what my response should be to Harry's absence. Me, simply unable to take advantage of Harry for trusting me alone in his house. I was reliving the moment but also watching myself as if in the midst of an out-of-body experience – my dual nature asserting itself once again. From inside myself I felt like a stranger to myself. But from outside, I liked what I saw, as if I was looking at myself in a mirror under the most flattering light.

I caught myself wondering how long ago it had been, this moment of trustworthiness on my part, and was flabbergasted to realize it had been only yesterday. It felt more like weeks, full and enjoyable and interesting weeks – nothing at all like the life I had been living right up until my latest visit to, of all places, this burg's local chess club. Before that the weeks flew past without distinction, like an endlessly recurring dream, devoid of color or meaning.

I pulled my hands out of my sleeves and started the car.

Charlie

By slow degrees it had gotten way past awkward with Dad. He could see I was falling asleep but he persisted in waiting up for Maddie except he didn't want to talk about Maddie. When I said something like, "I'm sure it will turn out to be nothing…car trouble, a dead battery, something like that," Dad would only frown at me darkly. There might as well have been a thought bubble bobbing above his head: *she may not carry a phone but she would have found a way to call.* To torture him even further, Dad's phone had rung twice more since Maddie's brother called. Both times Dad whipped the screen under his nose but, seeing the number – Maddie's brother again, I was guessing – Dad made no move to answer.

Finally, I said, "'Night, Dad," and pulled a blanket over my head and tried to sleep. Eventually Dad got the hint and he moved around the downstairs, turning off light after light. I heard him creep up the stairs. I heard him pacing slowly back and forth in his bedroom, pausing at the end of each circuit, no doubt to spy out the window.

Lying there in the darkened living room, I replayed in my mind the conversation I had had with Maddie. Was it foolish of me to open up like that with someone who was very nearly a complete stranger? – never mind the fact that she was involved with my father. Maybe. But it had felt so good to talk to a sympathetic listener about my troubles with Alexis. A huge relief actually. If anything, I wished I had found a way to tell Maddie even more. The strangest thing about Alexis was that he either refused to admit or didn't believe that he himself was gay. I mean, there are plenty of gay men in denial, of course, but I had never encountered a gay man who so aggressively wanted to be in a sexual relationship with another man – (and Alexis had been nothing if not ardent in his pursuit of me when we first met) – yet who still maintained that he himself was not gay. For Alexis, as I came to learn, the distinction had to do with the fact that, although he loved to penetrate other men, he never allowed himself to be penetrated in turn. He claimed it was a practice and a distinction that went back to the ancient Greeks. He claimed that he was in fact the extreme opposite of a gay man; he was a man so hyper-masculine that he could only take pleasure in possessing other men.

I turned over on the couch. I took a deep breath. I sighed. Okay, maybe it was better I hadn't shared all of *that* with Maddie.

For one thing, I could just imagine her asking, *You knew this about him but still you entered into a relationship with him?*

But that was the thing: I didn't know. Oh, I had certainly noticed the first few times in bed with Alexis that our lovemaking had been markedly *one-sided*: he would bring me off with his hands sometimes, no other way. But I didn't think too much about it, didn't let myself think too much about it, while he was sweeping me off my feet – and before I knew it we were living together.

How embarrassing it would have been to have to try and explain that to Maddie – or to anyone.

I must have fallen asleep. The next thing I knew I was dreaming of a very fast cat – a big cat, something on the order of a panther or a puma – bounding down the stairs. Then I was awake and the big cat rushed past me. I was too terrified to move. The front door flew open and, peeping from under my blanket, I saw Dad with his back to me and on the other side of the open doorframe I saw Maddie, smiling in the glow of the front porch light.

She handed him two items that I couldn't clearly see – Dad's body partially blocked my view. She said, "I got a little lost along the way." She said it like it was a private joke between the two of them which explained everything and which, of course, he would understand. And – odder still – Dad gave a soft chuckle as if this indeed were the case.

Maddie came through the door and I pulled the blanket down over my eyes but not before seeing Maddie give Dad a peck on the cheek. I heard the door close, the lock being set. I lay perfectly still as they walked past me. I heard Dad whisper, "Charlie's sleeping." I heard someone go into the kitchen and place something on a counter. I heard the faint clink of glass. I thought: *oh, the items she handed him was the wine, packed in separate grocery bags*. Perhaps both of them had gone into the kitchen. It was quiet in there, but it was a quiet packed with energy. I heard Maddie giggle. I heard Dad urgently whisper, "Not here!...Charlie..." I heard the two of them steal up the stairs. I grabbed a couch cushion and carefully arranged it above my head so as not to hear any other sounds, and I tried as hard as I could to plunge back into sleep.

V. Sunday

Harry

My radio alarm goes off every morning at five minutes past six. I'm almost always already awake, lying there with my eyes closed, thinking about the day ahead if it's a workday, or thinking about whatever book I happen to be reading, or thinking about old times, remembering. Since Maddie arrived in my life, I had been careful to override the alarm each morning before it went off.

That morning, Sunday morning, the alarm snuck up on me in my dreams. I untangled myself from Maddie, rolled over and hit the off button, silencing two earnest public radio voices as they discussed densely populated coastal regions in Southeast Asia and the ever-growing effects of climate change. Maddie didn't stir in the least.

It was cold in the house. (I had turned down the heat last night when I came upstairs, thinking that I would be sleeping alone.) Maddie lay slightly turned away from me, her body exposed almost to the waist, as I had inadvertently pulled most of the blankets along with me when I reached for the alarm. The light was dim; it was probably an hour till sunrise.

I could actually feel the force of habit, insisting that it was time to get up, get out of bed, get on with another day – like I had done every day, whether it was a workday or a holiday or a weekend, for as long as I could remember. The pull was so strong I found myself sitting up, swinging my legs out of bed, placing my feet on the cold floor. Maybe it was the jolt to the soles of my feet that brought me fully awake. I said to myself, *What the hell am I doing?*

I scrambled back into bed. Stretching the blankets before me, I covered Maddie and, snuggling in beside her, slipped my arms around her and gave her the gentlest of hugs. She sighed and turned away from me slightly more. I fitted the front of my body to the back of hers, taking in her warmth and her softness and her scent, and gave myself over to sleep.

**

Full sunlight was streaming through the window and there was some sort of commotion downstairs. I fumbled into my clothes from yesterday and raced toward the trouble. It turned out to be Charlie and Maddie facing off near the front door. When they caught sight of me, Maddie demanded, "Why didn't you tell me he was planning to go back to Alexis today?" – while Charlie cried, "You were supposed to tell her after I was asleep!" The best defense I could muster was: "Is there any coffee?"

Actually, I suspected there had to be coffee because I could smell it.

Both Maddie and Charlie continued to glare at me. I couldn't think of what to say to Charlie other than "I forgot" and that seemed lame, so I pled my case to Maddie instead: "What was I supposed to do, forbid him?"

Maddie was not appeased. "He won't even tell me if Alexis has made a single effort to communicate, much less apologize...you ask him, maybe he'll tell his father."

I said, "What does it matter whether or not Alexis tried to get in touch?"

"Hey," Charlie protested, "I'm standing right here – do you mind not treating me like I'm invisible?"

"It matters because silence is a classic control measure for an abuser like Alexis. If Charlie goes back to Alexis under these conditions, Alexis will consider that he won, that Charlie gave in first."

"Hey!" Charlie shouted.

I said, "Sorry, son...listen, do you have to go this minute?...could we maybe discuss it, the three of us?...over coffee?...I could really use a cup of coffee."

Reluctantly, Charlie moved away from the door; Maddie shadowed him. There were two coffee mugs already on the dining room table and half a pot of coffee in the kitchen. I filled a mug for myself, asked if anybody needed a refill, got no reply, puttered through the tasks of adding milk and sugar. When I emerged from the kitchen I found the two of them sitting in front of their coffee mugs, warily eyeing one another, as if they were two boxers each in a neutral corner, waiting for the referee to call the next round. Somehow or another in this scenario, I was the referee.

I was hardly seated before Maddie said, "At the very least you need to set conditions...I tried to tell you this the other day."

Charlie's usually pliant eyes took on a stony, obstinate look that I remembered all too well from when he was growing up.

"You still don't want to hear them, do you?" Maddie said accusingly.

Charlie shrugged. "Setting conditions just seems like the wrong approach to take with Alexis...his pride would be wounded."

I contemplated various remarks questioning how much pride a man could have who couldn't control his temper – but kept them all to myself.

"Let me tell you something, Charlie," Maddie said, leaning toward him and glancing my way. I took her body language to mean that whatever was coming next she wished she could say only to Charlie, wished I wasn't there to hear it. "My knowledge on this subject goes well beyond the academic. I've been in more than my share of abusive relationships, and I've known some gals who've been in worse situations than I ever went through, and I can tell you relationships like that mostly don't end well."

"You're saying you think I should give up on Alexis...that we're going to split up sooner or later anyway."

Maddie could not suppress a sharp, bitter laugh. "When I say these relationships mostly don't end well, believe me, I'm not talking about them ending in a nice, clean breakup – that would be a *happy* ending. No, what I'm talking about is when the victim, if she gets out of it at all, and far too many of them don't, gets out with serious damage, emotional of course and often physical as well, damage some people never recover from. The abuser sometimes suffers, too – sometimes he winds up in jail or sometimes his victim goes over the edge and murders him, or attempts to. I suppose that has to count toward a bad ending, although in my book any payback the abuser gets is well deserved.

"I'm saying all this like it's always he/she, but you get what I mean."

Charlie's eyes had softened. He gazed at Maddie now like they were kindred spirits. "When it was happening to you...did you ever feel like, if you could only solve this one thing, the two of you would be so perfect together?"

Another laugh from Maddie, this one less bitter and not sharp at all, almost sad. "That's what I think every time I get involved with a man, that the two of us are a perfect fit – but something always trips it up: I figured out a long time ago I'm naturally drawn to the wrong type."

Maddie seemed to have completely forgotten my presence. Charlie turned his big brown eyes toward me, showing me a mix of horror and sympathy. Maddie caught the direction of his gaze and the look in his eye, and she tried to save the situation. "Present company excepted, of course," she mumbled. It was a terribly awkward moment.

Charlie tried to move us all past it. "I hear what you're saying, Maddie...about it not being a good sign that Alexis never tried to make contact – and I can see him thinking along the lines you laid out...but dammit I have to go back...I can't give up on him, on what he and I could have together, not until I can look myself in the mirror and truly say I gave it my best shot...I'd never be able to live with myself otherwise, I'd always regret, always wonder..."

Maddie sighed: *been there, felt that.*

Charlie lifted one corner of his mouth. "So tell me these conditions already."

Maddie ticked them off on her fingers: "One, he must admit he has a problem – and no qualifications on this one, no blaming the victim, no bullshit about how it's really something *you* do that causes *him* to be violent – it's his problem and he has to own it.

"Two, he must agree to seek help. Immediately. It has to be a specific course of action that you and he agree on together. A professional counselor should be involved.

"Three, he must swear never to do it again.

"If he can't agree to all three of these conditions, Charlie – please listen to me on this – turn right around and walk out of there: you'll save yourself a lot of grief."

Charlie appeared to mull it over.

I said, "I like the first two conditions; I'm not sure how much water the third one holds."

Maddie gave Charlie a chance to answer. When he said nothing, she replied, "I'd agree with you, Harry, if we were talking about some random abuser. But this is a person Charlie obviously feels deeply about – so I'm going with the assumption that Alexis must have his good side, must have something on the ball, and that if he gives his word he intends to keep it."

Charlie flashed Maddie an appreciative smile.

At the door, Maddie and Charlie fell into a hug. I held out my hand and Charlie shook it, then he hugged me, too. I said, "If there's anything you need from me, son, anything at all, just say the word..."

"I'll be okay, Dad. Promise."

It was in my mind to tell him that he was welcome to come stay at my place anytime, but that contained a certain whiff of defeatism and I held it back.

As I watched Charlie walk toward his car, I stepped out onto the little concrete front porch and checked the weather – the habitual practice of a man who has spent his working life outdoors. The sky was clear; the air was brisk, no more. The tall pines on the far side of the parking lot betrayed a steady westerly breeze, although I couldn't feel it myself standing in the shelter of the apartment building. Clear skies today but were there storm clouds over the horizon?

Maddie

The first thing Harry asked me after Charlie left was: "Do you really think there might be a good side to Alexis?"

"Hell no."

Harry did a double-take and his face dropped with disappointment.

I patted his cheek. "Kidding," I said. "Sort of."

"Do you think so or not?"

"Probably not – but you never know."

Harry went into the kitchen and cleaned up the coffee things. "Hungry?" he called.

"You know I am."

"Biscuit Den?"

"Sure."

Before we left, Harry started a load of his work clothes in the combination washer/dryer tucked into the narrow space under his stairs.

When we got back, Harry moved the clothes into the dryer. He asked if I would like to do some laundry. That's how he said it: *would I like to.* Who *likes* to do laundry?

"Um, no. Maybe later."

"Everything okay?"

"Sure, everything's fine."

"Should we go out again? Find something to do together?"

"What do you usually do on a Sunday?" I asked.

"Usually on a Sunday I'll clean the house if it needs it – but I did that last Sunday. The other thing I do is I spend a couple of hours catching up on my reading."

"Sounds enchanting, why don't you do that?"

"What would you do?"

"I've been known to read a book from time to time."

Harry looked doubtful – not so much about my ability to read as about whether he was failing me somehow as a host. Nevertheless, he moved to his reading chair. It was a broken-down upholstered thing in a corner of the living room beside the front window with a floor lamp positioned behind it. It was so nondescript I had barely noticed it till now. Harry pulled a small footstool from under the chair and positioned it just so. He picked up a book from the seat of the chair.

"What'cha reading?" I queried.

He showed me the cover: *The Sumerians* by C. Leonard Woolley.

"I'm almost finished," he remarked.

"Interesting?"

"Oh yes…I think so, anyway."

"Why don't you ever read fiction?"

Harry made a face like I'd asked him a really hard question. But before he could answer, his phone buzzed. His troubled expression made me think it must be Charlie — and that Harry somehow was able to intuit that the news was bad.

He glanced fearfully in my direction. "You're going to be mad at me," he said. The phone continued to buzz.

"Why am I going to be mad at you?"

"This is your brother…Freeman?…he called for you several times last night while you were out…I, I forgot to tell you…I'm so sorry…"

He sprang up from the chair and quickly crossed the room with the phone. I took it from him and looked at the screen. It was Freeman's number alright. The phone buzzed once, twice, three times more, then stopped.

Harry gave me an astonished look. "Why didn't you answer? He must be worried sick."

"He'll get over it."

Confused, Harry muttered, "I wonder if he's leaving another voicemail…he left a couple last night."

"What did he say?"

"I didn't listen to messages meant for you…do you want to listen to them now?"

"Nah."

"I can't believe you're not going to let him know you're all right."

Harry

Maddie's reply was: "What's today?"

I said "huh" and she repeated the question.

"It's Sunday, of course."

"And when did I call Freeman?"

I had to think back. "It was the night of Thanksgiving, wasn't it? Thursday night."

"So let's see…" she counted on her fingers "…Friday, Saturday, Sunday – that's three. How worried could he be if he can't be bothered to return my call for three days?" She counted off three on her fingers again. "Maybe I'll call him on Wednesday."

"To be fair," I said, "he called on Saturday night – so that's only two days."

"Okay, so I'll call him on Tuesday."

"Is this how you and your brother communicate all the time?"

I said it in what I thought was a joking manner, so the force of Maddie's indignation surprised me. "You should talk! Your own son has to be put in the hospital before he will call you – and neither one of you thinks that's strange!"

That felt like a low blow and I opened my mouth to say something hurtful but I found I had nothing to say. Not because I'm such a nice guy. I had nothing to say because Maddie was still such a stranger to me I didn't know enough of her weak points – didn't know any, really, expect that she didn't have a job and was living out of her car.

I mumbled a half-hearted apology for making a bad joke, but Maddie was already moving away from me – apparently oblivious to how close we'd come to what would have been our first fight. She was headed for the stairs. She said, "Maybe I'll get on the internet while you're reading…I ought to check my email at least…do you mind if I use your computer?"

I watched her glide up the stairs. Her loose-fitting, multi-layered clothes obscured her wonderful figure but couldn't hide the graceful, forceful way she moved. She was right at the top before I thought to call after her with the password.

"Oh…right…thanks," she said. There was something odd in her tone but I couldn't figure out what it was.

**

Later, quite a bit later, Maddie, returning to the living room, said, "What are those crazy Sumerians up to?"

I told her that I'd finished the book.

"In other words," she observed, "the Sumerians are history."

I caught on to her joke a half-second too late and when I laughed it was awkward. "Wish I'd said that," I said.

Maddie smiled a kind of Mona Lisa smile.

"On to the Babylonians?"

"No," I said, "I jump around a lot with my reading. Now I'm reading about what they call the Age of Discovery." And I told her briefly about the hundred years or so before Darwin's *Origin of the Species* when new experimental methods along with new means of transportation and new political forces allowed scientists or "natural philosophers," as they tended to call themselves, to gather vast quantities of information and about how they tried to make sense of this new wealth of knowledge.

Maddie listened, I thought, with at least half an ear. When I concluded she said, "You never answered my question – from before."

"What question?"

"Why don't you ever read fiction?"

I scratched my forehead. "For me, reading is a bit like those natural philosophers gathering all of their specimens and data. I read because I'm trying to figure out where we are, what we're here for, if anything..."

"Oh, the M of L."

"The what?"

"The M of L, that's what we used to call it in late-night bull sessions in my undergraduate dorm: the Meaning of Life. Good luck with that quest. Can't think of anyone else who's gone down *that* road before. I'm sure you'll find the answer right 'round the next corner."

Unaccountably, Maddie's accent had taken on a slightly British cast. She noticed my questioning look and said, "Sorry for going all Monty Python on your ass."

"Not at all," I said, trying to retain a bit of dignity and not completely sure that Maddie was finished mocking me.

She said, "So, non-fiction tells you about the world but fiction doesn't?"

I thought that over, I nodded, I said, "Yes, that's been my feeling...it's a bit like the difference between a photograph and a painting: if you really want to know what something looks like, even to the smallest detail, the photograph is more helpful, isn't it?"

Maddie glanced back and forth between the two largest images on my walls, Van Gogh's *Starry Night* and my poster of colliding galaxies.

"That's a bad comparison," I insisted.

"Is it?"

"All right okay, you know what, maybe it isn't – I challenge you to tell me which one, really, gives us more information about what's actually going on up there in the sky?"

Maddie didn't answer right away. In hindsight, I'm guessing she was allowing me a chance to figure this one out for myself. When the silence threatened to grow too long, she said, "It isn't a competition. Each one is telling us something essential, something the other one can only hint at."

When I thought it over later I could see she had a point but, in the moment, that answer didn't satisfy me. I argued, "If you're looking up at a sky full of stars and you're wondering what they could possibly be – maybe you're living in the Dark Ages or something, maybe nobody knows – which would be more helpful to you: a painting of the sky, heck a *thousand* paintings of the sky, or a good telescope and a camera?"

Maddie blinked at me. "If they'd had telescopes and cameras it wouldn't have been the Dark Ages."

"No no, you're missing…"

But Maddie had already turned away. She was headed for the kitchen. "I'm hungry again. Didn't you order pizza last night? Are there any leftovers?" I heard her open and close the refrigerator, then do the same to a couple of the cabinets like she was looking for something – paper plates, I was guessing – then there was the hum of the microwave.

I put down my book and walked into the kitchen.

"Where'd you put the wine?" she asked.

I motioned with my head. "Lower cabinet, far corner."

She brought out one of the bottles she'd purchased the night before.

"Does it bother you that I don't read fiction?" I asked.

"Corkscrew?"

I opened a drawer at my elbow and took out a corkscrew. She held out her hand for it and I gave it to her.

"Does it?"

"It's your loss, Harry."

I opened a nearby upper cabinet and pulled out two wine glasses. Maddie poured. The microwave went *bing*. Maddie carried her pizza and her wine into the dining room, leaving me in the kitchen. I hadn't felt hungry but the smell of the heated up pizza was causing me to change my mind.

While my own slice was warming up I stood in the doorway and watched Maddie as she blew on her food and nibbled at the edges. She tossed back a big gulp of wine.

I said, "I feel like we're out of sync somehow today – do you feel it?" I took a first sip of the wine. It was thin and unpleasantly bitter. I wasn't surprised: I'd noticed the labels this morning when I was cleaning up the kitchen – this and the others Maddie bought were brands I usually avoided.

Maddie said, "You're probably just worried about Charlie."

"I'm definitely worried about Charlie," I agreed. "But that's not what's putting us out of sync – or am I imagining things?"

The microwave *bing*ed again but I ignored it.

"Get your pizza," Maddie said. "Sit with me."

Maddie

He was kind enough to fill my glass before he sat down and thoughtful enough to leave the bottle on the table. He was taking microscopic sips from his own glass.

I said, "Last night I was thinking how *full* our days have been together. Has it felt that way to you?"

Harry nodded eagerly.

"You don't like the wine, do you?"

He took a self-conscious swig. "I'm not making any complaints."

"Hmm," I said, and watched him try to swallow without making a face. "But then today rolled around and today doesn't feel so full, do you know what I mean? Today feels like we're marking time together."

Harry fretted, "We should have gone out somewhere instead of me sitting here, reading – I knew it!"

I patted the back of his hand. "It would have been the same either way – maybe it would have been worse if we'd gone out: the two of us traipsing around in public trying to fake it."

"Fake what?"

"Fake it that we're supposed to be together, that we're any kind of a good fit."

He tried to turn his face into a mask of stone, tried to put on the face that maybe he wore out in the cold all day laying block – and succeeded insofar as he turned himself into a gargoyle, an oddly handsome gargoyle, who happened to be listening to the saddest music in the world and who feared that the music was about to become far, far sadder.

"Any two people can have an off day...maybe that's all this is..."

I could see he didn't believe that was the problem anymore than I did.

"Harry, you're a sweet guy..."

"But I'm too old and too boring."

I sighed. "You probably wouldn't believe me if I told you that I'm finding that I *like* old and boring – not that you're *too* of either."

The sad, handsome, gray-haired gargoyle stretched out a rough claw. "What's the problem, then?"

I busied my hands lifting pizza to my mouth. The claw withdrew.

I said, "The main reason we're together is desperation. That's not a good foundation to build on...I'm telling you this from experience."

"Desperation's a strong word."

"It fits, Harry, you know it does. If your Suzanne hadn't died in a random car crash, if some sleazebag politicians hadn't axed the funding for my job, if last year I hadn't...well, never mind about what happened last year...the point is: bad things have happened to each of us and they've left us with no better options – temporary options – than each other."

The gargoyle's remote gray eyes betrayed a mortal wound.

"I'm sorry you feel that way," he said very softly.

"I don't want to lead you on, Harry. I don't want you thinking that this is going to be anything more than it is right now."

"Right now it sounds like you're leaving."

Jokes spring into my head at the most inopportune times. "Sure thing," I said, "That's my plan: stuff myself with pizza, swill a bunch of wine and I'm outta here!"

The stone mask cracked enough to let me see that Harry was alarmed, confused, perhaps even offended by my careless quip. I swilled wine, as advertised, toyed with my almost empty wine glass; Harry filled it. His own glass was practically untouched. "Sorry I didn't get the kind you like," I offered. He sipped, winced ever so slightly, said, "No, this is perfect...perfect for the occasion."

"Listen, Harry, all I'm saying is: sooner or later, probably sooner, I'll be leaving. Either you'll be sick of me and throw me out..." Harry wanted to object but I held up a hand "...it's happened before, Harry, believe me, with lesser men than you – or I'll find another job, and the chances of that job being in this town are slim – or I'll once again lose my nerve and once again go running home to my family, what's left of it.

"Those are the options for our future, Harry. Don't kid yourself into thinking anything else is possible."

"What if...?" he began? I shook my head to signal it was hopeless but he ignored me. "You say the chances are slim but what if you *do* get another job right here in town...?"

"Harry..."

"And what if I never get sick of you?"

We sat staring at one another like a pair of poker players playing an exceeding strange game – one player, me, was trying to show her hand and the other player was refusing to look.

Harry said, "Or is the truth, really, that you're already so sick of me?"

"You don't know me too well, do you?" I said.

"I'm sure I don't."

"If that was ever how I felt I'd have been long gone."

I caught a glimpse of the real Harry peeking around the edges of the stone mask. I had finally shown him a card that he was willing to look at, but he couldn't figure out how it fit with all the other cards he preferred to ignore.

I said, "Harry, promise me when I leave you won't be hurt."

An unhappy laugh escaped him. "I can't promise that."

Harry

I thought we were done talking about leaving, but Maddie wouldn't let it go. She said, "You know that day is coming same as I do – I wish you would admit it. I've seen how sad you get after we screw. At first, I couldn't figure it out. But then it dawned on me: you're thinking along the same lines I am."

Her wine glass was empty again, mine was halfway there. I poured a stream down my throat without tasting it and filled both our glasses, and that killed the bottle. Maddie tore into her by now cold pizza. Around a mouthful of food she said, "It kind of pisses me off you won't admit it – it makes whatever time we *do* have together less enjoyable for me, for both of us really."

I asked her what she meant by that.

"Anytime we're having a good time – and I don't just mean in bed – I don't like having the thought in the back of my mind that I can't make it *too* good a time for either one of us because you're going to be hurt that much worse when the inevitable happens and I go away."

I felt my eyes boggle. "Are you saying you've been holding back?!"

"Sometimes…a little."

I was incredulous. How much better could it possibly be? (I have to admit, despite Maddie's claim that she wasn't just talking about sex that I was thinking pretty exclusively about our time together in bed.) For an instant I felt almost dizzy – and I wondered if that was the same feeling someone gets when they say that their head is reeling. I felt, too, a powerful incentive to admit to anything Maddie required, if that would prevent her from holding back.

Of course I knew what she was talking about when she mentioned my sadness after sex. And I knew she was, uncharacteristically, misreading me. I had already made up my mind that I wasn't going to speak about Suzanne to Maddie. First of all I was pretty sure that Maddie didn't want to hear it. But more importantly, it would have felt like a betrayed of Suzanne to discuss our mutual inadequacies and dissatisfactions with anyone else – especially with another woman, especially in these circumstances. Oh most especially in these circumstances. So I couldn't see any way of setting Maddie straight as to the cause of my sadness.

Maddie said, "I hate it when you go into one of your long silences – you did that a couple of times our first night together and it really got under my skin."

That puzzled me for an instant, and then I recalled how Maddie had stormed out of my car into the rain. However, I did not recall going into any sort of a prolonged silence.

"Christ sake, Harry, say something!"

"Sorry."

Maddie took another big bite, finishing off her pizza except for the crust, which she dropped onto the grease-stained paper plate in front of her. I had done little more than nibble the end of my own slice.

She watched me with those pale blue eyes of hers. She said, "What are you thinking, Harry?"

"I'm thinking about how empty I felt last night when you didn't come back…"

Maddie started to say something but caught some signal from me that I had more to say.

"...It was a terrible feeling but, looking back at it, I can't say that I was also feeling anything like shock or surprise...so when you say it's inevitable that you'll be leaving...I guess I know that, I'm not happy about it but I know it's bound to happen...but don't ask me to not be hurt or sad when the time comes."

"It's going to make me sad, too, Harry."

"Do me one favor?if you can."

"What's that?"

"Give me fair warning, don't just walk out the door without a word."

Maddie spent some time thinking this over before gravely nodding her assent.

Charlie

Our building didn't have a parking lot like Dad's: it was every man for himself on the street. But there was almost always a spot within a block or two of our door. Sometimes I wished we lived in a bigger city with enough public transportation where car ownership would have been less of a necessity – but the wish was too vague: I didn't know if I wanted our city to be bigger or if I wanted to live in a different, bigger city so, of course, nothing ever came of it, by which I mean, I guess, I never took any action, if any were possible, to make my wish come true.

Despite my firm resolve to do otherwise, I'd driven around for hours after leaving Dad's. I drove past my old grammar school, then my old high school. I drove past the house where I first kissed another boy (he told me I was a freak but he let me kiss him again). I don't know what finally decided me to stop driving and to go have it out with Alexis. I found a spot and parked my car and noticed Alexis' car a few spots away – so it was a pretty good bet that he was home.

"Deep breaths, calming thoughts," I told myself, and people I passed on the street probably thought I was crazy, mumbling into the front of my shirt. Still, by the time I climbed the stairs to our door, I wasn't the least bit calm: my heart was racing and my head was full of fears and what if's. I thought I heard music inside, so that clinched it: Alexis was home.

The music turned out to actually be coming from next door. That's how wound up and disoriented I was standing in that hallway – I couldn't tell the difference. When I opened the door to our place I was greeted by the same mere hint of a beat and a melody that I'd experienced in the hallway except now it was being drowned by silence. I stepped inside, closed the door behind me. Alexis was dozing on the couch, curled up like a cat in the late afternoon sunshine streaming through the window. He was wearing his hospital scrubs. His feet were up on the couch and his shoes were on – a pet peeve of mine, since the couch belonged to me.

I slipped into the kitchen. The refrigerator was full of Alexis' super-healthy, minimally-processed, farm-fresh foods. I pretty much never brought home anything I liked – the looks of distain, not to mention the outright browbeating, were too hard to take. I fished around and the most palatable thing I could find was a cup of plain, organic, probiotic yogurt. There was a bag of walnuts on the counter, shelled and crushed. I mixed some of those in. The crunchiness helped but there still wasn't much flavor. I creaked open the door to our tiny pantry and pulled out a packet of sugar from my hidden stash. I added the sugar to the yogurt and buried the wrapper in the trashcan under the sink. I nudged the pantry door closed and it creaked once again and the second instance of this small noise was the thing that roused Alexis.

He woke abruptly, almost fearfully, as was his habit. When I first knew Alexis, I used to think he must be waking up from a dream of toppling over the edge of a cliff, but he always said that wasn't it. In fact, Alexis claimed that he never dreamed – not just that he didn't remember his dreams but that he, in fact, never dreamed. We used to have arguments about this. I was certain that everyone dreamed, certain that a person who never dreamed would go insane. Alexis would take offense, would accuse me of calling him either crazy or a liar. In any event, since he claimed to not be dreaming, whenever he would startle awake I was then left with the impression of a person who aspired never to sleep, who believed that silly old saw about sleep being for the weak, who would have claimed that he never slept if he could have possibly gotten away with it.

Alexis' eyes darted in every direction and he soon found me watching him through the small hatchway between the living room and the kitchen.

He grunted to acknowledge my return; I gave him what I hoped came off as a cold, unforgiving stare. He remained seated on the couch; I stayed in the kitchen.

"When did you get in from work?" I grudgingly inquired. So much for talking anything through, so much for laying down conditions.

He searched his pockets for his phone, found that it had fallen out onto the cushions of the couch. He checked the time.

"About two hours ago."

"When do you work again?"

"Not till Tuesday."

"Hmm," I said.

I finished the yogurt, left the spoon and the cup in the sink alongside of a few other dirty dishes.

Rising, Alexis said, "Want to go see a movie later?" Alexis' favorite kind of date: something we could do together out in public and not really be with other people.

"Sure."

Alexis stretched, said, "I'll be in the shower." But he didn't go into the bathroom; instead, he came into the kitchen, his intense blue eyes glittering black. He slid a hand around my neck, kissed me. His other hand moved to pull me into a hug. I winced against the pain and he released me.

"Let me see," he said.

I raised my shirt to show him the fading red welt and the long, thin, purple-yellow bruise along my rib. He made no comment and I lowered my shirt and gazed at him accusingly. He threw my gaze back at me.

He said, "I scored some pills for you last two shifts at the hospital."

I said, "I scored a few of my own – thanks to you."

Alexis smiled as if I had told a joke. "Bet mine are better," he winked and sauntered off to the shower.

Maddie

Strangely, a light-hearted feeling slowly took root between us. It was as if getting it out in the open that our days together were numbered somehow made each of us giddy with – not happiness, exactly, certainly not joy – but with a kind of imbecile, inexplicable elation: our time together was too precious to allow for any lesser feeling. Harry insisted we go out somewhere, almost as if we had earned a celebration. I resisted the idea: "Don't you have to go to work tomorrow?" But Harry would not take no for an answer – and in any case I wasn't too difficult to convince.

We took his car, of course. At the exit from the parking lot, Harry said,

"Where are we going?"

"I thought you had someplace in mind."

He didn't.

A car behind us tooted and Harry rolled into the street, turning right, toward the, to me, increasingly familiar commercial strip that contained the Biscuit Den, the supermarket, the chain drugstore. It was evening; the sun had set, and every car had its headlights on. We passed the spot where I'd attacked Mr. Tattoo's truck. I glanced along the curb but caught no sight of a crumpled antenna. We passed a lot of restaurants. Harry said, "Now I wish we hadn't eaten that pizza." I said, "We could stop in somewhere and split a salad." Harry: "Do you want to?" Me: "Sure." So we did that. Harry picked out an expensive-looking place which neither of us were really dressed for but we went in anyway. The waiter looked dour when we ordered one salad and an extra plate. I also ordered a glass of wine, the cheapest red on the list. Harry said, "No more wine for me – I'm driving." "You're a good scout," I said and pecked him on the cheek right there under the nose of the waiter. All this happened with that child-like elation still swirling between and around us.

We threw out ideas about where to go next. A movie, a play, the mall just to stroll around (neither of us knew how late shops stayed open at the mall on a Sunday but we were guessing that they were keeping longer hours, now that Thanksgiving was behind us and the Christmas shopping season must be gearing up). One of us suggested a bowling alley. I think it was Harry – but, who knows, it might have been me. Neither of us knew where to find a bowling alley. "There used to be one on Hamilton," Harry offered, "but it burned down years ago." "Let's ask our waiter," I said; "I bet he bowls all the time," and Harry got the joke immediately and his laughter was quiet and warm.

In the end, of course, we used Harry's phone to guide us. I had to show him how the map function worked.

The bowling alley turned out to be a lot of fun – who knew? I couldn't remember being in one since I was a child. In fact, my strongest impressions of a bowling alley came from the bowling scenes in *The Big Lebowski*, and it was kind of a relief to find that the real thing was not crawling with oddballs and crazies. The people who were there were an interesting mix: old and young, male and female, some intensely serious about their bowling, others, like us, just having a good time.

We had to rent shoes, of course. That put me briefly in mind of a boyfriend from years and years ago who would have died before he put on a pair of shoes that someone else had worn: his name was Howard – or Hector, something beginning with an "H" (but definitely not Harry) – and we broke up on the spot when I happened to mention in passing that I'd had other men before him.

Harry helped me select a bowling ball. He showed me how the finger holes were drilled with different sizes and different spacings from one ball to the next. He recommended that I start with a really light ball that I could comfortably grip. None of the balls was particularly light, but I quickly understood what Harry meant – some were much heavier than others. Harry himself chose a ball at least twice as heavy as the one I settled on. He informed me that he used to bowl in a league. I tried to act surprised but I wasn't fooling anyone, not even Harry.

"You must be pretty good, then," I said.

Harry shook his head. "It wasn't what you would call a very competitive league…just a bunch of guys, mostly in construction, who got together after work and drank a lot of beer…and I was never the star of any team I was on, not even close…and I haven't bowled in years, so…"

"Still," I said, "I bet if we were playing strip bowling, you'd have me naked in no time."

Harry shushed me, glancing nervously all around, scared out of his wits that someone might have overheard me.

They charged you by the game and there was an electronic scoring table that kept track of your scores and of how many games you played, but Harry had a word with the attendant and she let us warm up for a couple of minutes before she activated the scoring table.

Harry rolled the first ball, demonstrating for me where to stand, how to space out my steps, how to release the ball. He told me that really good bowlers put all kinds of spin on the ball but that the best thing to do as a beginner was to try to roll the ball straight down the middle of the lane; he himself had never gotten much beyond that approach. Harry knocked down a bunch of pins with that first ball, leaving only one standing in the far right corner – the ten-pin, he called it.

He said, "As soon as my ball comes back, I'll go for the spare, then you can give it a try with a full set of pins."

"I don't mind aiming at just that one," I said.

Harry was amused. "Go ahead and try if you want to," he said, "but it's easier to hit something if there's a whole bunch of pins standing."

I didn't care one way or the other if I hit the pin but, in just the short time we'd been there, I had seen several people roll what they called gutter-balls, and I was determined not to do that on my first try. I stood where Harry showed me, took one short step forward then three longer paces and, crouching, rolled the ball forward as straight as I possibly could. But I didn't put enough force into it and the ball wandered slowly, first left then right, as it made its listless was down the lane. I held my breath, fearful that the ball would not even make it to the end of the lane, that we would have to call over the attendant, that someone would have to walk out there and nudge the ball forward – an even more ignominious start than if I had rolled a simple gutter-ball. But the ball did make it to the end of the lane. It even nipped the side of the ten-pin so that the pin wobbled, righted itself, wobbled again and tipped over. I threw my hands in the air and gave a cheer like I had just won the state championship at bowling. Harry cheered for me, too.

When the pins were re-set, I rolled again. I threw the ball harder this time. The ball rumbled right down the center of the lane and the pins went flying – all except the seven-pin and the ten-pin.

"What do you do about that?" I asked.

Harry described how a good bowler would try to catch the side of one of the two pins really hard with the hopes of ricocheting it into the other.

"I'll just go for one," I said.

Harry explained the way bowling was scored, the importance of strikes and spares, why it was better to try for both pins. I listened to him patiently, then I plowed down the ten-pin.

By the time our warm up session was over I had learned a few things. Comparing Harry's rolls to mine, I saw that a heavier ball could do more damage to the pins – although of course it was harder to throw – also that accuracy was more important than brute force (a lesson I suspected Harry had never fully grasped: he threw the ball harder than he needed to). Also, I'd learned that, if you hit the head pin slightly off-center, you stood an excellent chance of scoring a strike, and in any case you almost always avoided the dreaded seven-ten split.

Harry signaled to the attendant and our scoring table lit up and I told Harry I'd be right back, I was going to go look for a heavier ball.

Harry

When Maddie returned, I asked if she wanted a few more warm ups, since she had just switched the ball she was using. She said no, the new ball felt right, she'd be okay — and wanted to know who went first.

"Beauty before age," I said, entering our names into the scoring table, and Maddie tweaked my nose as both thanks for the compliment and punishment for having dissed myself.

For her first official frame, Maddie rolled a sedate, straight-as-an-arrow strike. The pins laid down like blades of grass blown over by a gentle breeze. When she saw the last pin topple, Maddie's feet left the ground, she raised her fists and hallooed with excitement.

I threw a screamer down the middle but at the last second it veered to the left and I almost missed the head pin. I needed to pick up the five and seven pins for a spare, and I clobbered both of them.

In the second frame we each threw spares, and we each left the third frame open — Maddie scoring 8 and 1 against my 7 and 2, so that after three frames Maddie was leading 47 to 44. In the fourth frame, we each threw strikes. Once again, the pins laid down for Maddie as if she'd sung them a lullaby while I sent a great crashing peel of thunder echoing throughout the building. The fifth frame turned out to be decisive. Maddie again rolled a perfect, slow strike. I plowed down nine pins, then missed the remaining four-pin by a wide margin. After that, I could never catch up as Maddie rolled spares in the next two frames then another strike, whereas the best I could do was yet another open frame followed by two spares.

Maddie was poised to start off the ninth frame when I remarked that she'd left only one frame open so far all game. "That's amazing good luck for a beginner," I marveled. She frowned at me and rolled her worst ball of the night, easing over only five pins. She concentrated very hard on her next attempt but left one pin standing. She cried, "You jinxed me, Harry! Why did you do that?!" She seemed on the verge of tears. I said I was sorry then rolled my second strike of the game. Maddie went into a deep pout.

I showed her the score. She was up by over thirty points. I assured her that I had practically no chance to catch her. "You'd have to completely fall apart in the last frame," I said.

"Now you're trying to mess with my head!" she accused.

"I'm not, I'm not!" I pleaded, holding my open palms out in front of me.

Glaring at me, Maddie snatched up her ball and proceeded to throw two more unwavering strikes. She finished the tenth frame by knocking down eight pins and leaving herself for the first time all game with a seven-ten split – moot in this case. I didn't do badly in the tenth frame but it was too little too late – I wound up with a 169: about the same as I used to do when I bowled regularly, maybe even slightly above my old average. Maddie, on the other hand, had rolled a total of six strikes and three spares, scoring a 191 in the very first game of bowling in her adult life. I told her she was a natural and, grinning, she challenged me to another game.

Our second game went much like the first. Maddie kept rolling strikes and spares. She scored spares when she needed to because she almost never allowed a split and when one or two pins were standing close together her ball found them as if guided by remote control. I said, "Not trying to get inside your head or anything, but you have amazing accuracy." She thanked me and explained, like I was the beginner, that it was because she didn't throw the ball too hard. She didn't quite come out and say it, but she clearly intended to send the hint that maybe I should try throwing the ball a little softer. Well, how could I argue? She was beating the pants off me. I tried it – but it didn't work for me: it did not increase my accuracy and meanwhile the pins I did manage to hit no longer flew around with as much force as usual.

At the start of our third game, Maddie, peeling off a few of her flimsy layers, commented on how much of a sweat a person could work up at this silly pastime.

"Do you want something to drink?" I asked.

"A beer would be great right now – have one with me?"

I hesitated since I expected that I would be driving later.

"I'll only drink one if you will," Maddie insisted.

I went to get us each a beer, reflecting along the way on Maddie's sudden unwillingness to drink if I didn't, on her reluctance to give up any advantage at "this silly pastime."

Maddie

I give Harry a lot of credit. Most men would have thrown a tantrum. For a man to lose at a sport that he knows something about and even has a fair amount of experience playing, to lose to a woman, to a woman who is a rank beginner, to lose over and over again – most men would have gone apeshit. But sweet, dear Harry was genuinely pleased for my success. And he made no false claims about his own performance. Nothing along the lines of: "I'm usually much better than this but my back is acting up" or "these shoes don't quite fit" or "the lighting is bad" or "I don't like the music they're playing, it's distracting" or whatever. Harry was cheerfully forthright about the fact that he was bowling about as well as he ever did and that I, without any prior experience, was simply a better bowler.

As for me, I have to say, my own competitiveness at this essentially meaningless activity snuck up and surprised me. At first, I couldn't even acknowledge it: that I actually cared how I did at bowling. Then I tried to talk myself out of it. What would be next, golf? But the fact remained I took enormous satisfaction at knocking down more pins than Harry – and with a lighter ball, too!

Harry's easy attitude about the whole thing eventually won the day and the edge fell off of my need to win. I still *wanted* to win. I still enjoyed it when all the pins fell over. I especially liked watching the chain reaction of pin falling into pin while the ball angled away toward other pins: the best strikes were the ones where the ball clearly wasn't doing all the work.

After our third game we decided to take a breather. At each lane there was enough seating for a party of ten, and we sat side by side surrounded by empty seats, nursing our beers, gazing at the ten fresh pins at the end of our lane.

I said, "Bowling's a better game than chess."

"Better?"

"Absolutely."

"How do you figure?"

"With bowling we're in competition, sure, each trying to do our best, each trying to outdo the other, but, except for evil people who try to cast jinxes, we don't *interfere* with one another, not like in chess. In chess, each player is doing everything they can to frustrate the other's plans. That's what makes bowling better."

Harry thought about this. "Yes," he said, "chess is a more direct competition...or maybe confrontation is a better word...the same way tennis is more direct than something like golf."

"Don't tell me you play golf," I said in mock horror – without being entirely sure how much I was pretending.

"I tried it," Harry said. "I stunk at it. I guess you never played golf, huh?"

"Never! – and I've never had good luck with any man who did."

"In that case, I'm glad I don't play. What about tennis?"

"What about it? Are you asking did I ever date a guy who played tennis?"

"No, I'm asking did you ever play?"

"Not really, no, just batted the ball around a few times for kicks. You?"

"I never dated a guy who played tennis, either."

"Very funny." I slapped his arm.

He said, "No, I never played tennis, never even tried it, never got the chance."

"What sport did you play when you were growing up – baseball, right?"

Harry smiled, remembering, "Baseball, sure. I played Little League for three years, or maybe four. I wasn't much good at it, mostly 'cause I was small for my age. But what I *was* pretty good at was boxing."

"Boxing, really?"

"Yeah, it was a big thing in the parish where Fran and I grew up."

"And you were good at it?"

"Well, my small size kept me from having to fight any of the real bruisers...I always fought in the lightest weight classes – but I always won."

"Did you teach Charlie to box?"

"Funny you should mention that," Harry said. He regarded me like I was some gypsy woman who had just divined a secret from his past. "Charlie and I were talking the other night about things I taught him and things I wished I had taught him, and it was in my mind to mention boxing but I didn't say anything about it...I was scared he would take it wrong."

"Like: he can't stand up for himself against Alexis the way a real man would?"

"Yeah, that – but also I didn't want him to get the idea that he *should* stand up to Alexis that way."

I said, "I don't understand you, Harry. Isn't that what you'd do to Alexis if you got half a chance?"

Harry looked dead serious. "Oh sure, I'd knock him into next Tuesday if it was my fight — but the thing is: I'm not in a relationship with the son-of-a-bitch and Charlie is. Charlie can't solve it like I would solve it, what would be the point? How do you claim to be in love with someone if you have to physically intimidate them to get them to stop slapping you around? No, the only way for Charlie to solve it is the way you told him. If he can't solve it that way, he needs to get out."

"So, love's more like bowling than like chess...or boxing, is that what you're saying?"

"Love shouldn't be any kind of competition at all," Harry said.

I slowly shook my head.

"What?" Harry wanted to know.

I said, "Wish I'd run into you years ago, mister. I didn't know there were guys out there who thought like you."

Harry started to say something but just then the attendant called over and asked if we were done bowling.

"Heck no!" I said. "Ready for another game, Harry?"

Harry said sure but first he needed to make a pit stop. He promised to return with two more beers.

In his absence, a newly arrived party was assigned to the lane next to ours. The party consisted of Otto, from the chess club, and a woman whom I assumed was his wife, along with two other guys I also recognized from the chess club and two other women.

Charlie

Alexis let me pick the movie. Sort of. There was a sweet, low-key coming-of-age film playing at the downtown art theater that would have been just my cup of tea: the main character, of course, discovers that he is gay. Afterwards, Alexis and I might have stopped by someplace for drinks or a bite to eat and — who knows? — maybe run into a few of my old friends: downtown was where they liked to hang out. But Alexis had only allowed me the choice of any movie playing at the Cineplex across from the mall. The choices included horror, action-adventure, blockbuster superhero, children's animated, romantic comedy, and a sci-fi end-of-the-world thriller. Given those choices, I couldn't make up my mind — and not because they were all so fantastically appealing to me. It was not until we

174

174

M. JonquilM. Jonquil

were a few paces from the ticket booth that I chose the animated movie.

Alexis griped, "I'm not going to sit through that."

"Well, why don't you just tell me what movie you want to see?" I said, trying to make it sound like a joke. Unfortunately, it came out more like a peevish sneer.

It didn't matter: I knew I was perfectly safe. We were surrounded by other people. Not to mention the fact that I was cruising along on one of Alexis' scored pills – way better than the generic percocets I'd been issued – and a shot of tequila. I was feeling no pain and wouldn't have felt any, even if a truck had hit me, much less Alexis.

Alexis enquired if I was up for the horror movie: he was partial to that sort of thing.

"Hell no," I said, perceiving that I'd made some sort of joke or pun or something by using the word *hell* in connection with a horror movie, and I laughed more than I probably should have. Alexis subjected me to a cross stare.

We compromised on the superhero blockbuster.

It was an utterly empty experience but full of vast quantities of color and movement and sound. There were good guys and there were bad guys and, as a result of the conflict between them, a lot of perfectly innocent people were put in jeopardy, and many of those people probably died, what with bridges collapsing and trains derailing and large chunks of skyscrapers getting broken off and sent crashing into the streets, not to mention any number of other superpower-induced catastrophes, but the deaths were mostly implied, mostly happened off-camera, and the few deaths that the audience did witness were not terrible to watch, were in fact sort of entertaining to watch, the special effects being so amazing, and in the end the good guys won.

I typically found movies like that distracting enough while I was watching them, especially if I was in a chemically induced state of mind-lessness, but I often left the theater feeling like I'd wasted two perfectly good hours of my life. That was exactly how I felt at the end of this movie. Alexis, on the other hand, almost always came out of a superhero action film with a raging hard-on and an overwhelming urge to do something about it. I'd been so focused on how the codeine and the tequila were getting along in my bloodstream that I'd forgotten about that little quirk of Alexis' – or maybe it was in the back of my mind all along.

Of course he wanted to go straight to our apartment; meanwhile, I was acting like it was our first date and I let it be known that I expected Alexis to make more of an effort before there was even a chance he would have his way with me. Besides, this sort of *was* a first date...our first date since he'd broken my rib, our first date since I'd moved back in.

"Take me someplace nice," I demanded airily.

"How about if I fix us a great meal at home?"

"You can do that, too," I said. "But right now take me someplace for a drink."

Alexis, of course, was driving. I turned up my nose at the first two places he slowed down for. I could see he was fuming but it was not the dangerous kind of fuming; it was just his faux-Latin blood smoldering for sexual release. I said yes to a snooty-looking place that catered mostly to older, richer people. We took seats at the bar, which was practically empty. I ordered a Tequila Sour; Alexis drank club soda with a slice of lemon. He wouldn't even taste my drink. And not just because he was driving – more and more Alexis was buying into this notion that he must never pollute his body: he ate only natural, wholesome foods, and those in small quantities; he had taken to bathing with soap made from extra virgin olive oil (organic, no doubt) that he special-ordered through the internet and that probably cost a fortune; he worked out relentlessly. His physique had been pretty spectacular when I first met him. Now he might have passed for an Olympic gymnast or a porn star. Or a budding super-something – hero or villain, I couldn't tell which.

We chatted about the movie, mostly about the actors, what we thought of their performances – the movie itself, the plot for instance, being too farfetched to discuss. We agreed that the foreign actor playing the baddest of the bad guys had stolen the show. He was somebody who was apparently a big deal in India's Bollywood but neither Alexis nor I had ever heard of him. In the midst of our conversation, when Alexis thought no one was looking, he leaned in close to me, grabbed my ass, said in a hoarse whisper, "Hurry up and finish that...I can't wait to take you home."

The bartender was at the end of the bar, looking out a window, but just then he glanced our way, and I smiled as if Alexis had told an innocuous joke. When the bartended turned and resumed his study of the street, I said to Alexis, "Hey, Gladiator, I'm pretty sore: some super-badguy broke my rib the other night – I might not be up for any shenanigans." (Gladiator was the name of the superhero we'd just watched overpower and dominate a whole slew of evil villains.)

"I'll be gentle," Alexis promised. But the intense look in his eye told me something different. He saw my skepticism. "Take another pill," he urged.

Harry

When I returned with two fresh beers, I found Maddie sitting at the score table, her back ramrod stiff, her eyes fixed straight ahead. There was a group of six people bowling in the lane beside ours, three men and three women. All of a sudden I realized that I knew all three of the men: Otto and Dennis and Rob, all from the chess club. I even recognized Otto's wife, although I could not remember her name (except that it was something French-sounding – Yvette?, maybe). She used to stop by the club occasionally – never to play, just to "visit" – before she and Otto got married.

It was confusing on more than one level to run into these three guys outside the chess club. First, there was the usual strangeness of people you associate with a particular place turning up in a wholly different and unexpected place. Then there was the odd fact that Otto was even socializing with guys like Dennis and Rob. Otto was one of those players who believed that superior skill over the chessboard made him a superior person all around. At the club, Otto would barely give players like Dennis and Rob the time of day. Dennis was near the upper ranges of the class-C category – but that still put him about a hundred rating points below me and something like five or six hundred points below Otto. And Rob! – if he was in the class-C category at all it wasn't by much. The final bit of strangeness had to do with the looks all three of them made when they recognized me. I mean, their eyes fairly popped out of their heads.

I was so discombobulated that I did a really stupid thing: I greeted the three men by name then said, "Oh and this is my friend Maddie." No sooner were the words out of my mouth when it occurred to me that, of course, they all knew Maddie – Maddie, too, attended meetings of the chess club. Hell, Rob had been there last Wednesday when Maddie had asked in that suggestive tone of voice if I wanted to play with her. A flood of embarrassment washed over me and I felt myself blushing.

We all stood around looking confused and stupid until Maddie sprang from her seat and shook hands with each of the men, saying how mice it was to meet some of Harry's friends. She asked each man to repeat his name. "I have a terrible memory for names," she confided. Then she spoke directly to the three women, giving her name again as if they hadn't already heard, and asking for theirs. Otto's wife spoke up first – Colette was her name. The instant she said it, it came to me.

"I'm with Otto," she explained. "I'm his wife."

"Of course you are," Maddie beamed, shaking her by the hand.

Colette was barely more than five feet tall, a good six inches shorter than Maddie and well over a foot shorter than Otto. She'd put on weight since the last time I'd seen her, and that was unfortunate because even then she was chubby. She was in her late forties, about the same age as Otto, maybe a year or two older than Otto, but she projected an odd child-like (or perhaps doll-like) quality that made her sort of endearing and at the same time a little creepy.

Colette smiled uncertainly. She wasn't quite sure what to make of Maddie's slightly off-kilter remark. She said, "Oh um, and these are my friends, Mandy and Monique."

"Mandy and Monique!" Maddie fell on them as though she'd been reunited with a pair of long-lost compadres. She wanted to know everything. First off: who was with whom? It turned out that Monique was more or less with Rob but that Mandy and Dennis had each been hoodwinked into this outing and found themselves in the middle of an awkward and not very successful blind date, made worse by the fact that they were surrounded by company – and now here was Harry and Maddie to make the company even more extensive. None of this about Mandy and Dennis was said in so many words, but it was amazing how Maddie, when she turned on the charm, could get some people to open up and say or at least suggest the most revealing things. Not chess people, generally. But Maddie could work wonders on people like Colette and Monique and even Mandy. Hell, even Rob – but then Rob wasn't much of a chess player.

The men of the other party resumed bowling as the four women chattered. I waited for Maddie.

Monique and Rob must have been in their twenties, roughly Charlie's age; Mandy and Dennis were a bit older. Monique and Rob refused to use the words "boyfriend" and "girlfriend" or even the word "friends" when describing their relationship – all either of them would say was that they were "together." Rob always struck me as high-strung, with his unfortunate habit of chewing his nails and his incessant smoking. The smoking, at least, kept him thin. Monique, on the other hand, was heavy-set and phlegmatic; her upper eyelids drooped so that she looked perpetually sleepy, and she breathed through her mouth, which she never fully closed. The sense I got, from listening to Maddie's cheerful interrogation, was that Monique and Rob each thought they could do better and when they said they were "together," what they meant was they were "together for now." Who isn't,

I wanted to tell them – join the club. I was thinking of both Suzanne and Maddie and of all the various ways you could find out you were only "together for now."

Meanwhile, Otto and Dennis and Rob had each bowled a frame, Rob letting himself be drawn into the women's conversation when it wasn't his turn. It was plain to see that Otto was an excellent bowler. This did not particularly surprise me – it would have been unlike Otto to engage in any activity at which he was not better than all or most of the people around him. Excellent bowler he might be but his throwing motion, in my humble opinion, was overblown and showy. After his lunging approach and dramatic release, he held himself still with his bowling hand high over his head and his opposite foot stretched out behind him, toes pointed for God's sake, held the pose for far too long, turning himself into a hulking, unwitting caricature of a ballerina. He put enormous spin on the ball, allowing it to skitter along the edge of the gutter before hooking at the last moment and slamming into the head pin; he threw resounding, thunderous strikes.

I noticed Maddie sizing up Otto as a bowler and I could see she fairly itched to compete against him, to show him up.

Dennis was balding, overweight, out of shape. Bowling clearly wasn't his thing – but then it was hard to imagine what sort of physical activity would be his thing. He told me once at the club what kind of work he did. He worked for a company that contracted with the federal government – he audited federal agencies that provided oversight of other federal agencies: he was some sort of watchdog of the watchdogs. The whole idea of what he did made my head spin. For all I knew, his job represented nothing more than another layer of bureaucratic bullshit. On the other hand, this sad, paunchy man might be the lynchpin of our entire way of life. If he didn't do his job well and honorably and conscientiously, maybe our whole system of democratic government would rapidly crumble.

In terms of bowling, Dennis was doing his best but that wasn't much. It was heartbreaking in a way, because even a denser man than me could tell that at least one cause for the awkwardness between Dennis and Mandy was the fact that Dennis was interested in Mandy, perhaps strongly interested, while Mandy was making every effort to pretend that Dennis did not exist.

Mandy was tall and haughty, thin yet shapely, like some high-fashion model, imperiously beautiful. She was beautiful but, to my eye at least, her features were too hard and too cold to say that she was genuinely attractive – if that makes sense. She looked out of place in a bowling alley and thoroughly unhappy to be there. It occurred to me, too, that she looked more like a Monique whereas the real Monique, that plain, big-boned girl, looked more like a Mandy.

Dennis, meanwhile, was casting about for any means of impressing his nominal date, or at least of getting her attention. Prowess at bowling might have been the answer. Mandy, to my surprise, applauded Otto's splashy strike, then went on to comment to the group in general, clearly not to Dennis in particular, that her father and her two favorite uncles were ardent bowlers. If Dennis could only have bowled like Otto... Unfortunately for Dennis, he was more prone to throwing gutter balls than strikes. The timing of his approach was all wrong. Also he didn't throw the ball so much as awkwardly place it on the polished floor and push it. This technique – if it could be called that – gave him little power and less control. His frame consisted of a gutter ball followed by a meandering slow pitch – *the bowling equivalent of a knuckle ball* was the thought that crossed my mind while we all waited to see if it would ever find the end of the lane. The ball managed finally to blunder into six pins. After his second attempt, Dennis glanced nervously and dejectedly toward Mandy, who was busy looking somewhere else.

When it was Rob's turn he seemed to grab a ball randomly from the circular rack. He had no preliminary stance. He simply ran forward full-speed and pitched the ball into the air, sliding a good ten inches past the foul line. The ball hit the boards with an ugly crashing sound and raced toward the pins, which were still setting. I thought for sure his ball would collide with the reset bumper – but they just missed one another. Pins flew everywhere but somehow, perversely, the five pin was never touched. With his second ball, Rob contrived to miss the spare. A single pin in the center of the box and he missed it. I had the feeling that would be Rob's luck all night – or maybe it was his luck at bowling all the time: he was a hard luck kind of guy – nine pins down, then miss the spare.

Maddie

Harry's introducing me to this trio from the chess club as if I were a stranger to them, I would have bet my last dollar, was a complete social blunder on his part – but what a fucking brilliant move it turned out to be! It totally spoofed the cold shoulders they'd rebuffed me with when they first appeared. And the moment they played along – Otto and Rob at least – it somehow wrong-footed them in front of their women. I wasn't exactly sure how this worked but I could sense it. Maybe they had made comments at home about a "crazy Maddie" who sometimes showed up at the chess club. Now they had to worry from moment to moment whether crazy, unpredictable me would reveal that I was, in fact, that very person. Oh it was delicious.

Add in next the utter *wrongness* of this group. It attracted me like a moth to a flame, like a crowd to an accident – I had to know all there was to know about them. Why was Otto socializing with these two archetypal chess losers? – that was the first question. This violated every rule of the chess club's pecking order, as far as I understood it. Initially I wondered if perhaps they were also members of some bowling club. Was it possible that a different hierarchy existed within the bowling club, and that the pecking order of the bowling club somehow canceled out the chess club's? But even before I saw the three men bowl I knew that wasn't the case.

By asking, prodding, probing, I found out that these guys were socializing because their women had required it. Colette and Monique were family somehow, although neither was particularly coherent about the exact nature of the relationship. Monique's mother was Colette's... something. Cousin once removed or perhaps niece. Colette was probably keeping it fuzzy because she did not want it emphasized that she was a generation older than Monique. Monique, for her part, seemed genuinely confused on the subject. (It was all made a little more strange because Colette had first introduced both Monique and Mandy as her "friends," but in fact this was only true of Mandy.) In any case, I imagined this family that Colette and Monique were each members of must have French ancestry – or pretentions to such – given their first names.

Mandy was known to them from church. Colette had taken it upon herself to find Mandy not just a boyfriend but a soulmate, and had recruited Monique as her sidekick in this endeavor. Colette was unshakeable in her belief that everyone should have a soulmate. That was how she put it: not that everyone *had* a soulmate, but that everyone *should* have one. I thought there was an odd twist to that somehow – like a soulmate was an important accessory everyone ought to own, more or less akin to saying everyone should have a sturdy pair of shoes. Colette and Monique were mysterious about why they had chosen Mandy in particular to focus their attentions on. Surely, she was not the only single woman in their congregation. Colette hinted at some dark tragedy in Mandy's past, but in front of Mandy she would not say more. In any case, Colette had tasked her husband Otto with finding a suitable man, and Monique had followed suit and made the same request of her not-boyfriend Rob, and the best those two dunderheads could come up with was moon-faced Dennis.

So, you had two fat girls – it was hard to think of fortysomething Colette as anything other than a girl – setting up the slim, pretty girl for a blind date. That was strange in itself. Then you had the utter incompatibility of Mandy and Dennis; not to mention Dennis' unmistakable desire for Mandy and Mandy's clear lack of any similar feeling toward him; not to further mention their mutual discomfort, the only thing the two of them shared: each had been invited on this outing without being informed of the other's presence. Oh the layers of wrongness – as soon as you penetrated one there was another to explore.

Otto tried to break up our girl talk by pulling Colette away to bowl a frame. But as soon as Colette left, Rob took her place, sitting in the very seat she had occupied, and I started drilling in earnest into the tense, wary relationship between him and Monique. All the while Dennis hovered nearby, hoping Mandy would throw him a bone.

I had lost track of Harry. I glanced over my shoulder and caught sight of him quietly waiting for me at the top of our lane. He was unreadable: the gargoyle mask was in place again.

Otto was giving instruction to Colette, his little, round piglet of a wife, on how to bowl. He spoke to her the way you would speak to a simpleton. She huddled into herself at being talked to like this in front of other people – (was she okay with it when they were by themselves, I wondered) – and, short as she was, this huddling, cringing motion made her look even smaller, especially next to Otto's imposing figure. Otto had more to say but Colette clearly wanted to get the ordeal over with and she waddled forward, swinging her arm the way you would to sucker punch some guy in the nuts. Unfortunately, her chubby, short fingers got stuck in the ball's finger holes and, unable to separate her hand from the ball, she launched herself completely off her feet. She came down hard on her knees and her one free hand. The ball sputtered loose and rolled directly into the gutter and soon came to a halt. Otto let out a booming laugh, while everyone else emitted a horrified, collective gasp. Colette rolled onto her side and struggled to right herself. Otto rushed to help her. Colette gave him a dirty look, and Otto was taken aback – I think he was completely unconscious of the fact that he had just laughed. Both of them frowning, she let him help her to her feet. Leaning on him, Colette limped to the seats at the top of the lane. Monique chased Rob out of "Colette's chair," as if no other would do for her. Once she was settled, all the women, me included, fussed over her.

Harry, meanwhile, unobtrusively stepped over the foul line, slipped up the lane and shoved the stranded ball forward with the toe of his ma-roon-and-tan bowling shoe.

Harry

After Colette's mishap, before the confusion had a chance to com-pletely die down, I pulled Maddie aside and urgently whispered, "Don't you want to get out of here?!"

Her eyes looked bright and sharp, like the gleaming eyes of some predatory bird, and she was grinning like a hyena. She was intensely enjoying the spectacle of these six mismatched people. Maddie's expression struck me as a display of raw cruelty, innocent and pure as the cruelty of a child, and she was a stranger to me – while at the same time I caught glimpses of a familiar face, one she sometimes wore when we had sex and she was bringing herself close to orgasm.

"God, this is fun," she practically growled. I didn't think she heard me at all.

Behind Maddie, Otto was frantically trying to gain control of the situation, to engineer some sort of diversion or do-over. He suggested that Maddie and I join his group and that all eight of us make use of both lanes. "We can play team against team – Rob and Monique, you play with Harry and Maddie." Otto noticed the beers I had placed on our score table, and using that booming voice of his, called to the lounge attendant to bring over a pitcher and six glasses.

Rob said he needed to go outside and have a smoke first. Monique dutifully joined Maddie and me at the top of our lane.

My heart sank. I felt trapped, the way you sometimes feel in a slowly worsening nightmare.

Then Otto said, "No wait! – I have an even better idea: we'll make it boys versus girls."

Maddie

When Otto announced his "even better idea," poor Dennis looked crestfallen: he would not get to play on the same team as Mandy. But that was nothing compared to the look on Harry's face. Harry was utterly appalled, as if he had been handed an invitation to his own funeral. I didn't understand his distress but I didn't need to for it to yank me out of the petty bubble of spiteful *schadenfreude* that I had allowed myself to get trapped inside of.

I said immediately, "We won't be joining any team. We're leaving."

"Harry wasn't planning to leave," Otto observed; "he just came back with two beers."

I cast upon Otto an exaggerated smile which most men would have understood to be contemptuous but which merely confused this showy, vein, cerebral oaf. What on Earth did I ever see in him?

I said, "Good to have a plan – I hear that all the time at the chess club…but plans change."

This went over the heads of Mandy and Monique, but Colette came to attention as if she had received an electric shock. Oh, she had heard about "crazy Maddie" alright – and not just from Otto. Rob had no doubt witnessed a certain amount of flirting under the guise of "lessons" that had once gone on between me and Otto at the club. It was hardly a stretch to imagine Rob telling Monique, and Monique telling her older relation, Colette.

Otto flushed.

I turned to Harry and said in my sweetest, most innocent voice, "Don't you think it's time to go now, Harry, dear?"

Rob stood just outside the door, carelessly blowing smoke into the face of anyone who came or left. As we passed – I couldn't help myself – I gave him a hard, fast swat on his skinny butt. "Knock 'em dead in there!" I yelled into his ear. I startled him so badly he almost swallowed his cigarette. Harry managed to contain his laughter but I hooted all the way to the car.

Charlie

Alexis never fixed me the sumptuous meal he promised. He barely had the patience to put together a snack tray for the two of us, and then he took it away while I was still nibbling.

Alexis was really big into roleplaying and that's what he wanted to do that night. One of his favorites was when I played a straight kid, scared shitless because it was my first time going to jail. Alexis would either be a sadistic prison guard, doing my initial intake, subjecting me to a strip search, then a very thorough examination, then a prolonged demonstration of what was going to happen to me once I was on the inside; or he would be a mad dog prisoner, too dangerous for anything but strict solitary confinement, and I'd been tossed into his cell as punishment for bad behavior. Both of those games were too rough for me with my broken rib. So we came up with a variant. Alexis was a prisoner who didn't bother anybody else and who didn't let anybody bother him, and all the other prisoners feared and respected him; I was the newbie, still, and I was getting bullied mercilessly and made to do terrible things, and I had come to Alexis to beg for his protection; Alexis was reluctant to get involved, and I had to convince him that I would be a worthwhile bitch to own. I worked it in as a detail of the game that the bad prisoners had recently broken my rib – and what I was looking for was a certain gentleness in my protector. It turned out to be a good game for that night. Alexis got to feel, sort of, like a superhero, agreeing (after extensive coaxing) to stand up for the little guy, me, against all the imaginary bad guys.

The game concluded, of course, in bed, and after my protector drifted off to sleep I lay there looking up at the shadowy ceiling, bargaining with myself about whether or not to take one more pill. More and more I was falling into a pattern of use. About once every ten days to two weeks I allowed myself what I thought of as a "night of excess." A true night of excess was always followed by several days of complete abstinence, then a slow build up to the next big night. However, if I managed to stop short of complete excess, then I could save that last pill or two for the next day, which I thought of as a "winding down" day before the days of abstinence. If I took one more pill now, would there be any left for a winding down day tomorrow? I tried to remember how many pills and how many drinks I'd guzzled that night. I settled on a number and refused to question its accuracy, because it was a number that allowed me one more pill now and one saved for tomorrow.

I had taken only one of the new pills Alexis had scored for me during my recent absence. They were slow-acting but disquietingly powerful. I would have to be careful with them. Slipping out of bed, I found the percosets they'd given me at the hospital. I had a stash of older pills and usually I liked to use those up first but the percosets were the easiest to find in the dark. I went into the kitchen and pulled a bottle of tequila from under the sink and washed down the pill with one judiciously small gulp.

I wandered into the living room, moving slowly, feeling my way around the furniture, although there was dim light in the room. I half lowered myself, half fell onto the couch. Rain was gently pattering the window. When had it started to rain? It seemed the rain was tapping out some kind of code, trying to tell me something, but I couldn't make out what it was. Maybe it was *let-us-in, let-us-in, let-us-in*. Or maybe it was *come-out-and-play, come-out-and-play, come-out-and-play*. Whatever it was, it seemed harmless, child-like. A muffled shout emerged from the bedroom. I got to my feet and moved to the door. Alexis was clumsily thrashing, thoroughly asleep, twisted in the sheets, not dreaming of course because Alexis never dreamed. Was he fighting on my behalf against all the meanies in prison, in that not-dream of his? He mumbled someone's name, some co-worker whom he detested – and I decided: no, he's fighting his own fight, he's not fighting for me.

Maddie

Harry claimed not to know what I was talking about when I asked, "What was that look for back there?" I eyed him keenly while he drove. I couldn't tell if he was fibbing or not.

I asked, "You did want to leave, didn't you?"

"Oh hell yes!"

"I thought so. I mean, the look on your face told quite a story...when Otto suggested boys against girls you looked like you were seeing your own corpse."

"Did I? – I don't recall."

Oh he was fibbing alright, he was outright lying, I was sure of it now. There was little traffic on the road, and Harry threw me a glance. I was giving him a look that said *I can see right through you, mister* but it was partially a bluff because I still didn't know *why* Harry had looked so appalled. We cruised along the quiet streets in silence for several minutes. It was past time for most people in this backwater town to be home on a Sunday night – and gosh-darn it, that's exactly where they were. I thought about making a comment along those lines just to fill the silence.

Harry said, "It felt like my old life was coiling out a tentacle and trying to drag me back to the way I was before...that probably doesn't make any sense..."

"The way you were before...when?"

Harry cast another lingering glance in my direction. "Before last Wednesday."

I started to say something but Harry spoke first.

"I know I'm supposed to be preparing myself for the time when you leave. And clearly my reaction back there does not bode well for how prepared I'll ever be..." He laughed briefly, a dour, resigned laugh. "Hell, just the idea of us being separated onto two different teams was almost enough to send me into a panic – but that wasn't even the worst part of it..."

"What was the worst part?"

"The worst part was the feeling we were getting absorbed into their group and then it would only be a matter of time before they turned me back into who I was before you and turned you into who they think you are and then they would drive you off and that would be how it ended for us, not us ending it but them. The worst part was foreseeing all that and feeling so trapped, so helpless, and not being able to find inside myself the strength or the will or the courage or whatever it takes to resist it. It was like being in a nightmare."

I observed, "For a quiet guy, you sure have a lot going on inside."

"You're making fun of me – I guess I deserve it."

I laid a hand on his shoulder; he kept both his hands on the steering wheel. "Not making fun, just trying to lighten the mood."

"But you!" he said admiringly. "You even wanted to stay but the second it dawned on you that I didn't, you snapped your fingers and got us out of there. Nothing holds you back – you're the most daring person I've ever met, the most daring and the most courageous."

I couldn't help but laugh. "Oh Harry, you are so mistaking me for somebody else!"

"No, really, you are."

The laughter evaporated, deserting me, and I spoke in deadly earnest. "No, Harry, I'm not. I'm not courageous at all. And if at times I act in a way you call daring...well, that often blows up in my face, often causes me and people around me a lot of pain, sometimes real harm as well.

"You have more invested with those people back there, that's all it was. You *care* what they think about you; I don't give a flying fuck what they think about me – no courage required.

"Jeez, Harry, can't you see? You're living a life with any number of relationships like that – people you care about and people who care about you – your family, your work, the chess club – there are probably other groups you don't even think of: old friends from childhood or from school or from work who you keep up with, stores where you stop in all the time and they know you and you know them and you ask about each other and you know all kinds of details about each other's lives – I'm not living a life like that at all and I hate it: there's nobody I care about and nobody who cares about me...I dropped off of Facebook a long time ago because it felt like such a Sahara to me...I never make friends anywhere I go...I..."

Suddenly I was crying.

The next thing I knew, Harry was holding me in his arms. I panicked briefly, thinking that no one was driving the car. Then I saw that Harry had pulled over and parked. Tiny raindrops the size of fruit flies were flecking the windshield. Harry gently reminded me that I had a brother who cared about me.

"Who? – Freeman? Don't make me laugh," I said through my tears.

"Freeman gives me a place to run and hide when life gets too overwhelming, but he's never happy about it." My nose was dripping and I made a rather un-ladylike snorting noise and wiped the snot away with the back of my hand. "His wife barely tolerates me and neither would he if it didn't make him feel so smug that he's holding his shit together while my life keeps falling apart."

I was whining like a child. I hated the way I sounded but I couldn't stop. I told Harry my secret suspicion that my job ended at the hospital not because they'd lost funding but because too many of my co-workers thought I was a flake. I surprised myself when I said it: it was a suspicion I'd been keeping a secret even from myself, maybe especially from myself.

Harry was petting my hair, whispering into my neck, "I care about you, Maddie. I care about you." He said it over and over like he was calling to his own echo at the bottom of a well. His breath smelled like beer.

Eventually, the whining and the tears exhausted themselves. We sat there, awkwardly stretched toward one another, Harry still holding me. He had freed himself from his seatbelt; mine was still fastened — which meant Harry was stretching a lot further than I was. Rain trickled down the windshield in rivulets as delicate as the silk of a butterfly's cocoon.

Harry was gazing at me with a look of such deadly earnestness that I knew he was about to say something stupid about love or maybe even marriage, something he would sorely regret and probably as soon as tomorrow morning. I said simply, "Don't." And he knew what I meant. He let me go. He settled into his seat. He buckled himself in. We drove the rest of the way to his apartment in silence. Harry watched the traffic while I watched the rain on the windshield steadily increasing.

VI. Monday

Harry

Monday was a washout for work. Lying in bed, staring up at the ceiling, I could hear rain drumming on the roof – it drowned out the sound of Maddie's breathing, which was what I was listening for. Washout or not, it was a Monday and I could not resist the urge to get up at my usual hour: six o'clock. I made sure to turn off the alarm before it went off. I gazed for only a moment at the recurring miracle of Maddie in bed beside me, then I got up, slipped downstairs, and heated water for coffee. I considered brewing the real thing, but laziness overtook me and, glad that Charlie wasn't there to fuss about it, I fixed a cup of instant coffee.

Vile but well-sweetened coffee in hand, I settled into my reading chair. I was thirty or forty pages into *Wallace and Bates in the Tropics*. It was a wonderful book, consisting of an introductory prologue written by the editor, a Barbara G. Beddall, followed by long passages of concise, descriptive writing from the two men's diaries and journals. The two intrepid young naturalists were in the midst of exploring the Amazon River basin. The rain outside my window should have helped me imagine myself into the world they described. But I felt restless and for some reason the book didn't satisfy me. I had just read a passage concerning eerie sounds in the rain forest which even the natives could not explain. According to Bates, the natives attributed these sounds to the *curupira*, the wild man or spirit of the forest. I set the book aside and wandered over to my bookshelves. I came away with Lee Smolin's *Three Roads to Quantum Gravity*, a book I had wrestled with a few times before. I decided not to try to pick up reading it from where I had most recently left it off but to start over again from the beginning. Smolin starts with a question: "What are time and space?" Smolin says this is "the simplest of all questions," but I've never quite agreed with that. Okay, it's a question about two of the most basic, fundamental things, but when has a question about anything so fundamental been simple? I avoided getting hung up on this quibble the other times I attempted

Smolin's book, and I didn't get hung up on it this time either. The next thing Smolin says is that his question about time and space is "also one of the hardest questions to answer" – which I take to be a sort of verification, or acknowledgment at least, of my quibble – and he promises to spend the rest of the book brilliantly elaborating on the reasons why. Except somewhere along the way, in all my other attempts, Smolin had always lost me.

I was baffled by this reading selection of mine. I didn't expect to get very far into it. If *Wallace and Bates in the Tropics* wasn't going to hold my attention on this rainy morning with Maddie asleep in bed almost directly above where I was sitting, how was *Three Roads to Quantum Gravity* going to do the trick? I loved reading about the Age of Discovery for many reasons: it was a compelling story involving far-flung places and including an impressive collection of interesting characters. It was also a story about how one of the greatest of scientific riddles was solved. How to account for the vast abundance of life on earth? *God* was the standard answer, mysterious and unassailable, immune to evidence, a classic conversation-killer if there ever was one, not much different than the *curupira*, come to think of it; *evolution* ignited debate and as an added bonus happened to coincide with all the facts. And the theory of evolution was just one of several significant scientific advances made during the Age of Discovery.   What a time that must have been.

Meanwhile, I kept delving deeper into Smolin's book, into the mysteries of modern physics.

Maddie might mock all this delving as the search for the *M of L* which only silly college kids could take seriously. But dammit if thinking about the meaning of life, your own life and the lives of the people you loved, if thinking about that wasn't serious enough for you, what was? I was getting old enough to feel each second tick off the time I had remaining. This was a new feeling for me and I could imagine – or maybe not – how much more intense it was going to get. What were you supposed to do with this precious time that was given to you, that was remaining to you? Seek love. Yes, of course. Sitting there, having completed Smolin's prologue and pausing on the verge of chapter one, it occurred to me that people sought love like plants sought sunlight: this struck me as obviously true yet I had never understood it before. What else was essential? I supposed that different people might legitimately give different answers, but for me the next thing on the list, however silly, was to try to understand the ever elusive M of L, if it could be understood at all – and part of that undertaking involved trying to understand something about the nature of this world we live in.

The science of biology, emerging from the Age of Discovery with its theory of evolution, had already demonstrated that a deeper understanding of the natural world can lead to a deeper understanding of ourselves. Modern-day physics was potentially in an age of discovery of its own. Smolin certainly thought so. Physics had made two great leaps forward in the twentieth century: the theory of relativity and quantum theory. Each theory gives a far more accurate picture of the world than the older Newtonian physics; each theory's accuracy has been tested time and again through experimentation. And yet each theory gives an incomplete picture of the world and, even more alarming, each theory contradicts the other on a few important points. So now in the twenty-first century, physicists were in search of a new theory which would unite relativity and quantum theory. This new theory was what Smolin called quantum gravity.

Of course it was always possible that quantum gravity would prove to be unworkable. Perhaps relativity and quantum theory could not be reconciled. Perhaps one or both was a blind alley. Smolin was optimistic that this was not the case. But what if relativity and quantum theory were un-reconcilable and yet neither was a blind alley? What if the world was fundamentally dualistic and it was impossible for any single theory to encompass the whole? This was an approach to the problem Smolin did not seem to allow for, at least not in his early pages. I felt a small thrill, believing I had found an idea in this thicket that Smolin had missed, perhaps an important idea. I flipped to the index to be sure. Duality was discussed at length starting at page 113. Damn.

Maddie paused halfway down the stairs. "What are you damning about?"

She didn't startle me. I had been reading with the kind of effortless intensity that allowed for other sensory stimuli to work into the background, and I had been aware of Maddie moving around upstairs for the last few pages.

She was wearing a garment that looked exactly like one of the neglected dress shirts hanging in the back of my closet and I was struck by the similarity, then I realized that she actually was wearing one of my shirts. It covered her backside and her pubes just barely, leaving her thighs exposed almost to her hips. She'd rolled up the sleeves and had buttoned only the bottom two buttons.

I emitted a slow, quiet wolf whistle. "You look like a dame from the cover of some nineteen-sixties detective novel."

"I thought you didn't read fiction."

"My dad used to read novels like that...used to read them by the truckload."

"Oh yeah?" Maddie said. "You're dad sounds like an interesting man, just my type...maybe I'll look him up...you, you're still a bit too immature for my taste." She was at the bottom of the stairs now and with that she turned, flipped up the tail of the shirt, and mooned me.

I was smiling when I said, "You missed the old man by about twenty years, I'm afraid."

"Too bad," she said, flouncing past me into the kitchen. She called over her shoulder, "What did he die of?"

"Lung cancer – he was a smoker. A drinker, too."

"Weren't they all back then?"

She appeared at the door a moment later, holding up the container of instant coffee. "Yuk," she said and disappeared again. I heard her run water into the kettle, then I heard her grinding the coffee beans. I thought: *Charlie would have waited for the water to boil; Maddie doesn't have that kind of patience* – and I felt a bit more drawn to her because she didn't. I got up and walked to the door of the kitchen.

Last night, after we got home from the fiasco at the bowling alley, we cuddled, first on the couch then in bed, we talked, saying mostly the aimless, empty-headed things you say right before sleep, and then we slept – and there was no need for anything more. For my part, I felt relieved. A night off every now and then, I figured, had to serve to put off the inevitable day when Maddie would have grow utterly bored with me: she was simply a more creative spirit than I was in bed. Also, frankly, my aging body welcomed the break. For Maddie's part, I think it had more to do with a feeling that people were at heart not very attractive. Admittedly, I'm guessing on this – but I felt it the way you feel a strong hunch. The bowling alley left her in a mood that was shedding a very bad light on humanity, herself included. We were all a bunch of lunatic egomaniacs who simultaneously had no self-confidence – a world full of demented, super-intelligent monkeys, often given to violence. God help the planet.

Maybe I'm overstating.

While we cuddled and talked, Maddie's remarks were not nearly so bleak. Not that I remember what either of us said with much clarity. The one exchange that I do remember clearly was this: I made some comment about finding a different bowling alley the next time we went bowling – Maddie's only response was a sad smile and a kiss on my forehead.

Maddie

He stood in the doorway watching me, admiring me. He wore what I had already come to recognize as Harry's hanging-out-around- the-house outfit. It consisted of a worn cotton sweater (he seemed to have a collection of these: this one was green), faded khaki trousers, white socks, and a pair of flat-soled sneakers. I was engaged in the incredibly sexy act of eating a couple of dry Saltine crackers I'd found in a box in the back of one of the cupboards. The crackers were all I wanted – crackers and coffee. For the first morning since meeting Harry I wasn't ravenous with hunger, since I hadn't been ravaged in bed the night before. (The second morning, truth be told, but I wanted to believe it wasn't fair to count the night Harry and I had brought Charlie home from the hospital.) The crackers were slightly stale but edible.

It was good that we'd taken a break from sex last night – I think we both felt that way; I know I did. On the other hand, my period was only a few days off: I could sense it looming. Sometimes when I was in that part of my cycle, I'd get so horny it would be like the top of my head was getting ready to blow off. That morning, waking up alone in Harry's bed, with only the earthy, animal smell of him for company, I'd felt a tide pulling me in that direction. I'd masturbated myself, thinking that would satisfy the urge, and it did – or I thought it did. Except why then did I choose to parade myself in front of Harry wearing nothing more than one of his own shirts?

Now in the kitchen, it should have been easy to know what was on Harry's mind. The bulge in his khakis was certainly not difficult to interpret. And yet on his face was a look of such far-away distraction. This was not the obliterating sadness I had witnessed sometimes after our bouts of sex. This was a calmer look, detached, more thoughtful than sad, although not entirely devoid of sadness. It was all of that while at the same time Harry was taking in the sight of me with obvious relish. I felt almost like some great work of art, capable of inspiring both pleasure and the most refined reflections, while I slouched there leaning my butt against the sink with my tits practically hanging out of Harry's mostly unbuttoned shirt, munching crackers.

The kettle spluttered and whistled, erupting water all over the top of the stove – perhaps I had overfilled it. Harry stepped into the kitchen and shut off the burner. He cleaned up the spilled water while I made coffee. From time to time we brushed up against one another. It was a very small kitchen. Soon he was hugging me from behind while I tended to the pouring of the water over the grounds. He caught the scent of that self-induced orgasm on my fingers and, taking my unused hand in his, licked each one of my fingertips. His hands, first one then the other, went under my shirt (his shirt, actually). His desire for me was urgent and real, but somehow it felt half-hearted. I let his hands do what they liked. He touched me in ways that he knew excited me, and I responded. But the energy wasn't really there — not from him and not from me — and slowly our lovemaking subsided until he was merely hugging me from behind.

"Want some coffee?" I said.

His head was next to mine and he signaled yes by nodding. He kissed me on the ear and let me go. He left the kitchen and came back a few seconds later carrying a coffee mug, about a quarter full of milky, acrid coffee. I took the mug and dumped the contents into the sink. A sugary residue hung from the rim.

While I rinsed out his mug, Harry said, "Do you think it's possible for two contradictory things to be true at the same time?"

"Like...what do you mean?"

"Like let's say you had two groups of really bright people and each group formulated a system for how the world works and each system seemed true but in fundamental ways the two systems contradicted one another...could both systems somehow be true?"

"Is this a religious question?"

"Physics."

"That stuff's way over my head."

"Mine too!" Harry said. "But it's still fun to wrestle with...like trying to solve a really hard chess problem."

I poured the coffee. I turned and I kissed Harry on the tip of his nose. "You and I have different ideas about what fun is, mister."

"I guess what my question is is does the world make sense or doesn't it?"

"That's easy." I opened the refrigerator and took out the half-and-half for myself and the milk for Harry (I couldn't convince him that half-and-half was better in coffee: "too rich," he claimed).

"Well?" Harry said. "What's the answer?"

"Of course the world doesn't make any sense."

"You don't really believe that."

"Certainly I do."

"But...but...the whole scientific method depends on the fact that the world *does* make sense and that we can figure out how it works. If you didn't believe that, you'd never go see a doctor, you'd never fly on an airplane or drive across a bridge or ride an elevator to the top of a tall building."

Harry was neglecting his coffee so I fixed it for him, putting in perhaps *slightly* less sugar then he would have himself.

I said, "Oh I see what you're getting at…of course in that sense the world makes sense: if you mix together the right two chemicals you blow up the science lab – that's an experiment I personally performed on numerous occasions in my high school and even my college days and I'm here to tell you it works every time – *or* if you dissect a frog (this I was told – as I always made sure I was sick on the days the frogs were going to be butchered), all the little frog-parts are always there and always in the correct, scientifically diagrammed locations."

"So then, what's the answer? Does the world make sense or doesn't it?"

I said, "Both, silly." I poured the milk; I poured the half-and-half; using one spoon I stirred both mugs so that the liquid in each moved in opposing swirling circles.

Harry frowned. Before he could speak, I said, "If you don't mind, I'm going to use your computer to send out a bunch of resumes. Then I think I'll get dressed and go to the gym."

Harry

Her offhand comment about sending out resumes left me feeling as if a tiny lump of ice had formed inside me – in my heart or in my head, I couldn't tell which, maybe both. Taking up her mug, Maddie slipped past me and went upstairs. I put away the milk and the cream and the box of crackers, and I noticed the tiny lump of ice fading away. I wondered where the crackers had been hiding. I went to the front window and lifted the blind. There was Maddie's car parked crookedly next to mine. I'd lost my appetite for reading and just stood there gazing out the window. God, was I smitten. Even the crookedness of Maddie's parking enchanted me.

Maddie

I had two email accounts, one for personal messages and one I was using for my job search. Both inboxes were staying pretty empty. There was an email from Freeman: *You okay or what? Seriously, if I don't hear from you today I'm calling the police.* When had he sent that? — 3:14PM Pacific Time, yesterday. Hoo boy.

I clicked on the reply icon and typed *i'm fine you better not have called the police* and hit send.

My usual Monday morning routine was to visit job listing websites until I had sent out a dozen resumes. I maintained a log of places where I had already applied for work so that I didn't send out two resumes to the same place and count it toward my quota. Sometimes it was hard to find a dozen new job listings in my field; sometimes it was simply impossible. When that happened, I cheated. I made my quota by sending resumes for jobs that I had little chance of being qualified for. As time went by, I sent the quota resumes to more and more outlandish places. I stopped calling them quote resumes and started calling them joke resumes. I applied to work as a financial advisor, as a corrections officer, as a superintendant of schools, as a maintenance technician at a nuclear facility, on and on. Sometimes I would send my actual resume; sometimes I would make one up. I never got a response to a made-up resume but I did get a few unexpected responses to my actual resume. For instance, there was a company laying a crude oil pipeline that was interested in hiring me to work as a pipe welder based on my resume as a psychological counselor. Maybe their regular welders were having a hard time convincing the pipes that it was okay to bond with other pipes? (Actually, I suspect, this company was simply trying to fill a quota of its own and was willing to offer a job to any female applicant who came along.)

So, twelve resumes out and twelve follow-up emails for the twelve I had sent out the previous week, even the joke ones: that was my Monday morning routine. Admittedly, it wasn't the most efficient or effective way of looking for a job. I should have been checking websites and sending out resumes every day. But I'd found that that was too demoralizing. It wore me down to the point where I hardly sent my resume anywhere, no matter how promising a job listing looked. This way, the sending out of resumes and follow-ups to resumes was no more than an onerous weekly chore — it was manageable, sustainable. I did, occasionally, check my inbox for possible responses a bit more often than once a week.

I had just sent out my third resume of the morning when an instant message box connected to my personal email account opened in the lower right corner of the screen.

freemanofsteel003: How do I know this is really you?

freemanofsteel003 was one of Freeman's usernames. (He'd added the 003 for two reasons: first, because the name *freemanofsteel* without any numbers was already taken; and second, so that the end of the name would look like the number 1003 – October third was his birthday.)

My message back read:

saintmaddster666: its my email acct isnt it

freemanofsteel003: My question remains. How do I know it's you?

saintmaddster666: remember the time...

I described a few of the most embarrassing episodes from Freeman's childhood, mishaps and blunders he'd made me swear never to divulge to another living soul.

freemanofsteel003: Okay shut up! It's you!

saintmaddster666: tell me you didnt call the police

freemanofsteel003: I almost did.

That was a relief. My focus shifted to my other email account and I sent out another resume.

freemanofsteel003: Why are you so nervous about the police? What kind of trouble are you in this time?

saintmaddster666: no trouble things r great

freemanifsteel003: Why don't I believe you?

saintmaddster666: believe what you like

freemanofsteel003: Who was the guy who answered the phone the other day?

I wrote *just a guy* and crossed it out; I wrote *a friend* and crossed it out; I started to write *no one youd approve of* but crossed it out after the first few letters; I wrote *none of your business* and crossed it out; I wrote *a really sweet guy* and stared at the words on the screen a long time before hitting send.

Freeman fell silent. I went back to my job search, but part of my mind was imagining Freeman puzzling and fretting over my last message, writing messages of his own and crossing them out – warnings, reminders of all my past romantic train wrecks (all the ones he knew about anyway), snarky comments about my latest victims, predictions of yet another disaster.

I closed the tab on my personal email. Whatever Freeman had to say, I didn't want to hear it.

Harry wandered up the stairs and went into his bedroom. (I was sitting at the little desk in the second bedroom.) I heard quiet rustling: Harry making the bed.

A message appeared in my inbox. A company was interested in me. They were a US-based non-profit medical relief group; they contracted with the Federal Emergency Management Agency to provide on-the-ground assistance in the wake of all sorts of disasters. Would I be willing to travel within the fifty states (and potentially but rarely to such places as Puerto Rico and Guam) as the job required? Would I be available for a phone interview and, if so, how might I be reached? (I had found that it was better on a resume not to give any number than to give a disconnected one.)

My heart leapt, my mind started racing. This could be the perfect job for me. I tended to get antsy if a job got to feeling monotonous and that tended to bring out certain quirks in my personality which some people found off-putting, even unprofessional. But this job would never get monotonous – always a new place, always a new set of challenges. Even if some of my quirks did rise to the surface from time to time, my imagined new co-workers would see them as nothing more than my way of dealing with the stress of our wonderful and demanding (but uplifting) jobs. My hands flew across the keyboard as I typed out a response. They had not asked me to call them; they had asked me to provide a number so that they could call me. I would give them Harry's. When should I say I was available? Anytime? – or did that seem too desperate? Abruptly, I stopped typing. It occurred to be that maybe giving them Harry's number wasn't the best idea. Maybe I needed to reconnect my phone. Yes, that was definitely the thing to do. It was worth the money for a shot at this job. I'd run out and reconnect the phone, then race back here and answer their email. Or better yet – duh – once I had the phone working I could answer the email directly from my phone.

Harry appeared in the doorway. He smiled at me like I was his favorite pet – no, I was being unfair – he smiled at me, that's all: it was a nice smile, a trusting smile. He said, "I think I'll go run a few errands."

"Me, too," I said.

Harry looked perplexed. "I thought you were going to the gym."

"Yeah right, the gym – that's what I meant."

Alexis

Usually, my days off, if he was working, I kept still and waited for the little cocksucker to leave. He knew I was pretending, but he went along with it and pretended to be careful not to wake me. But that morning he decided to be cute. That morning he decided to carry on a conversation with me, a one-sided conversation, like I was sitting up against the headboard with my eyes wide open and my ears all pricked up, like I gave a shit about anything he had to say.

He started off harmless enough, gushing about how great it had been the night before, about how powerful I had been and yet so gentle, about how our new game was his favorite ever and how he hoped we would play it again. But then he started to stray onto shakier ground. To make matters worse, every now and then he would interrupt himself with a "don't you think so, too?" and then he would act like I'd answered him and he would say something like, "That's wonderful, Alexis darling, I was so hoping you would see it my way," or, "I'm so glad we agree." His voice started to crawl under my skin like an infestation of tiny spiders.

He suggested that one night we might try playing our new game with the roles reversed. He complained (not for the first time) that I'd never made my preferences clear to him when we started dating. He swore that he *loved* feeling me inside him but there were times when he longed to be the top and not the bottom and would I please consider it? "You will? – oh that's wonderful, Alexis, thank you so much!" I felt pressure building behind my eyes. It was becoming clearer to me with each passing day that Charlie was like all the other fags I ever fucked – trying to make *me* become just like *them*.

He announced that he was calling a halt to our other games, the rougher ones – and not just while his rib was healing. He wanted to stop them altogether, suspecting that they encouraged the violent tendencies I was more and more displaying. "You do understand, don't you, Alexis?...good, I knew you would." Under the covers, my hands balled into fists.

"And while we're on the subject of your violent behavior," he continued, "there are some ground rules we need to put in place." The little cocksucker ticked off his ground rules. There were three of them: I needed to admit I had a problem, I needed to seek help, I needed to promise never to hurt the little cocksucker again. The spiders under my skin grew larger, the points of their legs got a little sharper.

"Don't answer me now about the ground rules, give it some thought, okay? Maybe when I get home from work this evening you can have your answer ready for me, agreed? Oh good, I'm glad that's settled."

The whole time, he had been moving around the bedroom, getting himself fixed up for work. He kept going back and forth to the trunk under the window where he kept his clothes, trying on different things. (The closet and the chest of drawers were my territory.) The barrage of words stopped when he went into the bathroom, then he was back and the onslaught resumed.

"Maybe you could have dinner fixed when I come home, a real dinner, not just some snack tray. Could you do that for me, Alexis, dear? – oh thank you so much! That will be the plan for tonight. Then tomorrow night we'll go out and hit a few of the old haunts and visit with friends, isn't that a great idea? What's that? You were about to suggest the same thing yourself? Well, aren't you full of surprises? Oh, and one more thing concerning tonight's dinner, I'm going to throw you a challenge: I want you to surprise me with one unhealthy item on the menu and, whatever it is, we both have to share it equally. What do you say? Are you game? Life's too short to never pollute your body at least a little bit, don't you think?"

My stomach was churning. The little cocksucker had actually succeeded in raising my blood pressure: I could feel my veins throbbing.

"Oh, and one last thing. Can we please please please give up the pretense that we never dream? You were *so* dreaming last night. You were having a fight with that Barney guy you hate so much from work. I bet you're remembering that dream right now, aren't you? So can we please cut the crap about…"

I sprang from the bed. Tarantulas surged and clawed under my skin. One-handed, I grabbed the little cocksucker by the throat. He was too startled to be afraid. He cast those big brown eyes on me, wondering if we were playing one of our games. I reared back and hit him, landing a vicious open-handed blow to his temple. He gasped the way some people do at the scary parts of a horror movie. I hit him again, this time on the side of the mouth, and I shook him, my fingers digging in on either side of his windpipe.

Then the little cocksucker did something I wasn't expecting. He punched me in the gut. It wasn't a hard punch – he didn't have the muscle or the practice to put much force behind it – and it bounced harmlessly off me. He moved in close with the obvious intention of kneeing me in the groin. I stepped across his body as if trying to protect my privates, then I swept both his feet out from under him. I pushed his neck away hard, so that he would crack his head when he hit the floor — and that's exactly what happened. He lay there staring up at me, tears welling from those puppy dog eyes.

"Got anything else to say?" I growled.

His eyes rolled back in his sockets, just for a moment, then he was staring at me again, and I thought *oh great, he's on his way to work high as a fucking kite on oxycontin*. He struggled to his feet. He looked confused. He stood there, hunched and swaying. I was on guard in case the whole thing was an act and he was planning to lunge at me. He tried to speak but his words were slurred and they made no sense. He collapsed, falling heavily onto his knees then awkwardly backwards, his legs a tangle. His head hit the floor a second time.

"Goddammit!" I said.

"Motherfucker, don't do this to me!" I said.

His eyes were rolled back again. A narrow stream of saliva — or maybe it was vomit — ran from the little cocksucker's mouth, across his cheek and onto the floor.

"Charlie!" I said. "Charlie?"

Harry

She left before I did. I was in no particular rush. My errands were few: put gas in the truck, maybe get a haircut. Maddie, on the other hand, was really energized to go and hit the gym. When she got to the door, the rain was coming down so hard you could see it bouncing off the pavement in the parking lot. I urged her to take an umbrella but she laughed at the idea, pinched my belly and pecked me on the cheek, and dashed out into the storm. She was soaked by the time she got her car door open — soaked but smiling. One more thing to admire about her: the way she found something to enjoy in every moment. I couldn't help but smile myself. I watched her back out of the parking space. She'd been parked so crookedly, she nearly brushed the back bumper of my truck with her front bumper. She activated her headlights, started her windshield wipers furiously whipping back and

M. Jonquil

forth, and rolled away. Parked, her car had been sheltering a small rectangular patch of dry pavement. I watched the rain attack it, and in no more than a couple of heartbeats it was gone.

Maddie

I was in such a hurry to leave it didn't occur to me that I had no idea where to find a store operated by my phone carrier. Even after weeks without one, I was still accustomed to letting my phone guide me to wherever I wanted to go. Sitting in my car, idling at the exit from Harry's parking lot, wondering if I should turn left or right, I felt like such an idiot. Harry's computer could have told me what I needed to know in a second. Harry even kept the old-fashioned yellow pages in a drawer in his kitchen, but I didn't think to stop and consult that either. So, I had to make a detour to the library, where, old pro that I was at living out of my car, I knew they had not only computers with access to the internet but also the yellow pages. I used the yellow pages: it was faster.

The nearest phone store turned out to be in the shopping mall south of town. I raced to get there, even though my tires were too worn and slick to drive like that in the rain. I drove so fast I drew the attention of a police cruiser which followed me for maybe half a mile, forcing me to slow down. I think if it hadn't been raining so hard I would have gotten a ticket: lucky for me, the officer decided it wasn't worth his trouble to pull me over and have to get out of his car and get soaked.

There weren't many customers at the phone store. On the other hand there was only one sales associate – and each customer seemed to have a problem more complicated than an entire chapter out of one of Harry's physics books. But as minute after precious minute slipped away, it became increasingly apparent that the real problem was not with the customers but with Clyde, the sales associate. I knew both his name and his job title because he wore a large, orange nametag pinned to his even more orange company-issue polo shirt that read:

Hi! I'm **CLYDE**
<u>*your*</u>
sales associate

The name "Clyde" had been printed on the tag in thick, smudgy, black letters. Clyde was a young man — maybe mid-twenties — and he wore a size XX-large polo shirt despite the fact that he was half a foot shorter than I was, just to give you some idea of how large his belly was. He breathed through his mouth and, damn him to hell, was he ever a talker.

There I was, sick to my stomach that this errand was taking too long, that my dream job was slipping away, that I would finally pull up my email account on my newly activated phone and find that the request for an interview had been rescinded; and this rotund little sales associate, this *Clyde* would not stop blathering no matter how simple the question, no matter how obvious the answer. By the time he got to me I was ready to tear out his tongue. I quickly told him what I wanted. He started to innumerate the steps required to reactivate my phone. "*Just do it!*" I screamed, and people strolling in the wide mall corridor outside the store stopped and stared.

Alexis

My first impulse was to run. But it was my apartment — Charlie had moved in with me and not the other way around — so running was not an option, unfortunately. I cursed myself for my pigheadedness, for refusing to even consider moving into his larger space — if he'd been lying on the floor of his own apartment, I would have packed up all my shit and gotten the hell out of there.

His heartbeat was strong and regular. His breathing was shallow, sometimes ragged, sometimes steady. The muscles on the left side of his body — and particularly those in his left hand and forearm — jerked at random intervals. Tears streamed from his half-closed eyes and spit ran from his gaping mouth. His face, I thought, was slowly losing its color.

I knew I needed to call for an ambulance, but I hesitated. What would be my story? He suffered some kind of attack: one minute everything was fine then the next minute he was staggering, his legs buckled, and he hit his head when he fell. But what about the marks on his neck? He must have done that to himself — when the attack first came over him he was acting like something was caught in his throat and he was tearing at himself, crazy to get it out. Should I tell anyone about the pills he probably took that morning? I decided that I shouldn't. In fact, I did a quick sweep of the apartment, collecting all the pills I could find. Should I flush them or keep them? I decided to keep them — they might come in handy if I ever had to prove that whatever happened to Charlie was his own doing. I hid all the pills where I had found many of them — in Charlie's trunk.

Only then did I look for my phone. It wasn't on the bedside table where I often left it to charge overnight. It wasn't on the kitchen counter either — the other place I sometimes charged it. As I searched for the phone, a crazy idea was taking shape in my head.

Maddie

I sent the email providing my phone number while still in the store. My hands were shaking, I wanted that job so bad and I was so scared of missing out on it. However, I was immediately relieved to see that there were no new messages: the interview request had not been rescinded.

Message sent, I found myself strolling from one end of the mall to the other, mixing in with the few shoppers, mostly women, and with a small army of seniors who had no intention of buying anything: they were there simply to walk, simply to get in their recommended daily allowance of exercise. I could picture Harry among them in five or ten years — actually more like ten or twenty. The stroll was doing me good. It was helping to work off some of the stress of that morning.

My phone chirped, letting me know I had an incoming message. It was from Ekaterina, the HR person who had originally contacted me. She was emailing to ask when would be a good time to interview. Oops, I had forgotten to say. Impulsively, I typed: *now is good for me*. As soon as I pressed send, I worried that I had made a mistake — maybe Ekaterina would think I was too pushy, too desperate. A long couple of minutes passed. The response came back: *me too*. I felt elated — but also exposed. I didn't want to do this interview in a public place. This was potentially a major turning point in my life. I hurried away.

I did the interview in my car. Luckily, I had parked in the lower deck of the mall's parking garage, so there was no rain drumming on the roof. The car was a good setting: quiet and private and well-known to me. There were no other cars parked close by. Ekaterina's accent was hard to pin down – Midwestern, if I had to guess, with hints of the Northeast – like she had grown up in Iowa but gone to school in Boston. Her voice was vibrant and energetic, but I didn't picture her as youthful. Rather, she struck me as a woman who had experienced a lot, good and bad, and had learned along the way to celebrate the good and to dismiss the bad. From the start of our conversation I liked her, and I sensed that she liked me. Soon we were talking like old friends. She explained that what we were doing was a "pre-interview," so that we could "cover some basics," and that if the pre-interview went well, then the full hiring committee (Ekaterina plus three others) would want to talk to me, by phone or by Skype, perhaps as soon as later in the week. The basics had to do with the travel requirements of the job, the enormous range of emergencies their staff was called upon to respond to, the difficulties they often faced, sometimes even dangers, the crazy long hours when they were in the field, and the need for me, should I be offered the job, to relocate to the DC-area. On that last point, Ekaterina said, "It looks like you're about three hundred miles away…" (I had given Harry's address on all my recently sent resumes.) "…that going to be a problem?" I assured her that it would not be a problem.

At the end of our conversation, Ekaterina said, "So, normally at this point I tell a candidate I need to touch base with the other members of the hiring committee and I'll get back to you about scheduling a more complete interview – but in your case, given your background and how well we've hit it off, I feel confident enough to go ahead and schedule the interview. How about tomorrow right about this same time?"

I said that would be perfect.

Ekaterina asked, "Any chance we can do it by Skype?"

I hesitated, and Ekaterina laughed, saying, "I don't blame you…I know how it is…shouldn't be about looks, right?…looks and age…but how often does a potential boss size you up on just those two factors… believe me, I know, I've been there…I promise you that's not how we operate, but if you're more comfortable doing it by phone, we'll do it by phone. Once I've checked with the other committee members I'll send you a text confirming for tomorrow. Talk to you then!"

Harry

Only two barbers were working in the shop that morning. So there was a bit of a wait, but I didn't mind – I wasn't in any hurry. I knew both of the barbers, of course: I was a regular there, I had been going to that shop for years. I even knew one of the guys in the chair, another regular. We were all chatting.

My phone rang. I answered without looking to see who it was. It turned out to be Doug from work. He wanted to know if I was looking at the hour-by-hour forecast. I assured him that I was not.

"All this rain's going to clear out by one today...two o'clock at the latest."

"Doug, you're not seriously suggesting..."

"Listen, that developer is riding me like you wouldn't believe!"

"It's got to be a mudpit out there."

"We're mostly up on scaffolds now."

"It's getting dark earlier...we'd spend more time setting up and cleaning up than we would laying block."

"There's another big line of storms moving in right behind this one, and there's likely going to be some snow...we got to be out there every chance we get...it's the only way we'll ever get finished...I need you there, Harry."

I sighed. Was there any point in reminding Doug that it was the developer's own fault he was so far behind, not ours? No, there was not.

"All right," I said. "I'll see you when the rain stops."

Alexis

What if I could get Charlie out of here without anyone seeing? What if I could dump him somewhere? That was the idea that was coursing through my brain. If I could do that, if some stranger found him lying in an alley or maybe in a park, then it would look exactly like what it was: somebody had attacked him and Charlie had banged his head. My first story – that Charlie had had some kind of seizure – the more I thought about it, the more I worried it wouldn't fly. Too much history of this kind of thing in my past. Charlie knew nothing about it, of course, but I had been in court more than once on domestic violence charges. Worse than that was what happened with Wilfredo, the little cocksucker before Charlie – "my little Haitian fag," I used to call Wilfredo just to needle him because he was really from the Dominican Republic. Things ended very badly between me and Wilfredo – so badly in fact that the district attorney originally threatened to bring attempted murder charges against me. My lawyer worked them down to aggravated assault, and in the end I pled guilty to simple assault and never spent a single day in jail. I think it worked in my favor that Wilfredo's immigration status was not altogether clear. All this happened in a different town on the other end of the state.

I visualized hoisting Charlie onto my shoulder, carrying him down two flights of stairs and stuffing him into the backseat of one of our cars. It would have to be his car – mine was parked blocks away, but Charlie had been so pleased with himself the day before that he'd found a spot right in front of the door. I felt certain I could carry him that far – he was almost as tall as me but so much skinnier.

I decided it was worth a shot. If I could get him out of the apartment with no one seeing, I'd be practically in the clear. Finding a place to dump him couldn't be too hard. On the other hand, if anyone did see, then I'd go back to the original story and say Charlie had a seizure and I was taking him to the hospital. I'd be no worse off than if I called for an ambulance, which was really my only other option.

Charlie was twitching noticeably less. Also his breathing had fallen into a regular rhythm – no more ragged patches. It was almost as if he were asleep. If he would only stop drooling.

I hurriedly gathered my clothes, which were somewhat scattered about the place as a result of our game the night before. That's when I found my phone. It was in my pants pocket.

Maddie

I was in training mode. For the next twenty-four hours, I was in training to ace that interview. My plan was to eat healthy, get plenty of rest and plenty of exercise, take my antidepressants strictly on schedule. No unhappy thoughts, no troubling emotional exchanges, no stress of any kind. No booze (well, maybe a little red wine in the evening with Harry would be okay). And especially no crazy antics in bed, nothing so outlandish that it leaves you on edge, saying to yourself *did we really just do that?* The only sex I was interested in over the next twenty-four hours was the kind that leaves you feeling blissfully drained and utterly relaxed. Harry wouldn't mind: that was the kind of sex he liked best, and he and I were getting better and better at it all the time.

I left the mall and drove to the gym. Not only would I be getting a good start on my training but I would be somewhat nullifying the lie I'd told Harry earlier as to where I was going.

Driving from the mall to the gym, I cruised right past the entrance to Harry's apartment complex. There was no need to turn it: my gym clothes were already in the car. The rain seemed to be letting up a little. I wondered if Harry would be able to work the next day. I hoped he would. I hoped he'd be able to get up good and early, as usual, and be out the door long before the call came for my interview. I didn't want to have to lie to him again, didn't want the feeling again that I was sneaking out of the house. Of course, I'd sworn to myself not to breathe a word about the interview to Harry, not until it was a *fait accompli*. Maybe not even then – why cause him to worry about a job offer that, no matter how well the interview went, might never come?

I was standing in the women's locker room at the gym in my panties, just slipping a sports bra over my head, when I caught the faintest hint of my phone inside my gym bag signaling to me that I had a text message. I supposed it was Freeman and almost ignored it. But something made me check. It was Ekaterina.

> *Change of plans. But only if you're up for it! As it happens, the gang's all here right now. Tomorrow won't work for some on the team and the next window when all are available will be late next week. Any chance you can do the interview sooner? Like now? So sorry to spring this on you. And if you want to wait til next week, that is totally fine. Will not impact your chances of getting the job one way or the other, I promise. If possible, please let me know in the next half hour. Thanks. And once again my apologies. Kat*

Harry

I drove home. Maddie was still at the gym. I laid my work clothes across the bed and puttered around in my puttering around clothes. The flowers Maddie had placed on the nightstand on her side of the bed had wilted, and I carried them downstairs and threw them away and put into the recycling bin the wine bottle Maddie had transformed into a vase. The flowers on the dining room table looked like they still had a little life left in them and I gave them some water. There were no dishes to clean, as I had taken care of all that earlier. I flipped through the two books on the side table next to my reading chair, but could not concentrate on either of them, could not even bring myself to sit in the chair. I felt a restlessness, almost an uneasiness, that I couldn't quite define or explain − (I don't think I'm adding that in from hindsight: I truly believe I felt it). I paced, stopping every now and then to glance out the window, watching the rain turn to a light drizzle.

I fixed myself another cup of instant coffee, drinking it quickly and washing the mug and spoon so that no one would fuss at me about my abysmal lack of discernment when it came to coffee. I wondered how long Maddie would be at the gym.

My phone signaled that I had a text. It was Doug. *Clear skies in one hour.* About a minute later he called; I didn't answer. He left a voicemail, which I listened to − did I get his text? I texted back *roger that, preparing for blastoff in T minus one hour.*

I went upstairs to put on my work clothes, and while I was dressing I heard a car pull up in front of the apartment. From the sound of the engine − its minute, peculiar knocks and tings − I was certain it was Maddie's car.

Alexis

I heard people coming and going and I waited and waited until the building fell completely silent. I lost track of how long I waited.

It was a struggle to get Charlie off the floor. But once I had him over my shoulder, getting him to the car was almost easy. I had already pocketed my wallet and Charlie's keys. I opened the door and stepped into the hall. I glanced down the three flights of stairs. As far as I could see, they were empty. I made my way to the second floor landing, then to the lobby, moving without hurry. A feeling had come over me that there was no need to hurry: whatever was going to happen in the next few moments was fated to happen: I would either make it to the car unseen or I would be forced to take my chances bringing Charlie to the hospital: the decision was out of my hands.

Sometimes luck is with you. It was looking like it was with me that day.

At the car, I slipped Charlie from my shoulder, pinning him in a more or less upright position to the side of the car with my body. I opened the rear door of his little sedan, sat him down on the seat, bending his head forward so that he wouldn't bump it yet again. I held his wrists as he gently fell backwards then I scooted him onto the seat as far as he would go. I folded his legs until his feet were inside, and shut the door.

I stood there next to the car, looking all around, up and down the street and at every window in sight. Light rain was falling from a rapidly clearing sky. As far as I could tell, I had gotten away with it. While I stood there, I suddenly knew where I would dump Charlie – Greenleaf Park. The idea came to me almost like a revelation. It was nearby and he went there from time to time, so it would not be strange if he were found there. Also, there was one particular corner of the park where various drugs could be purchased. I wouldn't dump him right on that corner, in case the police were surveilling – but close enough to make it seem he might have come from there. Perhaps it would look like he'd been attacked and robbed.

I opened the rear door again and reached inside. I went through Charlie's pockets and removed his wallet, also the cash I knew he carried separately in his front pants pocket. It was good that he would be without his wallet – that might give me some additional time before he was identified. Of course, I took his phone as well. I briefly considered running upstairs and grabbing a few of his pills and planting them on him. Let them think he was a user or a dealer himself – he'd get less sympathy and no one would make much of an effort to find out who he was or who had attacked him. But I decided that leaving him in the car like that for any passerby to see was tempting fate a bit too far.

On the way to the park, I really regretted not being able to add that little touch with the pills. My mind kept circling back to it. A thought occurred to me, and at the next red light I quickly riffled through Charlie's glovebox. Sure enough, under a pile of old vehicle registration cards and of unused paper napkins from a variety of fast food restaurants, there was a clear, plastic baggie with a couple of pills. Perfect! It was like an omen that this crazy scheme was going to work. The light changed and I continued toward the park, strategizing about where I would plant the incriminating evidence. If I left them in one of his pockets, that might look strange – why hadn't his attacker also stolen the pills? I determined that I would stash them inside one of his socks.

Maddie

He was standing in the bedroom, pulling on a checkered flannel shirt over a thermal underwear top and a t-shirt. He also wore his thermal underwear bottoms and at least two layers of socks. His tough, loose-fitting work khakis lay on the bed.

"Why on earth are you putting on your work clothes?" I wondered.

He explained about the window of clear weather before the next batch of storms, the pressure his crew was under to get the job done.

"Does this pushy developer think you're building him an ark?"

"Maybe so," Harry laughed. He gazed at me appreciatively. "You must have showered at the gym. Did you have a good workout?"

There was not the least hint of suspicion in his comment: he was utterly trusting and guileless I opened my mouth to tell him the truth – I wanted so much to share with him my excitement about this possible new job – and not a word came out.

He said, "It must have been the best workout ever, judging by the look on your face."

But the look on my face was rapidly changing as excitement gave way to confusion – what was I going to tell Harry?

He noticed the change. "I'll never be able to figure you out," he murmured.

His gray hair was freshly cut, and I could smell the slightly musky, slightly antiseptic tang of barber's lotion. His hair was not military short but near enough so that with the hard, clean lines of his face and that trim, muscular body showing through his tight-fitting thermal underwear he was like the image of some military hero – a colonel, say, battle-hardened and ready for anything – preparing to lead his troops into yet one more fight. He possessed an air of command which, I suppose, I would have found attractive under any circumstances but which was causing me to feel a slow burn, and I knew it was only a matter of time before the slow burn would threaten to ignite. At least part of the appeal for me was that Harry was completely unaware of this air he possessed or of the power it held over me.

"Take that flannel shirt off for me," I said. My voice was deep and throaty.

"Do what?" Harry smiled.

"You heard me, mister." Sometimes I get bossy when I wouldn't mind being bossed myself.

"But I can't stay…Doug's counting on…"

"You heard me." After the flannel shirt came off, I said, "Now the t-shirt."

I couldn't get enough of the sight of him. Maybe somewhere in the back of my mind I was trying to memorize him, preparing for the time that was fast approaching when I wouldn't have him anymore. I studied his musculature, his legs and thighs, like those of a mountain-climber, his flat boxer's stomach, his swelling chest and shoulders, his sinewy, thick arms. I would have liked to move all around him, to study him like a statue. But I could tell that he was uneasy and somewhat embarrassed, also still impatient to get to work. I cooed into his ear, "You can be a few minutes late, can't you Harry?" "Sure," he whispered. It was plain from the lack of bulge between his legs that he wasn't at all turned on by this treatment I was giving him, but I didn't care – I was doing what I wanted to do. I was doing it while simultaneously wishing he would turn the tables on me and start giving me orders. Part of me still longed for him to bend me over his knee and spank me, although I had decided days ago that he wasn't the least bit into that sort of thing.

It was strange but the tight-fitting thermal underwear had the effect of idealizing him somehow. I have already mentioned that I would've liked to have treated him like a statue. But what he most reminded me of in that moment was a superhero. Don't get me wrong – I didn't lose sight of the reality before me: here was an older guy in amazing good shape, given his age, with a handsome but weather-beaten face standing reluctantly on display in his underwear. Actually maybe I did lose sight in that moment of who he really was. My strongest impression, looking back, is that I was profoundly confused. I think in that moment I came as close as I ever have to truly falling in love with a man. But there's something in me that always sabotages the process. Whatever that something is, it is powerful and subversive, and it kicks into high gear whenever an even vaguely attractive man comes into my life, much less someone like Harry. Typically what I do is I find the man's worst flaws, I take them into myself, then I attack him with them until I drive him away. (I tell you this as a mental health professional with years of analysis behind her, not to mention a lifetime of self-evaluation and self-diagnosis.) In Harry's case, my inner saboteur was finding a new method. It was making him into something unobtainable, something too far beyond me, a superman, a man without flaws — Super Harry! Maybe none of what I've just said makes any sense.

Harry

Maddie came home acting weird — you could even say "totally weird."

For instance, she told me that I looked like a superhero in what she called my "thermal underwear." I laughed at this and replied that I knew it for a fact that a guy had to be at least six feet tall and younger than forty to qualify for his superhero union card, and, besides, what I was wearing was just light cotton long-drawers and a long-sleeved undershirt: the real, heavy-duty thermal underwear didn't come out of storage until it was winter and the laborers started mixing anti-freeze into the mortar. Maddie reacted as if I'd said the most seductive thing a man ever thought to say to a woman. She threw herself onto me, kissing me furiously, and soon we were rolling together on the bed, entangled in each other's arms.

She begged me to tear her clothes off. She told me I could fuck her any way I liked, I could fuck her up the ass if I wanted, I could rape her, just so long as I didn't take off my long underwear. It was something like our first night together when Maddie was trying to get in touch with my dark side — like that but different: then, when she offered me "anything I wanted," it sprang naturally, it seemed to me, from a recklessness and curiosity that was at the core of her personality. This time, her offer – her offering of her body – was coming from somewhere else. I didn't know what to make of it, but instinctively I didn't like this new place it was coming from.

We continued to wrestle on the bed but suddenly I felt that I was in the midst of a minefield, that a single false move could blow us apart. *Should* I tear her clothes off? *Should* I get rough with her? Did Maddie really crave that kind of treatment? That first question about tearing off her clothes was rapidly becoming moot: I wasn't tearing anything, but I was industriously removing one of Maddie's flimsy layers after another with her enthusiastic assistance. But what to do about the second question? What if I attempted such a thing and she resisted? Would I be stepping on a mine if I forced the issue? Was there another mine to step on if I backed off? And what to make of her strange request concerning my long underwear?

Meanwhile, I had peeled away enough of her layers so that Maddie's midriff was exposed, and I was busy kissing and nipping and licking the skin all around her belly button. This was not a thing she taught me: this was something I had discovered on my own. The first time I did it, I was just being playful – and there was no nipping or licking involved, only kissing. Almost immediately, Maddie had started to squirm and to moan. She'd been no less surprised than I was to discover how turned on it made her. So, I had taught her something about her own body: I genuinely regarded it as one of my proudest moments. Since that first time, the technique had evolved and each time I did it it became more pleasurable for both of us.

This time, however, I had barely started when Maddie grabbed me by the hair – or tried to: my hair was too short to really get a hold of – failing that, she grabbed my ears and pulled me away.

She sat up and peered into my face. "You're thinking too hard," she accused.

I didn't know how to respond. It was true, of course. I was trying to understand that intuitive feeling that something was off, trying to figure out what I should do. But I couldn't find the words to say any of that to Maddie. I sat up opposite her.

Maddie continued to undress as she spoke. "Turn your mind off, Harry…I need you to just be with me…I need you to not ask any questions right now…"

"I don't understand…" I began but Maddie shushed me.

Since she was undressing I thought I should too. I started to pull my long-sleeved undershirt off over my head. Maddie grabbed my wrists. "Don't!" she whispered urgently. "I wasn't kidding about the underwear – I want you to keep it on."

"See, that's what I'm talking about..." I protested but again Maddie silenced me. She was topless now and she silenced me by pulling my face to her breasts and putting one of her nipples into my mouth.

She ran her hands through my hair and I thought I heard her murmur something about wishing she could put a cape and a mask on me. I was getting more and more confused.

Charlie

I woke up in the backseat of my car. I sat up. There was Alexis in the front seat, driving. He was very tense, very focused. His hands were gripping the steering wheel with such force...it reminded me of something but I couldn't remember what. He was holding onto that steering wheel so hard I actually worried that he might pull the thing loose – and *then* where would we be, I wondered. *We'd be up shit's creek*, I answered myself, *with plenty of paddle but no rudder*. Yee-hah!

I had intended to simply say *hi* to Alexis but I think instead I actually yelled out Y*ee-hah!* There was a buzzing in my head and it was confusing me. In any event, Alexis let out a yelp of his own and jumped so violently I thought he might have given himself whiplash straining against his seatbelt.

"You okay?" I asked.

He glanced back at me. "What?" he said.

"You okay?" I repeated.

"Yeah yeah, I'm fine. How about you, Charlie? You okay?"

"I'm fine, too," I said.

He threw me another worried glance.

Alexis

He was slurring his words. Not terribly but enough to make him hard to understand.

I probed to discover what he remembered from this morning. As far as I could tell, he was saying he didn't remember anything. I immediately lapsed into my story that he'd had a sudden seizure; I explained to him that I feared he was suffering from a stroke and I was rushing him to the hospital. (Of course, my plan of dumping him had to be abandoned the moment he sat up and spoke.)

He said, I think, "Oh okay, that's nice."

I kept an eye on him through the rear-view mirror. He had a look of blank innocence on his face that put me in mind of Stan Laurel from the old comedy team of Laurel & Hardy, also maybe the Scarecrow from *The Wizard of Oz*. Absently smiling, Charlie gazed at the passing scenery. A moment passed. He slurred, "Greenleaf Park isn't on the way to the hospital." Another moment. His eyes met mine in the rear-view mirror. He frowned at me; his fingers touched the bruises on his throat.

Maddie

Both our phones made various noises and were ignored.

When we finally came up for air, the last rays of afternoon sunlight were slanting through the windows. I remember hazily thinking: *well, would you look at that — the weather really did clear up*.

When I checked my phone, I found a *welcome back!* message from my service provider, electronically high-fiving me for reinstated my service. I also found a slew of junk messages, and a two-word message from Ekaterina: *You're hired!* My heart leapt.

Harry said, "Hey, your phone's working now!"

I gave him no explanations and he didn't ask for any.

There were some texts and a voicemail on Harry's phone, all from that boss of his, Doug. Harry listened to the voicemail, and I could hear Doug's tinny voice screeching in Harry's ear: *Goddammit, Harry, you said you'd be here, I was counting on you, where the fuck are you, you better have a damn good reason...* It went on and on. Harry listened to the entire message; his face was grave.

"Sorry," I said when it ended.

"Not your fault."

"Um, excuse me...?"

Harry gave me a weak smile. He reached out and stroked my thigh with the knuckles of a half-closed, upturned hand. "Just saying if I choose not to go to work, ultimately it's on me, you know?...I'm not trying to leave you out of the equation but I'm not blaming you, either... I'm just saying: at the end of the day, I'm responsible for my own actions."

"Of course you are."

Harry studied me, suspecting I was mocking him or teasing him. I wasn't.

I said, "Will he fire you?"

"Who? – Doug? I don't think so. Not while this big job is hanging over his head."

My own head was swimming, my heart was racing – *I'm hired!* – but I did my best to hold up my end of the conversation with Harry. "So, why the concerned look?"

Harry was at a loss, not knowing what "look" I was talking about. "I'm not concerned," he said; "I'm just bothered that I let Doug down, that's all. I can't say I think all that highly of the guy, but I told him I'd be there and then I let him down and it bothers me."

"Of course it does."

"Would you stop saying that!"

I leaned forward and planted a kiss between Harry's eyes. That was all I'd intended to do but my body must have had ideas of its own and an unconscious momentum kept me moving forward until I was on top of him. I was entirely naked; he still wore his long underwear, which was more than a little damp now from perspiration. I tried to mount him but he protested that he needed a break. I persisted until he lifted me off with those powerful arms of his and gently set me down beside him on the bed.

Harry

It was a little thing, an unimportant turn in our conversation, but it stuck with me. Maddie asked if Doug would fire me. I said I didn't think so, not while we still had this big rush job to do. And that satisfied her. She moved on. Most people, I think, would have asked one more question: *but what about after the big rush job — aren't you worried that you might get fired then?* But Maddie's mind didn't work that way. If a problem was solved in the short term, it was solved — case closed. The long-term was someone else's worry.

Alexis

"Lay down, Charlie, close your eyes, rest…I'll have you at the hospital in no time."

He tried to catch my eye again in the rear-view mirror but I wouldn't look at him. He did as he was told.

I turned at the next intersection and headed toward the hospital, but after a few blocks I veered off in a different direction. What was I doing?! I asked myself that question over and over. Part of me seriously didn't know what the plan was.

A voice that was mine but was not mine said inside my head *Charlie's going to be good as new, he just needs a little fresh air, that's all, we're just going to take him for a little drive in the country.*

"I can't believe I'm even joking around about this," I said to myself.

That other voice inside my head made no reply.

"We'll go a few more blocks, then that's it, joke's over, we're turning around for the hospital," I said to myself.

Silence.

"I refuse to be a party to this," I said to myself.

Harry

The sun must have dropped behind the trees on the far side of the parking lot. The light coming in through the windows was softer, cooler, grayer. "Supposed to get cold tonight – and more rain moving in," I said, still feeling bad about leaving Doug in the lurch. I turned my head to look at Maddie and found her looking at me. "What are you thinking?" I asked. "Nothing," she murmured.

She was lying on her side with her legs curled in front of her and her arms held close to her chest.

"Are you cold?" I asked. "I should go turn up the heat." I started to get up.

"No you don't!" Maddie insisted, "that's my job," and she sprang up onto her knees and pushed me back down. She leaned over me and kissed me, dangling her breasts before my eyes. She said, "Tonight I'm your servant, your naked bondslave, if you want the heat turned up all you have to do is order me to do it."

As she spoke, Maddie began to delicately peel the condom from my shrunken penis. She slipped off the bed and disposed of the thing in the bathroom. She returned and posed in the doorway, head down, hands clasped demurely before her pubic hairs.

"Does the Master wish for the heat to be turned up?" she asked in a low, servile voice.

"Yes," I said, stifling a "thanks."

"Does the Master wish for wine to be brought to the bedchamber?"

"Yes," I said.

"May his bondslave presume to bring a glass for herself?"

"Yes, she may."

She turned to leave, paused, glanced over her shoulder and said, "Will the Master have fresh orders for his bondslave when she returns?"

Alexis

How would we do it?
We'll get some rope maybe, strangle him.
Get some rope where?
At a store. They got rope in stores.
And then...what? Just dump the body?
Maybe better if we bury it.
What if somebody sees us?
No one will see us. We'll find a secluded spot.
You got a shovel in your back pocket I don't know about?
It's the same as the rope. We'll buy one in a store.

Sometimes it was a conversation in my head, sometimes I found myself speaking out loud.

I don't like it. What if somebody happens to remember our license plate number?

People don't sit around memorizing license plate numbers for no reason...anyway, it's his car, so how would that implicate us?

What if somebody remembers us from the store where we buy the rope and the shovel?

Not likely, especially if no one finds the body — or if no one finds it for a long time.

We were outside the city limit on a two-lane highway that was becoming more rural with every mile. I wondered where I'd be able to buy some rope and a shovel. I kept my eyes open for something like a hardware store or a farm supply store. Probably a good idea to also buy a pair of work gloves, I decided...

It can't be this easy to kill somebody, or people would be doing it all the time.
Who knows? Maybe they do.

...and a couple of plants, to make the other items look less suspicious. I hadn't bothered to count the cash I'd taken from Charlie's pants pocket. I wondered if there would be enough for everything I needed.

Harry

I tried to concoct orders for my servant, my naked bondslave, but my mind stayed stubbornly blank. Why was Maddie always putting me in these situations? I wondered if this roleplaying was something normal couples did all the time but I, somehow, had no aptitude for it — like dancing. I couldn't help remembering when Maddie had invited me to dance — a few days ago, half a lifetime ago — and I had had to confess I didn't dance. I remembered how clumsy and clueless I'd felt. I was feeling the same way now.

Almost imperceptibly, the curtains rippled and swayed as air flowed through the vent in the ceiling above the windows. It wasn't particularly warm air: the heat system in that apartment was slow to work. I felt uncomfortable in my damp cotton underwear, both too covered up and a little clammy, so I took them off, stripping naked, tossing them into a corner. I figured since I was the Master and Maddie was my bondslave, her orders regarding my underwear no longer applied. I propped the pillows against the headrest and arranged myself in a sitting position, an emperor on his improbably bed-shaped throne. I covered myself halfway with a sheet and one of the blankets.

Maddie

There was still plenty of daylight coming through the windows, and I moved about the kitchen without turning on any electric lights. I was getting myself worked up imagining any number of kinky things Harry might order me to do, while at the same time I was trying to stay in my role as bondslave and pretending to dread those same vile acts that I would soon be forced by my Master to perform. The only wine in the house was the inexpensive stuff I had purchased. I felt bad about that. I wished I could bring to the bedchamber of my Master something that would please him. But there was no helping it — at least there would be no need for a corkscrew: all the remaining bottles had twist-off caps. As I took down two wine glasses it occurred to me that perhaps my Master would want to punish his bondslave for this inferior offering. I felt my juices flow. Then suddenly I felt I was being watched.

My eyes darted from window to window then all around the room. No one there.

At the top of the stairs, an even stranger feeling came over me. I was just outside the open door to Harry's bedroom. There wasn't a sound coming from within yet something made me hesitate, some sense that Harry was not alone in there, that I would be walking in on something, interrupting something. I didn't know what to do. I felt foolish loitering bare-ass naked in that shadowy narrow hallway. But I couldn't move forward. I was certain – and it terrified me – that if I stepped through that doorway I would find Harry in the arms of the ghost of Suzanne.

A figure appeared in the doorway, silhouetted against the fading light coming in through the bedroom windows. I screamed, dropped the wine and the glasses. The figure gasped and recoiled.

It was Harry, of course, every bit as naked as I was. He stammered an apology for scaring me; he explained that he'd heard the stairs creek then became puzzled when I didn't appear. The bottle of wine remained intact and I had not yet screwed off the cap – so no damage there – but both glasses were broken, snapped in two at the stems. Harry picked up the bottle, which had rolled in his direction. He stepped forward and nudged the broken glasses aside with his bare foot. He held out a hand to me. "Step over the spot," he said, "in case there are shards." "You're naked," I all but accused: this was not how I wanted him; this was sabotaging my sabotage. While Harry cocked his head, no doubt trying to make sense of my odd tone, I muttered, "I should go – to the kitchen, I mean, to get more glasses." "Nah," Harry said. He held up the wine bottle as if to indicate that we had the essential thing, no need for anything more.

Inside the bedroom, I couldn't help myself, I looked all around for signs of Suzanne. Harry was still holding my hand and he led me to the bed. I felt cool air circulating from the vent in the ceiling. We sat and Harry opened the wine, twisting off the cap with an effortless slow turn of his wrist, and passed the bottle to me for the first taste. I wanted a big, sloppy pull of that wine but I took a lady-like sip. I held the bottle out to Harry but he wouldn't take it. "Drink," he said. Had he sensed the insufficiency of that sip? Was he starting to read me like I could read him? I filled my mouth with wine and let it run down my throat in a slow stream. I handed the bottle to Harry and heard the wine quietly go *glug-glug* as he drank.

Alexis

It must have been late afternoon. The rain had completely given way to blustery sunshine. Up ahead on the left was a promising-looking place for the supplies I needed. The closer I got, the more perfect it looked. According to the placard above the entrance, it was a Feed & Seed store – *Charlie's* Feed & Seed, in fact. I was finding that there was no such thing as a coincidence on the day you set out to kill somebody. Everything was an omen, either good or bad. After a little thought, I decided that the name of this place was a good omen: what do you do with a seed? – you plant it, and that was exactly what I was going to do with Charlie. There was not a single car in the gravel parking lot, but a glowing neon *open* sign in the front window of the run-down store gave me hope it was still in business. The empty parking lot was potentially yet another good omen: the fewer people who laid eyes on me the better.

I parked away from the front door. My thinking was: if anyone else happened by, they would not park near me, they would park closer to the front door, and therefore they would not notice Charlie sprawled across the backseat.

I checked on Charlie before I went into the store. His hands were tucked under his head. He was asleep – or unconscious – blowing little bubbles of spit between his lips every time he exhaled.

The gravel in the parking lot consisted of tiny white pebbles. Walking across that pea gravel was almost like walking on sand. It crunched and shifted under the soles of my shoes.

As I approached the store, it became clear that there was merchandise displayed in the dusty windows, and there were lights on inside. The front door was unlocked. A bell attached to the top of the door chimed as I entered. A long rack of shovels and other farm tools – pitch forks, hoes, mattocks – stood just beside the front door, as if they had been placed there exclusively for my convenience. There were shovels with long handles and shovels with short handles, shovels with square ends and shovels with pointy ends, shovels with wide digging blades and shovels so oddly curved or so narrow they had to be for some special purpose that I could only wonder at. I chose a pointy shovel, medium-width, with a short handle: I didn't think a long-handled one would fit inside the modest trunk of Charlie's car.

The voice of an elderly man beckoned from the back of the store. "Hey there! Who all's that?"

"Just me," I called. "Just a customer."

"If ya want help, Charlaine'll be back in bout half n'hour."

"I think I can find what I need – thanks!"

I heard the old man grumbling to himself. "Thinks he knows what he *needs*…ain't much a man *needs*…"

The shovel was marked twenty dollars – nineteen ninety-nine, to be exact. I reached into my pocket and brought out Charlie's money. Thirty-eight dollars. I found a display of work gloves next. The cheapest pair was four ninety-nine. I tried them on – they fit great: another good omen. I turned a corner and before me was every variety of rope. What else could this be but one more good omen? It was as if the very universe was conspiring with me to do this thing. The universe was telling me: *strangling is really the best way – no blood, little mess.* Surveying all the different kinds of rope, I found it hard to decide. I stood there wavering, knowing I was being stupid: the longer I stayed in that store, the more likely it was that someone else would walk in, and that would be one more person who might possibly recognize me. I just needed to decide. I picked a hundred-foot length of clothesline rope wrapped in clear plastic. It was, of course, far more rope than I needed – but it was on special for seven ninety-nine, and clothesline rope seemed so innocent. I remembered my own mother hanging clothes out on a clothesline: she must have bought clothesline rope.

Okay, so in round numbers I had a shovel for twenty, gloves for five, rope for eight. That was thirty-three dollars, not counting sales tax. That didn't leave a lot of money to buy plants.

Just then, the old man called out, "You still doin' okay?"

"Doing fine," I answered. "You got any two- or three-dollar plants?"

"Charlaine'll be back in bout half n'hour," the old man repeated, making it sound like a complaint.

I decided to ditch the plant idea and get the hell out of there. I brought my purchases to the counter at the back of the store.

Maddie

Harry held out the bottle. "More?" he offered.

"You're supposed to be ordering me around, not asking me what I want."

"In that case," he said, turning and setting the wine bottle on the nearest nightstand, "that's enough wine for now. Get under the covers."

"You're only telling me to do that because you see I'm cold."

"Yeah? So?"

"You should make me open the window and stand in front of it."

He thought it over, picturing me standing there naked. "The neighbors might like that," he said; "I don't think I would. Get under the covers."

I obeyed my Master.

Harry crawled in beside me and we huddled together, shivering in each other's arms.

Harry said, "You must have turned on the air conditioning by mistake."

I said, "I didn't turn anything on."

Harry pulled away to get a look at my face. "When you went to get the wine...weren't you going to turn up the heat?"

"I forgot," I said. "I thought you must have done it. When I came back to the bedroom I felt air coming out of the vent."

We both looked at the vent. From beneath the covers it was hard to tell if any air was coming out. Harry got out of bed and stood directly under the vent. "Nothing," he said. He ran a finger over the curtains, making them ripple. "That's strange," he said. He left the room and I heard him go softly down the stairs. A long moment later he returned to the room and quickly rejoined me under the covers. I could feel the cold on his skin.

He said, "The heat's turned up now...the place will warm up soon enough."

The curtains stirred.

Alexis

The old man behind the counter was blind. He sat in a wheelchair with one leg propped straight out in front of him in a kind of metal stirrup that was attached to the chair. He wasn't wearing shoes or socks on either foot, and the mottled skin of his feet, brown on top, gray on the edges and underneath, was as wrinkled as old parchment, and the big toe was missing from the foot that was propped. And he was blind! That old man was blind. Could there be a better omen? Could there be a better indication that I was about to commit the perfect crime?

"Find what ya' was lookin' for?"

"Yeah, I sure did."

"What ya' got there?"

His empty, pink-white eyes couldn't really be said to be looking at anything, but judging by the set of his neck, the direction of his face, he seemed to be addressing some invisible person a few feet to my left. I was tempted not to mention the shovel, to pay for the cheaper items and to walk out of there with the shovel, too. But it occurred to me that this old man's hearing might be exceptionally keen. He might well have heard me picking through the shovels – it was certainly possible that he'd heard me set the shovel again the counter just a moment ago.

I slipped the rope into my back pocket. "I got a shovel and a pair of work gloves," I said.

He asked me what the prices were and I told him.

He frowned at the price I reported for the gloves. "Must be them cheap cloth ones...they ain't good for nuthin', won't last one day of real work...might wanna think about switchin' them out."

I assured him they'd be fine for the job I had in mind.

He grumbled as if speaking to another invisible someone sitting right beside him, as if I weren't anywhere within earshot, "Cain't be much of a job if no 'count gloves like those is goin' be *fine*." He cocked his head like he was listening, then he cackled as if the person sitting next to him had made an outrageously funny joke. Then, peering once again at the invisible person standing to my left, he said that I should just add a dollar to the total as he wasn't good at figuring the sales tax, so that would be twenty-six dollars, and did I have the exact amount as he was no good at giving change either. The money I had taken from Charlie's pocket consisted of two tens, a five, and a bunch of ones – so I was able to hand over the exact amount. I did not hesitate even a moment over the possibility of slipping the old man three ones and telling him they were a twenty, a five and a one. I wanted this transaction to be as ordinary and as forgetful as it could be, at least from the old man's point-of-view. I didn't want Charlaine coming in later and informing him that he had been duped.

I picked up the shovel and gloves, said thanks and headed for the door.

"What about them plants?" the old man called after me.

"I'll come back for the plants," I promised brightly. "Maybe later today…I'll come back when Charlaine is here."

"Good idea!" the old man said. Then I heard him grumbling, "Man's got hisself a shovel and nuthin' to plant." As I left the store, I heard him cackling.

Maddie

There was an extra blanket and a quilt folded up at the foot of the bed. Harry arranged them both on top of us and we tunneled in under the mound of bed coverings and lay entwined together as if inside a cocoon.

I murmured, "What does my Master desire?"

Harry was quiet a long time.

He said, "Your master is a sultan with enormous power and wealth. He is a cruel man and all his people fear him. He owns a harem of a hundred bondslaves, and he chooses from among them a different victim each night to torment and to humiliate. And tonight he has chosen you. But tonight he finds he is bored with the old routine, and he tells you, 'Tonight I want to share my bed with an equal partner, not a victim, but an equal, loving partner.' What would you do?"

It was my turn to be quiet. "My master is asking for the impossible. Even a wife is a bondslave of sorts. If I were to truly be your equal partner, even for one night, the other bondslaves would turn against me, would tear me limb from limb."

Harry frowned at this, pondered. He said, "What if I were to dismiss the other bondslaves, set them free, scatter them to the four corners of the world?"

I kissed him delicately, sadly on his lips. "It is not in you power, oh Great Sultan, to dismiss the other bondslaves. Alas, I wish you could."

Harry

In late November, the interval between sunset and twilight can sometimes be fleeting. Even inside our cocoon, we could tell the light was fading.

I thought I was being cute with my story about the cruel and powerful sultan but somehow it turned out that Maddie had out-riddled me. Maybe that's what comes of not having any use for fiction. Worse, I wasn't at all sure I understood Maddie's meaning, but I had an uneasy feeling that it did not bode well for the two of us.

"Then is it always hopeless?" I asked. "Is every relationship doomed to fail?"

"For some people...yes."

Her arms were around my waist, her head on my chest. I stroked her hair and wished that time would stop, that the light would not continue to fade. She slid her hands to my shoulders and pulled herself along my body until we were face to face. She kissed me and, smiling, whispered, "But in this moment we're good, aren't we?"

I nodded.

Maddie gave my dick a squeeze then sat up and threw off the covers. It was in her mind to get a fresh condom from the nightstand, I imagine – perhaps also to take another swig of the wine. Instead, she gave a little scream and fell on top of me and hurriedly reformed our cocoon. "It freezing out there," she chattered.

"Really?" I said. But in fact I had felt more than a hint of the cold air myself when Maddie sat up. Still, I slipped a hand then an entire arm outside of the covers to test the air. "Jeez," I said, pulling my arm back in, "it's like the air conditioning is going full blast – but I know I turned up the heat..."

I moved to get out of bed but Maddie pounced on me.

"Don't go out there, Harry...don't leave me here by myself...I don't like this...this is spooky!"

"What's spooky?!"

Her nails were digging into my arm.

Alexis

I strolled across the gravel parking lot, popped the lid on the trunk, dropped the shovel and the gloves inside, pulled the rope from my back pocket and dropped that in, too. Not a car went by on that long, straight two-lane country highway: not a witness in sight. The sun had set and there was a pale hint of a crescent moon hanging low in the bright blue sky. The wind was steady and brisk, the kind of wind that promises to grow sharper with every hour until it starts to bite. I was wearing only a light jacket and wished I'd brought something heavier. *Oh well*, I thought, *the digging will keep me warm*. I moved around to the driver's side, glancing into the backseat to check on Charlie.

The little cocksucker was gone.

Maddie

Harry stared at me like I was crazy.

"It's true," I insisted. "I felt her presence in the kitchen – and that was by no means the first time! – and then again at the top of the stairs.... Remember? – when you came out into the hall to see what was keeping me?"

Gently, reasonably, Harry spoke my name. "There's something the matter with the heating system, that's all it is," he soothed. "I'll just go and shut it off and this cold air will stop blowing on us – okay? I'll only be gone a minute...you'll be fine by yourself for a minute, wont you?"

"Something's pissing her off," I said.

"Let's talk about it more when I get back," Harry said. I was familiar with that tone of voice he was using. In my line of work, I'd heard it often, used it many times myself – it was the tone you use when you're talking to a crazy person. Harry pried my fingers loose from his forearm (I hadn't realized I was clutching him so tightly) and plunged from under the covers into the cold.

Alexis

I circled the car – twice – spying all around for him. He was nowhere in sight. But in his condition, how far could he have gone? I checked inside the car again. Had he rolled onto the floorboard behind the front seats and had I failed to see him? He was not on the floorboard. Desperately, I confirmed once again that he was not on the backseat, nor was he was sitting in either of the front seats. I studied the gravel near the car for evidence that he had crawled away – but of course that was hopeless: short of being able, probably, to follow a set of footprints in virgin snow, I had not the slightest ability to read tracks. Absurdly, I felt the urge to reopen the trunk and check to see if Charlie could possibly be in there.

Don't panic, I told myself; *he really couldn't have gone far – keep a cool head, think clearly, and we'll get him back.*

I took a deep breath, then another. And all of a sudden I knew where he was. He had to be there. Given his condition, it was the only place that made sense. I felt a malicious smile spread across my face as I dropped to my knees and prepared to yank Charlie out from under the car. He wasn't there, damn him.

I jumped to my feet and yelled out, "This isn't funny, Charlie!"

An old pickup trailing white smoke trundled by on the two-lane road. The driver waved to me, as people often do out in the country. I turned my face away.

Maddie

Harry returned to bed and reported that the system was shut down and no more air was coming out of the vents. He called it an "h-vack" system.

"What's that mean?" I asked, finding that I had no tolerance for even the slightest mystery: I wanted everything just to be normal.

"H-V-A-C," Harry said. "Sorry – I thought everybody said it but maybe it's a word only guys in construction use. Stands for heating, venting, air conditioning. All those things are considered one system."

"And you pulled the plug on the h-vack thing?"

Harry glanced at me skeptically and saw that I wasn't joking. "I, uh...there's not exactly any plug to pull...I shut it off at the thermostat. It had been set to 'heat' but for whatever reason the system was blowing cold air...probably a computer chip inside the T-stat has got its wires crossed."

Harry was shivering. His feet were bricks of ice and his skin was covered in goosebumps. I folded him in the blankets and energetically set about warming him. He liked that, but I could tell he was distracted. After a few minutes he said, "Do we need to talk some more?...about ghosts?..."

"I don't think so," I said.

"Because if you're uneasy..."

"I'm not," I said. And mostly I meant it. "I guess I got a little carried away. I guess there's nothing too spooky about a thermostat messing up."

Harry kissed me. He said, "If the house warms up at all it won't be much: the weather's supposed to get nasty tonight: cold with more rain, or maybe even snow, moving in after midnight...maybe I'll carry the electric wood stove up here and get it going, would you like that?...or how about if I lit some candles for heat?" He turned us inside our cocoon so that he was on top of me, and we rubbed noses like a pair of Eskimos. The tip of Harry's nose was still far from warm. "Also for the atmosphere," he murmured suggestively, nibbling my ear.

There was a roaring over our heads and freezing air blasted out of the vent in the ceiling.

Alexis

He would have headed for the nearest cover — that's where we have to look for him.

The nearest cover was a ditch beside the road. I hurried to it and inspected it carefully, even doing my best to look inside two nearby culverts while avoiding the nasty water trapped in the bottom of the ill-draining ditch. God, was I scared a snake or a groundhog or something worse was going to spring out at me! There was no ditch on the other side of the road — just a recently harvested field, a flat expanse of brown dirt offering nowhere to hide.

The next nearest cover was Charlie's Feed & Seed store itself. I circled the building. But this was not something I could do in a hurry. Charlie's Feed & Seed was a highly irregular structure, a conglomerate of additions with sheds and pens and porches and covered alcoves attached willy-nilly to all the additions. Here, there was an endless supply of places to hide, and I had no choice but to take my time and check every one of them. Aside from the building itself and all its attachments, there was a collection of rusted-out vehicles, mostly trucks, not to mention discarded farm equipment, stacks of crates, rolls of fencing, barrels as big as refrigerators and, oh yes, even a collection of junk appliances, including a pair of actual refrigerators. Every single one of these things had to be checked under or inside of or around. It was tedious and infuriating and still there was no sign of Charlie.

By the time I worked my way around to the front of the building, there was another car in the parking lot. A white four-door sedan not much different from Charlie's. It was empty and parked by the entrance to the store.

Inside the store was the next logical place to look for Charlie but every fiber of me resisted going back in there. If Charlie *was* in there blabbing away, then how was I going to explain myself? *We were having a nice drive in the country when suddenly my friend had a weird fit, like a seizure, and he started spewing out nonsense about me planning to kill him...I was rushing him back to town to get him to a hospital...* Yeah, right – then why exactly was I stopped at a feed and seed store, and didn't I sound suspiciously like the guy who just a little while ago purchased gloves and a shovel? I could picture them calling the police or, more likely out here, the sheriff. I could picture some overweight bumpkin in a rumpled tan uniform with a seven-pointed star; I heard him drawling, "If you're not that fella' who bought the shovel and the gloves then a'course you wouldn't mind if we poked around inside that car of your'n, would'ya?" That sheriff's deputy was no more than a figment of my imagination, but I cursed him vehemently as a dishonest bastard, merely pretending with that drawl to be far more of a dimwit than he really was.

No, if Charlie was in the feed and seed, then I was done. Therefore, Charlie couldn't be in there. All the many good omens of the day could not be mistaken. I surveyed the other possibilities as to Charlie's whereabouts.

To the north was a chain link fence separating the feed and seed store property from the next business along the two-lane highway: a rough-looking bar. Charlie could have gone around the fence but that would have been a long walk for a man in his condition – and then it was still a long way to the bar itself, all across open ground. To the west was the two-lane road: I'd already checked the ditch line there. To the south was what looked like an abandoned business: possibly a machine shop or a small factory. Thin, scrubby pines had sprung up around the building. That way, too, was a long walk with not much cover. To the east, behind the feed and seed store was a greenhouse, cobbled together with salvaged sheets of corrugated plastic and old window panes, and beyond that was a dense stand of trees.

I circled around once again to the back of the store and made my way to the greenhouse.

Harry

Maddie was in her car with the engine running, warming herself. Also hiding from ghosts. She would have fled from the apartment stark raving naked if I hadn't practically tackled her and insisted she put on some clothes.

I'd told her earlier that there wasn't a plug to pull on the heating and cooling system – and that was true, of course – but there was in fact a pair of switches called circuit breakers I could have shut off inside the electrical panel. But I hadn't bothered, thinking that setting the thermostat to *off* was sufficient. The heating and cooling system consisted of a) a furnace and air handler, in the crawlspace beneath my apartment, controlled by a double 30-amp circuit breaker, and b) an outdoor condensing unit controlled by its own double 20-amp breaker. Both breakers were clearly marked, and, too late to matter, both were definitely switched off now.

I moved around the apartment wrapped in a blanket from the bed, checking every air vent, both supply and return. The system – needless to say – was completely deactivated, since such things as furnaces and air handlers and condensing units run on electricity and not spirit energy, and the laws of physics are not easily overwhelmed. But how to convince Maddie of that?

The last vents I checked were in my bedroom. The room was still icy cold. The windows there were fogged but when I touched them they were dry: the condensation was on the exterior side of the glass. Unusual for an evening when the outside temperature was rapidly dropping but in fact, given the conditions inside, it made sense. Once again, the laws of physics prevailed.

I got dressed but avoided putting on my long underwear, which still lay in a heap in the corner where I had tossed the upper and lower halves. I glanced out the front window to see if Maddie's car was still in the parking lot. It was, a faint hint of white smoke sputtering from the tailpipe. I wondered how I was going to talk Maddie into coming back inside the house. It was getting darker outside – maybe that would help to sway her. I'd turned on most of the lights in the apartment when I went around checking vents, and I would make sure to leave them all on when I went outside to attempt to reason with Maddie. Also, I switched on the electric wood stove: it wasn't much, didn't put out tons of heat, but I figured it was better than nothing.

The overhead light was on in the bedroom, and it cast my own see-through reflection back at me as I stood looking out the window. Then I saw the reflection of another person, a woman, standing a few paces behind me. Her image was partly hidden by my own. It might have been Maddie, part of me wanted to believe it was Maddie because there was no other rational possibility for who it might be, but I knew it wasn't Maddie, I knew in the pit of my stomach and in the way the small hairs at the back of my neck were suddenly standing on end. I turned to face Suzanne. The room was empty. I twisted toward the window, looking for Suzanne's reflection. I saw no one's reflection but my own. I scanned the room; I slowly approached the doorway; I peeped into the hall. No one.

Tentatively, I called Suzanne's name. Silence.

Maddie had said that she was able to feel Suzanne's presence. I stood just inside the bedroom and attempted to send out psychic antennae. Of course, I had no idea what I was doing and I immediately began to feel silly – until all of a sudden there was a jolt of something I'd never experienced before. *Jolt* is perhaps too strong a word. It was like being engulfed in a wave of emotion coming from somewhere other than myself. The emotion was…complex. Deep sadness, tenderness and longing and regret – and beneath all else a kind of fright, not for me, not for Suzanne herself, but for some other. The wave passed through me in an instant. I remained rooted in place, braced for another engulfment. But no other wave came.

As far as I could tell, I was not the least bit frightened but I was shaken and confused. I wished Maddie had been there with me, wished she and I had experienced it together. But as soon as I thought that, I knew it was a wrong idea. Suzanne would not have made contact, not with me, if Maddie had been in the room. A vivid image of Charlie popped into my mind. He wore an expression on his face that perfectly matched the wave of emotion I had just experienced. Charlie was the one I truly wished had been by my side to experience this thing with me. I considered calling him, telling him what had just happened – but I worried about how crazy I would sound and pushed the thought out of my head.

Above the ceiling, I heard faint popping sounds as the metal ductwork of the heating and cooling system dissipated its residual coldness into the relative warmth of the attic.

Alexis

I reached the greenhouse at a trot, my light jacket pulled tightly around me against the intensifying chill. I made a quick search of the perimeter then plunged inside. It was warm in there – warmer at least – but not humid like most greenhouses are. And it was quite a bit darker inside than out. In one corner of the greenhouse not far from the door was a table with a dozen or so wilted plantlings in tiny plastic flowerpots arranged in uneven rows. The entire greenhouse was crowded with tables, but all the other tables were empty or held stacks of empty plastic pots. Clearly, this was someone's great business idea, slowly dying and close to its last gasp.

It would have been perfectly quiet inside that greenhouse, except that whenever the air outside stirred even the slightest bit, loose sheets of corrugated plastic would rattle or some part of the structure would creek or even groan. Also, someone had come up with the bright idea of flooring the greenhouse with that same annoying pea gravel that they'd used to create the parking lot, so that it crunched under my feet with every step I took. Each time the outside air grew calm, I stood still and held my breath and listened for Charlie. Meanwhile, I crept forward through the maze of battered wooden tables. I wanted to kick myself for having taken Charlie's phone from him: it would have been so simple to be able to call his number and listen for the ring.

There had been no light switch near the door and as far as I could tell there were no electric lights hanging down from the bare rafters – probably no electric wiring at all in that sprawling makeshift structure. Just as well. I wasn't at all certain I would have flipped on a switch if I'd found one: too much chance of attracting attention from the store.

No sooner had that thought crossed my mind when I decided that I needed a light at any cost. If Charlie was in there I had to find him fast. And no sooner had *that* thought crossed my mind when I reached for my phone, which could be made to act as a flashlight. For that matter, so could Charlie's. I pulled Charlie's phone out of my pocket and activated the flashlight function. I felt a certain satisfaction doing this: one way or another, I was going to use Charlie's phone against him.

Maddie

Harry appeared, dressed, at the front door of his apartment. He looked troubled. He studied the sky. He walked to the passenger-side door of my car, opened it and got in.

"Warm in here," he said.

I was keeping both eyes focused straight ahead, watching for…I don't know what – some kind of entity, some hint of Suzanne following Harry out of his house. There was nothing to see but the ordinary front facade of an ordinary townhouse apartment.

"Feels good," he said. "The warmth."

He attempted to explain about the "h-vack" system – damn that word! I loathed it with a sudden irrational fury – he wanted to tell me how there were various switches that could shut the system down, how he had failed previously to deactivate them all, but now it was okay: we could go back inside: there wouldn't be any heat, aside from the fake wood stove which he assured me was churning away, but there would also be no further malfunctions of the h-vack system.

The ghost of Suzanne was keeping out of sight.

Harry said, "Clouds moving in – probably that rain Doug was scared of."

Harry had thrown on pants and a shirt, slippers and socks, and one of those hoodies he often wore to work under his outer jacket. He unzipped the hoodie. "Warm in here."

"You already said that."

"Doug said this rain that's coming might turn to snow – can you believe that?…or maybe I already say that, too…"

I turned to Harry, hoping that Suzanne would not pick that moment to come wafting out of the house. (I didn't know which was faster, a ghost or a car, and I really didn't want to have to find out.) I said, "I'm not going back inside there, Harry. I'm not."

Harry studied my face. He could read my determination but he attributed it, I think, entirely to fear. I let him be deceived in that way. He sighed and said, "Maybe in the morning."

I was a little surprised by that; I suppose I had expected Harry to try a bit harder to get me back into his house and into his bed. It was *my* turn to study *his* face. There was that troubled look again, the same one I'd noticed when Harry first stepped outside. He, too, seemed to be glancing nervously toward the apartment, as if he half expected someone or something to emerge at any moment.

"Harry, did you...sense something in there...?"

He neither confirmed nor denied that he had; instead, he vigorously contended that there could be no such things as ghosts – they were as unlikely as leprechauns or elves. I frowned at this and told him it was a weak argument. We got into a discussion over it which actually almost turned into a fight. My point was that simply calling a thing unlikely didn't make it so, and besides ghosts were a different class of phenomena altogether from leprechauns and elves, which, one might argue, were entirely imaginary beings, whereas ghosts had a firmer basis in reality, being the spirits of actual, once-living people – although, in fact, I also happened to believed in leprechauns and elves. Harry blathered on about the laws of physics and how they disproved essentially all things supernatural, but I let him know that I failed to see how the laws of physics even came into the picture, since it was well-known that scientists simply made up extra laws when confronted with new data which was otherwise inexplicable.

It had gotten so warm in my car that Harry had removed his hoodie and I a head scarf and a light shawl.

"What do you say we go for a drive?" Harry suggested.

Without another word having to be spoken, I backed out of that parking spot. The first cold droplets of rains were just beginning to splatter my windshield.

Alexis

I used only Charlie's phone for a flashlight, saving the battery in my own. I held the light down around my knees and pointed the beam toward the floor, hoping that would make it less visible outside the greenhouse and figuring that Charlie, if he was there, could not have climbed up onto anything but would be lying low. I moved as systematically as I could through the haphazard rows of wooden tables, dragging one out of my way from time to time so as to leave no portion of the greenhouse uninspected.

I was getting close to running out of places to look when I heard a faint noise to my right. I swung the light in that direction, and there was Charlie on the ground, trying to inch past me into the area where I had already searched. His big, round eyes reflected the light of his phone back at me. To compare him to a deer in someone's headlights would have missed the fact that his body was impaired and possessed a limited capacity to flee. He was more like a wounded, frightened rabbit caught in a trap.

"You got me," he said, matter-of-fact, un-slurred, like we were in our own living room shooting the breeze. The only hint in his voice that anything was wrong was an odd flatness of tone and a slight stammer at the beginning when he said "you."

Yes, I had him. Now the question was: what was I going to do with him?

I hadn't noticed when but, somewhere along the way, that other voice in my head had abandoned me – certainly the whole time I'd been in the greenhouse it had remained silent. Now suddenly it was back with a vengeance.

Get him to the car...then we take him someplace and carry out the plan. There's no other option this late in the game – we carry out the plan!

The voice was so sure of itself, so forceful. Meanwhile, I was saying to Charlie: "I can't tell you how sorry I am, this has all been a terrible mistake...I don't know what came over me, temporary insanity or something...but it's passed now, I'm back to normal...besides too many people have seen us together out here: even if I still wanted to hurt you I'd never be able to get away with it...so you can trust me...and I really *don't* want to hurt you anymore, Charlie, I want to help you...c'mon, give me your hand and I'll help you up and we'll get you to the car and I'll drive you to the hospital and everything will be fine, you'll see, and I hope over time I can find a way to make it all up to you and you can find it in your heart to forgive me…"

All the while I had been speaking I had been inching closer to Charlie. He sat wide-eyed and perfectly still, mesmerized by my words, letting himself be convinced – the same old dupe he had always been.

"Would you really try to make it up to me?" Charlie asked.

I promised I would.

"You'll stop hitting me? You'll see a counselor?"

More promises. "Take my hand, Charlie."

He smiled his goofiest, most loving, most hopeful smile. Then he threw two fistfuls of pea gravel into my face.

Maddie

I wanted so badly to tell Harry about the job interview, about how well it went, about Ekaterina's two-word text, about my amazing new job, about how perfect it was going to be for me – but that would mean telling him that I planned to leave tomorrow. And I couldn't do it. I remembered my promise to him that I wouldn't just disappear without warning. It was my *intention* to tell him. But I couldn't do it. Not while I was driving, anyway. I decided what I needed to do was to find a place to park and to invite Harry to crawl into the backseat with me, into the nest I had made for myself back there, then, holding him in my arms, I would tell him.

Harry was quiet – usual enough – but in an odd sort of way, a brooding sort of way. Did he somehow suspect my plans?

Alexis

I glimpsed the quick movement of Charlie's hands but in that dim light I never saw the tiny stones moving toward my face, never had the chance to blink, and the stones pelted my nose and my cheeks and struck both eyes directly and I saw an explosion of white light and then I was blinded and roaring in pain. Enraged, I lunged forward in an effort to grab him, to throttle him, but I must have become disoriented and lunged in the wrong direction because I cracked my head on a table leg that had not been between me and Charlie. I toppled over sideways, clutching at my eyes.

I felt something wet seeping around my fingers. I didn't know if it was blood or tears or both. The pain was excruciating, and my body was at the same time shivering and sweating. The voice in my head had abandoned me once again.

Maddie

There were a couple of truck stops out by the interstate where you could park a car overnight and sleep and nobody minded. Before Harry, I was always careful not to park at the same stop two nights in a row, or even two nights during the same week, just in case someone was checking for people living out of their cars. Maybe it didn't matter, but it was a point of pride with me to do everything I could to conceal my situation from as many people as possible, even total strangers, when I was without a roof over my head – a conventional roof, I mean; in my own mind, the roof of my car was always good enough.

I took Harry to the truck stop that was my favorite. It was the one with a diner that offered an all-you-could-eat lunch buffet for pretty cheap. Times when I was particularly worried about money, that would often be my only meal of the day. I parked in my favorite spot: just on the edge of the illumination thrown off by the all-night lighting at the gas pumps; far enough from the side entrance to the 24-hour convenience store so as not to be conspicuous, but near enough to be able to make a beeline for those doors in the event of any trouble; sort of close to the trucks that were, like me, parked for the night but also sort of separate from them.

I turned off the lights and the engine, and Harry and I sat there watching trucks roll in and trucks roll out, watching people gas up their cars and their pickup trucks and their SUV's, watching them walk stiff-legged in and out of the convenience store, watching a lazy, cold rain spatter the windshield.

Harry started to say something but fell silent. He looked perplexed.

"Random night, huh?" I prodded.

Harry shifted in his seat. "No," he said. "I mean, yeah sure, winding up here feels pretty random, now that you say it, but I was feeling something else…"

I waited.

"...like there's somewhere else I ought to be right now."

"Home asleep in your own bed," I suggested.

"Yeah...no...I don't know..." Harry murmured.

I suppose I could have taken offense. What did he mean he was thinking of somewhere else he ought to be?! What was wrong with being here with me? But Harry was so unguarded, so open in what he said, so trusting of me to understand him that I knew he in no way meant to offend me.

It was time to invite him into the backseat, to take him in my arms, to give him my news, to keep my promise to him. But he looked like such a lost sheep I couldn't bring myself to do it quite yet.

I said, "This place has a pretty good diner. We missed the lunch buffet but we could go in and get supper...I'm buying."

"Are you hungry?" he asked, turning to look at me.

"Yes and no, mostly no."

"Same here."

Yet another SUV pulled up to a pump. Before it even came to a complete stop, one of its back doors flew open and a kid jumped out. He sprinted toward the front entrance of the convenience store, holding his crotch with both hands. Out of the SUV's passenger-side front door leapt a woman trailing a head of wild red hair. I mean, it was like this woman's head was on fire. She chased after the boy, yelling, "Wait for Mommy! Wait for Mommy!" She wore only flip-flops on her feet, and I remember thinking what a poor choice that was for such a chilly evening.

Harry said, "We're spending the night here, aren't we?"

"Unless you got a truck stop you like better."

Harry gave a tired laugh. "Can't think of one," he said.

"How about if I go in and get us a six-pack?" (Boy, was I the big spender — first offering to buy dinner, now the beer — me with my new job looming: but really what I was was the big procrastinator — anything to keep us out of the backseat.)

Harry gave the notion of a six-pack some thought. "Sounds like a bad idea," he said. "We'd be running back and forth to the rest rooms all night."

"I'll just get us one each."

Harry tilted his chair back. It didn't go back very far, the way I had stuff piled behind it. "Get one for yourself if you like," he said. "I'm tired — I'm going to try to sleep."

Alexis

Pain tunneled from my battered eyeballs right into the depths of my brain. I kept my hands over my face, too afraid to take them away and test my sight. Wet stuff still dribbled between my fingers: I still didn't know what it was. The side of my head where I'd banged it throbbed. I groaned and wailed, nor caring who heard me, believing I was beaten.

After a time, the pain subsided – not completely but enough to let me get a partial grip on myself. I rolled onto my back. I peeked between my fingers. I saw nothing but darkness. Was I blind? Or had the evening light completely faded? I sat up, looked around for the glow of Charlie's phone, which I'd dropped. Darkness. Was I blind? Or had Charlie's flashlight function timed out? Or had Charlie snatched his phone before he fled? Had he fled? If he owned an ounce of sense he would have looked around for something heavy and bashed my head in while I was helpless – that's what I would have done in his situation. Maybe he was creeping up behind me at that very moment. I groped inside my pocket and pulled out my own phone. I activated the screen. Light! The light penetrated my eyes! One eye, at least: my left. My right eye didn't seem to be doing so well – also it was leaking worse than the left. I was further dismayed to realize that the glowing screen of my phone was a hopeless blur. I tried to use the light from the screen to look around for Charlie, but the light wasn't strong enough and my vision was too impaired. Also, the screen was set to turn itself off after about ten seconds – that was annoying. I longed to turn on my own flashlight function but couldn't see the screen well enough to make that happen.

I pocketed my phone. If Charlie's was still on the ground close by, I didn't care. Slowly, I made it to my hands and knees, then I managed to pull myself to my feet by clutching onto one of the wooden tables. The world teetered back and forth like one giant see-saw. It made me queasy. I was beginning to suspect that some of the wet stuff I felt around my right eye was actually coming from a cut on my head. I didn't know if that was good news or bad.

I wondered how long it would be before the police arrived to arrest me. I took it for granted that Charlie, having failed to bash my head in, would have made his way to the feed and seed store and raised an alarm. I had to fight the urge to lie back down in the pea gravel and curl up and wait. Eventually, I was able to convince myself that I wanted out of that damned greenhouse. Whatever was in the cards for me next, I didn't want to be taken inside that greenhouse. But my problem was: I couldn't see to find my way out. There was nothing to do but pick a random direction and lurch forward, and that's what I did, steadying myself against the tables. A wickedly chilly breeze cut through me. I wanted to huddle inside my flimsy jacket, but I couldn't spare my hands: I needed to keep hold of the tables.

Then it struck me: that breeze had to be coming from some sort of opening. I thought I had closed the greenhouse door behind me when I entered, but Charlie would almost certainly have left it open when he fled. I let my skin be my eyes and followed the breeze. It led me directly to the exit.

Harry

"Are you claustrophobic?" Maddie asked.

"A little," I admitted.

"It's not good to sleep in the front seat – you'll get cold, also it's too exposed. Climb into the backseat and see how that feels to you."

I reached for the door handle. Maddie shook her head. "You have to climb between the seats."

Once I was back there, I could see the reason why. Maddie had stacked various items against the rear doors to block anyone's vision. From the outside, it looked like the backseat was packed full to the ceiling. In fact, Maddie had constructed a network of strings and bungee cords to create a kind of netting to hold a few things against the rear doors and still leave the maximum clear space on the backseat. A short man like me could almost stretch out full length. Maddie had also densely packed the floorboards in front of the backseat with possessions, then covered them with a layer of cushions, so that the available area to lie in was almost the size of a double bed.

"How are you feeling back there?" Maddie wanted to know. "Not too closed in?"

"It's snug," I said.

"Snug in a good way or snug in a bad way?"

I glanced all around. This was Maddie's home – temporary perhaps, but her home. She was inviting me into her home with more good grace than I had first invited her into mine.

"Snug in a good way," I said.

"How about if I join you?"

"I think the snugness will get even better."

She locked both front doors, then she climbed in beside me.

We each had to bend our legs a little: Maddie slightly more than me. We quickly learned that lying face to face was doable but our legs had to inter-tangle and, while that felt good at first, it soon became uncomfortable for whoever's legs were in the middle of the tangle. Spooning turned out to be the best position. It worked either way but, maybe because it was her space, the most natural arrangement seemed to be for Maddie to spoon me.

"Thought you were going to get yourself a beer," I reminded.

"Not my style to drink alone," she whispered. Her hot breath tickled the back of my neck.

I felt her reaching back, stretching her arm up to the ceiling. I glanced over my shoulder to see what she was doing. She untied a pair of strings and a black curtain made of cloth unrolled itself, dropping into place just behind the front seats. No one outside the car had any way to see us now.

"Still okay?" Maddie asked, checking to see if I felt too closed in.

I nodded, and Maddie kissed the back of my neck to signal that she had felt my response.

It was not completely dark in there. A hint of light made its way through the barricades of stuff strapped to the side doors, especially from the side of the car closest to the lights at the gas pumps. As we lay there, my eyes adjusted enough so that I could see my hand in silhouette if I held it directly before my face. I felt Maddie reaching again, this time into the mass of belongings she had stowed between the back seat and the rear hatch.

"Pillow?" she offered, and I felt a pillow beside my head. I lifted my head and Maddie slid the pillow underneath. I breathed in her scent on the pillow with deep satisfaction.

"Blanket?"

"A blanket would be nice," I said.

Maddie covered us both with a blanket.

"Did you get a pillow for yourself?"

"I'm using a rolled up blanket...I have plenty of blankets."

There was the faintest patter of rain on the roof.

"Cozy in here," I said.

Another kiss on the back of my neck, then a lazy nibbling at my ear. She whispered, "Do you know, you're the first person I've ever...brought home like this?" And I knew what she meant: *brought home to her car.* (I thought it was interesting, but not too surprising, that she said "person" and not "man.")

"I'm honored," I said, quite sincerely.

Out on the interstate a truck applied its air brakes, and the distant hum of traffic was punctuated momentarily by that distant hammering.

"I used to dream of this," Maddie said, "nights alone in this car. Having someone to hold in my arms."

I pictured Maddie lying there alone; I pictured the dreams she must have had. A question occurred to me. "Did you dream of holding someone or of being held?"

"Just like this," Maddie breathed into my ear. "I dreamed of holding someone...especially a man. I dreamed of a man who would let me hold him, a guy who didn't always have to have it the other way around."

Her hands had worked their way under my shirt. My body chimed at her touch. Had there been a similar chiming at Suzanne's touch? Dimly I supposed there must have been, but I could not in the backseat of Maddie's car remember specifics. A darker question occurred to me: had I been, the whole time with Suzanne, that guy who had to have it the other way around? No, I had not been that guy. I was certain that I had not been that guy: I always treated Suzanne as an equal, I never imposed my will on Suzanne. But these last few days with Maddie had taught me that I had been a guy who had missed something, a guy who had missed too much. I was still uncertain about what it was, exactly, that I had missed, believing that whatever Suzanne and I might have found together would have been different in its essential character from the dizzying heights and unspeakably pleasurable depths that Maddie and I were reaching, but I knew without doubt that it was something profoundly important to Suzanne, something that would have made Suzanne's existence on this earth more fulfilling, or at least more pleasurable. I regretted deeply not giving her that fulfillment or pleasure or whatever it might have been. I wished for a way to tell Suzanne how sorry I was.

Maddie's voice was in my ear. "Hey, stay with me...don't drift away."

Slowly, languidly, piece by piece, our clothes came off. Maddie was the one who undressed us both.

Alexis

When I stepped outside the greenhouse, I found that it was raining. It was dark, too – or at least it seemed so to me. I ducked back into the greenhouse to test my vision once again using my phone. There was not much change. The left eye detected light; the right eye detected nothing. Perhaps the left eye was focusing a little better – I wasn't sure: perhaps it was only wishful thinking. The left eye certainly didn't hurt as much as it did when I was lying in the pea gravel. The same could not be said for the right eye, which still hurt like a motherfucker and continued to ooze some kind of fluid. At least the flow of blood from my forehead seemed to have stopped.

I shut off the phone and ventured forward into the rain. It was not a downpour, but a cold, miserable rain that dampened your hair and sent little tendrils of wet through your clothes like slow torture until you were soaked. I thought I could make out with my left eye the low loom of the feed and seed store. I moved in that direction, placing my feet cautiously on the uneven ground. It bothered me that I could see no light from the store – was it really in front of me or was I wandering off into the trees? After maybe a dozen steps, I heard a car go by on the two-lane highway. It was somewhere in front of me, moving from my left to my right. A few minutes later, I heard another moving from right to left. These sounds reassured me that I was creeping along in generally the right direction. I watched eagerly for headlights but saw none.

I walked straight into something large and metallic – possibly one of the junked vehicles I had seen earlier behind the feed and seed store. I cracked my knee on it before running into it less forcefully against my stomach and then my cheek. I stood there cursing, shivering, rubbing my knee through my sodden pants. By then the rain had soaked me through. I began to move even more slowly, walking with my hands out in front of me. *Like a Frankenstein monster or a sleepwalker or a zombie*, I thought, comparing myself to anything and everything except the most obvious – *like a blind man*.

Slowly slowly I made my way around to the front of the feed and seed store. I turned the final corner and encountered the soft glow of diffused light. It was like waking up out of a nightmare – (well, coming half-awake anyway: all in all the day was still scoring pretty high on the nightmare scale). The glow was coming from a security light attached to the top of a not very tall telephone pole at one edge of the feed and seed store's parking lot. No! actually, there were two lights, perched on two different poles! – I could make them out, with my left eye I could make that much out! I probably would have seen them sooner except the feed and seed store had been blocking them from my line of sight. The store itself seemed to be completely dark, shut up, closed for business. I wondered what time it was. I wondered, for that matter, where the police were: a warm jail cell would have suited me just fine. I noticed the blurry image of Charlie's car parked almost directly under one of the security lights. I peered all around the parking lot. I did not see another car, not even the white sedan that had looked so much like Charlie's car and that had been parked near the front door. I moved toward Charlie's car. My knee was stiffening. Driving the car was out of the question but it promised shelter and, once the engine heated up, warmth. I limped across the parking lot through the pitiless rain and through that miraculous glow of light; already in my imagination I was basking in the car's warmth.

Maddie

We didn't have any condoms with us. No doubt, there was an ample supply in that truck stop. But it was cold and rainy outside in the big, mean world and we were snug and warm and content together in our little world, not to mention the happy circumstance that we were as naked as Adam and Eve before the Fall. I wanted Harry to go off inside me, this being our last night together. Minus a condom, and not taking into account diseases only the possibility of getting pregnant, there were two safe options available and, given how close I was to starting my period, one very unsafe option. Of the two safe options, I vastly preferred taking Harry in my mouth – an activity I very much enjoyed, in fact – to the other option, which I frankly didn't much care for.

Harry was not aware of any of these machinations. He understood well enough the essential problem of not having a condom, of course, but he did not know about my resolve to satisfy him, which, I admit, had not always been at the top of my agenda when I was with Harry, and rarely ever was close to the top of the agenda when I was with any other man.

(I had so far failed to tell Harry this was our last night.)

It took me a while to work out the best position for oral sex. If I was lying on my back, then Harry had to straddle my chest and poke his dick into my face: I was okay with that arrangement, but Harry was uneasy dominating a woman in such a manner, more's the pity. If Harry was lying on his back and I tried to give him a standard blowjob, then I had no legroom and became too scrunched against a side door. The legroom problem was slightly better if we attempted to mutually blow one another, but that was a position neither of us much liked, having tried it in the roomy comfort of Harry's bed. Harry, particularly, got too distracted by what I was doing to him to fully concentrate on what he was supposed to be doing to me and, new as he most assuredly was to the wonderful world of cunnilingus, this made him even more inept than usual, and it frustrated and embarrassed him and he would pull away from me, losing his erection. The solution, there in the car, was to have Harry sit with his back against one of the side doors. He could fully stretch out his legs, while I lay between them and played with his dick, bending my own legs as needed and resting my feet against the other side door.

The next problem to overcome was Harry's deep-seated reluctance to go off in my mouth. No matter how many times I told him I liked it – and I had told him many times before – he resisted. He simply could not get it through his thick skull that a woman could allow such a thing to be done to her and not feel demeaned and disgusted. My attempted solution – and I wouldn't have risked this with any other man but I trusted Harry so much – involved riding him until he was straining to hold himself back, then lifting myself clear of him, shoving him against the side door, and going to work on his throbbing cock with my mouth and hands. But, damn him, he would not go off. He bucked and moaned but he would not go off.

Meanwhile, he had brought me to orgasm several times already, once even with his mouth. It was starting to feel, from my point of view at least, like a contest – a contest I was losing – and the longer it went on, the grimmer it felt.

Alexis

Charlie's car was locked. I searched in pocket after pocket but could not find the key. It was impossible for Charlie's car to be locked. It was impossible that I had lost the key. But the universe, apparently, was not interested in my pronouncements regarding what was possible and what was impossible.

Still, I attempted to argue my case with the universe:

Charlie's car did not have automatic locks or even electronic windows. To lock Charlie's car, you had to physically press down the little, square button on the door. Had I done this when I left the car – eons ago – to buy the shovel and gloves and rope? Okay, yes, maybe so. I could not clearly remember doing it, but maybe. But picture Charlie making his escape. Charlie would have opened one of the back doors, slipped out and dragged himself away as fast as his damaged body would allow. Charlie would not have taken the time to so much as close that door much less lock it. Therefore, it was impossible for all the doors of Charlie's car to be locked.

The universe hummed along, utterly ignoring me.

I, however, could not help but remember that when I came out of the feed and seed store, carrying the implements necessary to bring about Charlie's demise, I had found Charlie missing and all the doors of the car closed. So, yes, in fact Charlie had taken the time to close the door behind him and, goddamn it, he must have locked it out of force of habit.

But where was the key?!

A sudden flash of memory: me, standing at that counter, pulling Charlie's money out of my pocket: the faintest *clink* against the floor, so faint it did not register in my brain when it happened: that old man laughing laughing laughing.

Only then did I start to cry real tears. Whatever fluids had fallen from my eyes since Charlie had blinded me had been the result of physical damage; these now, these present tears, were the real thing. The rain drummed a little harder against the hood and roof of the car and against the top of my head. I lifted my damaged eyes to the heavens and I howled and the cold rain stung my eyes, especially my right eye, and I howled until my throat was raw, I howled and howled until the howling turned to laughter. If I could have opened the trunk of Charlie's car, I would have taken out the rope that was in there and hung myself, laughing, from the nearest tree. For some reason, I found that thought uproariously funny.

Then whatever had come over me – call it a tide of despair – ebbed away, left me hunched and empty, drenched and shivering, wondering what to do next.

Far down the highway, blurry headlights appeared. As they approached I concentrated on bringing them into focus, with little success. Before they reached me, they turned off onto my side of the highway and were lost to my sight. Distances were hard to judge but it seemed to me they had turned off not too far away from where I was standing. I tried to remember what lay in that direction. I recalled that on one side of the feed and seed store was an abandoned garage or factory and on the other side was a rundown bar. I was pretty sure it was the bar that was ahead of me.

What else was there to do? Wander off into the trees and slowly freeze to death? Was it cold enough for that? I didn't think so – I wasn't completely sure but I didn't think so. Anyway, thoughts of suicide had ebbed away along with the howling and the laughter. I started walking toward the bar.

Harry

Our bodies were the only source of heat in that car and we were covered by no more than a single, oversized blanket, but what a sweat we managed to work up while the cold rain pattered on the roof. Our lovemaking started out as playful and satisfying as it had ever been. I think we both felt an illicit excitement at doing it in her car, even more so because the car was parked in a kind of semi-public space – I know I felt it. But somewhere along the way the mood shifted. Maddie grew uncharacteristically serious, emotionally withdrawn – while physically she continued to be anything but withdrawn. It was perplexing.

Finally, she threw off the blanket and started rooting around in the stuff she kept behind the backseat.

"What are you looking for?" I asked.

"There's some lotion back here somewhere," she said fiercely.

"Lotion?"

"Here it is." She found my dick with her hand and I felt her smearing me with lotion.

"Yikes!" I complained, jerking away.

"What?"

"It's freezing!"

"It is not, don't be a baby."

"It's really cold, I'm telling you."

Maddie paused. She was hard to see in the dim light but she appeared to be testing the lotion on some hidden part of her own anatomy.

"Okay you're right, it *is* pretty cold. Sorry. I should have warmed it first." She laughed and for a second I thought that the odd mood might be dissipating.

"Um...Maddie...um, what are you..."

"Shut up!" she commanded.

"Maddie...?"

"I'm taking one last shot at getting you to go off."

I bent forward and kissed her. "This has been wonderful. I don't have to go off every time..."

"Shut up," she said. This time it was more of a plea than a command.

She was half kneeling half sitting, straddling my upper legs. She squirted lotion into her hand then, setting the tube aside, rubbed her hands together to warm the lotion. I thought she was getting ready to give me a really slippery handjob. I thought that the whole time she lathered me up. I thought that right up to the moment she lifted herself off me and scooted forward on her knees and started guiding me into her, but not into her vagina.

"Hey hey wait a minute!" I protested, lifting her off, accidentally bumping her head against the top of the car. "You don't have to do that."

"I thought you said you wanted to try it."

"I thought you said you didn't much like it."

"Did I? I don't recall saying that."

"You said something like that...I'm pretty sure you did..."

I was holding her by the hips. She grabbed my wrists and, giving her bottom a shake, she tried to pull my hands away. Giggling, she said, "Unhand me, you brute. Let me impale myself on that massive pole of yours."

It was tempting. I won't say I wasn't tempted. But there was that feeling again, like earlier in the evening, that some hidden danger was lurking, that it would be easy to go terribly wrong here. I moved her away and set her down on my upper legs.

"There's something you're not telling me," I said.

Alexis

I had forgotten there was a chain-link fence between the feed and seed store and the bar. I walked right into it. It didn't hurt nearly as much as the large metallic object I had walked into earlier. I made my way around the fence, using it for guidance and support. I forgot, too, that there was a ditch beside the road. As it happened, the ditch must have been particularly steep right there at the end of the fence. As I made my way around, one foot slipped out from under me, my injured knee buckled, I landed awkwardly and rolled completely into the ditch, which was full of sour-smelling water. The smell was so rank, it crossed my mind that some of the patrons of the bar up ahead might be using that ditch for a latrine. I struggled desperately to keep my face out of the water. I prayed none of it had gotten into my eyes — I didn't think any had but I was so wet I couldn't tell for sure.

I dragged myself out of the ditch, staggered to me feet, and plodded forward.

Maddie

It all came tumbling out of me: the fantastic new job, the way I aced the interview, their need for me to start right away, my determination to leave tomorrow morning. Harry became very quiet. I was still sitting on top of him; his poor, once-eager dick was completely deflated. I was growing goosebumps against the seeping chill of the night.

Harry said, "Do you have something to wipe this goop off with?"

I pulled another blanket from the back of the car and used that to tidy up both Harry's crotch and my own hands. As I was finishing, Harry reached behind me and took hold of the blanket we had been using to keep warm. "You're cold," he said, and he pulled me down on top of him and covered me with the blanket. *How did he know that?* He felt as warm as a fever patient.

"You weren't going to tell me, were you?"

I snuggled against him and made no reply.

"You promised you would."

I kissed his neck. "I'm a liar. A coward and a liar." It was on the tip of my tongue to add *I should be severely punished*, but this was neither the time nor place – sadly, games like that we were destined to miss out on. Poor me, poor Harry. Most of all poor Suzanne.

That seemed the end of it, the end of Harry and me.

I lay on top of him. The blanket on my back was cold, and a cold rain drummed overhead on the roof of my car, but Harry, beneath, me, was as warm as that ludicrously charming fake wood stove of his. He whispered my name. He told me I was as true a person as he had ever met. He said the word "true" as opposed to "truthful," touching me. He assured me that I was no coward. I snorted quietly against his neck to express my abject amusement at that last remark.

He said, "Maddie, if I had half your courage…" but his voice trailed off.

He said, "Maddie, you're not that little girl on the rope swing anymore. Somewhere along the way you conquered your fear of sailing off into the unknown."

I arched away from him. "Who told you that?" I demanded. "Who told you about the rope swing? Have you been talking to Freeman behind my back?"

"You told me," Harry said. I could hear as much as I could see the perplexed smile on his lips.

"When did I tell you?"

"Our first night together…when we were playing at the club."

"I told you *that*?"

Harry's hand came up and curled around my neck and gently he pulled me down until I was once again lying on top of him, swaddled in the warmth of his body. He murmured, "Don't you remember?"

I thought back to that first night with Harry. I vividly recalled our first reckless sexual adventures – reckless on my part at any rate. I recalled, too, all the earlier unpleasantness: Mr. Tattoo and that nasty bar, me turning my ankle in the rain. But beyond those memories, or rather preceding those memories, there we were: me and Harry playing a couple of innocent games of chess, and there was I opening up to a man I hardly knew in a way I had never done before.

The rain was drumming even louder on the roof of the car, but Harry's warmth had entirely driven away the cold, had enveloped me. I heard myself saying, "Come with me, Harry, let's stay together…what's keeping you here?"

Mournfully, Harry said, "You don't mean that."

"I do! Harry, that's the answer! Run away with me! Now it all makes sense."

"What makes sense?"

"Why she drove us out of your house tonight. She was trying to get you into my car. She was trying to tell us to run away together."

Harry made some noise to the effect that he didn't know what I was talking about, but he couldn't even convince himself. Finally, uncertainly, he said, "I don't believe in ghosts."

"Are you saying you won't come with me?"

"My life is here."

"What life?"

Harry took a long time to answer. "Charlie's here."

"You'd only be a couple hundred miles away from him...you two live like that anyway."

Harry laughed. Unconsciously, he slipped a hand from under the blanket and gave me a swift, sharp, playful swat on the bottom. *There's hope for him yet*, I schemed.

"What if..." he said and I put a finger to his lips.

"Don't play chess with this, Harry. Don't think too many moves ahead. Time for you to find the courage to sail off into the unknown. Right now, for me, in this moment of my life, you make me happy, you make me whole somehow...I can't even explain it and, worse, I don't know if what I feel will last until tomorrow. But I've been feeling these feelings day after day all week and every morning I wake up and there they are, they won't go away. And one other thing I can tell you, Harry: I've never met another man like you, and I don't want you to slip out of my life — not just yet."

In the dim light, I could only guess at Harry's expression. Maybe the idea of running away with me frightened him. Or appalled him. Maybe this was the final proof he needed that I was certifiably nuts. My instinct told me different, however. He was turning the idea over in his imagination, he was actually considering it. I let him have his quiet spell for as long as I could stand — but patience is not one of my virtues. I said, "I bet they have a really good chess club up there."

Harry laughed. "You probably meet a better class of people in the bowling alleys up there, too."

"That's two great reasons for you to say yes."

Harry laughed again and gave me a massive hug. "I've got all the reason I need right here."

Charlie

The door flew open and in walked an honest-to-God zombie – a zombie who had just clawed its way out of the grave. There was blood on one side of its face, smeared by the rain. There was a trail of blood down the front of its oddly familiar jacket. One eye of the creature was a purplish, swollen mess. It quivered and its lips were blue, no doubt from having been buried in the cold ground. The rest of it was covered in muddy slime.

There was almost nobody in the place: the bartender, one or two couples, a few guys in the back playing pool, a few other guys sitting alone at the bar. They were a rough-looking bunch, even the women, but they treated me okay when I stumbled in. They listened to my story, showing a lot of patience – I wasn't slurring so much anymore, as far as I could tell, but words were coming slowly to my mind, even simple words like "kill" and "scared" and "run." I think about half of the people in that bar believed my story and half of them didn't. Believe me or not, the bartender was nice enough to lend me a heavy coat (out of the lost and found, I guess) so I could try to get warm, and to steer me to a seat next to the wall heater. He even brought me a can of beer and a shot of whiskey. I fumbled in my pockets but came up empty. He just shrugged. "You'll need to come back and settle up when you're on your feet again...nuthin's on the house in this place." He also obliged me by putting in a call to the sheriff.

Everyone froze when the zombie walked in. One of the women gasped. One of the men murmured, "Holy shit!"

After a long moment, I said, "Alexis?"

Another pause. Then someone said, "Is that the guy who's trying to kill you?"

Someone else said, "Holy fucking shit, our man here wasn't lying."

Someone else said, "Who's been trying to kill who, that's what I want to know."

It *was* Alexis and not a zombie – I was almost sure of it. I kind of recognized the creature's one undamaged eye as belonging to Alexis (also, there was the jacket). I caught a glimpse of Alexis' quick, wounded mind working behind that eye. He raised an arm, pointed at me and wailed, "It's him! He's the one who's been trying to kill *me*!"

The sheriff's deputy arrived a few minutes later.

VII. Tuesday

Maddie

We breakfasted at the truck stop diner. They advertised "endless refills" of coffee. We ordered two big plates of food and, while we ate, we tested the meaning of the word "endless." I have to say, the waitress was a sweetheart about it. She was a young thing, probably fresh out of high school. In her eyes, Harry and I were in the same class of people – old. She took us for a married couple. I couldn't find it in myself to get upset, Harry was obviously so pleased by how she treated us. She was plainly perplexed when Harry and I tussled over the bill. In the end Harry won, and I agreed to let him pay. This was a place where you paid at the counter by the door. Getting up from the table, I left the tip. It was a good tip, generous even. Harry, exuberantly, reached into his pocket and slapped down the same amount of cash, doubling the tip. All I could do was smile: it felt so right, we were both so happy.

We had discussed some of the logistics of the move, wrapped in each other's arms, at various times during the night. I was determined to leave town that very morning. I would drive Harry back to his apartment and be on my way. I had no plans to set foot inside that apartment again. I was convinced now that Suzanne's visitation of the previous night had not been malicious – but why take chances? Very few of my things were there, and whatever I was leaving behind Harry could bring. He figured he needed at least a week to tie up loose ends. He was even willing to give two weeks notice at his work, assuming Doug hadn't already fired him. That would give me time on the other end to find a place for us and to settle into my new job. Harry was going to send me money to help pay for deposits, utility fees, the first month's rent, etc. He was paying month by month at his place, so there would be no worries about breaking a lease. In any case, Harry had decided to keep the apartment for at least another month; we both agreed that was a good idea.

We drove to his place through wet sleet. The promised snow (or threatened, depending on how you look at it) had never materialized. I parked in front of his door and we kissed and said our goodbyes. I pulled out my phone.

"What's your number?" I asked.

He told me. I dialed it. When the voicemail kicked in, I said, "Boo!" and hung up. "Now you're number's in my phone and mine is in yours."

And with that Harry got out of the car. He stood there in the freezing rain, waving, as I pulled away.

Harry

It was only marginally warmer inside the apartment than it was outside. The electric wood stove had been churning away all night, but it simply didn't put out much heat.

The first thing I did was to look for my phone. Not so much to call the landlord about the heat as to confirm that Maddie's number was there — already I was fretting that I'd let her slip away, never to be seen again. I found her voicemail and played it. *Boo!* I played it again. *Boo!* I wrote Maddie's number down on a piece of paper and put it in my pocket. I was puzzled to see a couple of missed calls and a voicemail from numbers I did not recognize. Not many people ever called my phone, especially not from strange numbers. It occurred to me that maybe something had happened to Fran and Milt on that cruise they were taking.

I didn't bother with the missed calls right away but went looking for the landlord's number. I recalled Charlie teasing me about still keeping a handwritten phone book, not to mention various notes in drawers with numbers on them — old habits. I fished out the note with the landlord's phone number but didn't call right away. Instead, just for the hell of it, I flipped on the circuit breakers for the heating and cooling system and set the thermostat to warm the place to seventy degrees. I heard the outside heat pump kick on. A minute or so later, I heard the air handler in the crawlspace start to work. I placed my hand over a supply vent. Air, flowing air, warm flowing air. How to explain that?

Well, I was going to need some time to think over the events of last night: the trouble with the heat system, the weird sensation and other ghostly encounters Maddie reported, the sensation I myself felt or thought I felt. But now was not the time. I was too buzzed from all the coffee, not to mention from the prospect of my new life with Maddie, the hopes and fears that were swirling in my heart and my head. I checked the time – quarter past eight. I wondered if this would be an okay time to call Charlie. I decided to chance it.

A woman answered. A black lady, I think. I started to say that I must have dialed a wrong number – although that wasn't likely since Charlie's number was one of the few my phone was set up to speed dial: Charlie had set it up himself – when the voice on the other end cut me off.

"You know whose phone this is?!" It was both a question and an accusation.

I told her yes. I told her the phone belonged to my son. I told her Charlie's name. I asked who she was. She seemed offended that I would ask such a thing but she told me that her name was Charlaine. She'd found the phone just a few minutes ago "making a racket" in her greenhouse and she figured whoever it belonged to must be stealing things out of the green-house or was homeless and sleeping in it, one. I assured her that Charlie was neither homeless nor a thief. I had to ask, just to be sure I heard her right, "Did you say 'greenhouse'?" Yes, that's what she said. I told her that I would be happy to come by and pick up the phone: I'd be willing to pay a reward. She didn't want to give me her location. I suggested she mail the phone to me, that I would pay the postage plus a reward.

She said, "How about I call the sheriff and let him come get it for evidence?"

"Okay good, that would be fine," I told her; " Would you please call him right away? And please ask the sheriff to call this number I'm calling from as soon as he gets there."

I ended the connection and started for the door. I figured I'd better drop by Charlie's place and let him know about his phone. Then, with a sinking feeling, I thought about the missed calls and the voicemail on my own phone. I stopped in my tracks. I listened to the message.

VIII. Epilog
Three Months Later

He'd been expecting an unannounced visit from Maddie or a summons to DC. Or even a phone call — he could picture her ending it over the phone. It had never occurred to him she might do it by text.

> *Found somebody new, wasn't looking didn't mean to it just happened, sorry, hes a sweet guy a lot like you, never would have believed there were guys like him out there if not for you Harry, best of everything to you and Charlie*

A few minutes later, another text followed.

> *Hope you find somebody new yourself, you wont have any trouble your such a catch xoxo*

He called, but her phone sent him straight to voicemail. He considered going up there to DC, to plead with her if necessary. Rather, he pretended to consider. Deep down, he knew he would not make the trip. He knew it the same way he had known for over a month now that it was ending between him and Maddie. He told himself that he would be all right: the adjustment from ending to over couldn't be so great, could it? Besides, there was Charlie to look after. Who had time for self-pity?

On that day in November when Maddie had left for DC, Charlie had been admitted to the county hospital. After three days undergoing tests and observation, Charlie had been released and Harry had brought him home. Charlie seemed to be improving. He was even able to navigate the stairs, which was good because it meant he could have the second bedroom as his own room and not be forced to sleep on the couch. Harry cleaned all the junk out of that room, found a sturdy bed frame in a Salvation Army store, purchased a new mattress and box spring, and fixed the place up nice for his wounded son. Charlie's speech was slow, his balance was iffy, his hands often trembled. But his mind was intact. He was still the same Charlie: same warm smile, same puppy dog eyes, same gentle, off-beat sense of humor.

Then Christmas Day.

There was no sign of trouble until evening. They were sitting together in the living room watching a football game. Charlie went silent. Harry didn't think too much of it at first. But the silence continued and Charlie's eyes took on a glassy sheen. Harry tried not to panic, he thought maybe they could ride it out, whatever it was. Then, slowly, methodically, Charlie vomited his Christmas lunch. (They were saving dinner for Maddie, who was on the way from DC.) Charlie showed no distress or even awareness of what he was doing. It was like watching a snake in the act of swallowing another snake, only in reverse. Harry called for an ambulance.

The whole month of December, Maddie and Harry had been making contingency plans. His reunion with Maddie in DC had been delayed, of course. Also, he'd been unable to send any money to help Maddie secure an apartment. She tried to find something big enough to accommodate all three of them, but that turned out to be impossible in the DC-area housing market, given Maddie's limited resources and Harry's inability to help. She settled on a one-bedroom studio apartment as a "temporary" solution, refusing to reveal any details about the lease.

Why couldn't she sleep in her car for a while, Harry never directly asked but often wondered...until they could work things out around Charlie? Okay, yes, winter was fast approaching and Maddie was further north, but still.

All of January was taken up seeing to Charlie – first in the hospital ICU, then in a recovery ward, then a rehab facility; meanwhile Harry spent time looking for a ground-floor, single-level apartment for the two of them when it became plain that Charlie would not be climbing stairs, not for a long time, if ever again.

Then, too, there was all the legal trouble with Alexis. Alexis continued to claim that Charlie had tried to kill him. Charlie, of course, contended – right up until Christmas – that it was the other way around. Admittedly, neither story made much sense. To accept either you had to believe that the would-be murderer had gone temporarily insane. But Charlie's story was at least consistent, whereas Alexis' story seemed to shift around a lot. Alexis was also bringing suit against Charlie in civil court for blinding him. Harry expected the suit to be tossed out, or at least put on hold while the authorities tried to sort out who might have been trying to kill whom, but that didn't happen, and Harry was forced to hire an attorney to countersue Alexis for the damage he had inflicted on Charlie. What was particularly galling to Harry were the reports he received that Alexis, with partial sight in one eye, was managing fairly well on his own. He was blind only in some technical, legal sense. How did that compare to Charlie's situation? Harry was convinced that Charlie's second episode, the result of a lingering blood clot, would never have happened if he had gotten immediate care for the initial aneurism. Needless to say, Harry believed Charlie's account of the events of that day and not Alexis'.

Harry felt his connection with Maddie evaporating away all that month. If there was one thing he knew about Maddie it was that she lived in the moment: let too many moments slip past while they were apart and her attention would wander. But what could he do? He needed to work as much as possible to bring in as much money as possible. Fran and Milt were a godsend helping out with Charlie while Harry worked, especially Fran.

There was a CD Harry played a lot those days, one that Charlie had given him, a Van Morrison CD. The song that hit Harry the hardest, that caused him to compulsively play the CD over and over, was about "precious time," about it slipping away.

Of course Maddie knew about Charlie's second episode. She had used her key to Harry's apartment and had walked in that Christmas night to find the place empty and the mess made by Charlie and a hastily scribbled note from Harry. (In his distress and confusion, Harry had not thought to use his phone to call and warn her.) But Harry kept the news of Charlie's worsened condition from Maddie as long as he could. Why burden her with this additional bad news? For all anyone knew, it might be temporary, Charlie might bounce back at any time. Harry pretended to himself that this was his sole reason for not telling her. What he couldn't face was the possibility that, once she knew, it would be over between them. He couldn't face it and he refused to allow such thoughts to even be formulated in his mind, however much they were present nonetheless. But how else to explain why he looked only locally for the new apartment? He did not even glance at apartments in the DC area. Instinctively, he knew he needed to stay close to Fran and Milt. Maddie was cut out to be no one's nursemaid. She'd be no help taking care of Charlie, and she would quickly lose patience with Harry if Charlie consumed too much of his time, which inevitably he would.

Maddie, meanwhile, was settling into her new job. When she wasn't in the field, she worked at a government-funded clinic in suburban Maryland, where disaster victims from around the country received medical and psychological treatment. It was a small clinic since the general practice was not to relocate disaster victims but to minister to them in their own surroundings, and Harry never clearly understood what the criteria were for bringing some victims to Maryland, but Maddie seemed to think it all made sense. She had been in the field one time so far. For two and a half weeks in January, Maddie had counseled survivors of a horrific train derailment near a little prairie town in Deaf Smith County, Texas. The derailment involved two freight trains, one of which was carrying chlorine gas and sodium hydroxide; the other was carrying something call cresol, not to be confused with creosol. The derailment happened in the middle of the day on the outskirts of the town. A grammar school was nearby. Dozens of people were killed; hundreds were seriously injured. Many children were among the killed and injured. In a place so small, essentially the whole town was affected. For those two and a half weeks, Maddie lived out of a cramped two-bedroom hotel room she shared with two HAZMAT nurses who had also been sent from Maryland. There was a bunk set up between the two beds, but the bunk was almost never used, as it was rare for all three of them to be sleeping at the same time. The hotel was near Hereford, the county seat, over an hour's drive from the devastated town. Including the commute, Maddie worked twenty-hour days, grabbing snacks and naps when she could. Mostly she worked with people who were grieving over the loss of a loved one: a spouse, a child, a parent, a grandparent, a sibling, a cousin, an aunt, an uncle, a lover, a life-long friend. There seemed to be no end to the losses. And some of the people Maddie counseled were grieving multiple losses. Some had also been injured themselves. Maddie called Harry sometimes late at night, sobbing into the phone. When it was over and she was back in Maryland, she told him that she couldn't wait for her next chance to get out into the field.

Then came February. They released Charlie from rehab. To Harry, it seemed too soon. Charlie still had such a long way to go. Were they giving up on him? Harry signed a lease on a one-story apartment. It was more expensive than made sense for his budget but time was up: no more bargain hunting. Once he signed the lease, Harry felt he had to tell Maddie. About the move, of course: he couldn't very well up and change his address and not tell her – not that she ever sent him anything as archaic as actual mail – but, who knew, maybe one day she would take it into her head to pay him a surprise visit. It hadn't happened so far, but with Maddie you had to be ready for any surprise. Harry also felt it was past time to tell Maddie about Charlie's condition: he simply couldn't bear to hide it from her anymore.

One evening, toward the end of the first week of February, Harry dialed Maddie's number. Charlie was napping on the couch. This was now common behavior for Charlie: since getting out of rehab he slept at least twelve hours a day. The television was on with the sound turned low.

Charlie watched a lot of television now – any program, it didn't matter, so long as there were people talking – and the television pacified him during his naps on the couch. Music was good, too, as long as it included people singing. Harry was worn out. He'd spent that day moving the last of the furniture and truckloads of books out of the old place and into the new apartment – (it had been too cold to lay block) – then giving the old place a final cleaning in hopes of getting his full deposit back – (he'd heard from other former tenants that the landlord looked for any excuse to keep some of the deposit) – then grocery shopping, then racing home to relieve Fran, then doing all the chores that Charlie required and Fran wouldn't do, then feeding Charlie, then talking to Charlie, which was supposed to be good for him, then more chores.

Maddie answered on the sixth ring. She pretended to be surprised to hear Harry's voice. Harry tried to picture the scene on her end. Had she been far from the phone and snatched it up quickly without looking to see who it was? Harry didn't think so. More likely, the phone had been close by and she knew perfectly well who was calling and she needed a moment or two to think it over before answering.

They chatted awkwardly. Harry did most of the talking. "Is this a bad time?" he asked.

"N-no," Maddie muffed her chance of escape.

Harry gave his news, first telling about the new apartment, then mentioning Charlie.

"What about Charlie?" Maddie asked.

"He's bad."

"How bad?"

Harry told her. Charlie rarely spoke now. The few words he did produce were hopelessly tangled. He didn't seem to care if his words were understood or not. It was as if he simply made the noises his brain told him to make then he stopped making noises. He often choked on solid food. This was a shame because he wanted solid food: he clearly enjoyed it and he could eat it himself: both hands were shaky now, the left far worse than the right, but he could manage right-handed to laboriously lift a fork to his mouth. But then he choked. The only answer was to feed him liquid foods – soup, oatmeal, yogurt, applesauce: essentially baby food – all of which he hated because there was no good way to eat these things with his shaky hands, and he hated to be spoon fed.

Charlie, asleep on the couch, spoke the word "opposable." He spoke much more clearly when he was asleep, although his speech was limited to single words, randomly chosen as far as Harry could tell, at random intervals. Still, Charlie's clear pronunciation of these words gave Harry some small hope that over time Charlie's waking speech would improve.

Maddie said something and Harry had to ask her to repeat it.

"Is he ambulatory?"

"He moves very slowly. His left side is especially weak. When he walks it's better if someone is there for him to lean on."

"Other than trying to talk, does he communicate – does he write notes?"

"So far he has no interest in writing notes, he won't even hold a pencil in his hand – we've tried, both in rehab and at home."

"At least he's talking," Maddie said, trying to sound upbeat.

"He listens, too," Harry said. "There are times I'm talking to him I'm sure he's listening."

"That's good," Maddie said, without the least conviction.

"Porcupine," Charlie said, in a voice as high and clear as a choir boy's.

"Can he go to the bathroom on his own? Is he continent?"

"Sometimes," Harry said, hoping that Maddie would not press him for details.

She did not. In fact, Maddie seemed to have run out of questions. After a moment, Harry said, "I thought you should know what the situation was – I needed to tell you."

Maddie said, "Yes thanks. Thanks for telling me."

Their conversation petered out soon afterwards. Maddie did not seem to want to talk about herself, and she asked no questions about Harry. At the end of the call, Harry said, "I miss you," and Maddie said, "You shouldn't."

The next day when Harry called, he was directed to voicemail.

On Valentine's Day, Harry sent a text: *Happy St. V's Day! Love, Harry.* Hours later came a reply: *in the field again call you later.* There was no call, there were no further texts, not that day or the next day or the week after.

So, it was hardly a surprise when the final text arrived. It hurt, of course, but it was almost a relief. A little like having an infected tooth yanked from your mouth. It was late at night. Harry had put Charlie to bed about an hour earlier. Usually, Charlie was almost enthusiastic about going to bed – he really liked to sleep – and usually he slept through the night with no trouble. But tonight Charlie had seemed reluctant, resistant even, and Harry had felt himself growing cross with his son. And now this. This text from Maddie.

Fran had already graduated from dropping hints to flat out saying, "Perhaps it might be best if Charlie received full-time professional care, in the proper setting." And of course the thought had crossed Harry's mind even before Fran mentioned it, especially in those weeks when he felt Maddie slipping away. Why not put Charlie in a home or institution of some sort? Fran had already started looking into the feasibility of getting Charlie's health insurance to pay for it. Harry agonized over the decision.

Tonight was a perfect instance of why the decision was so tough. Charlie resisted going to bed: it was such a small thing, yet Harry got cross with him. There had been no need for anger — a little patience would have done the trick. Harry worried how he would be acting in six months or, God forbid, six years. Would he be angry at Charlie all the time? Would he resent the burden of a grown son who was a perpetual infant? Would he resent the chance of happiness with Maddie that had been stolen from him? Of course he would — only a saint could overcome such resentments — the real question was: how much would his anger own him? Would he become abusive? Turn into some kind of monster? It had probably happened to better men than him. And yet, returning to the root instance, before Charlie had resisted going to bed, he had simply been reluctant. He had displayed emotion which Harry could read. There was communication there. And as the scene played out Charlie had sensed his father's rising unhappiness and gone to bed in the end with little fuss. Communication. At the moment there didn't seem to be a lot of Charlie behind those big, empty, brown eyes of his — but there still was some of him there. And maybe over time he would get better. How could Harry give up on that? What if keeping him home would eventually bring him back? What if sending him to an institution would lose him forever?

It wasn't a decision Harry could simply make once and for all. It was going to be a battle he fought inside himself day after day.

He'd had a life with Suzanne and sometimes they were happy together and sometimes they were not. All in all it was a life they would have continued, out of habit if for no other reason. But that shared life got cut short when Suzanne's time was cut short. Then Maddie came along and he'd had a chance for a second life with Maddie, but he missed the chance or the chance was taken from him or some combination of both. The difference between the two lives — the one with Suzanne and the one with Maddie — was that he had actually lived the first: he could only imagine what the other might have turned out to be. Naturally, in his imagination, life with

Maddie would have been some sort of emotional and sexual Shangri-la. His more reasoning mind understood that he and Maddie would have had their difficulties, to say the least. His most utterly cynical mind placed odds of nine-to-one they could not have stayed together a month once they found themselves in a living arrangement where they had to actually make long-term commitments to one another. Still, his imagination, fueled by his memories, distilled an endless number of tantalizing Shangri-la's.

Harry's books were piled in boxes along the long wall in the new living room, also in his bedroom and in the kitchen, more spacious than the kitchen in the old place, and even a few in Charlie's room. He had disassembled the bookshelves from the old place: they were now a pile of wooden parts stacked under a tarp outside his patio door. He didn't know when he would find time to reassemble the bookshelves or to re-shelve the books, much less sit down and read one of them. But he longed to do it. He longed to read again, to delve into the nature of things, to attempt to figure out what it was all for, what it all meant, if indeed it meant anything.

Maddie gone, Suzanne departed, Charlie profoundly wounded, Harry felt it would be easy to conclude that life, the world, human existence didn't mean anything, was just one damned thing after another until everyone you knew was dead, including yourself; and while you were alive you should scramble for every scrap of happiness you could find and leave all the others, whoever they may be, to fend for themselves. A lot of people seemed to be of that opinion: perhaps this was true of any age. It seemed likely that Maddie was of that opinion. But Harry resisted. He clung to the hope that somehow it all mattered. He didn't know how: he didn't believe in any sort of afterlife, no eternal reward, no punishment. Even so, he clung to his forlorn hope as tenaciously as he clung to the hope that his son would recover.

M. Jonquil has been a store clerk, a construction laborer, a teacher, a cashier, a grant writer, a babysitter, a highway maintenance worker, a ghost writer, a fortune-teller, a fruit picker, a vagabond on a bicycle living out of a tent. Among other things. Jonquil's stories have appeared in *The Literary Hatchet* and *Every Day Fiction*.

www.ingramcontent.com/pod-product-compliance
Lightning Source LLC
Chambersburg PA
CBHW031710170626
46808CB00005B/1685